KISS FROM A MONSTER SERIES

VOLUME ONE

CHARLOTTE SWAN

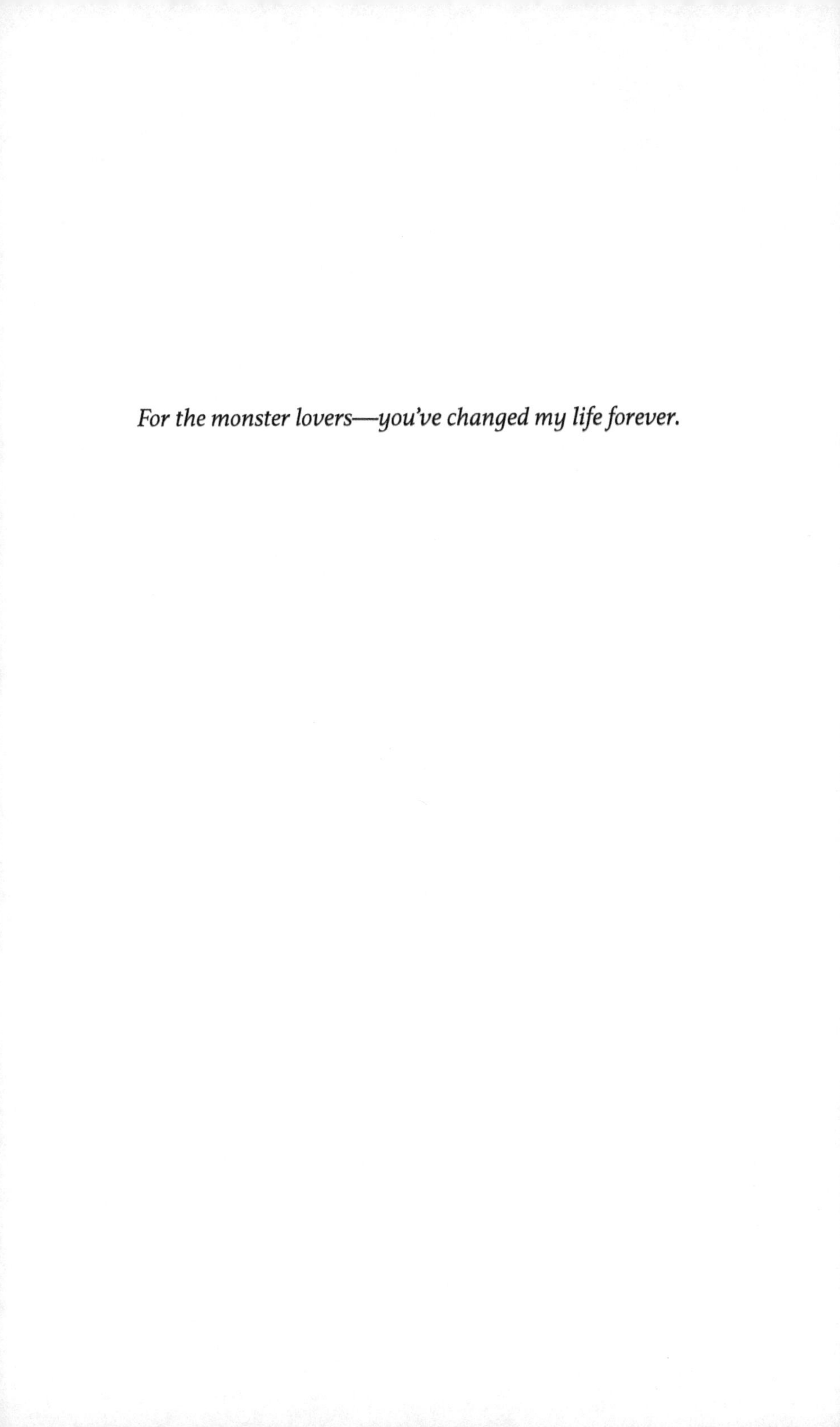

For the monster lovers—you've changed my life forever.

TABLE OF CONTENTS

A KISS FROM A DEMON

A KISS FROM A KRAKEN

A KISS FROM A DRAGON LORD

A KISS FROM A FAERIE KING

A KISS FROM A DEMON

KISS FROM A MONSTER SERIES BOOK 1

1

IRYS

It is desperation that sends me out into *The Woods* tonight. A desperation laced with fear that has me walking into this cursed land as the sky above fades from warm gold to poisoned black. It is as if the sky is warning me to turn back. To stick with the demon I already know and find a way to defeat it with a more conventional method.

I am all ears if the sky could tell me how I get out of marrying Duke Brayborne.

However, I suspect it would offer the same advice everyone else in our village has: to grin and bear it. To be happy in the knowledge that, while my husband may be old and cruel, at least I will have a home. I will have food in my belly this winter and I will eventually have his children. That is the only true joy a woman can look forward to in her life. By becoming a vessel to produce heirs and enjoying their love until they are old enough to leave home and start their own families. Continuing this whole hideous cycle again for a new generation.

Well, I want no part of it. If making a bargain with the demon they say dwells in this forest is the only way to save myself then I will take that risk. Why must I suffer for my father's mistakes? All of my older sisters were married off to men at least close to their age. Men that they may not love but at least have respect for. Duke Brayborne has lusted after me for as long as I can remember. It is remarkable I was able to avoid him and reach my twenty-second birthday.

Unfortunately, my luck had run out. With the Duke in attendance at my birthday dinner, my stomach sank as my father announced that I was to marry him. My father, Lord Evergrove, has an affinity for drunk card games. An addiction that led him to gamble away all his tenants' money. Duke Brayborne was willing to overlook the debt if my father gave me to him as his wife.

A trade my father contemplated on for a few moments until Duke Brayborne threw in a keg of ale and one-hundred gold pieces. That is all I was worth to my father. Ale and some gold he gambled away within the hour. When my mother died on my seventh birthday he began to sink deeper into himself. He never cared whether I came or went, and refused to have a tutor brought in to see to my education so he could spend more gold on his drink. When the townsfolk began remarking on my beauty as I grew he saw an opportunity. Especially when Duke Brayborne was the one who began showing the most interest in me.

I shudder and shake myself from that train of thought. No point in dwelling on my misfortunes, I will get the life I deserve no matter what it costs. Anything is better than being the wife of that horrid man.

The sun has fully set now and the moon has taken its place high in the sky. Its pale light and the soft glow from my lantern are the only things guiding me through *The Woods*. Shrouded in myth and mystery, no one dares spend enough time in here to create a map of its layout. I only know about the creatures in this forest thanks to a healer woman who goes into these parts to find the herbs that will not grow in town.

When I confided my plight to her she took pity on me and informed me that something in these woods helps desperate humans for a price. I am hopeless enough to believe she is telling the truth.

I do not have much money. Only a few gold pieces I was able to hide away when my father wasn't looking. I can only pray that it is enough.

The healer said to head in from the north side of *The Woods* and walk until I reach a house with a twelve-pointed star on the door. She said that if I felt like I was getting lost, I was on the right path. Which is not very helpful seeing as how I have felt lost the moment I crossed under the first mangled oak tree.

The snow and ice that has covered our village does not dare go into these woods. My long, brown cloak snags on branches from the gnarled trees above. The boots I am wearing are a size too small and I can already feel a blister forming on my heel as I sidestep thick roots bursting through the forest floor like vengeful fingers. A wind blows through *The Woods*, rustling the leaves and tugging at my braided back dark hair. It holds a bite that makes my cheeks sting. The scent of dank earth over-whelms my senses.

I keep walking, listening for anything that may tell me I'm on the right path. Even with its lack of snow, the forest is colder than our village. The dangerous magic that permeates the air has me pulling my cloak tighter around myself. Passing by another tree I swear I have already walked by, the breeze picks up again. Only this time it seems to push me in a new direction. I'm so desperate for anything to guide me that I let myself be led by whatever invisible force this is.

After a few moments on this path I see it.

For a moment, I doubt myself and wonder if it is too late to turn back. This cabin, if it can even be called that, is built into the base of a massive hill. Roots make up the thatch roof and curl their way around the door like veins. Obsidian stones chart a path up to the dark wood door that is marred with the marking the healer mentioned. There is an odd scent in the air and a soft glow peeks out from beneath the door.

Something is definitely home.

Perhaps this was a trick? Maybe the healer woman has a deal with this creature to lure unsuspecting young women to its door to devour them. If that's the case then I might as well meet my end. If it won't eat me, something definitely will if I try to find my way back to town.

I hesitate for another moment as I look up at the door. I remember Brayborne's wrinkled face and stale breath as he whispered in my ear how he's been waiting to bed me since his wife died. His wife...who had passed just over ten years ago.

Swallowing down the bile in my throat I march towards the door and knock once.

The sound echoes into the cabin beyond. I wait for a sound; I wait for something to stir behind the door. Half expecting it to be ripped from the hinges and me to be picked up by a monster and swallowed whole but nothing happens. I knock again, the old, wooden door soft against my knuckles. It is rotted through enough that, coupled with the rusted latch, it swings open.

I do not know if demons have the same type of manners we do but I can imagine they wouldn't take kindly to someone walking uninvited into their home. Left with no other choice, I do just that. As soon as I cross the threshold I know I have made a mistake. The heavy door slams shut behind me and it feels like I'll never get the chance to walk out of it again.

Even as the temperature inside the cabin warms my bones I know I have to keep on my guard. I set my lantern down on a small wooden table by the door and take in my surroundings. The cabin is...nice. There are tools scattered along what seems to be a workbench. The kitchen is sparse with a few pots and pans hanging from the walls. The wooden floor is maintained and the rugs are clean. A few potted plants and books for herb cataloging sit along a counter that faces a small glass window. A lingering scent of stewed meat wafts through the air.

This cabin feels otherworldly. A tingle forms at the base of my neck as I take a step deeper into the cabin. It is so quiet in here, the only noise coming from my breathing. It's enough to make me believe I am alone. Until I see him.

How had I missed him before?

I gasp and my heart beats faster. He stands in front of a roaring fireplace. A massive figure that almost entirely blocks the flickering flames from my eyes. Dressed in a heavy, wool cloak he turns towards me. His massive horns are gnarled like the branches of the trees outside, almost brushing the high ceiling of the cabin. The fire behind him illuminates his ghastly features.

His face is a skull made of weathered gray bones. The only sign of life are the flames from the fire pouring into his eye sockets to illuminate him from within. The room seems to glow even brighter and my feet are carrying me closer to him despite my fear. There is something else I am feeling as I get a better look at him. Something I have never experienced before.

It started out as fear tightening my belly but it is some other emotion tickling it now. Maybe it is the powerful form and just how unknown his kind is to me. That unknown feeling has traveled lower, to my most feminine flesh and heated it. My body is rebelling from the warnings my brain is issuing.

The figure turns fully towards me now, his expression unreadable. Though I suspect it is hard for a skull to emote.

"Who are you?" He asks, his voice is deep and skates over my skin making me clench my teeth and thighs together. I should not tell him my name. The healer woman warned me against it but for some reason I cannot recall why.

"Irys Evergrove." The answer spills from my lips. Well, so much for keeping secrets. The demon tilts his head as if assessing this answer to see if I am lying. He hasn't tried to eat me yet so I take that to mean I should press on with my demands. "I have come to make a bargain with the demon of *The Woods*."

A sound rasps out of him and I think he is laughing.

"I do not make deals with little girls." He waves a clawed hand, dismissing me.

"I am not a little girl. I am a woman of twenty-two. One who is being forced to marry a hideous man in the morning if I do not find some way to stop it. I've come to bargain with you to stop my marriage."

I take a deep breath unsure why I feel compelled to say the next bit.

What is wrong with sharing the deepest desire of my heart if I am already bargaining with a demon?

"I wish to bargain for the chance to marry someone I truly love."

The cabin has grown hotter. My palms are beginning to sweat and I wipe them on the soft material of my cloak. Those fiery sockets track the movement without saying anything. They linger on my hands before traveling up the length of my stomach, to my chest, and then to my face. It is not in the same manner in which the Duke looks at me and maybe that is the reason more wet heat has found its way into my most intimate parts.

"And what did you bring to bargain with?" I reach into my satchel under my cloak and dig around before my fingers close over the crushed velvet pouch. Pulling it from my bag, I hold the purse out toward him. My meager ten gold pieces barely jingle as he extends his hand and the purse floats towards him on an invisible breeze.

His claws sift through the bag counting each coin. Shame makes me hang my head and look at the toe of my boots. I count the scuffs on the wooden floor until I hear him laugh again. The sound curls my toes and I know the tips of my ears are pink.

"I have no interest in the gold of men. Especially not this...*humble* amount."

Shame floods me. Even a demon will not help me escape my fate. I truly am doomed to endure that horrible cycle that took my own mother from me. Forced to pass this curse on to my own children. No, this cannot be it. I will find another way.

I have to find another way.

"Thank you, demon. I'll see myself out." Turning to leave his voice booms behind me.

"There is something else you can offer me." He extends the clawed hand holding my purse toward me. "Something I find much more valuable than a small bag of coins."

I furrow my brows in confusion. "I have nothing else. You hold in your hand all of my worldly possessions."

"That is not true. You possess something much more precious than gold."

His gaze rakes down my body again, devouring it with that eyeless stare, and then it clicks. No, surely this demon cannot mean...But did not the healer woman warn me? He may ask for something more than money. I never thought it would be that.

My sisters always said I was too gullible and I would pay the price for it one day.

"I am not bargaining with that. If I wished to be defiled for my first time I would stick with the Duke," I spit. Even as the words leave me I cannot help but feel that I am wrong to categorize these two in the same way. Would it be defilement with this creature?

Why does it feel like I would enjoy it?

The demon bares his teeth in a feral grin. Each one is pointed and razor sharp as he takes a thunderous step towards me. The wooden boards groan under his massive frame until he is only a few feet away from me. I have to crane my neck all the way up to be able to look at him in those flame-filled eyes.

"Defile? I would give you pleasure no mortal would ever be able to, little human. I would have you shaking around my cock, begging for my seed, while my tongue fucked your ass." My breath hitches at his vulgar words. Those are the types of words I have only heard my sisters whisper. They're coarse...*dirty* and yet the flesh between my thighs grows even damper. Why did I like to hear that? Surely this demon wields a power to make me desire this profanity.

"If you agree to lie with me tonight, to give me your maiden-head, I will agree to your bargain. That you will only be able to marry someone you truly love." He leans down even closer to me, his warm breath smells like pine trees and sends a tingle down my spine.

One night. All he is asking is one night of my life and I will be able to get what I want. Perhaps I do not marry the man of my dreams as a virgin but it is a small price to pay to be able to marry him at all. If I let this monster have me tonight, hope-fully these odd feelings I am having towards him will be sati-ated. My curiosity will be fulfilled and I will be able to live out my life in a marriage of my choosing.

There is one thing I have to ask before making my decision.

"How would that even work? How would we even"—I swallow—"fit together?" The demon chuckles and the fireplace flares behind his frame. A breeze kicks up and makes his cloak swirl around him. One moment I am looking up at a flaming skull the next, a pair of black eyes are peering down at me. Long, dark hair tangles in the horns on his head and has two sharply pointed ears sticking out from the mass of it. Skin of the palest gray and lips peel back to reveal normal teeth aside from two extra sharp fangs. He is still massive but he has shrunk by at least a foot.

This figure is more human but no less monstrous.

"Better?" He asks, his voice softer too. There is that dark part of me that preferred his rougher tone.

I shake my head and I can feel a blush warming my cheeks. This will be the man—the creature—to whom I will give myself to. Who I will lie with of my own choosing if that is what I wish. Do I wish for this? As if he read my mind, my demon speaks.

"Do we have an agreement?" He holds out a clawed hand for me to take. An ominous offering that will bind my fate to his tonight.

One night. Just one night. I repeat that to myself as I stare at his hand. *Think of all you are gaining for just one night.*

"We have an agreement," I say, clasping his hand. I watch as he traces his clawed thumb over the back of my palm. Even as I repeat to myself this is only one night, something tells me that that will not be the case.

2

———

ASGORATH

It has been a millennium since a human has interested me and found its way to my door.

However, none of them have ever intrigued me as much as this Irys does. Normally humans beg me for the same mortal requests: eternal life, unending wealth, and undying love. Pathetic, really. Those things can be so easily taken away. They are normally so desperate and self-absorbed that they do not even realize they have bargained over their soul to me in the process.

Alas, that is all a part of the job. You cannot get everything your heart desires without paying a price. A price I have never wanted anyone to pay more than Irys. For some reason, I entered into this bargain with her without one of my failsafe curses. Something I use to make sure that no matter how powerful the humans I work with figure themselves to be, I am the one who gets the last laugh. They will toil in service to me for all of eternity.

My desire for Irys has me wanting her to serve me in a different way.

It is truly unfortunate that the only human I have wanted to keep in my whole existence is the one who bargained with me for her freedom. I cannot put my finger on why I want her so much. Maybe it is those green eyes of hers that would give even the most bloodthirsty creature pause before feasting on her flesh. Maybe it is those full lips that I am desperate to see wrapped around my cock. Or maybe, just maybe, it is because she is the first human to come to me and not be repulsed by my form.

Irys fears me, to be sure, but I excite her as well. Does she think that I cannot smell how wet her cunt grows in my presence? That her sweet scent has not been tempting me since she walked through the door? Men and women, old and young come to bargain and each one of them are disgusted by me. I taste it on their scents even as they beg me to pity them. Their condemnation of who I am seeps from every pore.

They do not look at me with thinly veiled lust like Irys does.

Knowing that she is still in possession of her virtue, I had to be the one to claim it. Before some other mortal got to her, my treasure. My Irys. Convincing her with pretty words that he loved her only so he could take what belongs to me. I will give her pleasure no mortal man could ever live up to.

She will be begging me to keep her once I get my cock inside her.

Looking at her now as she stands before me, her small hand still pressed in mine, there is an innocence about her that goes beyond her sexual inexperience. A shyness. That makes my heart, something so shriveled and worn out I am surprised it still works, beats faster. It demands I claim her, keep her, kill for her so she never wishes to leave. To protect her from the darkness of the world and keep her safe in my cabin for eternity.

We have a long night ahead of us and while she may desire me, it is clear she does not know why. Her thighs will welcome me when that part of the night comes, for now, I need to work on gaining her trust. In the morning, I will worry about making her mine.

Reluctantly I drop her hand and she uses it to grip the side of her cloak.

"So...what now?" she asks in a timid voice. Time to test her limits.

"Where do you want me to take you first?" Her green eyes widen and pink stains her cheeks. Her hand trembles where it grips her cloak even as her arousal turns her scent sweeter. My poor little human. Who taught her to be ashamed of these urges? Soon she will give in to her desires. She will see there is nothing to be afraid of when I am the one who has the honor of pleasuring her.

"I—I don't know. The bed, I guess? That's where my sisters did it." The soft timber of her voice makes my cock harden. I would love to capture the sound and bottle it. It would be something I would bargain away all of my power to keep.

"We have all night," I say softly, reaching out to run one of my claws along her soft cheek. Her answering shiver has me biting my tongue before I rethink my idea to take this slow. "A creature like me wants to take his time savoring his prize."

My claws reach for the tie of her cloak. Her hands fly up as if to stop me but they pause mid-air as I undo the delicate bow. The brown cloak falls open leaving her in a light blue gown. It is made of a sturdy, cotton material but the hem and stitching are fraying. When she is mine I will have her draped in the finest silks, encrust her in the finest jewels mortals are so eager to part with in return for some selfish wish.

I would not part from Irys for all the jewels and gold in the world.

"Pretty girl," I growl and she shyly looks down at her boots

Reaching behind her, she stiffens before my claws find the thin leather band holding her braided hair back. With one gentle tug, the long, dark strands are freed. My fingers itch to embed themselves in it. For my claws to prick her scalp and to wind the length of it around my fist, snatching her head back while I pound into her from behind.

Patience. She robs me of all of it.

"Have you ever been kissed, little human?" I ask and her answering blush tells me all I need to know even before she shakes her head. This pleases me greatly. I will reward her for this with my tongue later.

"Are you hungry?" Her stomach growls at my question. She needs her strength for what I have planned. I grasp her by her upper arm, even as she struggles in my grip, and steer her toward the old, oak dining table. Her slight resistance only hardens my cock further in my pants.

Irys sits at one side of my table and I sit on the other. My cloak drapes down to my feet and I brush my hand over the dust collected on the table's surface. I cannot recall the last time I sat and had a meal here. Irys and I will dine here every night going forward.

With a wave of my hand, a wide array of food appears. Steaming bowls of broth filled with all types of vegetables. Roasted meats drenched in rich sauces and paired with mashed potatoes. Even a three-layer cake sits at the far end, decorated in pink and yellow icing. There is a goblet of wine for each of us but not enough to make her drunk. I want...no, I need Irys to remember everything that happens tonight.

To remember why she should stay with me.

"I've never seen this much food," Irys mumbles, half dazed as I spoon a portion of everything on her plate. My claws clink on the dish as I set it down in front of her. I watch as she picks up the metal fork I forged and begins to dive in. As much as I love her eating the food I prepared for her, my teeth bare at the fact that she has not been taken care of.

Mistaking my displeasure as being directed towards her,

she sets her fork down and wipes her mouth, tucking a strand of dark hair behind her delicate ear.

"I apologize, where are my manners? It's just been so long since I've been served this much. The winter has been hard for us all. Even with my father being the lord we've only had a few plates of food between the two of us. Though I guess that has more to do with—" She stops talking and looks down, twisting her hands in her lap.

"More to do with what, Irys?" I am eager to know more—anything—about her.

"Nothing, I shouldn't have said anything. I should be grateful my father has kept a roof over my head all these years." She picks up her fork again but she is eating slower, more measured. "My father is a good man, deep down. He just lost his way."

"You are starving," I say. "Your father let you starve."

"It's more complicated than that," she says, but I see the shock in her eyes. Uncertainty coloring her features as she considers what I've said. "Isn't it? I honestly don't know anymore. I was taught to be grateful. That so many people have it worse than me. My father said he was the only one to have my best interests at heart but then he marries me off to the Duke for..." She trails off again, the color leaching from her face.

"Tell me, Irys, how did this marriage come to be? A marriage you felt so trapped by you sought me out." Without her pathetic excuse for a father, Irys and I may have never met. That is the only thing I will be ever grateful to him for.

It still may not be enough to spare his life should his path cross with mine.

"My father gambles and he owes the Duke money." The truth comes pouring out of her like someone uncorking a barrel of wine. "The Duke has been after me since I was a child. Always staring at me, always following me when he wasn't supposed to. He never touched me, even though I could see that he wanted to. I thought I had avoided him. That surely some nice man from the village would catch my eye and marry me before the Duke had the chance to."

My teeth clench at the mention of her desiring other men but I do not interrupt. Irys clearly needs to share.

"I should've known something was wrong when the Duke attended my birthday dinner a few nights ago. How my father proclaimed that we would wed in one week's time. I can still feel the Duke's hand on my arm as he told me how long he's been desiring me. How it was only a matter of time before my drunkard father toiled away too much coin and it was up to me to help my father by performing the duties of a wife."

Her voice is soft and I see the tears shining in those wonderful eyes of hers. The Duke will be dead, even if the bargain did not necessarily hinge on his death, I will make it so just for scaring her this way.

She laughs but it holds no humor.

"Ale and some gold pieces are all it took for the Duke to secure my hand. No matter how much I begged and pleaded, my father wouldn't hear of it. The truth is, he never had much time for any of his daughters. Our mother took on that responsibility alone and when she passed, and all my sisters were grown and out of the house, there was no one left to raise me. No one has ever cared much about what happens to me. No one has ever wanted to keep me for me." Her green eyes find mine and they are so sincere. "The Duke wants me for my beauty, he does not want me."

"Then he is a fool. And the only good fool is a dead fool." Irys rears back her eyes wide.

"What do you—"

"Eat your dinner, Irys. You have a long night ahead of you." I drop my fork before picking up a leg of chicken and ripping through it with my claws. "Besides, you already walked into my cabin uninvited. Proper manners have no place in a demon's dwelling."

Irys smiles shyly at me and that may be where my obsession with her turns into love.

Regardless, pride blooms in my chest as I watch her tuck into her meal with gusto. She eats spoonful after spoonful, polishes off a massive piece of chocolate cake, and finishes her wine. In the warm light of the fire, I watch her eyes grow heavy and soon her head lays against the back of the chair.

I could stare and watch her like this for the rest of my days but, I do not want her to injure that lovely neck of hers. Scooping her up I marvel at how small she is. No matter how hard I wish to fuck her I have to remember to exercise a bit of restraint, lest I risk bruising this unblemished skin. Irys does not stir as I carry her deeper into my home.

She barely makes a sound as I make my way into the bedroom and lay her down on the dark sheets. Rolling over onto her side I watch as my massive bed cocoons around her. Waving my claws, the fireplace is set ablaze. Irys is about to spend a considerable amount of time naked and I will not have her cold.

I stand over her, marveling at her one last time. She needs her rest, to regain her strength for what will be a night she will never forget.

3

IRYS

I want to stay wrapped in this delicious warmth forever.

My father has not had the money for firewood in weeks so this is a real treat. Usually, I go to sleep bundled in at least three layers. When did he get the money for this? A gift from the Duke?

That thought has me shooting up as I take in my surroundings. I am in an unfamiliar place. An ornately carved fireplace is on my right illuminating a room I have never been in before. I am tangled in dark sheets that are so soft I imagine this is what sleeping on a cloud would be like. Especially when I am in this massive mattress that is high off the ground, with over a dozen pillows decorating it.

I am not in my father's home.

The intensity of the fire seems to double and suddenly I am being suffocated. I rip off my thick gown and toss it aside, my socks and boots follow shortly after that. Dressed only in my shift I can finally breathe deeply. The fire licks along the bare skin of my arms and then I remember.

The Woods. The demon. Our bargain.

He let me sleep after dinner? The demon seemed so singularly focused earlier. With a shaking hand, I feel my way down my body. Slowly taking into account everything until I reach the apex of my thighs. I do not feel as though anything about me is different.

My flesh down there is damp and I know it is not all from sweat. As my own hand grazes up my inner thighs I let out a soft moan. Everything seems to be in order. That is at least a small relief.

Laughter echoes from the corner of the room and I gasp, nearly jumping out of my skin.

"Believe me, little human, I want you wide awake when I claim your maidenhead. To hear the scream you make when my cock enters your unused, little hole."

He rises from a chair placed against the far wall. How long has he been watching me? The demon moves slowly, his horns dragging along the low ceiling as his cloak opens to reveal a hint of his muscular torso. Gray lips are pulled back into a predatory smile as he advances toward me, stopping at the foot of the massive bed.

"Wait," I say and his dark eyes survey me. "I don't even know your name."

Shame makes me drop my eyes. I am going to let this demon inside of me and I did not even ask for his name.

"Asgorath."

"Asgorath," I repeat back and his nostrils flare as a shiver wracks his body.

"You'll be moaning it soon enough." Asgorath unbelts his cloak and it drops away revealing pale gray skin stretched over a heavily muscled body. His upper arms bulge with every movement, and his powerful thighs are clad only in dark pants. There are markings that decorate his stomach and chest. Intricate symbols I have never seen before.

Another reminder that my first time is not going to be with a human.

I watch with uneven breath as he kneels upon the bed and makes his way toward me. Apprehension has me slipping back towards the headboard. That only makes him chuckle, the sound damping my flesh even more.

"Did you put something in the food?" I ask. "Why does my body respond to you like this?"

His horns glow in the firelight, reaching towards me like hands.

"You already agreed to give yourself to me. I have no need to rely on the tricks of man to make you willing," he says. I know he is right. There is something about Asgorath that makes me feel safe. Like at dinner, somehow telling him all of that stuff made me feel lighter. Made me feel like I finally had someone who cared enough about me to listen.

That realization sends another batch of moisture slicking out of me. Asgorath inhales deeply and wraps a clawed hand around my ankle. He pulls me gently so I slip down the bed, laying fully on my back in the center of the massive mattress. I squirm but it is of no use, his strong hands are there pinning my arms to the bed.

"Are you ashamed at how wet you grow for me? For the beast that will rut you—fuck you as your virgin blood runs down my cock—until you are a quivering mess?" His voice has grown deeper, more gravely. "You should be disgusted with yourself. Shouldn't you?"

Asgorath's claws pull my arms over my head as he crawls on top of my body. His hard muscles press into my breasts and I cannot help but moan. I have never been touched like this, never been this close to anyone or anything before. Unkissed and untouched and my first ones will be claimed by this demon.

He rocks against me gently, something hard presses into my damp center and my hands strain, seeking anything to hold on to.

"I am a creature so feared and reviled, but your pussy gets wet all the same. A disgusting creature holding you down makes you drip down your thighs. Admit it."

I shake my head but that only causes more of the hardness to rub against me. It feels so good I need more. This need is so potent I am writhing underneath him, trying anything to get more friction. His teeth coast down my neck.

"Use your words," he teases, pullings his lower half away from me and that wonderful hardness is gone. My whines reach my own ears and it is clear all logical thought has left me. I am solely focused on the pleasure that he was giving me. I care about nothing else but getting it back.

I will say anything, even though what he is asking me to admit to is the truth.

"Yes. Yes!" I yell, lifting my hips to try and get him to press back against me.

"Your pussy gets wet for a monster. Say it." I shake my head, I am not that far gone. I do not use language like that. I never have.

"Say it, and I'll let you rub your greedy cunt all over my cock until you come." Asgorath's hips drop down just slightly and I feel him against my center again. My pussy, he called it. Pressing against me once, twice until I am shaking. Only for him to pull away from me again. Tears of desperation sting my eyes and I thrash again in his grip.

"My pu...pussy gets wet for a monster," I bite out and I am instantly rewarded. His hips slam back against me and then he is moving. Slamming our lower halves together as his teeth nip at my skin. His dark hair tangles with my own, getting caught in my sweat and tickling my face. I am obsessed with his woodsy scent which has gotten even deeper since he crawled into bed with me.

My legs rest on either side of his hips and my shift rides up. Dangerously close to baring me completely but I am too lost to care. He continues his movements, the seam of his pants and that hard bulge behind it keep grinding against me. The pleasure builds in my stomach, and my thighs begin to shake but Asgorath keeps going.

"I'll keep your secret," he says into my neck. I can feel his muscles constricting with each thrust against me. "No one from your village knows that you're the demon's pretty little whore. Begging to rub your clit on his cock. Dry-fucking me for all you're worth."

The words are my undoing. My muscles seize and I feel new moisture leak from my pussy and course down my thighs. My eyes bore into his as he looms above me. A thin layer of sweat covers his forehead and I do not know what expression is on my face. All I know is that I lean up to capture his mouth and suddenly my body is no longer coming down.

It is flaring back to life.

As if in shock it takes my demon a minute to realize his mouth is on mine but he does. Asgorath's tongue tangles with my own. My inexperience is clearly showing but he does not seem to care in the slightest. The flavor of his mouth is wonderful, so crisp and delicious I want to drink it down. His growls rumble through me as he lets go of my wrists to spear his hands in my hair. My own hands find their way to his back and dig into the corded muscle, eliciting a deep groan.

I will do anything to get that sound out of him again.

We come up for air and I think that the kissing portion may be over but once I have sucked down a few breaths Asgorath is back. His tongue invades my mouth only to slip in deep, passing my own tongue until I feel him tickle the back of my throat. My eyes fly open but he continues. Sliding his tongue farther down until I choke, my eyes watering.

"That's good to know," he says softly. Before I get the chance to ask what he means or how he did that with his tongue, his hands leave my hair and tangle in the top part of my shift. With one harsh tug, Asgorath rips it clean down the center, baring my naked body to his eyes.

When I was still covered my shyness had been kept at bay. In the heat of the moment, when pleasure had been my sole motivation my brain temporarily forgot where we were and who we were with. It all comes flooding back to me now and I make to cover myself.

That was the wrong move.

Asgorath growls and pulls my arms away from where they went to shield my naked breasts.

"Never hide this body from me." He uses his magic to pin my arms to my sides and I squirm. This is when the apprehension creeps in. I do not know if I am ready for the full thing yet. Panic starts to turn my breathing ragged. As if he can read it on my face, Asgorath leans down and places a soft kiss on my lips. "Relax, my little human. You came so hard on my pants I need to see it. Need to lick it all up and drink down your pleasure."

He kisses me softly again before nipping at my bottom lip. "When it's time for me to put my cock in you, you'll be begging for it."

Asgorath moves down my body, peppering kisses along my neck and throat. Stopping to swirl his tongue around my left nipple while he rolls the other one between his claws. Pinching and twisting it so that my back arches off the bed. The pain only heightens my pleasure. His sharp teeth scrape over the first nipple before he switches to the other. As he comes away from them, I see the pale pink buds slick with his saliva.

He lifts his head and gazes into my eyes. My chest is rising and falling; I try to free my arms again but it is futile. Without breaking eye contact I watch as his jaw drops open. Lower than any man's jaw ever could. Then slowly, I watch his tongue unfurl. Dark red and forked, wet with saliva that drips onto my stomach in soft splashes. He drags that long tongue around each of my breasts, squeezing them as he goes while licking my nipple.

I gasp, my hands pulling at the sheets. There is a euphoria unlocking in me. A heady sense of belonging and righteousness as I watch his tongue trace down my stomach, leaving behind a trail of spit. No man would ever be able to give me what I know he is about to. They simply do not have the motivation or the equipment to.

When I stopped being unsure of Asgorath seeing me naked I do not know. But whenever it was, my body has already decided that here and now, we belong to him.

I will worry about what that means in the morning, as far as my future is concerned.

If I thought him licking my breasts was amazing, when his tongue laps over my pussy I feel like I am going to bust out of my skin. His eyes are still locked on mine as his tongue drags over the top of my pussy, taking a moment to circle around a bundle of nerves that has my toes curling, before licking through my folds. I can hear how wet I am, the sloppy sounds his tongue makes as he licks up my first climax all the while preparing me for my next one.

My eyelids become heavy as the sensation becomes too much. My sisters have definitely never mentioned their husbands ever doing this to them.

Asgorath growls and his tongue pulls away from my wet flesh, curling it back into his mouth. My eyes fly open and I let out a whimper, wanting more of his attention, wanting to reach that peak that only he has ever brought me to. Magic releases my hands and he slides down my body, kissing below my navel, the top of my pussy, before looking up at me between my legs.

My thighs rest on either side of his cheeks, and his horns loop up toward me.

"Oh, Irys. Only naughty little girls have pussies this wet." He licks up my center and my hands fly to his horns to keep him there. "Sweeter than anything. It's a wonder you've kept this cunt untouched. You knew it belonged to me, didn't you?"

I nod my head. "Yes, yes. Please keep licking me."

"Beg me to eat your pussy. Beg me like the greedy slut you are." His tongue licks me again and I scream in frustration. I need it. If I do not get it I am going to die.

"Eat my pussy, please. It's yours!"

He attacks my pussy with renewed vigor. He rubs his nose against that sensitive bundle and laps at me over and over. I am not prepared for what it feels like when his tongue enters me. The overwhelming sense of fullness as he pushes past my entrance has me jerking on the bed. His clawed hands lock under my thighs and press them up and back towards my body, baring me fully to his mouth.

I grip his horns harder and I'm afraid I might break them. My screams echo off the cabin walls as I feel his tongue expand wider inside of me. Asgorath licks along the barrier of my maidenhead and I try to squeeze his head with my thighs. His tongue retreats and he looks up at me. His mouth and chin are wet from my arousal.

"Going to be such a tight fuck. You're going to be my pretty, human plaything. Even if this is wrong, your little pussy wouldn't listen. Isn't that right?"

"Yes, it needs you! I need you, please." The words slip from my lips but they are true. I need him, in this moment and perhaps even beyond it. He has unlocked something inside of me. Something I will never be able to hide away with shame again.

The wet, messy sounds my pussy makes as he continues his work help propel my body into climax. He rubs his face all through my wetness before sucking on that bundle of nerves again. My thighs squeeze him even tighter than before. He does not stop, does not once come up for air until my release barrels into me. The breath is knocked out of me and I scream his name. My back has arched clean off the bed and I feel like I am weightless.

Floating forever until I am able to reenter my body.

Asgorath gives me one final lick that causes me to shutter before kissing his way back up my body. My mind is fogged with lust but I know one thing to be true. I do not fear this demon. No man would be so thorough in my pleasure, would not even know how to give me this. Asgorath is also letting me set the pace. He knew I was not ready and gave me pleasure all the same, instead of demanding I open my legs so he could find his own release.

I do not know if I am ready for him to be inside me like that yet, but I do want to show him I appreciate what he did. More than that, I want to be able to give him the pleasure he just gave me.

He will just have to teach me how to do it.

Reaching my face he presses a soft kiss to my lips and I can taste myself on him. Even after coming so hard, I feel myself grow wet again. His long tongue licks up my cheek and I smile up at him, letting my hand trail down his muscled stomach. I stop at the waistband of his pants and look into his dark eyes.

"May I lick you?"

4

ASGORATH

If this human was not already mine, that soft question out of her mouth sealed her fate.

May I lick you?

My cock is the only one that will ever feel the soft, wet cavern of her mouth. To push all the way down her throat until she is choking, tears leaking from her beautiful eyes. I tested her gag reflex earlier and she should be able to get me down a good distance. I will push her, though. Her limits are mine alone to test.

"You want to put your virgin mouth on my cock?" I ask and I love watching her blush. That same delicate pink matches her nipples and the soft skin of her knees. Her pussy is red and swollen from my efforts. Begging for more of my attention as my gaze lingers on it.

"Yes," she says, eyes bright.

"Do you think I should allow you to do that? Have you earned the right to service my cock?" Her breathing picks up and her breasts rise and fall faster.

"I want to give you pleasure like you gave me." She swallows. "I want you to teach me how to pleasure you."

"Will you let me come inside that pretty mouth of yours? Will you swallow it down like a good girl even if you're choking?"

She nods, her eyes straying down to the top of my pants. Irys moves slowly, trailing unsure fingers down past the waistband. Her slender fingers undo the simple lacing and they sag around my hips. Dipping her hand inside, I growl loud enough to shake the bed.

Her small fist rubs my cock and stars shoot off behind my eyes. Gripping my own pants. I rip them off and bring my cock into view. Irys's hand flies to her mouth and she scrambles back, no doubt wondering how she is going to accomplish the task she has set out to complete.

My cock sticks out from my body, already seeking the warm, tightness of her cunt. It points at her like an accusation. In this form, it resembles more of a human male's cock. The head and shaft are smooth, and decorated with only a few dark veins. A bead of my come already sits at the tip and I hear her gasp as more rushes out in front of her eyes. Warm, stickiness slipping down the side of my shaft and dripping onto the sheets.

"Do not be scared, little one. My cock will only give you pleasure, even when you are not sure you can take it." I wrap my hands around her ankles and pull her down the bed, her dark hair fanning out behind her. "Now get on your knees."

Dropping Irys to the floor, the fire from the hearth illuminates her in a warm glow. She sits back on her heels looking up at me. Her full lips are open and she runs her tongue along the bottom one. I stand above her, jerking my cock in my clawed hand over her face. This act is deliciously crude. She is an angel I am about to sully for my own pleasure.

An angel who I can see dripping onto the carpet.

I sit on the edge of the bed and spread my thighs. Waving a clawed hand, I motion her forwards. Irys crawls towards me, that ass of hers swaying with each movement. Damning myself for not tasting that hole earlier, I make a mental note to explore it later.

"Look at how you tremble. My greedy cock whore wants to taste her demon's dick. To drink his seed until it fills her belly," I say and her moan in response is all the confirmation I need. "Kiss it, little one. Kiss it how you kissed my mouth, we will go from there."

Irys slides closer until her mouth is level with my lap. Her small hand replaces mine around my shaft. I watch her hesitate for only a moment before her pink lips kiss the crown of my cock. My come already there coats her lips and I growl as she licks it off. As she tastes me her eyes grow more unfocused, the sound of her arousal hitting the carpet is music to my ears.

Kissing the tip again I watch her grow bolder. Tentatively slipping her pink tongue out to run along one vein and caption more of my spend to drink down. She moves her fist up and down and my balls hit against my inner thighs. Irys discovers them at the same time and runs that curious tongue along them as well.

"Do...do I only kiss you here?" Another perfect blush. "You did more than just kiss my pussy."

"I licked you until you creamed all over my face. Lick my cock, feast on it my beautiful slut, and I'll treat your face to the same reward." Irys loves how I speak to her. I felt it when I was growling those same words against her pussy, being rewarded by more of her delicious juices.

A growl rips from my chest as she flattens her tongue and licks the underside of my cock. Over and over again she tastes each side of my cock, coating them in her spit. She licks at my tip and is rewarded with more of my seed that she drinks down. Licking lower she runs her tongue along each ball before returning to my shaft.

"Such a hungry little girl. You were starved for food but

more importantly, you were starved for cock. Don't worry, I'll make sure you get your fill of each every night."

Moaning around the tip of my cock, her eyes connect with mine once more. The flush of her cheeks, her wild expression, and the saliva running down the corner of her lips is beautiful.

Irys smiles at me as she opens wide and takes me fully into her mouth.

I pitch forward on the edge of the bed which causes my cock to go deeper into her throat. Gagging slightly, she does not stop. The muscles of her mouth work in tandem with her hand, sucking and tugging me until my vision blurs.

"My perfect little cock-slut. You were born to suck cock." I growl as she takes me deeper, watching tears leak from her eyes. "Only my cock. Mine. No man will ever get to see you like this."

Her nod is frantic as she continues to work me. Never stopping, only more and more eager to taste me. My self-control is in short supply. My claws tangle in the soft strands of her hair and grip her skull. I want to get deeper, but she is so small I do not know if she is ready for that.

Irys's hand squeezes my knee and she nods her head. She knows what I want to do and she is giving me permission. *Mine.* I will brand her name on my skin.

Gripping her head even tighter, I release myself. I bring my hips up to meet her mouth as I drive her face down into my lap. My cock not only bumps the back of her throat but goes down it. She swallows and the pressure makes my teeth grind. She does not protest, she does not stop me.

Irys holds on to my knees and lets me face-fuck her for all that she is worth.

The sounds from her mouth are wet and obscene. I feel her nose bump up against my stomach and my toes curl. I slam her down harder, not sure how much longer I can last.

"You're perfect, my perfect little toy. I said I wouldn't defile you but that's exactly what I'm doing." Irys lets out a moan and then chokes around my length again. Her tears land on my thighs, the salty smell of them an aphrodisiac to me. I feel myself start to spray more come into her mouth that she greedily drinks down until she is gagging again.

Her nails dig into my knees and I know she is at her limit. My brave little human.

I rip her off my cock and she tries to catch her breath. Those green eyes are bloodshot and wet, her mouth is smeared with a mixture of her spit and my seed. Those plush lips are bright red and swollen. I should have come down her throat but my possessiveness demands I claim her in a more primal way.

After all, I did promise to come on her face like she came on mine.

"Sit back on your knees and open your mouth." Irys does so immediately. "Good girl."

My clawed hand moves in a frenzy as I tug on it over her face. Her breathing is turning ragged again, her nipples are pebbling under my stare and I watch a stream of wetness coasts down her parted thighs.

"Please give me your come, Asgorath. Please reward me with it."

Her soft voice saying my name is all it takes. I let out a bellow that has the birds nested in the ceiling scattering off. The first rope of my come lands on her tongue, before sliding down her chin. The next ones land lower on her chest, dripping down on her breasts. I come and come and come until her mouth and chin are painted in my release. The white, sticky substance clings to her skin and her dark hair. My scent mingles with hers.

My chest moves with labored breaths as I watch Irys run a finger through the seed on her collarbone. She lifts that finger to her mouth before swallowing it, licking the extra from her lips. What a picture she makes. Covered in my come and dripping her own.

"Thank you," she says. "Did I please you enough to let me suck your cock again?"

I growl and scoop her off the floor.

"You'll be sucking my cock every day for the rest of your life." Irys giggles before nuzzling into my neck. Stickiness coats me but I do not mind it. I am just grateful that I have her in my arms, so trusting and content.

I will keep her this way for eternity.

With a wave of my hand the antique copper tub turns on and hot water fills the basin. Grabbing a handful of herbs and salts I throw them into the water until it is cloudy and emitting a woodsy scent. Irys is still in my arms, watching me from half-closed eyes. Once the bath is full the water switches off and I lower both of us into the warm water.

Irys lets out a soft moan and stretches her legs out in front of her. My cock is wedged between the cheeks of her ass and I grit my teeth. I wash her gently, cleaning away my spend, secure in the knowledge that I will be covering her in more of it in the coming hours. Scrubbing her scalp she sighs and tilts her neck to give me better access. The silence between us is comfortable. A comfort that I am already attached to.

"Asgorath," Irys says softly. I hum as I reach for a basin of fresh water to rinse the soap from her hair. "You know I do not have much experience...with any of this."

I nod, setting the basin down and reaching for a towel to keep her clean hair out of the dirty water.

"My sisters always said I was gullible and it would get me in trouble but, I don't have anyone else to ask."

"Ask me, little one. I'll tell you whatever you wish to know." I feel her take a deep breath.

"Is this normal? The way I feel towards you? My sisters respect their husbands but they never have spoken of this...

desire. This need to be pleasured is all I can think about. I can't imagine them feeling this way and being able to keep it quiet."

My heart thunders in my chest. My little human desires me. Irys wants me to pleasure her and can think of nothing else. This warms me and my claws slip down her sides, dragging along her smooth skin, before coming to rest on her hips.

"Your sisters are not married to men who could give them this. No mortal man can give you this." My claws slip lower until they part her folds eliciting another sweet moan. "Your pussy recognizes this. Your heart does too. It understands and desires to be kept by me even when your brain still believes it wants a normal man. You've never truly wanted a human man and you never will."

I slip a claw just into her entrance and she throws her head back against my shoulder. She is ready for me. Finally.

"Now it's time for me to prove it to you."

5

———

IRYS

Asgorath dries me with a plush towel before leading me back into the bedroom.

I do not know when he became so handsome to me but he is. I love the way his dark hair tickles my sensitive skin. Love the way his claws tease me and pinch my nipples.

But most of all I love how much he wants me.

Call it wrong, given what he is and how we met, but I am beginning to realize that maybe I want him to keep me. I do believe him when he says no man could ever satisfy me and it is evident to me that I can never live without this pleasure. Sometime between when he was licking my pussy to me sucking on his cock I made the decision that I would remain here in the morning.

To see what life could be like with him.

As someone who grew up unwanted and passed around, his possessiveness over me makes my hunger for him grow. No one has ever wanted me. My sisters abandoned me to start their own lives, my father used me as a bargaining piece but Asgorath…

Asgorath could have demanded I stay with him. Could have put that into the bargain and I would have had to agree but he did not. He told me he would give me pleasure and then I could do as I wanted. To marry who I wanted.

Is it wrong that I can no longer see that person being anyone other than him?

Perhaps I should desire freedom. To be able to start a life where I am able to pick and choose what I want and where I want to go. But hasn't Asgorath given me that? Would he keep me locked in this cabin? Would I even want to leave?

These are all things I will grapple with in the morning. Right now I will sink into this deep pool of lust and give myself fully to my demon.

Walking into the bedroom I see that the sheets have been changed. Unlike the dark ones before, these are bright white, tightly tucked into the mattress. I look up at Asgorath with a raised brow. He sets me down gently, leaving me covered only in the towel.

"I want the proof that I was your first time. Your virgin blood will soak these sheets and I will keep them as my most treasured possession." My answering blush makes me dip my head. I look at the soft bed and drop my covering. The wet strands of my hair tickle my back as I crawl onto it face first.

My first time. I should be as nervous as I was at the start of the night but I am not. This is the right time. This is who I want and who I know will take care of my needs. I am not afraid, I am ready to give myself to him.

The *real* him.

Asgorath makes a move to join me but I sit up.

"I want you to take me in your true form. The one that I first saw you in." Shock has his dark eyes widening.

"Are you sure? That form can be even more...demanding than this one." I nod my head and he steps back from the bed.

With a deep breath, he begins to transform. His body glows with a warm light pulsing, shimmering and shaking as it reveals his true form. His skin begins to tear to reveal black hands the color of the night sky that tapers down into deadly sharp claws. With a few groans and snaps, his horns lengthen and become even more gnarled. The skin of his face peels back, ripping through bone and flesh until a skull is all that's left behind. The fire from the hearth is pulled through the air. It threads itself through one dark eye socket until his gray skull is lit from within.

"It seems my greedy little human demands more from her demon lover." He runs that extra-long tongue over his sharp teeth. My pussy starts to drip and I watch him inhale the scent. "Be warned, little one. My other form had a bit more control. I cannot promise that when I am like this I will be able to be gentle."

In this form, he towers over the bed. At least another foot taller than he was before and wider too. His cock is definitely larger, I can barely make it out in the firelight but I know it will be even more magnificent. My thighs rub together and those fiery eyes track the movement. I should be scared, should change my mind and have him switch back to that more palatable form. However, I do not ask for that. Instead, I crawl forward on my hands and knees and grasp one of his clawed hands, falling on my back and pulling him down on top of me.

"However you fuck me will be right. I want you to ruin me for anyone else." Kissing a skull is a new sensation. There is no give and it feels like I am kissing a warm, smooth stone. I do not care though. Not as my tongue glides under those sharp teeth to pet his. His growl shakes the bed, the air turning thick with desire.

"My seed has made you bold, little human. Let me give you more of it."

"Please," I whine. "I miss your taste."

His cock stretches between us, rubbing up and down my stomach, already seeking to enter me. My earlier suspicions were confirmed when I feel its size. It spans the length from my hips to my breasts. As well as it being adorned with ridges along his shaft and tip. How will those feel inside of me? My thighs squeeze at the question and I know I cannot wait any longer to find out.

I push up on my heels to try and align him to my entrance, but his clawed hand wraps around my jaw and forces me to look at him.

"Once I am inside you and I have your blood running down my cock, that is it for you. I will own you. Your cunt, your body, your heart. It will belong to me. Should you try and run from me..." His deep voice grows rough, coasting over my skin and turning my nipples hard. "I'll find you and keep you locked in this bedroom for all of eternity."

"Please, I want to be kept." The truth tumbles from me before I have a chance to suck the words back in.

"You better mean that, Irys. Besides, I can't have my little fucktoy wandering too far, someone might try and take her from me." His hand moves from my jaw down to my throat. "And I do mean try, for if anyone succeeded I'd kill them with my bare hands."

The violence, the vulgar words, it is too much for me to bear.

"Please, Asgorath, I need you inside me. I can't wait any longer."

"Oh Irys, we haven't even begun and already you're a soaking, pathetic mess." His clawed hand leaves my throat and trails down the center of my body. He stops briefly to tug at my nipples, scraping his sharp teeth over each of them. His hand goes lower, over my pussy before cupping my folds. I moan and grind myself against his palm.

Lust has taken over and I need him more than I need my next breath.

"Wet and soft. That's how you'll always be in my presence. Wet and waiting for me to pound this tight pussy." Asgorath gives my feminine flesh another squeeze and my eyes roll to the back of my head. His tongue extends from his mouth, licking up my chest and leaving behind a trail of moisture.

"Please, Asgorath."

"You need me to fuck this cunt?"

"Yes!" I scream. "Please."

"I told you you'd beg me," he laughs, his claws slowly sinking into my entrance. "Now let me get this little, pink pussy ready to take this demon cock."

With one finger inside of me, the pressure is almost too much. When he adds a second one I almost come clean off the mattress. His fingers are thick, and those dangerous claws scrape softly inside me, not too far as to break my maidenhead but enough to have my toes curling. Unfurling his jaw once more, that long tongue slips out as it licks a path down to where his fingers are parting me.

"Your greedy little clit is begging for my attention and it's too sweet for me to ignore." His magic lifts my legs, tilting my hips so I am completely exposed to his face. My fingers grip the white sheets as his tongue laps at that bundle of nerves, my clit, and works it over and over in tandem with his claws. He fucks me with his fingers, while his tongue makes love to the rest of me.

"I wonder if this hole is just as sweet."

His tongue pushes against my back entrance and I scream. My skin breaks out in a hot rash as I thrash on the bed, trying to break out of his hold. *Not there, oh my...anywhere else but there.*

"Embarrassed? You shouldn't be. As my whore you will give me entrance into all your holes whenever I want to use them.

Whether it's for my pleasure or to give you yours." He smirks even as his tongue presses harder against my forbidden entrance. "Maybe I'll fuck your ass tonight as well to rid you of this shame."

"Please...d—d—don't, not there!" I thrash as his tongue pushes past the tight ring of muscle. Those fingers of his have not stopped pumping into me but the added fullness of his tongue makes my muscles strain. It's too much, way too much. Tears leak from my eyes. The pleasure barreling into me will break me. Snap me in half and I am scared of it.

The fear is what propels me forward.

Asgorath's tongue pushes in deeper, his fingers tickle the walls of my pussy and I start shaking.

"Come on my fingers, greedy girl. Come while my tongue is stuffed in your pretty little asshole." As if I can do anything but obey. My thighs shake and squeeze his head, my knuckles turning white where they grip the sheet. Perspiration breaks out of my skin as my climax hits me. A fresh wave of my come coats his hand and he growls. My stomach is in knots as my muscles continue to lock.

It takes me a moment to regain control of my breathing. It takes me another moment to realize Asgorath has removed his fingers and is pushing the tip of his cock into my entrance. My muscles are relaxed and my thighs are still held in place by his magic. He bares down on me as he feeds me one magnificent inch at a time. The fire in his eyes rages. Whatever emotion he is feeling it is a strong one.

The first shallow thrust is pleasant. The second one is filled with pressure. On the third one, I feel him break through my virginity, I look down to see the red drops sink into the sheets. Asgorath's tongue sneaks out to lick over another nipple again.

"You belong to me now, your purpose in life is to serve me in this bed."

My brain is fogged and I absentmindedly realize he is not

even halfway inside me and it already feels like I am being split in half.

"My purpose is to serve you." Another inch of his cock fills me, those ridges making my head fall back on the bed. "Forever."

"Even if it hurts?" he asks and I nod. He grits his teeth and leans down to meld his mouth to mine. "Forgive me, little one. This is the only pain I'll ever cause you."

That is the only warning I get before he jerks forward, burying himself completely inside of me.

The scream I let out is inhuman. I buck underneath him to try and move away from him and the pressure he's caused inside of me. There is pain, but he does not try and move. His fire-filled eyes bore into me as his clawed hand wraps around my throat.

"Hold still. Hold still. The pain will be over soon, let yourself adjust."

His hard mouth rains kisses all over my cheeks and mouth. The longer we stay still the more the pain begins to subside. Those ridges inside of him caused me discomfort but now I need to know what they feel like as he thrusts inside of me.

"This naughty pussy couldn't resist me for long. It needs a good pounding and that's what I'm going to give it." His mouth returns to mine and his hips retreat before slowly pushing back in.

The sensation is everything. I am so incredibly full I could burst. I feel his warm tongue slip into my mouth and it keeps pace with his thrusts. His wonderful pine scent fills my lungs and I want to be consumed by it. The hard skin of his body rubs against my nipples and it only adds more to the pleasure.

"Tiny and tight. If I wasn't already from Hell, fucking your cunt like this would surely damn me there for eternity." Picking up the pace, his hips rear back and slam into me. The muscles of my ass jiggle with the impact as the sound of our bodies slapping together only increases my arousal. I can hear the wet slurping sounds my pussy is making as he pounds into me.

His tongue creeps deeper into my mouth, past my teeth, and tickles the back of it. I gag and cough around it but that only spurs him on further. Licking up the back of my throat tears blur my vision as he increases his brutal fucking. My breasts bounce in time with the impact.

"Open your mouth," he says, pulling his tongue from my throat. I obey without question parting my lips and sticking out my tongue. His face looms over me as his tongue hangs out, grazing my own. I watch as a trail of saliva slides down it and into my waiting mouth. So much pours from him and I can feel it slip down my throat and spill out over my lips.

"Swallow," he commands and I all too happily obliged. He spits down, another patch of saliva lands on my lips that he promptly rubs in with his clawed hand. It's vile and disgusting to be degraded in this way, but I crave it all the same.

He sees it in my eyes and his mouth widens into a grin exposing those sharp teeth.

"Dirty, little human. Letting me defile her virgin cunt with my demon cock. Watching her swallow down my seed and my spit. You're a vessel for my pleasure, that's all you'll ever be."

"Yes, please. I want more of your come."

"Inside of you, little one?" he asks. "Inside this pretty pussy."

"Yes, inside of me. Anywhere!" I scream. His pace hasn't slowed down. The force with which his hips slam against mine leads me to believe I'll be bruised in the morning. Bruises I'll be wearing with pride.

"I'm going to fill you up. My come will flood your tiny cunt."

Taking both my wrist in one clawed hand he pins them down above my head. My body is taut on the bed and can do nothing but absorb his rough fucking. The posters of the bed creak and groan with each of his thrusts as the headboard smacks against the wall. He leans down to lick up my neck before nipping at it with his teeth. My muscles are cranking tighter and tighter. My hips tilt as much as they can to get him even deeper. His ridges press against a secret spot inside of me and my nails dig into his hand.

"Clenching down on me so you can receive my come. This greedy pussy will be drowning in my seed." He slams into me once, twice, and on the third time, my climax hits me. "Take it. Take every last drop, good girl."

My screams echo around us and mingle with his groan. I feel his warm come shoot into me over and over again. True to his promise he floods me. The hot liquid slips out around where we are joined and joins my blood on the sheets. Asgorath still pushes into me even as his cock softens, the squelching sound makes my cheeks heat.

As he continues to fill me I am struck by how right this feels. Everything about this moment is perfect.

"Asgorath," I say, my voice hoarse from screaming. "Thank you. That was beyond anything I could've imagined."

"Was?" he chuckles. "Oh, little one, we are not done yet."

Before I can react, his strong forearm is wrapped around my middle and flips me onto my hands and knees. His claws snag at my hips and he pulls my ass up toward his face.

"Did you really think I was only going to have one round with this pretty cunt?" He runs a claw through my folds and I watch as he sucks our mingling releases into his mouth.

"But our bargain—"

"Said you would give me your virginity and that you would spend the night with me. The sun is not rising anytime soon." Asgorath squeezes one of the cheeks of my ass. "And I will be inside each one of your holes tonight."

I don't get the chance to protest before I feel him pushing into me again.

"You should see the mess I made in your pussy. My seed

makes sliding into you so much easier. Your only purpose is to take my come, isn't it?"

"Yes, Asgorath," I say, my ass tipping up toward him. Reaching down he winds the length of my hair around his fist, making my spine curve even more and my eyes look up at the wood beams of the ceiling.

"Did you mean it?" I choke out as he continues slamming into me from behind. My arms feel like mush but I support myself, absorbing each brutal impact.

"Mean what, greedy girl?"

"That you're keeping me?" All movement stops and the bed quits its creaking. Shame makes me stay quiet. I should not have asked. Perhaps this is what all lovers say in the heat of the moment and in the morning light both parties part ways.

If he rejects me now, in this state, I will never recover from the embarrassment. From the vulnerability I am showing him in this moment.

His chest comes down on top of my back and I feel it shake with laughter. Is he laughing at me? Heat presses against my closed eyes.

"See what happens when someone tries to take you from me," he whispers in my ear. "Then you'll know if I mean it or not."

Asgorath's warm breath tickles my cheek as I feel his tongue lick down my back. Tasting the sweat that lingers on my spine until slipping through my parted ass cheeks.

He said he would claim both holes tonight. He said he would keep me. Asgorath is a demon that keeps his end of the bargain.

That wet tongue pushes through my back entrance, stretching me until my muscles burn. It goes deeper than before. With Asgorath fully sheathed inside of me, I've never experienced being this full. This pleasure is not meant for this world, it is not meant for humankind.

But I have tasted it and I will never live without it again.

"Only naughty whores question their master." He drops my hair and pushes my chest down towards the bed. "Cheek to the mattress while I fuck those doubts out of you."

My demon does just that.

6

IRYS

oft sunlight filters into my eyes, waking me from the deepest sleep of my life.

Groaning, I bury myself under my pillow, stretching out my legs beneath the sheets. It is tempting to believe I dreamed Asgorath up. The story is certainly absurd enough. A woman wandering into *The Woods* in order to escape her marriage. Only to be pleasured by a demon who wants to keep her forever.

If it was not for the soreness between my legs I may have believed that it was all just a figment of my imagination.

Disentangling from my sheets I wake up to find that I am alone in this massive bed. I could not tell you how many times Asgorath buried himself inside of me, but by the final time, I could barely keep my eyes open. My demon pulled himself from me despite my hissing from the lack of connection and gathered me to his side, careful not to impale me with his horns.

The whole night I slept safe and wanted in his arms. Arms I want to be in again right now.

I swing my feet over the side of the bed and stand. All at

once a rush of his comes leaks out of me and drips down my thighs. Smiling, I take a tentative step toward the bathroom, gritting my teeth at the discomfort. I need a pain reliever herb, the healer woman told me those are the ones she comes into *The Woods* to find. If those plant cataloging supplies were anything to go by, I am sure some is grown around here.

Wetting a towel with warm water I gently wipe away the blood and stickiness from my thighs. I find a stack of clean clothes laid out for me. Ones made of much finer material than the ones I arrived in. Making my way upstairs I wonder where Asgorath is.

The cottage is quiet and I can smell fresh bread baking. He probably just stepped out for a moment. Collecting my cloak I fasten it around myself before pushing through the door and standing in the front lawn. *The Woods* are still dangerous but in the morning rays they are not quite so ominous.

Or maybe that is because I have Asgorath to protect me now. Perhaps *The Woods* are just welcoming me as their new inhabitant.

A quick survey of the yard and I find the bright blue leaves of the plant I am looking for. There is only enough for two cups of tea but that should be all I need to soothe this ache. I smile, realizing I should probably plan to collect some extra to have on hand.

Pulling it from the ground I go to put it in my satchel when I hear it.

Gallops from horses. I stand there frozen until they come into view. My heart beats wildly and I cannot register what I am seeing. No, it cannot be.

My father and the Duke are here. They have come to collect me.

Both sit atop white stallions, flanked by two soldiers on their opposite sides. My father's eyes are bloodshot and his skin is greenish in color. His normal look after a night where he found himself particularly deep in his cups. While my father is battling a hangover, the Duke looks livid. His wrinkled skin is red and his eyes pierce right through me.

My skin crawls at the reminder that I was supposed to marry him today.

Not anymore though, Asgorath saved me from that. He gave me my freedom back and I am using it to choose to stay with him. With that newfound resolve, I square my shoulders and face both men.

"Lady Evergrove," Duke Brayborne calls out. "Your presence is required in town. Did you think *The Woods* would keep you from fulfilling our marriage arrangement?"

"I do not have to marry you." My father seems to be coming out of his stupor and slides down from his horse.

"Daughter, why have you dishonored me? I gave you to Duke Brayborne to wife and you fled? If we hadn't gotten it out of that healer woman where you might be, we may never have found you." My lord father walks closer to me and I back up a step. "You're coming home to be married. Running away from your duty is unbecoming of a woman your age. You are lucky the Duke still wishes for your hand after you dishonored him."

Where is Asgorath? Surely he would not allow them to take me.

"I do not have to marry him, father. I made a bargain with the demon in these woods."

"And what, pray tell, did you offer this creature, daughter? You have no money to tempt him with."

Heat rises to my cheeks but I refuse to feel shame over what Asgorath and I did.

"Myself." Father rears back as if he has been struck, shock contorts his features. The Duke lets out a deep laugh and shakes his head, his beady eyes narrowing with disgust.

"Foolish girl!" My father makes a grab for me but I jump back out of his reach.

"Selling yourself to that beast will not save you from me." The Duke dismounts from his horse, the last three strands of white hair he has blowing in the wind. His yellowed teeth bare in a grin at me. "I will delight in punishing you for your desertion, you traitorous whore."

Dropping my satchel I look around. *Asgorath please show yourself and make good on your half of the bargain.* Both the Duke and my father advance on me. I could make it back into the cottage but they may catch me in there and drag me out. I was never very quick at climbing trees either.

A gentle wind tugs at my hair, the same wind that propelled me to Asgorath's door in the first place. It pushes me to *The Woods* behind the cottage as if urging me to run as fast as I can. That is when I remember Asgorath's words from the night before.

Should you try to run...I'll find you.

I have to believe he was serious in his threat. Without a moment to lose, I turn from my father and the Duke and sprint deeper into the heart of *The Woods*. I hear the Duke shout something behind me but I am already moving too fast. The breeze is pushing me as I pump my arms and legs. My cloak and hair snag on the branches as my feet jump over the uneven ground. I keep going, willing Asgorath to realize something is wrong and save me.

The sound of hooves hitting the ground pound in time with my heart.

There is a break in the trees up ahead and I know I just have to make it there. I keep going, even as I feel them closing in on me.

"Get back here, Irys. I'll wring your neck once I get my hands on you." The Duke's threat sends a chill of fear down my spine and makes me run even faster. My heart is racing and my legs are throbbing from the effort.

I burst through the clearing and that is when I see him.

Still, in his demon form, his cloak drawn tight around himself. In his hands I see a large bushel, the telltale blue leaves of the pain reliever plant. Relief and happiness make my steps falter and tears rush to my eyes. The glow in his eye sockets sparks.

"Were you trying to run from me, little one?" He calls across the clearing just as I hear the gallops close in on me. His head snaps to look behind me and without giving him an answer I run straight toward him until my arms are wrapped tightly around him.

"Don't let them take me, please. Don't let them take me back." I sob into his chest, relishing his warmth and strength. "He still wants to marry me, Asgorath. He'll kill me if I go back, please don't let him!"

The thunderous sound of hooves has stopped and I hear a loud gasp behind me. Opening my eyes I look over my shoulder to see all of the men frozen in fear. Even the Duke has paled and he reaches for the sword at his side, brandishing it Asgorath. The two other soldiers follow suit

Asgorath is unruffled by them. Waving a clawed hand I watch as the Duke's sword is yanked from his grasp. Asgorath flicks his wrist and the blade spins in time with his hand, flying high above the Duke's head until it stops with the blade pointing down.

"This is for tainting her scent with fear." It is the only warning my demon gives before the sword drops, impaling the Duke. Crimson blood leaks off the tip of the blade as it protrudes down his chest. With a meaty thud, he hits the forest floor.

The soldiers in the Duke's employ meet a similar fate.

My father's eyes are as round as teacups as he takes in the gore. He looks up at me, at how I am grasping this demon like he is my lifeline. Father shakes himself and then drops to his knees. He clasps his hands in front of him and raises them towards me.

"My daughter, my beautiful Irys. I have been a terrible father to you. Letting that lecherous duke anywhere near you was my fault. I am sorry. I am so sorry for how you have suffered in my care." His green eyes, the same color as mine, beseech me. "Spare my life and come home with me. Away from that creature and you have my word that you can marry whoever you want."

Asgorath stiffens next to me. Does he think I would so easily leave him? Silly demon, he is mine for all eternity as well. I wrap my arms tighter around his middle.

"I am sorry too, father, but my bargain states I can only marry someone I love." I tilt my face up towards my demon, his fire-filled eyes warming my face. "And I've already found that."

A clawed hand cups my cheek and tilts my head up before hard lips caress mine. I break the kiss needing to end this once and for all. To sever all ties to my old life.

"I will have my demon spare your life if you agree to tell everyone in the village I ran away. That the Duke and his men tried to find me but met with an unfortunate accident. You will promise to never come and look for me again. You will tell no one what has happened to me." My father is already nodding his head. "Do you agree?"

"Yes, yes please just spare me."

My eyes meet Asgorath's and he nods.

"Be gone father, the daughter you knew died in *The Woods* last night. Who I am now is someone else."

Without so much as a backward glance, my father scrambles to his feet. Quickly mounting one of the white stallions he turns on his tail and gallops out of the clearing.

He always was pathetic. I realize that now.

There is a stretch of silence before Asgorath breaks it.

"Did you mean it?" he asks. I nuzzle my face into his chest, inhaling his earthly scent.

"Of course I meant it. I'm waiting for you to say it back." My face heats and I shake my head. "Unless of course, you don't. Which is fine. I don't know why I expected you—"

"Irys, what I feel for you is stronger than love. It is an obsession. One that will completely consume me if I let it." His claws tangle in my hair and gently scratch my scalp. "I'll live every day for you. For your pleasure."

His mouth descends on mine and I moan into our kiss. That wonderful tongue of his tickles mine. Leaving my hair, his claws tangle in the tie of my cloak, undoing the bow and letting it pool at my feet.

"Well then, don't let me keep you from your life's purpose." Reaching behind me I undo the laces to my gown, letting it drop and join my cloak at my feet. I stand there under his fiery stare completely naked. He lets loose a growl before taking one of my breasts in his hands.

"Should we enter into another bargain?" Asgorath asks, licking my nipple until I squirm.

"What did you have in mind?"

"That you'll spend all eternity telling me how much you love me...and I'll spend an eternity showing you how much I love you." I bark out a laugh. Gripping the sides of his cloak I pull until he too is gloriously naked. Dropping to my knees I take his magnificent cock in my hand, roughly pumping him twice. Licking up the come that has already beaded at the tip.

"This may be the second easiest bargain I've ever agreed to," I say, before taking his cock all the way down my throat.

EPILOGUE

ASGORATH

Five Years Later

The *Woods* have never felt more like my home than they have in the past few years.

I always viewed this realm as a part of my job. A job that has experienced an uptick in customers recently. I guess the story of a young woman finding her way into the path of a demon who bargained to get the life of her dreams will do wonders for business. My purpose in this land is to fulfill bargains and gain more power.

But it does not truly satisfy me like Irys does. Nothing ever will.

Once this latest bargain is done I can get back to her. Already my mouth waters for a taste of her sweet skin. Over the last five years, my desire for her has only increased. I need to be inside her every moment of the day. If there were no bargains to make or food to prepare I sometimes think I would never pull out of her. Living out the rest of eternity in the warmth of her pussy.

Speaking of bargains, I watch as the elderly fisherman in

front of me hands over his bag of saltwater pearls. The last of his late wife's possessions so that I will grant him his favor. I shake the bag in my clawed hand. His red hair is graying around the sides and his face is weathered by a life spent at sea.

"Your offering pleases me. In exchange for these pearls, I will grant you luck on the high seas. That your catches will be bountiful. You will be the envy of every other sailor in your company."

He gives a surprised gasp and clasps his hands.

"Thank you, thank you. It is for me and my daughter. She is only sixteen. This is to keep her fed."

I grunt at him ready for this exchange to be done. Besides, this fisherman is a fool and will soon have to face the wrath of Kraken of the Darksea. A fate he should have taken into consideration before coming to me.

"Your reasons are your own. Our business is done here."

Tucking the pearls into my cloak I let my magic wash over me and suddenly I am at the door of my cottage. Our cottage. A life the two of us have built. No more cold, solitary nights when she is with me. We spend countless hours a day getting lost in each other. I've taken her on every surface of this home and it is still not enough. It will never be enough.

Irys has blossomed in the short time she has been with me. After her father departed it became apparent to me that he did not think to give her an education. She was embarrassed by her lack of ability to read or write when I asked her to help me catalog some of the plants that grow around the cottage. I kissed away her embarrassment and made it my goal to teach her everything. True to my word I have.

From the history of the world to how she can take me in her ass for hours on end. She has become the best pupil any teacher could hope for.

I wonder what Irys is up to now. Studying? Cataloging some more of the wildlife? Pushing through the door, she is not immediately in front of me and that displeases me. Normally, when I return from a bargain she can't wait to get her hands on me.

The bag of pearls is removed from my satchel and I study it. I had planned on giving it as a gift to Irys but the more I think about it, surely it is bad luck to give your own wife the pearls of another man's dead one. I set them at the table by the door and call out to my obsession.

"Irys?"

"Down here." Her soft voice reaches me and my cock instantly hardens.

My Irys wants to play. I know she is in our bedroom and I quickly shed my humanoid form. After all these years, Irys still prefers my true face. It makes her so wet I only use my other form when I am making a bargain.

My feet stomp through the house until I am outside our bedroom. There she is, my beautiful wife. Lying on our bed completely naked. Her dark hair is fanned out around her and her delicate wrists are bound to the headboard by a thin scrap of ribbon. A soft, shy smile on her full mouth.

Instantly I am salivating over her. I shed my cloak so I am just as naked as her and I watch her rub those smooth thighs together. Circling around the bed I drag one of my claws up the center of her body, swirling around each nipple, before slipping it into her parted mouth. She moans as she sucks on my finger, with the same vigor she gives my cock.

Leaning down I whisper in her ear.

"You know I love you?" I ask.

"Yes," she says around my finger, continuing to take it deeper into her mouth.

"Good because for the next few hours"—I rip my finger from her mouth and use my thumb to keep it open—"I am going to fuck you like I don't. Like you are nothing more than a naughty human slut who wandered into the demon's lair."

My jaw unlocks and I watch as my tongue licks over her chest and through the dusting of dark hair on her pussy. I watch her eyes go glassy as she pulls against the restraints when my tongue finds her slick folds. Delicious. I lick and lick until sweat breaks out along her forehead.

Pushing my tongue into her entrance, I lick along her walls until I butt up against her womb. She moans, her thighs squeezing against my ears.

"Such a beautiful whore. You'll let me put my tongue in your ass as punishment, yes?" I ask. She was shy about it in the beginning but she loves her ass being fucked now.

"Y—yes," she stutters out.

"Won't be much of a punishment, will it? Naughty girls like you like having their two holes stretched at once, don't they?" Her head nods vigorously. My tongue coasts lower until it meets her little asshole. It takes nothing for my tongue to slip in now, though she is still as tight as the day I first claimed it.

I push my claws into her, scissoring both fingers and stretching her tight pussy while my tongue fills her ass. Irys moans my name and begs me in an incoherent voice until I feel her cunt clamp down over my fingers. She soaks my palm, her come shooting out of her and drenching the sheets below.

Pulling my tongue out of her, I eagerly lap up her moisture before crawling up the bed to straddle her lovely face. I am careful not to rest my weight on her as I push my cock into her warm wet mouth. In this position, she cannot take me as long but she sure tries.

"Cock-hungry slut, aren't you? You suck me so good, little one. You want to earn my come."

"I do," she garbles around my length. My hands grip the headboard for leverage as I slam myself down her tight throat. Irys chokes, her nose and eyes leaking to mix with some of my come already spread on her face. The bed creaks under the force of my thrusts as I drill her face into the pillow. It is obscene what I am doing to this beautiful creature but she craves it just as much as I do.

Feeling my spine tingle I pull myself from her mouth and stroke my cock in front of her face. She keeps her eyes open as her lips part and she sticks out her waiting tongue. My come lands with a splat on her chest, painting her breasts in my release. I spread some of it along her lips before pushing the tip back into her mouth.

"There you go. Good girl for cleaning up my cock like that."

Her green eyes are dazed but she smiles at me, preening under my praise. As much as she loves being my greedy, little whore, she loves being my good girl just as much.

Reaching up I untie her wrists before sliding down her body. Gripping her hips I flip her on her hands and knees. I fold her arms behind her back before tying them so that her shoulders are the only thing supporting her upper half on the bed.

At this angle, both her holes are presented so nicely to me. Asking me which one I would like to fuck this evening. With Irys, I never have to choose.

I have been waiting on showing her this surprise but it feels right to give it to her now. My tongue licks a path up her spine, before dipping once into her ass and once into her pussy. I spit on her pink asshole and watch as it drips into her already wet folds.

"Irys?"

"Yes?"

"Will you let this monster take both your holes at once?" I ask, gripping one pale ass cheek.

"You know I love your tongue in my ass," she whispers, as if she is still shy to admit that.

"Not my tongue this time, little one. I've been working on a surprise for you." My magic zips through me and I can feel myself take on the transformation. I watch as my lower half glows faintly and then it sprouts out. A second cock, identical to my first one, only placed a little higher.

Gripping her hips I press both cocks to each of her respective holes.

Irys lets out a moan and writhes on the bed. Powerless to do anything while I have her immobilized.

"Asgorath...what is—how?" she asks, already leaking even more moisture from her pretty pussy, coating the head of my cock nudging her there.

"My girl loves my cock so much I had to give her a second one. So that I can fuck both her ass and pussy at the same time. Thank me for giving you what you need." Irys moans and tries to push back. My clawed hand smacks her ass, leaving behind a bright red handprint. I spank her again, digging my claws in to heighten the sting.

"Thank you, thank you!" she babbles.

Without warning, I plunge both cocks inside her. The feeling is incredible. She grips me so tightly in her cunt and ass that it is like having two fists wrapped around the most sensitive part of me. I pull back gently and can feel the twin ridges on my cock rub each other through the thin barrier that separates her ass from her pussy.

"Asgorath, it's too much! I can't—"

"You can take it. You were made to take my pounding. That is the only thing you are good for." Irys lets out another shriek as I retreat farther out of her before slamming all the way back in. This is some of the roughest fucking I have ever given her. It may be too much.

Just as I think that I watch her push back to meet my thrusts. Her breathing comes in pants not from fear but from arousal. She wants this. My greedy girl just needs to be fucked by me. It is what she always needs.

"I don't know if two cocks will be enough to satisfy you. There's still one hole left open." My tongue unleashes and snakes around her front, slipping into her parted mouth. I hear her gasp of surprise but it is soon swallowed up by her moans as my tongue fucks her throat in time with my cocks. Working in tandem to dominate every hole she has. Over and over again my hips slam into her. The globes of her ass cushion each blow. The wet suck of her pussy grips me and pulls me deeper inside her.

Irys is so wet that her arousal is dripping down my cock and slapping back against her ass. Messy. Just the way I like her. Her cunt begins to tighten around me and I know she's close.

Slipping my tongue from her mouth, her moans are even louder. She is delirious with pleasure. My tongue snakes back and dances over her clit and it is all over for her. Both her ass and pussy grip my cocks and I come the hardest I ever have.

I pitch forward and grip her hips, my claws digging in hard enough that I know I broke her skin. She screams as I shutter, filling both holes with rope after rope of my seed. Pulling out of her I watch it spray back out onto me and the sheets below. It runs down both of her openings in a continuous leak, coating the inside of both her thighs.

Absolutely perfect.

My magic zips again and my regular form has returned. I use my tongue to lick up the blood on her hips, my claws left behind and that has my cock hardening again. But my little Irys needs a break. Using one finger I sever the ribbon binding her arms and pull her up against my chest. Using my hands to rub the feeling back into her arm.

"That was incredible," she slurs, still floating on her orgasmic high.

"I'm glad you enjoyed that. I had been saving it for a special occasion but now felt special enough."

"Every time with you is special," Irys says, turning to press a kiss to my lips. Her arms circle around my neck and her legs wrap around my waist. A yawn sneaks up on her and I stand

while she still clings to me. I turn to make my way to the bathroom but she squeezes my waist to make me stop.

"Fuck me again."

I laugh in surprise. "Irys, you're exhausted, I'll be inside you
again soon enough. Let me clean you up and you can rest."

"I don't want to sleep. I want to come again."

"Greedy little slut," I say and kiss her brow. "But you're my
greedy little slut. The only one who's privilege it is to serve this
cunt."

"Only you, you'll own me forever." I grip her ass in my claws
and notch my cock at her entrance. We will go slow this time
and then I will put her to bed so she can be rested for another
round tonight.

"Wrap your arms tighter around my neck." She does so
immediately.

"Now be a good little girl and let me fuck you against the
wall."

I would not be surprised if every creature who calls *The
Woods* home could hear her scream.

The End

BONUS SCENE

IRYS

The smell of freshly baked bread tickles my nose.

I'd love nothing more than to retreat back to the peaceful darkness of sleep. However, my growling stomach has other ideas. With a deep sigh, I stretch out in my demon's bed. *Our bed*, I think with a smile.

My fingers and legs glide against the soft fabric even as my aching muscles protest. I'm deliciously sore all over. Rolling onto my back, my braid has come loose, and the long, dark strands of my hair tickle my bare shoulders.

Our bedroom is deep within Asgorath's cottage, and it's hard to tell what time of day it is. From the golden sunlight streaming in from the stairs above, I'd say it has to be late morning. It's no surprise that I'm so spent. Throwing back the covers, I take stock of my body.

Seed and saliva have dried along my thighs and stomach. Red marks from my demon's tongue and teeth decorate my chest. My lips curl as I take in my wrist, the silk ribbon still wrapped loosely around it.

Binding me to the headboard had been a particular delight. Has it really only been a day since my father departed? A day since that horrid duke came to claim me and my Asgorath saved me from a fate worse than death like any valiant knight. He is a monster, my monster, and I have no regrets in declaring my love for him in front of my father.

A love that mirrors the same kind my demon has for me.

All the ways he had me yesterday and into the early hours of this morning blur together in one erotic dream. My body has never experienced such pleasure—if this is a taste of what an eternity as Asgorath's lover will be, then I am eager for more.

Lover. The word brings a reluctant frown to my lips. It's a perfectly normal word, yet it doesn't feel right to apply it to the union I share with my demon. It feels too fleeting—too mundane. I want us bound together in every way.

As lovers, yes, but also as husband and wife.

I all but said it yesterday when my father had come to collect me. To fulfill my bargain, I can only marry someone I love and that is Asgorath. Do demons marry? While he loves me, does he want to be tied to me in that way?

Unease creeps up my neck as I feel a familiar sense of uncertainty. Asgorath has made me confident in my pleasure, but it will take time to let go of the fears that burdened me during the years I lived under my father's thumb.

Time. It is another simple word that is causing me untold distress. How much time will Asgorath and I have together? He is life eternal, and I am...well, me. A human—one whose life span is not particularly long in the face of eternity.

Will he want me when I'm old and gray? Will sickness or fate give us only a few decades together?

I'm spared from my unsavory thoughts as heavy footsteps echo on the stairs. My body, despite my muscle's protest, flames to life. With my heart racing, my nipples harden in anticipation of seeing my demon. The skin between my thighs turns slippery and warm.

I don't bother pulling the sheet back over myself. It's not as if my demon hasn't had his tongue or claws on every inch of my skin. My decision proves correct when Asgorath steps into the bedroom, the flames of his eyes blazing to life at the sight of me.

"Oh, little one," he growls. "Laid out amongst our bed looking thoroughly fucked with my come coating your precious skin. How am I to resist such a sight?"

My cheeks warm at his crude words—words I cherish hearing—as I raise my stiff arms toward him in invitation.

"You don't have to. I always want you."

The heat in his gaze burns away my lingering doubts as he advances toward me. He still wears his old cloak, letting me know that he had been off bargaining this morning. I feel ridiculous as a pout pulls at my lips. I want him just as naked as I am.

My mouth waters in anticipation of seeing his glorious cock —of taking it into my mouth once more until tear spill from my eyes. His imposing figure only causes more liquid arousal to slide out of me and collect on my thighs. With each heavy foot-step, my breaths become more halting.

Letting my arms fall to the bed beside me, it's not long before Asgorath's haunting face looms over me. I love him in this form. A human man could never satisfy me, I need my monster.

As if he's read my thoughts, Asgorath's lips pull into a feral grin, showing off sharp teeth. Gently, his clawed hand falls to my chest where he gently traces over a few lingering marks.

"I was rough, little one. Too rough for someone as delicate as you."

Despite his words, he grips one of my breasts firmly. His sharp claws press into my soft skin, and I gasp. When his thumb teases my peaked nipple, I thrust my hips on the bed in an obvious invitation.

"You love it, don't you? You need it rough—hard." His hold

on my breast tightens as I let out a soft moan. "Use your words, little one, or I'll remove my hand."

Making a sound of protest in my throat, the words my demon wants spill from my lips.

"Yes, I love it rough. You could fuck me on the floor, in the dirt outside this cottage, until my knees bruise, and I'd love every moment of it."

His grin widens as he releases my breast. With a deep groan, I use my hand to replace his and worry my nipple. It's barely a moment later that my hands are pinned to the bed by some invisible force. I thrash against his magic, but it is of no use.

"Naughty girl, you don't touch yourself without my permission. How should I punish you?"

"By touching me," I whine.

My body is molten with need more potent than any wine. If my demon doesn't touch me, I'll die on this bed. I need him, now and always. My legs scissors on the bed in desperate need of any friction I can get.

"More poor, aching, Irys. Are you in pain?" he asks.

His claws skim down my outer thighs, and I nearly come out of my skin.

"Yes," I say, watching goosebumps break out along my flesh.

"I see," he whispers. "You only misbehaved because you're in distress. I shouldn't punish you, should I? No, I know what you need."

"You," I lament. "I need you to touch me, to kiss me—to use me however you want."

"And I will, little one." His smile becomes even more sinister. "But not yet. Let me soothe you before the real fun begins."

Before I can ask what he means, he's suddenly at the foot of the bed. Using his claws, he yanks my legs apart before tossing them over his broad shoulders. I watch, entranced, as his jaw unhinges and the wet slither of his tongue echoes in the room.

Anticipation burns me as the wet muscle trails up my inner thigh.

I'm panting and shivering on the bed. His power holds firm as his tongue continues its exploration of my naked form. Slowly, deliciously, it reaches the place where I need him the most. His claws dig harder into my flesh as my moan is ripped from my lip.

Licking up my slit, Asgorath rumbles with pleasure. The fire in his eyes flames and bathes my naked skin in even more heat—a thin layer of sweat beads along my forehead and chest. My nipples are painfully hard as I thrust my lower body towards his face.

His tongue is gentle—reverent—as it tastes me fully. Parting my wet flesh, he teases my clit with a firm lick. Instantly, I'm on edge, and we've only just begun.

"Asgorath," I whine. "Please."

Giving my clit another lick, his tongue drifts lower to my entrance. He traces it once, twice, and then, without warning, plunges inside me. My hips rise off the bed as his tongue tunnels into me. The slippery feeling of his salvia mixes with my arousal, causing each thrust of his tongue to sound indecently wet.

Asgorath pumps into me, his tongue reaching an impossible depth as he curls it upwards. This far inside me, it pushes against that secret spot that has my toes curling into the crumpled sheets.

He plays with it until my thighs start to tremble in his grasp. Just a few more moments like this, and I'll reach my peak. My muscles begin to tighten as his claws trail higher on my legs. Faint red marks linger from the sharp points of his claws.

With a wicked gleam in his smoldering eyes, his fingers find my clit and rub gentle circles. It's too much, it's not nearly enough. I need more, and Asgorath will give it to me.

"I'm close," I whimper, my muscles tightening further.

His lips twist, and before I can utter another word, Asgortah pulls his tongue from inside me and stops his gentle ministrations on my clit. A frustrated growl leaves me as I fight against his power that still has me tethered to the bed.

"Patience, little one. Even a greedy slut like you should know the value of patience."

My cheeks heat at his crude words as more arousal slips from me. Another graze of his claws against me, and I'll reach my climax. I'm desperate, burning alive with my need.

"Make me come, Asgorath!" I scream.

Asgorath merely laughs—the cruel monster that he is.

"Beg."

The command is simple, and I cease my struggle. My eyes find his as he lowers himself fully to the bed. His claws slide down to cup me under my knees and lift them towards my chest. Baring me fully to his fiery gaze, his warm breath ghosts over my wet flesh.

"Did you hear me, Irys?" My heart pounds as I take in his severe gaze. "Beg me to make you come. Show me what a good little fucktoy you can be now that I've claimed for eternity."

A new emotion kindles in his eyes. One more dangerous and potent than his ravenous lust. Love. While his words are harsh—demanding—each one drips with love and possession.

I let him see the love I have for him reflected back in my own gaze as I lick over my dry lips.

"Please, Asgorath—my demon, my love—make me come. I need you. You own me. Taste my desire for you. Claim my pussy, it's only ever belonged to you." Tears of desperation burn the corners of my eyes. "If you don't touch me, I'll surely die. Every day, I need you. Every day I need you touching me, licking me, fucking me—loving me. There's nothing I want more than—"

My tirade of incoherent babbling is cut off as Asgorath growls.

Lowering his head, his horns press into my stomach as his mouth descends on me fully. He's everywhere at once. The wonderful wet tongue of him returns to my clit as his fingers spear into my core. He pumps them into me ruthlessly as my moans become choppy.

The tremble to my thighs returns with full force as liquid heat covers my body. I was on edge before, and my body is racing back towards that peak, desperate to be thrown off it.

A weight leaves my body, and I realize his power is no longer holding my hands to the bed. Raising them, I grip his horns and hold him to my pussy. I roll my hips into his thrusting fingers, and my teeth clench together.

"Perfect," Asgorath snarls against me. "My perfect girl. Look at how greedy your cunt is—sucking my fingers deeper inside you."

"Please," I mewl, my vision blurring.

"I know what you need, little one. Let me give it to you."

He hooks his fingers inside me, coating them in my arousal. Slipping them from my entrance, I cry out a the loss. Only for my groan of protest to swiftly become a shriek of pleasure as he spears a finger into my ass.

The burn is delicious, and that pain is mixed with pleasure as my body comes clean off the mattress as my climax tears through me. Tears flow from my eyes as I hold on to his horns to weather the storm. Love and lust and possession and obsession wage a war inside of me. I'm helpless to succumb to my baser needs as I grind out my orgasm against my demon's face.

Asgorath is there, guiding me through it all. His mouth is on my pussy, greedily drinking down every drop of my come. He rubs his face against me and spreads my wetness all over my hot flesh. My heart overflows with love as he looks up at me.

Asgorath is a dominant lover, but once our climaxes are reached, there is only tenderness remaining between us. He pumps his fingers into my back entrance one more before slipping them free.

Pressing soft kisses against my pussy, his mouth trails up my body. He stops briefly at each of my breasts, tonguing my nipples until my body is heating up once more. My legs lock around his hips as my arms wind around his neck.

His mouth comes down on mine, and I taste myself. Tongue tangling, our kiss is lazy and filled with connection. I'll never regret choosing him—I meant what I said: I can never live without this or without him.

Pressing one last kiss to my lips, my hand cups his cheek.

"Good morning," I whisper, my cheeks heating.

"It's well into the evening, little one," my demon chuckles.

"Is it?" I ask, noting that the bright light from the stairs has turned dark and golden.

"I've been waiting for you to wake up." His tongue licks up my neck.

I feel his hardness pressing against me, and I raise my hips to rub against it.

"My apologies. It seems a beast ravished me all night and well into the morning," I say with a smile.

"A beast?" he asks, lowering his hips to grind against me. "What kind of beast?"

Our bodies rub together, and I'm desperate for more.

"A demon—a terrifying creature that I was warned to avoid at all costs."

"A warning you did not heed?"

My tongue traces down his jaw as our bodies rock together.

"I did not, and now I am his forever."

His clawed hand cups my breast and gently thumbs my nipple.

"Are you content with his ownership?"

The question is heated, and while our banter may be light, I can hear the earnestness in his words. My eyes meet his as I press a chaste kiss to his lips.

"I love his ownership—I love him."

"Just as he loves you," Asgorath whispers, meeting my lips with his.

Our bodies grind together, desperate to be fused together once more. My demon gives me one more pump of his hips before he pulls back. His claws go under my back as he cradles me to his chest.

"We have to stop, little one before I end up fucking you and ruining the surprise I have been carefully crafting while you've slept."

My fingers trail the rough skin of his cheek.

"A surprise? For me?"

Asgorath presses a kiss to my forehead. "Yes. Now, let me dress you before this beast decides to ravish you once more."

Rising from the bed, Asgorath carries me to the wardrobe he's had stocked with new clothes for me. Gently, he sets me on my feet before selecting a robe. It's made of the finest blue silk and coats over my naked skin like a caress. The material is almost sheet enough to make out the color of my nipples.

My demon belts it loosely for me as his claw drags up to my breasts. Squeezing one gently, I fall into his touch.

"Tempting little thing you are. Let's go now before I change my mind about surprising you."

His hand encircles my wrist and gently severs the lingering ribbon.

"As you wish, my demon," I say, fluttering my eyelashes.

With a growl, Asgorath sweeps me into his arms and carries me towards the stairs. The scent of freshly baked bread that woke me causes my stomach to growl once more. Despite the smells emanating from the kitchen, my demon keeps walking us through the cottage and out the front door.

The sun has set, and darkness is all around. The pale moon

looms above, casting *The Woods* in a blueish glow. Creatures scurry amongst the trees, but no predator would dare interrupt us. Fireflies illuminate the wildflowers and overgrown grass of the front lawn.

The smell of smoke tickles my nose as I see a roaring fire a few feet from the cottage entrance. Next to it lays a large silk sheet the glimmers in the low light. Arranged on the silk is a basket and two glasses of dark wine.

With care, Asgorath lowers me gently to the blanket before settling behind me. My back falls against his chest as his arm slips around my waist locking me to him. Through my thin robe, I can feel the cool night breeze and his hard body. His warmth seeps into me as I snuggle deeper into his hold.

"I thought we could dine out here tonight," Asgorath whispers into my hair. "To celebrate you becoming mine."

"Was last night not enough celebrating for you?" I ask as he hands me a glass of wine.

Taking a small sip, the sweet flavor explodes on my tongue.

"That was different. It's important to me that you know I want you for far more than just your body."

I look up at him, his face harsh and yet so perfect to me.

"I know you do, Asgorath."

My worries from earlier come crawling back. I should voice them. There is no better time than right now, on this perfect night. Our souls are one, and there is no room for secrets between us.

"Irys, you are a gift. One that I will try to be worthy of each and every day. I never want you to regret choosing me over your human life," Asgorath says.

He curls a strand of my dark hair around his finger.

"I won't, my love. I meant what I said to my father yesterday: I love you. You have me for forever." Taking a deep breath, I look into his eyes. "But I must ask, what does forever look like for us? I am human, and naturally, I will grow older. Will I eventually d—"

"No." Asgorath's snarl cuts through the peaceful evening. "I would never allow death to separate us. You will stay just as you are now, perfectly preserved for eternity."

My heart beats wildly in my chest.

"You mean I'm no longer human?"

"You are human, but the mortal lifespan no longer applies to you. By choosing to live here with me—by binding yourself and your soul to mine—my magic and the magic of *The Woods* will keep you alive as long as you will it. As long as you want it."

Taking another sip of my wine to soothe my dry throat, I take Asgorath's hand in mine.

"I was worried that our time together would be so short. The thought of you forgetting me and living as if I've never existed broke my heart."

"Never," Asgorath growls. His hand cups my jaw and forces me to look up at him. "I will never forget you—when you no longer wish to be a part of the living realm, I follow you into that unknown next adventure. I have no wish to be parted from you. You are mine—in life and in death."

"Yes," I sigh. "Forever, my love."

"Then you will bind yourself to me. Tonight, I must lay claim to you in every way."

I nod my head before biting my lip. This is everything I've wanted to hear, and yet there's still that final nagging question. Is marriage a ridiculous notion to my demon? What is a ring and a few vows in comparison to a soul-binding?

"Irys," he says, the fire in his eyes cooling. "What's wrong? Do you not want to be bound to me?"

My eyes widen as I burrow deeper into his delicious warmth. Holding him tight to me, the rough contours of his chest graze my sensitive breasts.

"Of course I do, Asgorath, it's just that..." I trail off before taking a deep breath. His earnest eyes decide me as I take his face in my hands once more. "I want to marry you. I know that is a silly human desire, but I want us to be husband and wife. You are more than my lover. You are everything to me."

His eyes flame to life inside his skull-shaped face. The burning of his gaze causes my eyes to water. His arms come around me as he takes my wine glass from my hand and drags me to my feet.

Without another word, he lowers himself to his knees before me as I inhale sharply. Reaching into his cloak, he pulls out a small bag. The tinkling of metal echoes around us as his claws grasp something inside. My mouth goes dry as he pulls the ring out.

It's a simple gold band with a large diamond in the center surrounded by sapphires. Even in the dim light of the fire, its brilliance cannot be denied. Asgorath takes my hand in his gently as he stares up at me.

"My surprise, dear Irys. The vows we make to each other tonight during the binding ceremony are akin to a human wedding. When it is done, you shall be my wife, and I will be your husband. The first bargain we ever struck will be complete." His eyes glow even more intensely. "Will you marry me, little one?"

"Yes," I say, tears sliding down my cheeks. "A million times, yes."

Asgorath slips the ring on my finger, and it is a perfect fit. Rising to his full height, his claws slice through the belt of my robe as I lock my arms around his neck. The fabric gapes open as his hand trails up my stomach and cups my left breast in his hand.

His lips find mine and it is not long before our mouths are nothing more than a tangle of tongues and teeth. My lips already feel swollen by the time his mouth descends to my neck, biting and sucking as he goes. Liquid arousal pools between my legs and slips down my thighs.

Asgorath bites the soft skin of my throat, and a moan slips from my lips.

"We will leave this yard as one. With the moon as our witness, I will bind our souls together, and we will never live another day apart. Do you want that, my Irys?"

His tongue licks over the shell of my ear as I lean into his warm body.

"Make me yours, my love."

"First, I need you naked." Asgorath's hands strip my robe from my shoulders, and it falls to my feet.

He's seen me naked countless times, and yet the thrill is just like the first. My cheeks warm as he looks his fill from my toes to my head. His chest vibrates with a growl as a gentle breeze tousles my unbound hair.

"Beautiful."

Biting my lip, my hands go to his cloak.

"It's only fair you're naked as well," I say, helping him shed the thick fabric.

As soon as his form is bared to me, my mouth goes dry. He's so powerful, and my thighs rub together in anticipation of having him inside me again. His cock juts from his body, and I long for a taste of him. It's thick and long, the head slightly darker gray than the rest of his proud length.

"Soon, little one. I'll fuck you until the sun crests the horizon. Would your greedy pussy like that?"

"More than anything," I sigh as his hands play with my breasts once more.

"Then let us commence with the binding so I can reward your sweet little cunt with my cock."

The wind picks up around us as Asgorath takes both my hands in his. His musky scent mixes with the fire and the scent of evergreens nearby. I shiver slightly in the chilly breeze and step closer to Asgorath's warmth. His claws trace over my hands as he threads our fingers together.

My heart is overflowing with love for my demon. I do not fear eternity—not when Asgorath will be there to guide me. A life without him isn't a life at all. For so long, I've felt alone, abandoned by my family, and made to suffer under my father's reckless choices. Now all I feel is loved. Asgorath tends to me in every way that I need.

Loving a monster was the easiest thing I've ever done.

"With the moon as my witness," Asgorath begins, his deep voice rising above the wind. "I hereby take Irys to be my lover, my wife, my mate. I promise to love her and keep her safe and thoroughly well-fucked for the duration of our eternal lives. There will never be a moment with her that I will take for granted. I give her my soul and ask for hers in return."

My throat burns as tears slide down my cheeks.

"Your turn, little one." Asgorath's burning gaze heats my blood.

"With the moon as my witness, I, Irys, take my demon Asgorath's soul and offer mine to him. I take him as my lover, my husband, my mate. I promise to show you how much you mean to me every day. Together, we will face eternity together. Every day, I want to wake beside you, and every night, I want to fall asleep with you inside of me. I am yours, and you are mine. Eternally."

The wind roars in time with Asgorath's possessive growl. His mouth swoops down on mine with a kiss so intense it steals my breath. There's a metallic scent of magic in the air, and I feel an invisible weight settle along my bones. A shift in my blood tells me the ritual is complete, but I care little about that.

My hands hook around Asgorath's—my husband's—back, and I pull him closer to me. His claws cup my face as he devastates my lips. His glorious tongue teases mine in a delicious slide. His hard cock prods my stomach, and I rub my thighs together.

Asgorath's hand travels to the back of my head and holds me there while our mouths continue to work together to heighten our pleasure. The prick of his claws on my scalp makes me moan into his mouth. His other hand reaches down to my backside and hauls me against him. He palms my fleshy mound, squeezing it until my head spins.

"How should I take you first, wife?" I shiver at the new title. "Would you like me to lick your pretty pussy?"

I moan again as his lips taste my neck.

"Do you want to suck my cock while I fuck this perfect little mouth?" he whispers against me as his clawed hand slips from my hair to graze my swollen lips. "Or, wicked girl, shall I fuck all of your greedy holes until my comes is dripping dripping out of you?"

"Yes." It's the only word I can manage over the tremors shaking my body. I'm drunk on the erotic images his words have called forth—I want them all.

"Yes? To which option, beloved?"

"All of them," I say, biting down gently on his finger. "Would you deny your wife the pleasure she demands, husband?"

The new title affects him in the same manner it did me. His claws tangle in my waist as he lifts me into his arms. Rubbing my aching nipples against his chest, I capture his lips once more in a hungry kiss. His claws dig into my ass, and I know I'll wear his marks in the morning. I rub myself along the hard planes of his stomach, greedy for more friction.

"Wanton woman, perfect for me in every way. My greedy little slut needs her mouth fucked?"

"More than anything," I say, breaking our kiss.

"I need to taste this sweet pussy before anything else."

As much as I love his mouth on me, I want to take care of him. I need to pleasure him as much as he needs to pleasure me. My lips twist into a pout as my hands trail down his chest. Wrapping a fist between his thickening length, my thumb finds the tip and the wetness lingering there.

The sight of my wedding ring glittering as I stroke him causes us both to groan.

"But I need your cock in my mouth. Please, Asgorath, let me pleasure you. Let me show you how grateful I am to be used for your pleasure."

Asgorath snarls as I continue to stroke him in my hand. His tongue licks over my cheek before his jaw unhinges and glides wetly to my breast. Licking over my nipple, I give him a harder squeeze that has him shaking.

"My whore wants to please me? Very well, we shall just have to compromise."

My husband lowers himself to the silk sheet. Without a word, his hands grip my waist and twist me until I'm facing away from him. Throwing me around as if I weigh nothing, he pulls my hips back until my wet flesh is just above his mouth.

In this position, his cock looms large and commanding in front of me.

Licking my lips, I place a gentle kiss on the tip of his hard cock. I'm rewarded by more sticky seed leaking from the tip that I quickly lick up. His salty flavor explodes on my tongue, eliciting a moan from me.

"Suck my cock, little one, while I feast on your pink cunt."

A squeak of surprise leaves me as his tongue trails up my slit from below. The warm muscle swirls around my entrance as his claws keep hold of my hips. The sensation is obscenely decadent. The night breeze whips around us, and the thought of being outdoors where anyone could happen upon us only heightens my pleasure.

As easy as it would be to lose myself in the pleasure I gain from his mouth, I want to taste my husband fully. My hand grips his heavy cock as I bring it towards my lips. Running my tongue up the length of him, I delight in the velvety soft texture of his cock. My other hand finds his balls and gently palms them.

"Naughty girl, you were made to suck my cock. That's all your mouth is meant to do—bring me pleasure."

"It is," I agree. "Let me give it to you, husband."

Without another word, I take his length fully into my mouth. I slide my tongue along him until I feel the head of his cock hit the back of my throat. I cough slightly but keep going until tears burn in my eyes. Saliva pools and slides down his delicious length. Using my hand to stroke him in time with bobbing my head I give myself over to the task.

I keep sucking him as far as I can, letting him lift his hips to push farther into my mouth. It's decadent, and he is by far my favorite flavor. Giving him pleasure only heights my own, and with Asgorath's skillful tongue working me into a frenzy, I won't last much longer.

My hips wriggle as he alternates between sucking on my clit and fucking me with his tongue. I moan on his length before pulling him from my mouth. I graze his head gently with my teeth before skimming my tongue up along the side. I roughly pump him in my hand before taking him back inside my throat again.

"Perfect little slut. Are you close to coming, Irys?"

His tongue spears into me again, deep and curling against that spot that drives me wild. I nod my head, garbling against his cock. His claws leave my hip to rub gentle circles on my clit. His length hardens in my mouth as I suck him harder.

One more maddening thrust of his tongue, and I'm coming with his cock in my mouth. My thighs tremble, and my pussy locks around his tongue, milking it and soaking his face in a rush of my come. I continue working Asgorath in my mouth as he licks me clean.

"Now that I wear your come on my face, it's only fair that you wear mine."

Once again, as if I weigh nothing, Asgorath rolls me until I'm on my back. The night sky greets me as I pant up at the twinkling stars. In an instant, Asgorath is looming over me, roughly pumping his length inches from my face.

"Stick that pretty tongue out, little one. Taste my desire for you."

He doesn't have to tell me twice. Opening my mouth wide, I thrust my tongue out as he jerks himself harder. With a ragged groan, his first rope of come lands on my chest. The next lands on my tongue and lips, painting me with creamy stickiness. Rope after rope decorates my face until Asgorath slips the tip of cock against my tongue.

I suck him clean, swirling my tongue around his head until he pulls it free. I lick his saltiness from my lips and chin. My skin is flushed as I stare up at him. The love in his gaze makes me feel even more exposed than my nudity. It is as if he can see straight to my soul, and I suppose after the vows we've just spoken, he can.

Asgorath moves down my body, and my thighs part immediately. He settles between them. His claws skim up the smooth skin of my calves and thighs. The touch is gentle, but there is no mistaking the ownership in it.

"You're beautiful, little one. I have to fuck you—I need my seed inside of you."

"Make love to me, husband. Come inside of me."

My demon's gaze turns molten as he grips his hard cock. He rubs it gently through my wetness, coating himself in me. Pressing that hardness against my clit, he teases me until I'm panting.

With one swift motion, he slides himself inside of me, not stopping until our hips meet. The stretch of him is decadent, and my teeth clench. He's so large and hard inside of me. The fullness I feel is otherworldly. My hands fall to his backside and hold him still inside of me. Our breaths mix as our foreheads press together.

"Fuck me, husband. Claim what is yours."

Our mouths fuse together as his hips rear back. With one harsh thrust, he impales me on his impressive length. His tongue slides into my mouth and down my throat, mimicking the thrusting of his cock. Saliva coats my lips as my wetness squelches from where we are joined between my thighs.

Claws drag along my chest before he roughly palms my aching breasts. Teasing my nipples, I thrust them further into his hands. The slight pain from his claws pressing into my sensitive skin heightens my pleasure.

He withdraws—almost completely pulling out of me— before slamming back in one claiming thrust. Over and over, he fucks me, my breasts jostling in time with each thrust as he cups them in his palms. His ownership is clear, as is his claiming. With each pump of his hips, my soul gives way to him, and we become one creature together.

"This tight cunt is too fucking perfect. In a thousand years, you'll feel just like this, and I'll fuck you just the same. Come on my cock, pretty girl."

His thrusts become ever more intense. My muscles tighten, and liquid heat pools in my belly. My nails rake down his back as he pulls his mouth from mine. I watch rapt as his jaws unhinge and his long red tongue licks down my stomach until it finds my clit. He licks over it until I'm tightening on his cock.

My muscles want him as deep as they can get him. I feel him harden inside of me as his tongue flicks over my clit one last time. He pumps into me two more times before my body erupts. Throwing my head back, I let out a scream that has birds scattering from the nearest tree.

With another jerky thrust, Asgorath's seed fills me in a warm rush. He comes deep within me, bathing my walls in his heat until, at last, he pulls free from me. I feel the stickiness pool on my thighs and soak the blanket beneath me.

Warmth has my muscles feeling languid. I am unattached to my body as I float on the most wondrous cloud. My demon, however, does not look relaxed as he stares down at me. His cock is still hard, glimmering with the remnants of both of our arousals.

His earlier words float back to me, and I smile. Summoning the last of my strength, I roll onto my front and hoist myself up on my knees. Using my shoulders as leverage, I use my hands to cup the cheeks of my ass and gently pull them apart. His come flows from me and drops to the sheet below.

"You promised to fuck all of my holes, my love. A good husband never breaks a promise to his wife."

Asgorath's claws replace my hand and holds me open to his gaze. His mouth lowers to me as he tongues my back entrance. The tight ring of muscle is slow to give way, but after a few rotations of his tongue inside of me, my muscles begin to loosen. He gathers some of his come leaking out of me and coats his fingers in it. Using that wetness, he slips two fingers into my ass, scissoring them to stretch me.

My hips rock back and forth on his hand. Pleasure is building inside of me once more as I bring my hands down to snag in the silk sheet.

"Do you want me in your ass, Irys?"

"Desperately," I confess.

"Say you want a monster to fuck your ass."

My face flames, but embarrassment never has a place between two people who love each other.

"I want a monster to fuck my ass. I want my husband to fill me with more of his seed."

"Yes," he growls.

Removing his fingers, his hard cock presses against me. The burn is intense as he slowly slides inside. Our lingering mutual releases aid him, but it's still a tight fight. My muscles squeeze his length, and I feel every inch of him.

"Perfect fucking mouth, sweet fucking cunt, and the tightest ass—I am one lucky demon to call you mine."

My agreement is a babbling of incoherent words as he slides deeper into me. My breath catches at the feeling as he fully sheathes himself. His hand slips around to play with my clit. Pleasure and pain dance inside of me and race me to another climax.

He retreats his hips slowly before thrusting back in. Careful not to hurt me, our lovemaking this time is much slower and yet somehow more intense. The connection here brings him closer to me.

Our hearts beat as one, and our souls tie together.

"I love you, Irys," Asgorath says, leaning down to run his tongue along my spine. "I love fucking you, I love being with you. I can't wait to uncover everything about you and keep you as my most treasured possession."

"I love you, Asgorath." His claws work my clit, and my body crests its peak. "I'm coming—come with me, my love."

White hot pleasure licks my sweaty skin as Asgorath freezes above me. His seed releases a torrent of warmth inside me. He pumps into me gently, wringing every bit of pleasure from my body. Withdrawing gently, his release leaks out of me as I slump forward into a graceless heap.

My body shudders with the aftershocks of my pleasure-filled evening. His release is hot on my skin as I lay on the cool silk sheets. It's not long before Asgorath settles beside me and drags me into his arms. I huddle into his chest and listen to the rhythmic beating of his heart.

He smells of smoke and musk, and my pussy heats once more. I nuzzle into his side and my hands trace down his muscular side. His lips skim over my forehead as he presses gentle kisses to my cheeks and lips.

"How are you feeling, my wife?" Asgorath asks.

"Amazing," I say, planting a soft kiss to his lips. "Ready for more."

"Greedy girl," he says, love dancing in his eyes.

Despite his words, his hand grips my breast, and I lean into the touch. Unfortunately, my stomach chooses that moment to growl and break the headiness brewing between us.

"I need to feed you before I ravish you again."

Asgorath drags over the basket and opens the top. Crusty bread loaves and cured meats are nestled amongst shiny red apples and glistening grapes. Rising, he gathers me in his lap and brings a piece of cheese to my lips. Taking a bite, I moan over the savory taste.

"I don't know what the future holds," Asgorath says, feeding me another piece of cheese. "I never much cared to consider it. There was nothing for me beyond making bargains and finding delight in my deals."

Settling a grape on my tongue, I break threw the firm skin and drink down the sweet juice.

"Then there was you. From the first moment you appeared to me, I wanted you more than reason. You are my future now, the two of us."

"Or three," I say softly, cheeks heating. "Or four."

"Irys." Asgorath goes still behind me, cupping my cheek. "Surely you don't mean you're—"

"Pregnant? No, my love. I've been taking the contraceptive herbs and will continue to do so. For a while, I'd say. There's so much I want to experience in life—with you. Not to mention, I'm far too greedy for you to bring a child into our union just yet." My smile widens. "But one day. Would you like that?"

"Yes," he breathes. "One day, we will have a family."

"My future was as miserable as it was predictable. My father was to sell me off to clear his debts, and I would've never felt a bit of the love we share. Every day, I'm grateful I ventured into *The Woods*. Without you, my life would be meaningless."

Asgorath reaches for a loaf of bread and tears off a chunk before presenting it to me.

"Eat quickly, wife. My cock needs to be back in your pussy. Immediately."

I giggle as I devour the warm bread.

What is life without love? I am fortunate never to have to learn the answer. The future is unpredictable, but one thing that will never change is the love I have for my demon.

As Asgorath rolls me onto my back and falls between my thighs once more, he shows me how much he loves me. With each thrust into my body, our hearts and souls become one. Just the way they should be—just the way they will be.

Forever.

A KISS FROM A KRAKEN

KISS FROM A MONSTER SERIES BOOK 2

1

MELODY

This party was not my idea.

Well, none of them are, however, this one I was particularly against. My father didn't listen, something he's all too comfortable with doing these days. Once upon a time, my father would've rather cut off his right hand than see me sad. Would've tried tirelessly to coax a smile from me and we would've laughed together over this disgusting display of opulence in front of us tonight.

Four years ago, the dress I'm wearing right now would've fed us for months.

Four years ago, my father was a humble fisherman, one that was unluckier than most. He would come back every night with a few measly fish and a few gold coins to keep a rickety roof over our heads. After my mother passed he did everything to preserve her memory and to try and raise me to be a smart, strong young woman just like her.

To speak my mind, to never ever doubt my worth.

Then one night everything changed. I still remember it like it was yesterday. The barrels of fish he came in with that night.

Fresh catches of lobsters, mussels, and even some shellfish that we hadn't seen in decades. All of which would fetch a high price with the nobility who ruled over our town.

Precious pearls were cleaved from the hard shells of oysters and sold at the market.

Overnight we became millionaires. By the end of the week, I had been ushered into this grand house on the Lord's Row, given a lady's maid and a governess to teach me how to function within our new wealth and standing. By the end of the month, my father was different. The wealth had turned him into a greedy, egotistical man and I realized the life I had known, the one my mother had wanted for me, was gone.

Just like her precious bag of pearls.

My father said they were lost in the move, but he couldn't meet my eyes when he told me. Whether it be from shame or something else I don't know. The only thing for certain is that those were her most prized possessions, one of the last things I have of her.

A loud crack of thunder breaks me from my thoughts. I tilt my head to the side and stare out of our massive window. The rain is coming down in sheets, and people below scurry to try and save their hair and clothes but it is useless. This storm is foreboding, the sky an inky black, illuminated by the swift strikes of lightning.

No one at this party seems to take notice.

Turning back to the room before me I suppress the urge to groan. Instead, I force my face into a cold mask of indifference. This is my father's third annual Fisherman's Ball, the title a mockery of our former lives as no one here has ever cast a net, let alone felt the salty spray of ocean water sting their sunburned skin after spending hours at sea. This is just another excuse for my father to revel in his greed and arrogance.

Our ballroom is adorned in all types of gaudy fashioning. Eight solid gold candelabras decorate the long, wood dining table I am sitting at. Dinner ended over an hour ago but I cannot bear to mingle with these people. I take a sip of wine and survey the scene before me.

I watch from behind one of our ridiculous place settings, a bouquet of white roses dotted with real pearls and seashells, as our attendees float around the room. Perfumed lords and ladies dance in their finery. Dresses that look like pastries swish along our marble floors; men dressed in overcoats that are cinched so tight it's a wonder they can breathe. Everyone is primped and polished and using this as a chance to flaunt their own wealth.

Reaching for my glass I catch myself in the mirror hanging across the ballroom. I barely recognize myself anymore. Physically I look the same. My red hair is curled, and the front pieces are pulled back from my face to highlight the pearl earrings I am wearing. Those same pearls are stitched into my light blue gown, matching the color of my eyes and making my fair complexion glow.

However, this creature staring back at me isn't the child who enjoyed the mud and swimming at low tide off our old dock. Who stayed up late while their mother told them legends of the monsters who lived in the sea. Who saw each day as a gift, a wondrous opportunity to explore new things.

Our new wealth has sucked that from me. Turned me into this manicured, docile version of myself that is meant to sit still and smile during meaningless pleasantries. This is not who I am, this is not who my father is.

Does this show of wealth not disgust him? Does he no longer remember who we used to be?

I cannot keep living like this. I have become his doll. A prop he introduces to men, in the hopes that my marriage to them will secure him more connections. He made that evident last year after I turned eighteen. I was a woman and my job is to become a wife and mother, my dreams, if I had any, were all to be forgotten.

Reaching for my wine glass, I look away from the mirror only to lock eyes with the one person I have been trying to avoid most this evening. Prince Edwind is the most repulsive man I have ever met. When he kissed my cheek at the beginning of the evening my nerve endings screamed. I had to hold myself back from rushing to the nearest washroom and scrubbing my skin raw to rid myself of his contact.

He is a few years older than me but already shows signs of decaying. An opulent life has allowed him to indulge in all things and his health suffers greatly for it. If Edwind makes it to fifty years of age the gods have been more than merciful.

"Lady Melody, will you do me the privilege of letting me lead you in this next dance?"

His breath smells of sweet wine and roasted meat. From my chair, I have to look up to meet his unfocused stare. Those bloodshot brown eyes wander down my chest, where the swells of my breasts have been pushed up due to the tight lacing of my gown. The Prince does not even try to hide his leer, licking his stained yellow teeth. Repulsive.

His gold cloak is starched, stitched with an even finer gold thread. His whole outfit sparkles in the candlelight. Greasy brown hair has been swept back from his reddish face. Rings dot every finger as he holds his sweaty palm out to me.

The question is a formality, the Prince would never think to be denied. Especially not by the likes of me.

Perhaps I have partaken in too much wine, perhaps this time sitting with myself, watching this all unfold has afforded me some clarity. I look past the Prince and see my father's eyes watching us. He nods slowly and silently orders me to accept the Prince's dance request.

Last year I would've done it; this year I refuse to take part in this any longer.

My father must still have some love for me. His only child. He is not so far lost to me that he would make me entertain this disgusting creature, prince or not. I have to believe somewhere deep down he is still that poor fisherman my mother loved. That poor fisherman, who loved our family more than anything.

That thought strengthens me and I straighten my spine.

"Unfortunately, Your Majesty, I have no desire to dance with anyone tonight. I am sure another young lady would be a more willing partner for you." I cut a glance over to the ten young women watching our exchange with rapt expressions. Shock widens the Prince's eyes as if this outcome was completely unexpected.

This should be interesting, I think as I take my final sip of wine.

"I don't understand."

"What is it you don't understand?" I ask. "I thought I spoke quite plainly."

"You are rejecting...my invitation to dance?"

"Yes."

"You cannot do that."

"And yet I have." Rising from the table, I snatch up my glass, intent on getting a refill of wine and effectively ending this conversation. Thick fingers grip my upper arm and I let out a gasp.

"No one rejects me, you cold wench," he sneers at me. "Who do you think you are? I am your *Prince*, you and your family are nothing. You found fortune but that doesn't change the fact that you will always be beneath me."

"Get your hand off of—"

"Perhaps beneath me is where you are destined to stay." His

grin is pure lecherous evil as he licks over his lips. My stomach rolls as I try again to yank my arm from his grasp. Prince Edwind tightens his grip on me and instinct takes over. My leg kicks out, directly into his most private, albeit *underwhelming*, parts.

The Prince crumples to the floor, crying in agony and clutching at his groin.

"Never," I spit out, "*never* touch me again."

"How dare you, traitorous bitch! I'll have your head for this!"

Death would be better than marrying that beast.

Loud footsteps sound as my father approaches. Our matching eyes connect, his are akin to blue flames as he takes in the scene. Tension tightens his muscles and I think for a second my old father is back. Anger on my behalf and he will surely kick this prince from our home for daring to touch me. He will comfort me and tell me he is sorry he did not protect me better.

"Melody!" my father yells. From his tone alone I can tell that my hopes of my old father's return are dashed. "Explain yourself, why have you hurt the Prince in this way? He sought me out this evening in the hopes of me approving your courtship, which I did! You ungrateful child, you have hurt your potential husband."

"He grabbed me, Father, made it seem like he would—"

"It does not matter." My father is quick to cut me off. "You need to do your duty, child. You have dishonored me tonight. What man of standing will take you now?"

Shock puts ice in my veins. *He does not care what the Prince planned on doing to me. That whatever he wanted I need to go along with so long as he gave his word to my father that he would marry me.* With that sinking realization I understand now just how stupid I had been.

My father is lost. I lost him that day he came home with all the fish and the jewels. The man I once knew, the man I had loved, my true father died that morning.

I open my mouth to finally unleash all the things I've been holding back from saying when another crack of thunder sounds. This time it seems to come from right over the house, shaking the walls so hard portraits crash to the floor. On the second boom, my glass slides from my hand, shattering at my feet. Everyone is crying out trying to determine what could be the cause of this when our front door bursts open.

The heavy oak door slams against the wall and we watch in horror as salty, seawater begins to free-flow into our house. It is impossible, we are several hundred feet above sea level. If we are flooding, the people below us have no hope of surviving this storm.

A few cries of outrage can be heard as people start scrambling up on tables. My delicate shoes are soaked through, and the icy water stops just below my knees, making my dress feel extra heavy.

Immediately I start to shiver, the temperature plummeting until I can see my breath curling in front of me.

A few partygoers begin to shout that we should call for help when it happens. Another flash of lightning illuminates the scene before us. Massive blue, meaty tentacles come slipping through the front door. Slithering through the cold water in soft ripples. Stretching over the door frame, taking up the whole entryway until it pushes through, its enormous suckers sticking onto the sides for leverage.

The tentacles twist over each other, like a massive ball of suckers and muscles rolling towards us through the water. A pair of blazing red eyes peers out from inside of them. Completely red, with no pupils or whites. They survey the room, landing on me for a moment. A shiver runs down my spine but I note with some mild horror that it is not fear making my stomach tighten. Before I can examine that emotion too deeply, its eyes drift from me and lock in on my father.

This creature can only be one thing. A mythical creature, used as a cautionary tale to scare children into behaving and sailors to be wary on the high seas. However, there is no denying what is in front of us now. And if it is here…

"Percy Rivers." The voice sounds straight out of a nightmare. As deep and resounding as a fog horn. My eyes shoot over to my father whose fair skin has turned even paler.

"That's him!" Someone shouts from the crowd and my father's knees wobble as he takes a step forward toward the creature. Breathing rapidly, each of his exhales are white puffs that form in sync with the beat of my heart. Turning towards the creature, I try my best to keep my spine straight as I take in the sight before me.

One thing is clear: my father must have done something terrible for this creature to be seeking him out.

"Do you know who I am?" The voice booms again, scraping over my skin and freezing the blood in my veins. The sound is so ancient and evil, so raw and…powerful. My own knees threaten to buckle under the weight of it.

"Y—yes—s," stutters my father.

"Say it," the creature commands.

"You—you're the Kraken of the Darksea. God of the Tides and of the Ocean."

A few gasps go up in the room. Despite their distance from the actual work of fishermen, this is a seaside town. All children, regardless of wealth and title, are taught the stories of the Kraken. To not swim in dark water or it will drag you down to live in its cursed kingdom, feasting on your bones for eternity.

Within each myth is a bit of truth and it seems the legend of the Kraken of the Darksea hadn't been exaggerated at all.

"A god, he calls me," snickers the Kraken, "yet you so recklessly steal from me. Thinking you will avoid all punishment for doing so."

A small sound leaves me as I turn towards my father. He is a lot of things, especially as of late, but a thief? I guess he is an idiot as well because who in this world would think to rob the Kraken of all beings?

"I don't know what you are—"

"Do not deny it," the Kraken cuts him off. "Lying will not help your case, nothing will. I know every step you have taken since I first became aware of your treachery, Percy Rivers. The sea rewards those who deserve to be rewarded. You took more from it, from me, than you were owed through a trick. A bargain with that fiend in *The Woods*. A demon you sought out in a moment of greed." He pauses, his tentacles slipping and sliding around him through the dark water. "Bargained away a bag of pearls, if I'm not mistaken."

My world stops.

"No!" I shout. My father's muscles tense even further. "How could you? They were hers, *hers* and you gave them away without a second thought?"

My mind is racing. Does his treachery know no end? That was the price he paid for all of this? My outburst has caused the Kraken's eyes to turn on me, appraising me under those fiery orbs. I meet his stare, unafraid. My world has already been changed forever, what is a stare-down with a Kraken?

I want to launch myself at my father. To scream and kick and punch him, to hurt him, to make him understand the rage I have carried with me all these years. However, the Kraken of the Darksea moves faster. His eyes refocus on my father and his tentacles reach out, slipping along the marble floor beneath the shallow pool of water. They seem to grow larger as they expand until they finally wrap around the base of my father's legs.

"You will pay for your theft with your life."

My father screams, a blood-curdling sound that hurts my ears.

"Please, please," he begs, "please, Kraken of the Darksea, spare me. I only did it to save her." My father throws his arm out towards me, finally acknowledging my presence. How dare he claim this was all for me. "We were starving, I did it to keep her fed, to keep her clothed and safe."

Doesn't he understand I would've rather died than have lost that last piece of my mother? Instead, he parted with it in order to gain his change in luck, this new fortune, this house...all of it gotten by a bargain with the demon of *The Woods*.

The Kraken's red eyes land on me once more, appraising me from head to toe. A predator assessing its prey. Perhaps it finds me as culpable as my father and I shall be killed here too.

That thought makes me shake where I stand.

The dark water in front of me ripples and slowly, almost cautiously, a slimmer tentacle reaches out toward me. It skims up the side of my body before brushing along my cheek. The tentacle tucks some of my hair behind my ear, playing with my dangling pearl earring, before gently suctioning onto my earlobe. I try not to weaken under his attention. If he means to kill me, I will face my death bravely.

Though a deep, dark part of me does not wish to recoil from his touch. There is something obscenely soothing about it. His tentacle is warm, his touch gentle and firm. The events of this night have clearly rendered me in shock.

That can be the only explanation.

"She is sweet," the Kraken rumbles, the sound tightening my nipples in my gown. What is happening to me?

"I'll offer this deal only once, fisherman." His tentacle leaves my cheek, falling gently into the water at my feet. "Since you stole something of mine, I will take something of yours. I will spare your life if you give your daughter to me instead."

A shocked sound falls from my lips.

Please, don't let him take me, I am your daughter. I will him to hear my plea, but it seems like my fate is already sealed. As I watch a spark of remorse cloud his blue eyes before they harden and I know his decision has been made.

He mouths *I'm sorry* before turning back to the Kraken of the Darksea.

"I agree to your deal, Kraken." The tentacle at my feet moves quickly, looping and tightening around my legs in a vice grip.

"No!" I scream. "You can't do this! You can't! Father, *father* please, you can't let him take me." My father is silent as I hear the splashes coming from more tentacles entering the water. "Somebody! Any of you, help me please!" No one moves a muscle. I watch in horror as more begin to loop around me, covering my legs completely. The creature only laughs, while my father remains silent.

"Fuck you!" I scream at my father. "Fuck all of you for not doing anything! For not helping me!"

I turn back to the creature as more water laps up against my legs. His massive form twists and rolls toward me, a mass of suckers and blue muscles. From inside the chaos, I hear the stomps of thick leather boots. My knees buckle as long, strong human legs are revealed clad in thick leather breeches, take confident steps toward me.

Refusing to look weak in the face of the Kraken, I try and hold my body still and lock eyes with his red gaze. He stands in front of me, so tall that I have to crane my neck back to keep eye contact with him. The tentacles wrapped around me have dissipated. All of them have retreated back towards where his head would be. Shorter, stopping just under his shoulders like he has a beard.

A beard of blue tentacles that move and snap on their own accord.

Those red eyes bore into mine. A stray tentacle coasts over

my forehead as a blue, damp hand cups my chin. The warning is clear, his power is absolute. This is who my father gave me to. This is who holds my future in his hands.

"You're mine, sweet one." He gently pulls my chin down and a slippery tentacle takes a shallow thrust into my mouth. I cannot scream, I cannot move all I can do is stand there. One sucker attaches to my tongue and that is the last thing I remember before my shaking knees finally give out, and I plunge into the waiting darkness.

2

<hr>

ZALENYK

O f all the wonders I have seen over the years, this human in my arms is the most precious.

Her pathetic thief of a father never desired this jewel. She is a treasure, one I will safeguard for the rest of eternity. I will protect her, shield her and she will belong to me. Everything I had before today means as much as old fish bones.

She is all there is for me now.

My tentacles tangle in her long, red hair. Such a wonderful color, something that you don't find in the sea. I can feel her softness everywhere with her wrapped in my limbs like this. The soft press of her breasts and the supple curve of her ass warm my skin as I hold her. When she fainted in my presence, I wasted no time scooping her up and getting into the long boat. One of my servants, a drowned pirate with an exposed jawbone and one missing eye, steers us carefully to my palace.

A watery death puts your soul into my eternal servitude.

My human shivers against me and I tighten my hold on her. She is so small I will have to remind myself to be gentle when the time comes. Already my body is screaming, clutching so much of her delicate softness has my cock hard. How easy would it be to rip her from her soaked gown, to fit my tentacles into the snug hole between her legs, her mouth...her ass.

I must be patient, for as much as I would like to do those things, I need to wait for her to be willing. I will not behave like my kind used to. Just like my father when he found his human bride, the thought of my treasure in pain is abhorrent to me.

So I will wait. For her to want me as much as I want her. She fears me, I tasted it on her skin when I first laid my suckers on her. I will not have her sweet scent polluted with it.

Drowning would be more palatable to me than hurting my treasure.

She shivers again and I bring her closer to my center, where she will hopefully find some sort of relief. We are still a ways from my palace and I will not have her freezing on me. Truth be told, as we move through the dark water the evening birds cawing overhead, her coloring only gets paler. Her fingers start turning blue as do her full lips, no longer that tasty red they were at her father's house.

I never realized what a cold life I led until now.

The chill of the water seeps into my own muscles. I would offer her my servant's clothing—my clothing—but they are both waterlogged. That would only add to her chill.

There is only one thing to do and hopefully, my sweet human will not hate me for it.

Gripping her fancy gown with my suckers I pull it from her body. The material tears away easily and I feast on the sight before me. Pale skin, glowing in the moonlight, freckles dotting her slender arms and shoulders. Her shift is thin and soaked, clinging like a second skin, I decide to leave her in this measly layer to preserve some of her modesty. The garment is translucent, her small, pale pink nipples pushing against the front. Try as I might I cannot stop my eyes from drifting lower to the shadowy place between her thighs.

My eyes can make out just a hint of red hair down there as well.

Even with my mouth watering I shake myself, pulling her even closer to me. My human stirs, letting out a soft moan and lifting her arms. They wrap around my neck as best as they can and she burrows into me. My tentacles encircle her legs and waist, trying to warm up as much of her as I can. My human shifts slightly and nuzzles in deep letting out another soft moan. My cock hardens against her and I grit my teeth as she slides against it.

We stay locked together like that for several moments. The soft sound of the waves lapping against the side of the boat, a slight breeze tugging at her hair. Being able to touch so much of her soft skin is making my head spin. I need to see all of her, to taste her pretty cunt, to shove myself so—

No, I will not give in to instinct. I will be patient with my treasure.

Her blue eyes blink up at me and she smiles softly, making this moment even better. The way she looks at me thinks that perhaps my lust is not just one-sided and that maybe—

"What the fuck!" She cries, her eyes flying wide and she pushes at me, trying to free herself from my hold. "Let go, get your tentacles off me! Why am I naked? Oh, gods...*oh gods!*"

I relax my grip on her slightly but not enough for her to get away. I'm still surrounding her but she can slide back from me and she does so immediately. Missing her warmth already, my tentacles fan out around her to make sure she doesn't try and slip into the water.

"Calm down before you tip us over."

"What is going on, where are we?" She swallows loudly. "Why did you undress me?"

That stench of fear invades my nostrils and I know I must reassure her, that this isn't what it looks like.

"You were cold, sweet one. I had to find some way to warm you or you would've frozen to death."

She opens her mouth to say something but then stops before springing into action. Turning to her side she begins to hoist herself up over the edge of the boat. My tentacles snap out gripping her around the waist once more and pulling her back in towards me. I ensnare her wrists and ankles so she is unable to move once more.

"Let me go, Kraken. Release me!"

"No," I say. She is never leaving me, someone would steal her, recognize what a treasure she is and take her from me. But they would not be careful with her, they would not treat her as the precious jewel she is. This human is *mine* and she will have to stay with me so I can make sure she is safe.

"You can't say no. Please, please, just let me go. Kill my father, he's the one you want."

"I want nothing of your father." My tentacle curls around her cheek, my suckers sticking to her soft skin and suctioning gently. She lets out a small gasp and begins to squirm again. I find I rather like her like this, restrained, mine completely for the taking. "You, my sweet one, are mine for eternity."

"It's not fair." Thrashing again, my little human tries to free herself from my grasp.

"Stop moving about like that, you will hurt yourself." My tentacles curl tighter around her. "That would displease me greatly."

"I don't care what you want. Hear me, Kraken, the second I get free I will kill you. I will not be kept here."

"I like your spirit." And it is true, I do. She is lively and a challenge, one I will delight in bringing under my control. My human can say she hates and wants to kill me, but I can smell her. Her arousal scents the air, as sweet as honey, and I long for a taste of it. To taste her rage and fire, to feast on it between her legs.

The long boat comes to a halt, my human distracted me, I hadn't even realized we were close to the palace.

My Drowned Palace is lit with glowing shells and aquatic fish. Eels swim along the pathways or are trapped in jars to keep the inside lit. Half of it is completely sunken, allowing for easy access into the ocean, my true domain. I do not know how this came to be in my family but it has been our home for centuries.

A few servants are milling around the front: a woman who drowned herself by stuffing rocks in her pocket, a couple who got caught in a storm, and a fisherman who crashed into the side of a cliff. All of them turn to note our arrival and I growl, I do not want any of them to see my human while she is basically naked. Her flesh is only for me to see.

My treasure. Mine.

"Fetch her some warm clothes," I bark at my servant who scurries off.

I watch as my treasure takes in my palace. Her sea blue eyes absorb everything, scanning along the weathered grays rocks, to the great metal door that has rusted from exposure to sea air. The wild seagrass that grows out in front and the fish that swim around us, illuminating the black water below us. A small part of me is worried that it won't be up to her standard. The house I took her from was opulent to be sure, perhaps she will see this as beneath her?

I will just have to shower her in precious pearls and jewels if that is the case.

"Where are we?" she asks, softly. I note that she is no longer trying to escape and that pleases me greatly.

"We are at my home. The Drowned Palace, built on an alcove at the edge of *The Woods*, its wild magic was said to have helped the first Kraken King forge this place. Who had it before us I do not know, I assume some long-forgotten human king."

She nods and squares her shoulders as if preparing for

battle. My cock hardens even further. "And how long am I to remain here for?"

"Forever. Your father stole from me. I took you as payment, you belong to me for eternity." Her small hands shove at my chest and I hold back my chuckle. Even as her little fist pound against me I barely feel it.

"How is any of this fair?" she cries.

"It is not. But the world is not fair."

"And what are you planning on doing with me?" That determined look settles over her soft features again. "What could I possibly do for you?"

"Isn't it obvious?" My tentacle skims down her face, snagging on her plump lips and gently pulling them apart. "You will be my bride. My human pleasure vessel that I will fill nightly with my seed. I will keep you warm and fed and wet, begging for me to pleasure you with my cock and tentacles."

Her mouth pops open and I'm tempted to sneak my tentacle in there again, to feel the warm, wetness of her tongue. A broken sound leaves her and then she starts to shake. At first, I think she is shivering again so I move to wrap her in my embrace but it is not the cold making her move in this way. She is laughing. Giggles are bubbling out of her like air pockets coming to the surface.

She tries to cover her mouth but her laughter gets louder, more uncontrolled.

"Doesn't that just figure." Before I can ask what she means, she throws an arm over her eyes and flops down on the boat bench, trapping a few of my tentacles under her shaking body. Not that I would dare move them.

My human keeps laughing, sitting up I see that tears have begun leaking from her eyes. The moisture courses down her cheeks and our eyes lock. Whatever she sees turns her chuckles into sobs. Her eyes grow red and she starts crying in earnest now, her body being wrecked by uncontrollable wailing.

I slide a tentacle over her cheek to catch some of the wetness. There is a new scent tainting her honeyed smell. The sharp, metallic bite of despair.

"It is alright, my treasure. Do not be scared, do not get upset."

I should tell her now that the barbaric practice of taking human brides is not what this is. A voice inside of me whispers that I should reassure her but I do not know how. Not when she is looking at me like that. So scared and vulnerable. Words will not soothe her so I must show her through action.

Wiping away her tears, I watch in horror as she goes pliant in my grasp. The fire that has lit her blue eyes is gone. The defiant set to her red brows has been smoothed out. She is limp, as lifeless as my drowned servants.

I do not like this. Taming her spirit is one thing. To be able to tame that fire is what I crave, but to have her completely void of it...

This disturbs me, I must find a way to bring her spark back.

"Well, I'm basically naked already. Might as well get this over with." My horror grows as her face remains emotionless. I watch in shock as she reaches for the hem of her shift. No, not like this. I do not want her like this. My tentacles wrap around her wrist to stop her movements.

The first time I see her, see all of her, she will be willing. Her scent will not carry any notes other than arousal. I vow this in my heart.

With a sinking feeling, I realize that I must stay true to my purpose and protect her from anything that could cause her harm. Even if that something she believes is me.

I can be patient for my little human, I have to be.

"Not like this, sweet one. I will wait until you are willing." Relief floods her features and my stomach sours even more. Does she really hate the idea of me touching her that much? I suppose I could've been a little bit gentler in my approach when she asked me what I wanted her for.

"And what if I am never willing?" she asks carefully. I grit my teeth but I stay firm in my resolve.

"I have all of eternity to prove to you that I am worthy of sharing your bed."

My human is quiet for a moment and then opens her mouth but the sounds of footsteps make her stop and glance over.

The servants have arrived. I take the clothes from their outstretched hands, a warm wool dress and matching cloak and boots, and expand my form so that my human has privacy from prying eyes to change. I will myself not to sneak a glance and I don't. Within seconds, my human is dressed and exiting the boat.

She tightly curls the cloak around her, the muted brown in sharp contrast with the soft curls of her vibrant hair. My treasure is so beautiful, if I am lucky enough to just be able to look at her all day then that will be enough for me.

"Are you hungry?" I ask and her stomach growls at the question.

With one tentacle draped along her back, I guide her toward the palace. "Come, let us see what has been prepared for dinner."

As we make our way into my home, I reach out with one of my tentacles. It slithers up her back and curls a lock of her hair around it while I inhale her scent. This little human will give herself to me completely. From this moment forward everything I do is to ensure that one day she will desire me the way I already desire her.

I just hope that day is sooner than it seems.

3

MELODY

No one would ever accuse this underwater palace of being too lively.

Not with the servants all being half-rotted corpses, skin blue and damp, missing eyes, and bones eaten by some creature. The woman who'd brought me my plate of roasted fish was missing several fingerbones, her hollowed-out skin drug along the table as she set my meal down. I shiver at the thought.

My stomach turns at the memory of watching my captor tear into his raw salmon dinner. Devouring it with sharp teeth, swallowing it down whole. Descaling it with a wipe of his tentacles, eating the heads and fins and all.

We had eaten our meals in silence, truth be told I was too scared to say anything. Waking up on that boat, half-dressed, I had assumed the worst and I thank the gods that, while my captive seems keen on keeping me trapped here, he will not abuse me in that way at least. I thought for sure after we had finished our meals he would instruct me to go to his chambers but he did not.

Instead, that same servant that had given me my dinner led

me down a long damp hall. The walls were covered in shells and seaweed, my feet squelching along the wet carpet, before reaching this room. A room with a heavy door and a lock. Motioning me inside I saw that the room was mostly dry. With an ornately carved fireplace that already had a roaring fire burning in it.

The bed is carved in the same style with soft-looking blue sheets and a dozen pillows. My servant left a few moments ago after telling me fresh clothes would be brought tomorrow and asked me if I needed anything else. I dismissed her, not able to stomach looking at her macabre form.

I feel bad for my reaction to all of them, after all, they are trapped here just the same as me.

This room is nice but I am no less a prisoner. Brought here by that creature and proclaimed to be his bedmate for eternity. Still, try as I might I cannot hate him for it. I should, I really should. Make no mistake, I am angry, but I have been so angry for so long it is buried so deep beneath the surface I can hardly reach for it anymore.

My governess had quite a time, trying to teach me to be a proper lady. To be poised and polite. To smile and make myself small and quiet, something all men of good breeding loved in a future wife. Those strong emotions I felt so fiercely as a child were not permitted and thus all of them were buried deep inside me.

Especially my growing resentment towards my father.

He is the one I should blame. This creature took me from an unpleasant life. Here I have been afforded all the comforts I could want. Despite the dress ripping, he has been kind to me. Gentle with his touches even though I can tell he desires more. Would a human man be as understanding?

Any human man that my father had wed me to would've demanded I open my legs to him without a second thought. To get pregnant and produce his heirs. At least my captor, the

Kraken, wants to wait until I desire him. That earns him a little bit of redemption in my eyes.

Perhaps it is the shock of the evening, the way in which my world has just been turned upside down but I cannot seem to process what I am feeling. Besides the anger, there is curiosity. Maybe once he trusts me a bit more he will let me go exploring. Maybe I can live out my days an untouched virgin, kept by a sea creature, and be able to explore the grounds and take up a new hobby.

While it may not be the freedom I envisioned for myself it is better than the life I would've lived at home.

There is a darker part of me though. One that recalls what it felt like to be surrounded by him, sucked into the warm, slick mass of his muscles and tentacles. To be held so tightly and overpowered. It had made me wet between my legs, a fact that I would rather die than admit to him. When his tentacle had grazed my lips I had wanted him to push it into my mouth, like he had before I fainted. To push it past my teeth and tongue and keep going until...

Until I don't know what.

It is a dark desire, one I am not ready to confront yet. He is my captor. He is a creature of the sea and I should be repulsed by him. So why am I not? Why does the thought of him holding me down and restraining me, have my nipples pressing into the front of my gown?

Have I finally found the one thing that has alluded me? A male who does not want a meager woman who has nothing to say for herself and lets him completely control her with no resistance. Males who called me half-wild and said I was unfit to wed when they thought I couldn't hear. They were right, I was unfit to wed some sniveling lord like them. Why were they worthy of my submission? Even my attention?

The Kraken did not like it when I put my mask on in front of him. When I fell back on those lessons and became sullen and pliant. He hated it. He said he liked my spirit and now in the mix of all those emotions I am feeling, a small glimmer of hope is snaking its way through me as well.

Needing to distract myself from these thoughts, and from the boredom settling in, I warm myself one last time by the fire and exit the room.

My new boots stomp along the dank carpet, the hallway illuminated in a soft blue light. Glowing eels are trapped in jars along the walls, swimming back and forth to highlight the path. Shells and starfish glow as well, showing off the rotted wood of the walls. Some old portraits that were once mounted to the wall have been torn and shriveled up. Who owned this castle before it became the Kraken's home? His theory of it being an old human king looks to be correct.

The air carries salty notes of the sea, I can hear distant splashing. Being so close to the water, I am shocked that it isn't muggier. No, if anything the air is crisp and fresh, less polluted than the air of the city I was living in. It reminds me of the air at our cottage along the sea.

Nostalgia tightens my throat but I walk on.

The water at my feet is getting deeper, sneaking up to my ankles and soaking the hem of my gown. The water is cool, less frigid than the open ocean I experienced when we first arrived here. The hallway thins and more creatures begin to glow until I realize the walls of the hallway have faded away. In front of me is a small lagoon, a few glittering fish swim through the shallow water, lily pads glow the same color as the moon above, and night-blooming flowers perfume the air.

It is truly magical and I edge my way toward it. Perhaps this will be my new hobby, exploring my new home. Finding what treasures have lurked here for centuries and cataloging them.

I kneel down near the edge, my dress soaking through, and gently finger one of the plants. It curls around my finger and releases an even more intoxicating scent. My eyes catch on movement below, three of the most gorgeous fish I have ever seen swim towards me. They are a torrent of brightly colored scales. Blues, pinks, golds, and silvers all streak through the water, glittering and inviting.

They have mesmerized me so much that I do not even realize I am being stalked.

An eel with oily black scales and even darker eyes has slithered through the water. Those fathomless eyes lock on me and by the time I spy its movements, it has already struck, wrapping its body around my wrist and yanking me forward.

Down into the dark water below.

I manage to scream just before I was pulled under, my mouth and lungs filled with salty water. The temperature of the water is a shock. Even as I thrash, the creature's grip on me is too strong, I can't fight it. I am going to die, there is no way for me to survive this.

We rip through the water. Bubbles fly passed me at the speed we are going. My eyes burn so I close them, it is not like I can see much of anything anyway. Lungs burning, I make peace with my final moments in the world of the living.

Suddenly there is a shift.

A hum of power radiates through the water so overwhelming even the eel pauses its movements. With the last of my strength, I peel my eyes open and am met with a terrifying sight. Glowing red eyes are coming towards me, faster than lightning.

Blue tentacles unfurl towards me and rip me from the creatures grasp. I watch in horror as the eel is wrapped in the Kraken's limb and squeezed and squeezed and...popped. His insides floating around me.

I should be disturbed and alarmed, but I find that I am only aroused. Again, I will blame this on the lack of oxygen. My brain is shutting down, it is the only logical explanation.

The next thing I know is that I am being ripped toward the

surface. The tentacles push me the final distance before we break through. I suck down lungfuls of air, coughing and spitting up salt water.

Gently, I am slid back onto the safety of the shore, the glowing plants of the lagoon finally coming into focus. My chest is rising and falling so fast, and my wet hair is plastered to my face just like my dress is to my body.

The salty taste of the water still lingers in my mouth and burns my eyes. It is only by some miracle, I survived this.

My miracle is hanging at the edge of the water. He's shed semi-human form. The Kraken is just a mass of meaty tentacles and a round head with those glowing red eyes. His mouth is parted slightly and I can make out a few sharp teeth.

I should be disgusted and repulsed but I am not. When looking at him, I find that I am only grateful that he got to me in time. One of his tentacles lay by my side and I gently grasp it in my hand. It pulses with life, the suckers attaching to my palm in a firm press.

"What happened out here, sweet one?"

My hand squeezes his limb gently, curiously. I hear him let out a low moan but I cannot stop touching him. The tentacle is smooth and slick. Something other than water coats it in a fine, oily sheen. I wonder what that substance would feel like on my own body. My arms, my legs, my breasts...

"That eel grabbed me. I was exploring the lagoon and it just attacked me. If you hadn't gotten to me in time..." I don't need to finish the sentence, we both know what would've happened.

"My palace is not safe. Especially for someone like you." I crawl towards him on my hands and knees until we are face to face at the edge of the lagoon. "If you wish to go exploring tell me and I will keep you safe."

Smiling slightly I nod. I want to thank him for saving me but then I remember something. Something that I should've asked hours before now.

"I'm Melody, by the way. I should've asked earlier, but what is your name? I assume you were not born, Kraken of the Dark-sea?" I ask.

He is quiet for a moment and I fear he is not going to tell me but then he opens his mouth.

"My name is Zalenyk, sweet one. No one has called me that in centuries."

"Zalenyk." I like the way it tastes on my tongue. His tentacles shiver at my utterance of it, he seems to like me saying it as well. "Zalenyk you saved me."

I like the way he looks at me. The protective way in which some of his tentacles still hold me. Like the threat to my safety is still present, that he is the only one who can keep me safe. And I truly believe that he is.

To be so utterly desired is something I have never experienced.

My oxygen-deprived brain decides that is all the reason we need. Leaning forward towards his massive form I brush my mouth over his. I've never kissed anyone before but I am sure whatever technique I used with a human man would've needed adjustment to kiss a Kraken anyways.

Zalenyk is frozen. His mouth is unmoving as my lips meet his cool, slick ones. I pull back slightly, self-consciousness seeping in, causing me to question if I've just embarrassed myself.

Then he moves.

All at once his massive body is over the side of the lagoon and I am being consumed. His mouth is on mine kissing me with renewed vigor. His tentacles tangle in my hair, around my waist and arms, gripping me tightly, rubbing me up and down. That oil substance coats my mouth and it is as crisp as the evening air.

My pussy is obscenely wet, the moisture running down

along my thighs I know has very little to do with the water I was just pulled from.

One of his suckers grazes my nipple still covered in my gown and I moan. He uses the opportunity to push his tongue into my mouth. The warm wet muscle dances with my own, fighting with mine as his tentacle moves back and forth against my breast.

I shiver and I'm not sure if it is from my damp clothes or the assault he is having on my sense. This is wrong, in so many ways, but I can't find it in myself to stop. Or to care for that matter. This has stoked a fire in me; he has stoked a fire in me.

I'll do anything I can to keep it roaring.

A particularly strong shake passes through me and Zalenyk halts his movements.

"You are cold, sweet Melody. Come let us go inside, I must get you warm."

Crying out, I desperately want his tentacle back on my breast.

"Warm me yourself," I gasp, trying to capture his mouth again.

He growls in answer. Somehow when he had first come over the ledge of the lagoon, my legs had opened to accommodate his massive size. Now that we have stopped kissing, I can still feel his tentacles coasting up and down my gown-soaked legs. Tentatively grazing the sensitive skin of my inner thighs. A few of them have slid beneath my hem, inching higher to the most intimate part of me.

They are careful as if seeking my permission.

I nod my head and smash my lips against his again.

A tentacle grazes my slick folds and I cry out. The sensation is hot and cold, firm yet soft. It is an exploring touch, one that causes more moisture to leak out of me.

"Wetter than a rainstorm, my treasure. Are you ready to let me have you this way?" Zalenyk asks.

Despite the immense amount of lust, I am feeling, his question clears some of it from my head. Am I ready to have him inside me? To lose my virginity like this? With him?

"I do not know if I am ready for everything," I say carefully. "But I would like to do some exploring. With you. I don't know much of anything really, all I know is that you feel good"

"Have you ever been with a man, sweet one?" I shake my head now, a blush warming my cheeks. A shutter racks him and the tentacle grazing my folds presses down harder, the sucker suctioning onto a little bundle of nerves, and my back arches, a scream pulled from my lips.

I've touched myself before but nothing like this. I overheard one of our servants say the stable boy did something like this with his mouth on her clit but I cannot imagine it felt anything like this.

"We will explore each other, Melody. And once you are comfortable with me, you will let me have you."

Two tentacles tangle in the top of my gown and tug gently, asking if he can remove it for me. I'm so overwhelmed by the sensation all I can do is nod my head again. In a moment the gown is shredded, my thin shift the only thing between us.

"You are pink and pretty everywhere, little human."

I see now what he was doing, a torrent of tentacles underneath the hem of my undergarments. Some are wrapped around my ankles holding my legs apart, keeping them open even as I try to close them as his sucker works my clit again. It's too much.

"Do not hide your pretty cunt from me when I seek to pleasure it." Another tentacle comes up and circles around my hole gently, my whole body tenses as I wait for the intrusion. "Not tonight, sweet one, but soon. Soon you will beg for my cock to fill you. To have all your holes stuffed with me, and trust when I say I will not deny you that honor."

More moisture leaks out of me and flows down through the cheeks of my ass.

I can hear the slick slide of his tentacles through me as he returns his attention to my clit. That substance he has been secreting only adds to the wetness. My gown is pushed up and slowly my naked skin comes into view. Freckles dot along my bare stomach, and my nipples are pale and peaked under his gaze. The growl he emanates causes all his tentacles to vibrate adding even more pleasure.

Here I am, being held open by this creature and all I can do is wait for my orgasm to decimate me. It had always taken me a while to find completion with my hand but Zalenyk has already mastered my body. A few more rubs of my clit and I will be done for.

"Zalenyk, I'm—"

"Close?"

"Yes!" I scream, his tentacle sucking on me with a new intensity. My toes curl and my head is thrown back. His tentacles wrap around my arm and my throat, not choking me but making sure I know who is in control here. He keeps sucking on me and his mouth swoops down to kiss me once more. Zalenyk's tongue slips into my mouth and I'm panting, my hips writhing in time with his tentacle.

"Come for me, Melody. When you do it scream my name so all the fish in the sea can hear who pleasures this little pussy."

I'm powerless to do anything else.

My orgasm takes me to a high that is almost painful. Muscles flexing, I clench down around nothing as wave after wave of euphoria hits me. It's too much, this creature...no Zalenyk has broken me. Ruined using my own hand for me because I surely could never replicate this.

"Zalenyk, Zalenyk." Babbling his name incoherently he only chuckles, realizing the tight hold along my limbs. His form sneaks down my body, those red eyes looking up at me over the mound of my pussy.

The smile on my face is small.

"Let me taste it, let me find out if you are just as sweet here as I imagine you are."

"Whatever you want." The words are barely out before I feel his tongue lick up my center. He laps at me, and attacks my clit, sucking on it the way his suckers did. Two tentacles come up to attack my breasts, squeezing the mounts before the suckers attach to my nipples and begin sucking on them as well.

My body is quickly being brought to another peak.

I fear this orgasm may actually be the one to break me. Zalenyk rubs his face in my wetness, his own wetness mingling with mine and heightening my sensations.

"I am marking you in my scent, sweet one. That way, anyone who gets close enough to smell you knows I will kill them for touching you. For attempting to take what is mine."

That thought warms me, a funny feeling settling in my stomach. My legs are hoisted up by his tentacles. They push them back towards my chest so I am on full display for him. He licks from my asshole to my pussy in one clean sweep that has me moaning even louder.

"Come again, come now."

Further solidifying his control over my body, I do so on command. Violently, my body goes up in flames once more. I thrash in his grip, screaming his name as I come and Zalenyk is there. His tentacles hold me through it as he feasts between my legs.

Drinking down every drop of my pleasure.

I do not know what occurred here tonight, but one thing is sure. Zalenyk is a creature to me no more. I no longer want to escape him but to get closer to him, to feel him within me. If I could move I would suggest we go the whole way tonight but that last orgasm has me spent.

My eyes turn heavy. With one last kiss to my pussy, Zalenyk slips up my body once more and wraps me in a warm cocoon of his tentacles.

He licks his lips, a smile playing on them. "Your cunt is delicious."

I bark a laugh and my face heats. This Kraken, Zalenyk, also seems to be the only being I've ever felt shy around. He seems to know that and revels in it.

"Come now little one, let me put you to bed."

There is a faint metallic smell of magic and suddenly I am being carried by two very strong human arms. Zalenyk's steps are sturdy as he marches me back into the castle. His tentacles have shrunk to be beard size and they stroke over my cheek.

I fight to stay awake but as he settles me onto the bed, stripping me out of my wet shift, I find that I am losing the battle. The room is deliciously hot and I sink into the plush mattress. Zalenyk covers me with the comforter and steps back from the bed.

"I will see you in the morning, Melody." He turns on his heel and makes for the door.

Let him leave, you need sleep and time to think about what happened out there. Time to think about escaping. I should listen to those thoughts, should turn into the warmth of this bed, and let this night fade away like sugar in water.

I should do all of those things but I don't.

"Wait," I call, Zalenyk freezes on the threshold. Turning to me, I pull back the comforter and pat the bed beside me. "Stay with me. Hold me while I sleep, this place is new to me and you..." *Don't say it.* "I like being near you"

To admit such weakness causes me to close my eyes. Surely he will be like every other man and use this need as a bargaining chip. To exploit it for their own gain.

Zalenyk is quiet and I look up at him, he gestures toward the fire, his blue human arm glowing in the light.

"The fire is painful to me. I cannot sleep exposed to that much heat, but I want you comfortable above all else."

"You can keep me warm better than any fire." *What is happening to me?*

"Are you sure?"

Am I sure? Yes.

For the first time in a long time, I let go. Those doubts I had a moment ago, I decide to let fade. They were born from a life my father stole for me to have. A life I never truly wanted. In his own way, albeit perhaps not the most selfless act, Zalenyk gave me my freedom back. There are no rules with him, no tricks.

I refuse to live with my mask and guard up any longer.

"Stay with me, Zalenyk. I want you to."

Rushing water sounds from behind him and my Kraken catches it in his hand. It is a small bubble of water that he tosses into the fire. The fireplace goes out with a sizzle and plunges the room into darkness. His footsteps are light on the carpet as the bed dips under his weight.

I must admit he is easier to cuddle in this form.

Sliding on my side, I throw my leg over his middle and curl my arm around his neck. His arms come up to circle my back, tracing his fingers down my arm, my spine. All the while his tentacles tangle in my hair.

Feeling safe and relaxed I close my eyes and feel his rhythmic breathing, letting it seep into my bones and soothe me.

"You are the most precious thing in the world to me, Melody. You do not know the gift you have just given me, to let me hold you like this."

That decides me then and there. I will lean into what this is between Zalenyk and me. I owe it to him and myself to make a real go at this life here.

With that thought in mind, I give in and sink into the familiar waters of *sleep.*

4

―――――

ZALENYK

y Melody is beyond compare.

There are no words that can describe her. No words are worthy of her. It is not enough for me to keep her safe and treasured in my care, not after last night. No, I must win her affection and her kindness. Her desire. Her love.

It is apparent to me that she desires the responses I can coax from her body. Her thighs could not have been more eager and I can still feel her slender thighs squeezing the sides of my head. Her honeyed taste dripped on my tongue as my tentacles coasted over, squeezing every ounce of her delicious skin on display.

I must win Melody over, to show her that her place is here with me, that I will do anything to make her blue eyes sparkle. To have her look at me, not in fear, but in reverence knowing I'm the only one worthy enough to pleasure her.

And I have set about doing that this morning.

We sit at the breakfast table and I watch with fiendish joy as every type of fish is brought in and sat down in front of my human. Salmon, rainbow fish, and shellfish that live deep below the surface, are all plated and presented to her as an offering. The sailors may worship me but I worship Melody and I always will.

This morning had been a first for me. While I have had lovers in the past, none of which I will ever recall now that I have Melody. I had never felt this overwhelming sense of rightness as I did when I woke up this morning. She had held on to me throughout the night, her soft skin fitting against my muscles. Deliciously warm, my tentacles had traced her cheeks and eyelids, committing each freckle to memory.

Melody's blue eyes had blinked open, wary and unsure, her cheeks staining pink. My fiery human is shy in the morning light. Hopefully, she is recalling what it felt like to have me feasting on her pink cunt. I want her to think about that for the rest of her days.

Before I could ask if I could eat her for breakfast, however, a servant came in to deliver Melody fresh clothing. Human clothes aren't in great supply here but I should be fixing that shortly. In the warm glow of the morning, I pressed a kiss to her forehead and told her to join me for breakfast.

I'll cherish the soft smile she gave me for the rest of my life.

While her body is a treat, I want to know about her. To show her that she is safe with me, to be who she is. That I will not keep her trapped. My human is adventurous and I have something planned for her this morning that I think she will really enjoy.

Unfortunately for me, it does not look like she is enjoying her breakfast at the moment.

"What's wrong, Melody? Is the fish not to your liking? I wanted you to have a wide variety so I could learn your favorites." If she hates all of these I will simply have to go out and catch her more. Rare fishes that seek to evade even me.

She is more than worth the hassle if only for her to smile at me again.

"No, these are wonderful. You are too generous…it's just that…" My sweet human squirms in her seat, a blush rising to her cheeks. She doesn't wish to tell me but I will have no secrets between us.

"Tell me, my treasure. Whatever it is you can tell me."

Wrinkling her freckled nose, she grimaces. "I'm not the biggest fan of fish."

Not a fan of fish? Oh, my sweet human. I must fix this at once. She will want for nothing under my care.

"I am sorry, Melody. I did not know." I call for my servants, who appear in the doorway of the dining room. "I will fix this at once. Make sure human food is found, in addition to new clothes. Do you have any preferences, sweet one?"

"Um," she hums, thinking. "For breakfast, bacon if you can find it. If not, my mother used to make oatcakes, it's quite simple. I can even make them if you can find the ingredients."

"I will cook these oatcakes for you, you will not be made to work in my care." She giggles at my words but one look at my face lets her know I am serious. It is my honor to wait on her hand and foot. To provide her with whatever she needs.

"Zalenyk, I don't mind really."

Dismissing my servants with a wave of my tentacles, I have Melody's plate taken away. The room grows quiet as I sulk over what I've done. Not even a day and already my sweet one is going hungry under my roof.

"So," Melody says, interrupting my thoughts. "Will you show me around the palace today?"

In a second my mood is lifted as I remember my plan.

"Yes, I have something to show you that I think will please you."

"You already seem to know how to do that quite well," Melody responds, a small smile curving her lips. Already there is a change in her, and it warms me to know that I had some part of it. When I brought her here she was scared and sad but underneath all of that was a fire, one I can tell she had been suppressing for years. That icy facade of hers is slowly being melted away and I wonder how much more of a treasure she will be when it is all gone.

"When someone is in possession of a treat such as yourself, it would be wrong not to enjoy it."

"But you didn't...enjoy yourself. It was me who got all the...pleasuring."

"You don't think it pleases me to make you come?" She looks away, her face hot. I extend out a tentacle and wrap it around her chin, pulling her back to face me. "You don't think getting to feast on your sweet pussy, to drink down your pleasure, gives me pleasure in turn? To know that I am the only one who's seen you that way. Touched you that way. It makes me feel like a god."

"You are already a god," she points out.

"No, little human. Men may have called me one, but I became one last night with your come dripping off of my chin and your scream of my name ringing in my ears."

"Does that make me a god too? Since I had the power to make you one."

"I'll worship you like one." Her teeth sink into her plump lower lip, I can smell her honeyed scent becoming richer. My little human is wet, just like she should always be around me.

Tossing back her long mane of red hair, she leans her elbows on the table.

"So how did you actually become the Kraken of the Darksea?"

So curious, my Melody.

"My father was the Kraken before me. When he died centuries ago I inherited this place and his powers. There used to be more of my kind, but most of them fled deeper into the ocean. Into their own aquatic kingdoms along the ocean floor." My mouth twists into a grin. "But someone had to stay here and watch over the humans. To keep them in line and that task fell to me."

"Must be lonely, being the only one of your kind left."

"It's not so bad." Melody raises a scarlet brow at me. "Besides, I am not alone now. If more of my kind still existed here I'd have to kill them all to keep you."

Her mouth pops open. "Kill them? Why?"

My laugh is dark, my tentacle tracing over her lips.

"They get one smell of your sweetness in the water and they would want to take you from me. To claim you as their own. You are mine, Melody. Anyone who seeks to take you will wish for death."

Her chest rises and falls, nipples pressing against the wool material of her brown gown. She likes the idea, of belonging to me, her body already knows it. Knows that it is mine, that it belongs to me.

"You want me that much?"

"I need you that much."

"Why?"

"Why?" I echo. "You are a treasure, Melody. Your bastard father should've seen it. Should've protected you and kept you safe but he didn't. I will not make the same mistake."

A harsh shiver passes through Melody, whether from the chill in the air or something else makes no difference to me. It is time to show her my surprise.

"I thought I might take you to the hot spring. It's located just over here and the water will warm you." Melody's mouth opens in a wide grin and she claps her hands lightly. Warmth unfurls within me that I have pleased her.

"That sounds wonderful. I have been in need of a bath."

She takes my offered tentacle and I wrap it around her waist. Pulling her up against my side I lead her from the dining room. It is a short journey to the hot spring, as we walk through the palace I keep her close, casting warning growls at any of my servants whose gaze lingers on her too long.

Melody is mine, only mine.

Through the back of the castle, there is an opening to the spring. Already the air has turned muggy, as white steam billows over the lip of the pool. There is a riot of brightly colored flowers and plants dotting the sides of the spring, I hope that they please my sweet human. She deserves beautiful things.

"Zalenyk this is incredible," Melody says, stepping away from my side to investigate the spring closer. Always so curious.

"I thought you would like it. This will also warm you up, especially when we get into the colder months. The water is so hot, no other creatures can stand it besides me so you should be safe in here."

Melody nods, her blue eyes unfocused as she stares at the pool.

I watch as she begins to undress and my mouth goes dry. While I already have had my mouth and tentacles on every part of her body, seeing it on display like this in the morning sun unlocks something inside me. Her heavy wool gown is cast aside, and the long mane of her red hair drapes down her back. Next goes her thin shift, leaving me to feast on the sight of her smooth back, down to the pert little cheeks of her ass.

There's a freckle just at her hip and I want to lick it. To memorize every single one and kiss them all until she squirms.

As if hearing my thoughts she turns, her red lips tilted in a small smile. I can just see a hint of her breast and I growl as she turns back and jumps into the spring. Warm water goes everywhere and I hurry to join her. Her redhead resurfaces and she holds on to the side of the spring.

The water is shallow over here but Melody is tiny, of course, she cannot stand.

Reaching out one of my tentacles, I suction to her waist and hold her aloft.

"Thank you, it's been a while since I've been swimming. I fear I am not as good at it as I used to be."

"Do you like to swim?" I ask, hungry to know if this is something we can do together in the future.

"I loved it as a girl. To tell you the truth Zalenyk, I was a bit of a wild child. If you thought you captured a lady, I'm afraid you'd be mistaken." Melody laughs but there is no joy in it. She dips her chin and I use another tentacle to tilt her head back up so I can look into her eyes.

"Melody you're perfect. I want you, not a lady, you. I knew it from the moment I saw you." My sweet human opens her mouth as if to argue but I cut her off. "Tell me more about you as a girl."

"Oh! Well…" she trails off, "we were poor. Even as a child, I knew that. We barely had anything to eat, even before my mother died things were hard. But we had love. So much of it that I wonder if my father also bargained away some of his soul that day in *The Woods.* My mother was the heart of our family and she encouraged me to be free, to run, and have fun. To be curious and adventurous."

"She sounds wonderful," I say and Melody rewards me with another smile.

"She was wonderful. She would tell me stories about you, you know? The cautionary tales of not swimming in dark water, which I had a fondness for as a child. My mother believed in the legends and said they were real. If she could see me now, I think she wouldn't find this situation odd in the slightest, just smug that she had always been right about your existence."

Her blue eyes go a little damp and my grip tightens on her. Using my tentacle at her chin, I wipe away a few stray tears that have leaked out. My sweet Melody, so lonely and lost, not so unlike myself.

But I have found her now and she will never feel that way again.

"What about you? Where's your mother?"

"My mother is…" I search for the right words but none come. My mother? I hardly remember her. "She died. Shortly after I was born."

"Oh Zalenyk, I'm so sorry."

"She was human," I say carefully and watch Melody's eyes fly open.

"Human?" she asks.

"Yes, Krakens cannot breed with each other, so it used to be commonplace to steal a human bride in order to get her with child."

"Is that why you stole me? To further your line?" her voice is small, and she won't look at me.

"No, Melody. That is not the reason." I slide closer to her in the water, my tentacles latching onto her arms and legs in a gentle hold. Forcing her to look up at me I let her see the truth in my eyes. "My father loved my mother. Loved her more than anything in this world. When he took her to be his underwater bride she was so frightened, and he realized he could not harm her. Could not sit back as tradition carried on. Our kind would be better than pulling unwilling women under the water in order to procreate with them."

"So what happened?"

"He outlawed the practice and our race slowly died off. I'm one of the last Krakens, Melody. I intend to keep it that way."

"And if I wanted a child? Wanted a child between us?"

Her question throws me. She would want a child? My child.

"When you're ready to finally let me have you, finally ready to let me plant myself so deep inside of you that I soak you with my seed, then we can talk about having a child." I curl a lot of her red hair around my tentacle. "For now, let me show you something. Do you trust me?"

Despite our conversation topic, she nods without pause. Still wrapped in my tentacles, I lead her away from the edge of the pool and deep down into it. Melody's warm naked body is pressed into mine, her nipples hard as they graze over my flesh.

I want to suck them, bite them, and play with them but that will all have to wait.

We go deeper beneath the surface and I watch her start to get nervous, quickly losing air in her lungs. Summoning some of my magic I cast it forward, creating a Melody-sized air bubble rich in oxygen. The pocket covers her and the tentacles I hold her with.

Melody sucks down lungfuls of air and her eyes grow wide as she takes in the sights.

"Zalenyk, what is this?"

"I can do a few tricks here and there, sweet one. Would you like to explore more of the spring?"

"Yes!" Excitement colors her words, my curious little one. I knew she would be eager.

So together, with my treasure wrapped tightly in my embrace, we swim the depths of the spring. At this depth, the water is cooler, so there are a few schools of fish that pass us. Their scales glittering in the faint light. Melody runs her hand along a few waving locks of seaweed that passes us by. Our bare feet drag along the sandy bottom.

The deeper we go the darker it gets. I can see her perfectly, her eyes wide inside her air bubble, taking everything in. When she is completely unable to see she grips my tentacle, holding on to me as if I am a lifeline.

Like she trusts me to keep her safe.

I can feel Melody begin to sag in my arms and I know she is tired. With one last push, we make our way back up to the spring and break through the surface. Her air pocket is popped and she leans against the lip of the pool. Chest rising and falling out of the water, her pale pink nipples coming in and out of view.

Her expression is carefree, her guard finally gone for the first time since I brought her here. That mask has been smashed and I am seeing the real Melody. Gods, she is so beautiful.

We are quiet for a few moments, basking in the warmth of the sun and in each other's company. My tentacle traces up and down her spine, tangling in her hair, and sucking on her shoulders.

"What if I'm ready now? For more," she says, quietly.

My heart stops beating, and time around me slows.

"Are you sure?" I ask my grip on her tightening involuntarily. She nods, her blue eyes bright and trusting.

In the water, we move closer, as if our bodies have given up fighting even the smallest distance between us. Her red hair floats around her and her ruby lips part, waiting, inviting me in to taste them. I'll taste every bit of her, right here right now—

Footsteps sound behind us, and Melody gasps.

Covering her completely with my body, I turn, ready to strangle whoever dares to interrupt us. A couple of my servants rush in, their milky eyes are unblinking. This one had a particularly gruesome death, with half his face missing from being smashed against a cliff before drowning. The words that leave his mouth are garbled.

"Your Majesty, the merchant ship you requested we find has been secured. We are unloading all of their cargo now. It was on course for a human lord and his family so it is filled with all the human things you required."

"Stealing? Really?" Melody chastises me but I see her amused small smile.

"Only the best for you, sweet one." A giggle burst from her lips and I want to drink the sound. Before I get the chance there is a loud ruckus from inside the palace. A few curses and shouts make my servant grimace.

"The captain and his crew of the vessel were not...easy to subdue."

Another sharp yell sounds and Melody pulls on my tentacle to get my attention.

"Seems like we better go and investigate."

I nod solemnly and dismiss my servant. As much as I would love to sink into her right now in this pool, I will not be able to focus until I know that these sailors do not pose a threat to her. I will dispatch them by any means necessary to keep them away from my treasure.

My treasure...who I help rise from the hot spring and watch as she dresses. It is agony watching her naked skin being taken away from me. Even after I had this ship captured in hopes they had fresh clothes for Melody a secret part of me wishes I could burn them all and force her to walk around naked.

However, that would mean my servants may also see her body, and then I would have to drown them all. Again.

Tucking into my side we make our way back into the palace, Melody's damp hair curling and tickly my face. The shouting gets louder until we come into the front room. The captain, an older man with graying hair and wrinkled skin, is already gagged and restrained on the floor. There is blood trickling from his temple indicating some sort of altercation took place.

His crew of five other men looks in the same condition.

One look at me and their eyes widen, fresh sweat breaking out along their brow. It seems they know me and my reputation.

"It may be best to leave them like this and let the tide take them, Your Majesty," one of my servants says. "No loose ends, since they know the location of this place."

The humans on the floor crying out around their gags.

Thrashing on the floor. I nod my head, that would be the easiest course of action.

"No, Zalenyk," Melody says at my side. "Do not kill them. Not for just doing their job. You're not the monster of those legends. We'll take their cargo but spare their lives."

"Melody, you don't understand, I can't just let them—"

"Please spare them," she whispers, her small hand coasting down my front, dangerously close to my hard cock. She knows it too, the little siren. Melody rubs her breasts along my side, her lips tickling the short tentacles of my beard. "Please, for me."

Her hand continues its torture. Rubbing all over me, letting her tongue trace along a tentacle. I groan brokenly, she does not fight fair.

"Fine, sweet one. I will spare them. For you and only for you." Clearing my throat I dismiss the human men.

"Your Majesty, do you wish to see the items recovered?"

I only wish to sink my cock so deep into Melody's tight cunt that there would be no way to pull us apart.

However, that will have to wait. I need to make sure she has everything she could ever want. To prove to her that giving me a chance was not a mistake and that I will make sure she wants for nothing.

Melody must see how conflicted I am because she presses up on her toes and kisses my cheek. Her lips are warm and smooth and I instantly want them back.

"Check on everything, I'll see you at dinner." Melody's smile widens and her eyes become twin blue flames. "And then tonight we'll do more exploring. On land this time."

Turning from the room she doesn't see my tentacles expand and reach after her. Wishing to drag her back to my side and hold her and keep her. Already I miss her but this task is important.

Tonight, I will have my treasure in every way imaginable.

5

MELODY

Despite the feast before me, I find I'm not that hungry. Well, that is for food at least. Lust has stolen my appetite, but I know I will need my energy for what is to come. Taking bite after bite, I tuck into my meal. It really is no hard feat when there are perfectly cooked chunks of beef swimming in rich wine sauces. Fluffy mashed potatoes and roasted vegetables. Stealing is wrong and uncalled for but I cannot deny that it warmed my heart that Zalenyk went through all of this trouble for me.

I take a sip of my wine, my belly full, and look at my dinner companion who tears into another raw piece of fish.

Did I think him hideously ugly before? Surely not. There's more to Zalenyk than meets the eye. Mainly how caring and protective he is of me. I can still hear the growl he leveled at the human captain who came up to retrieve some food for him and his men. The way his eyes lingered on me for too long.

Zalenyk stopped it, something not even my father could've claimed to do.

Maybe that's the cause of these feelings inside of me, the

ones only he is able to stir. The protectiveness, the care, the understanding. All of the things I've been missing out on for so long. Zalenyk fulfills those needs and these new ones I am experiencing.

As if he can feel my eyes on him he looks up from his plate and tilts his head.

"Is the food pleasing to you, my sweet one?"

"Yes, it's delicious. That was the only good thing about my father's new wealth." I laugh without humor. "My health improved greatly after being on the brink of starvation for so long."

"Never again," Zalenyk vows, "will you want for anything. I promise."

My thighs grow damp.

"I know."

"I wish to learn," he pauses, "more about your life after your father's bargain."

I take another sip of wine. This conversation is uncomfortable but Zalenyk looks at me so honestly, it is clear he just wants to know as much as possible about me. That thought allows me to clear my suddenly dry throat.

"Initially, I was happy. My father was still my father in those early days, only now we had the means to actually enjoy the comforts of life. We were happy, before it all, but living hand to mouth can take a lot out of even the happiest of people."

Zalenyk nods and I continue.

"I believed his wealth would afford me some sort of freedom, girls in our old village were being married off at the age I was. This new rise in station meant I would be educated, and we had the means to travel something my mother had always wanted to do, but it became apparent that my future was not mine after all. Especially after the first lord remarked on how lovely of a young woman I was. That was when my father began to change. The wealth had changed him into someone greedy and now he saw me as a new way to gain more wealth."

The growl that comes from across the table shakes the table. A tentative tentacle reaches out to brush against my cheek.

"And now, I've trapped you here." There is a note of self-loathing in his tone. I should agree, tell him that yes my prison has changed from my father's home to his drowned palace but that doesn't seem right. Zalenyk has been kind to me in his own way and helped me explore things I would've never seen before.

"It's not the same, Zalenyk. Not anymore at least," I say but his brow remains furrowed. "Will you show me the world? Take me on adventures, show me the sea that you rule over?"

"Yes." His answer is immediate. "Whatever you wish I will give to you."

"Then perhaps it is a good thing you took me. Lest I become a breeding mare to a cruel, aging prince who thinks the best thing about me is that I can provide him, with children." Taking another sip of wine, I look Zalenyk directly in the eye. "Why did you take me, Zalenyk? Why didn't you just kill my father outright?"

"Because" —he hesitates— "when I saw you there, so beautiful and afraid, I realized you were mine. Something inside me clicked and I knew I had to have you. Perhaps it was years of tradition that even I wasn't immune to but I had to take you. Make you my bride. You feared me, yes, but you weren't disgusted by me. Beneath all of that, I saw you, your fire, and I knew I had to claim it for myself."

"Most men don't like my fire."

"I do. I want to feast on it between your legs, to have it glow in your eyes when I'm inside you."

My thighs clench together, my nipples hard and chafing against my gown.

"There are so many things that I want to give you, sweet one. So many ways in which I want to claim you I don't know which one I want to do first."

"We can do all of them," I say, my voice rough.

"Are you sure?"

"Yes."

I don't know where this boldness comes from but it has me rising from the table. Rounding over to Zalenyk's side I slide on his lap. His short tentacles coast over my face, playing with my hair. Shivering into his touch my fingers explore his face, his groan vibrating me and causing more wetness to slip out of me.

"You know I've never been with anyone before. What will it be like for us?"

"I do not know, I've never been with a human."

"Really?"

"It will be our first time together in a sense."

A small smile curves my lips. "I like that."

We stay silent for a moment, exploring each other. My hands stroke over his face, his chest, tangling in his mass of tentacles. That oily substance I felt yesterday coats my fingers, making them slick. His tentacles have grown and expanded, coasting over my chest, rubbing my hard nipples softly eliciting a moan from my mouth.

Suddenly, I feel it. That hardness beneath my ass pressing against me impatiently. I give a little wiggle and Zalenyk grits his teeth, his tentacles coasting over me faster.

"Zalenyk?"

"Yes, sweet one," he says, his own voice deeper with arousal.

"I want to please you like you pleased me yesterday. You know, with my mouth." My Kraken stops breathing, stops moving, and still I press on. "Will you show me how?"

He doesn't answer, but he moves quickly. Wrapping me up in his arms he takes me from the dining room, so quickly the world is a blur around me. We go deep into the bowels of the castle, and with a wave of his tentacles, the deep water subsides and I find myself in a bedroom.

Not unlike the one I stayed in upstairs but this one seems to find itself submerged quite often. The walls and bedding are wet. The once fine carpet is pulling away and seaweed litters the floor.

Zalenyk's bedroom will definitely need some renovating if we are to be sharing it regularly. That is a problem for another time. Right now I need to be naked, I need him to be naked.

Gently, he lays me on the bed, the waterlogged sheets soaking into my gown. Looming above me I watch with glee as he sheds his more human form and twists into that mass of tentacles and power. The blue muscles slip up along my body, the bed, touching me everywhere.

"Zalenyk." I moan as one tentacle suctions to my nipple over my gown. "I want you so much. Please, I ache for you."

"Melody," he groans, his mouth swooping down on mine. He is soft and slippery, so strong that he could easily crush me. Zalenyk's touches are gentle and exploratory and his tentacles join my own hands as I rip at my gown. Tearing it off of my body until my breasts are free, then my stomach, until I am totally bare.

I feel his tentacles loop around my calves, and my thighs, holding them open as he slips between my legs. My pussy is so wet and sensitive I can't help myself and rub it along him. My own wetness mixed with his own secretions, making my body so sensitive and slick it's a wonder some part of him hasn't already slipped inside of me.

My hands come up to tangle in his tentacles. His tongue dances with mine, licking into my mouth and drinking my moans. I grip the shorter ones around his face until I start moving lower, into the mass of them below. Pulling and tugging to bring him closer to me. My nipples are so hard they are painful and when one of his tentacles suctions onto the tight buds I scream, gripping another tentacle tightly in my hand.

Zalenyk jerks and I feel a rush of more secretion on my hand. Only this one is thicker, stickier, not the clear oily substance as the rest of him.

My eyes fly open and I look into his face, those red eyes clouded with lust.

"You want to please me, little human?"

"Yes."

"That's my cock in your hand. Keep touching it and I'll reward you with my seed."

My smile is so wide it hurts my mouth and I tug at his cock over and over again. It is massive and decorated with smooth ridges and bumps. Looking down I can see it is a darker blue than the rest of him, especially the bulbous head. A trail of white come, coats my hand but I keep moving my fist up and down on him.

His tentacles continue coursing along my body. One sneaks up to wrap around my neck loosely, holding me in place.

"Open your mouth, Melody." I do so immediately. "I love your fire, how strong you are, but make no mistake. In this bed, you are mine. My little human toy whose only purpose is to please me. I will use all of your holes when I see fit and you will beg me for it."

I start to shake my head, the way he's talking, ignites something inside of me. The want to fight him, to scratch, to claw, to make him work to pleasure me.

"I don't beg, Kraken," I say, giving his cock an extra firm tug. He is at my mercy, I am the one with the power here.

His mouth curves into a cruel smile. "Oh my sweet one, that couldn't be farther from the truth. Would you like me to prove it to you?"

"Do your worst." Zalenyk pauses for a second, his eyes growing serious.

"If anything we do—if anything I do—that is too much for you, Melody, tell me to stop. I want complete control of you, but that doesn't mean I just get to have it. Tell me to stop and I stop, understand."

"I want to give you complete control." My Kraken chuckles softly.

"Then tell me you understand what I just said."

"I understand. I say stop you stop." I look him in the eyes while I say the words and part of me melts like sugar in water. Now I just have to see what he does with this new dynamic established between us. A wicked smile curves his lips.

Without warning my hands are ripped away from him. Tentacles wrap around my wrists, pinning them above my head, my chest rising slightly from the bed. The limb wrapped around my throat tightens slightly, as another one snakes along my chest, over my chin, and into my mouth. The tentacles suction onto my tongue and I moan around it, at this new invasion.

It slips in deeper, down my throat until it bumps along the back. My eyes water, and saliva pools in my mouth and along my chin but it keeps going, deep and then retreating, over and over again.

"Take it, my pretty little slut, get it nice and wet so when I put it in your asshole it slides in nicely."

I start to thrash in his grip. My *ass*? Surely not.

When it finally subsides from my mouth, I cough and sputter. His eyes gleam with a wickedness I have not seen before.

"I can do whatever I want to you. Restrain you, choke you, and you know that you'll still walk away from this being my treasure. Don't you?"

Shaking my head again his grip on my throat tightens.

"Don't lie to me."

"Yes, yes I'm still your treasure."

"That's right," he purrs, feeling more tentacles loop around my legs they are hoisted into the air and pushed back against my chest. I'm completely exposed to his eyes, my glistening pussy swollen and begging for his attention. "But right now you're my human whore and I have to remind you who owns you."

That is all the warning I get before his tongue reaches out and licks me from pussy to asshole. It delves between the cheeks of my ass and prods the tight ring of muscles. Dipping in slightly and then retreating.

"Zalenyk, not there!" I scream, the sensation is foreign but not altogether unpleasant. I like what he is doing, I realize. His harsh words and degradation should be a turn-off to me, as they would be from any man, but Zalenyk is right. Here I can find him and let him own me. It is the one place I feel safe being overpowered. He is the one person who can overpower me and yet when this is over will treat me like I am his most prized treasure.

That knowledge lets me sink into this, into him, and lose myself to this coupling.

"Here." His tongue presses in deeper, his saliva coating my hole. "There." A tentacle comes up to gently dip into my pussy. His oily substance makes me even wetter. I am so full and so completely owned it is glorious.

"Wherever I want, whenever I want."

"No." I could tell him to stop if I really wanted to and I know he would, but stopping him is the last thing I want to do.

"Yes. Here you submit to me."

"Make me."

Zalenyk chuckles darkly and then it begins. His tongue leaves my ass only to be replaced by the tentacle that was in my mouth. It circles me there, once, then twice until it slips in gently. The burn makes my back arch.

His tongue is at my pussy, lapping up my entrance before moving up to suck on my clit.

"Such a pretty pussy, Melody. You're lucky no man ever had you. If he had, if he dared to see this pussy, my pussy, I'd have to kill him. Drown him in the sea and make him watch as I fucked you."

I cry out, my hands straining to grab onto anything, but I am powerless. At the mercy of my Kraken, all I can do is ride out this experience and hope I come out the other side in one piece.

His tongue parts me, tasting me as my moisture leaks out of me. The tentacles wrapped around my legs push them back even further until my hips raise off the bed. I am a meal to this creature and he is going to feast on me. Over and over again he licks me, dipping inside and then giving the same treatment to my clit.

The tentacle at my ass spears in deeper and I cry out. Another one sneaks up to sink gently into my pussy. They work me in tandem, in shallow thrusts as Zalenyk sucks on my clit. My muscles tighten, my pussy clenching down on.

"My little slut has the tightest cunt known to man. Are you close? Do you want me to make you come?"

"Yes!" I'm desperate too, my eyes water and I pull against his hold on my arms. My thighs begin to shake, and I move my hips in time with his tentacles, needing that extra bit of friction to push me over the edge.

"Hmmm," Zalenyk hums in his throat. "I don't think my little fucktoy has earned it yet. After all, she hasn't made me come as a good girl should."

Everything stops.

His tentacles leave me, and so does his mouth. My muscles quiver and I scream, trying desperately to get him back, to throw myself over the edge. Tears burn in my eyes from disappointment from denial.

"What the fuck? Make me come, Kraken!" I scream, foul language slipping from me again.

Zalenyk only laughs before using his tentacles to flip me. I'm suspended in the air while he slips up into the bed. He brings me back down so my face is on top of his great mass of tentacles and my ass is in his face. A sharp sting hits my backside and I realized he's smacked my ass with his tentacle. I feel the heat from it bloom ling on my skin.

"Naughty girl, you don't speak to your master like that."

"My master is supposed to make me come!" I cry. My lip juts out and I feel sweat beading at my brow. I'm not above throwing a temper tantrum right now. The denial of my orgasm burns so hotly inside me. I try to rock back onto his face but he stops me.

"I'll make you come, my sweet. After you behave like a good girl and make me come down your pretty little throat."

With that new goal in mind, my arms are free, and fling myself down into his massive body. It's not hard to find his cock, it stands out from the rest of his tentacles. Thicker than the rest of his tentacles and devoid of all suckers. It's darker in color and decorated with ridges and bumps along the shaft. I've never done anything like this before but I let instinct take over.

Giving him a tentative lick I taste his salty sweetness and decide I could dine on this. I lick him again before taking the head into my mouth. Sucking lightly I use my hand to circle his shaft, stroking at the same time. He's so large I doubt I'll get him all the way down my throat but I am determined to try.

"So good, my treasure. So perfect, I knew you were born to suck my cock."

I moan around his length, my own wetness leaking out of me. As if he can't help himself I feel his tongue sneak up to lick between my slit. Groaning at my taste and renewed by that bit of pleasure I work his cock harder. My head bobs as I cram him down my throat further.

My lips stretch wide and I feel him bump against the back of my throat. My eyes burn but I keep going, briefly realizing he was testing me earlier like this with his tentacle. Getting me prepared for this exact moment. I fight past the burn and feel him slip down my throat, more salty goodness spurts into my mouth.

Swallowing down eagerly, he groans and that's when I feel him at my entrances. A tentacle probes my pussy and my ass, his tongue tickling my clit. Not with the vigor he did before but enough to know that my reward is coming soon.

I double my efforts, licking and sucking, running my tongue along each bump and ridge. How will this feel inside of me? I can't wait to find out.

"Do you want me to fill your holes, Melody?"

"Yes," I gasp, finally releasing his length with a pop.

"Then ask me." I grit my teeth, and my old vow that I don't beg rings in my ears but I'm done pretending that's not true. I'll beg if he lets me come.

"Please, Zalenyk, please use my holes. Make me come, master, please."

Zalenyk chuckles and then his mouth is on me. Glancing over my shoulder, I watch his massive blue tentacles push into me, in and out. Moving in fluid motions together. I hear him sucking on my clit, the wet and sloppy sounds my pussy is making. The sight before me is so erotically beautiful, I fall back on his cock and work him with the same intensity.

My thighs shake once more. This orgasm feels more intense as if being denied the first time has caused my body to rage. I might snap in half once he finally lets me come but I won't stop sucking on his cock. It hardens in my mouth and his tentacles seem to pulse around me.

"Close, Melody?"

Nodding, I don't dare release him from my mouth.

"Me too. Swallow it all down, sweet one." That's the only warning I get before a roar so loud it shakes the room around me. Then I'm drowning in his seed. So much sprays from his cock and shoots down my throat. I try and swallow all of it down but I can't quite manage it. It leaks from every tentacle, coating me in that sticky substance.

It covers my face and chest, some is in my hair, and of course in my stomach. There's so much of it I can only moan and writhe as it coats me completely.

Then my own orgasm hits me.

Sneaking up on me like an eel in the water, I go up in flames. My muscles seize, my body shakes and I scream. Scream for Zalenyk, scream for mercy, scream for anything. The warm press of his tongue is at my entrance as he drinks down my come.

I lay there on him, shaking with little aftershocks, sticky from his seed, and panting.

My throat and eyes burn, my muscles are aching, and there are red sucker marks all over my body. Yet, I have never, ever been happier.

Tentacles flip me and suddenly I am staring at Zalenyk's face. He wipes some of his seed from my cheek with a gentle touch. There is a soft rushing sound before warm water glides through the air washing away his seed from my body and hair and off him as well. There is a wariness to him.

"Are you alright, my treasure? I didn't hurt you did I?"

I shake my head no and bury it into his warmth.

"I need the words, Melody." His tone is firm and almost pleading.

"Zalenyk," I murmur into his chest. "I loved it. Every second of it. You gave me something I never knew I needed."

"What's that?" He pulls me closer to him.

"An outlet. To be wild and free; to be able to fight you and you still want me after."

"I more than want you, Melody." Kissing the top of my head, I want to tell him that I more than want him too. "I promised to give you everything that you need and I will not fail you on that."

"There is one thing I need though." My fingers tangle in his tentacles, wrapping a few of them around my fist.

"What is that, my sweet?"

I smile, running my tongue along the side of his face. Salty and sweet, maybe I should call him sweet one as well.

"I need you to come inside me this time."

6

———

MELODY

Zalenyk freezes, his tentacles pausing they're playing along my hair.

Surely this can't be a surprise to him. Sucking him off was nice, but it just made me want to feel him inside me even more. Slinging my leg over him, I straddle his massive form. Red splotches decorate my chest where his tentacles sucked on me.

"Don't you want to give me that?" I pout. "Haven't I been good enough to earn more of your come?"

His tentacles come up to dig into my backside, wrap around my hips and hold me in place to stop my wiggling.

"You have been good," he says. "Do you want me inside that little pussy? My tentacle wasn't enough, was it? You need to be stuffed with my cock, greedy slut."

"Yes." Nodding my head vigorously. "I want your cock so bad, please. I've saved myself for you."

"When I come inside you, Melody, you know what could happen?" he asks.

"Yes," I answer, trying in vain to move my hips.

"You'd want that? Me to breed you?"

"Isn't that why you stole me? Deep, deep down that was always your plan?" I ask, even if we are playing this game between us I want to hear his answer. It will determine where I take it from here.

"Did I take you so I could fill you with my come, over and over again?" He curls a lock of hair around his tentacle. "Yes, I suppose I did. The thought did occur to me that I could get you pregnant, despite me telling you that I wanted my kind to end with me."

"Do you still want that?"

"I want you," he says, firmly. "If you want us to have a child, I will love it just as I love you." My eyes water at his confession. "If you do not, I will procure you herbs that will stop your womb from quickening. Your choice, sweet one, always yours."

I lean down and press my mouth to his.

"I love you too," I say, it feels too soon but I'm about to fuck a Kraken. I think I can let my human reflex to play aloof fade. It is the truth, it is how I really feel. No mask, no guard. I will only be my true self in front of Zalenyk. "I'll take the herbs, there are so many things I want to see. To experience with you."

"I'll show you everything, Melody. My treasure, my love." Zalenyk kisses me again, his tongue slipping in my mouth, his body raising beneath me. I pull back slightly, running a hand down over my pale, flat stomach.

"One day, though, I want us to have a child. I want us to have a family."

"Anything you want, Melody."

"I knew you'd say that," I laugh. "Now fuck me until I can't walk."

I'm rolled onto my back, my arms and legs wrapped up in his tentacles. Splayed open wide like an offering. One limb sneaks around and slithers into my opening. My wetness mixed with Zalenyk's own has the tentacle easily pushing inside of me. A second one is added but even that I realize pales in comparison to Zalenyk's actual size.

The sensation still makes me moan, feeling so full I could burst. His tongue licks over my breast, circling each pale pink nipple until it is a stiff peak. My mouth is empty for a moment and as if he realizes that, my Kraken pushes one of his tentacles inside. I suck on it like I did his cock and he growls, as it tickles the back of my throat.

"Would you like to be filled now?" Zalenyk asks. I nod my head vigorously. "The words, Melody. Don't make me remind you again."

"Yes, Zalenyk, my love, my master, fill me. I'm so empty without you."

He groans and my legs are pushed apart even wider. Something hard rubs along my entrance. It presses firmly against my clit and I squirm before I feel it dip inside of me. The head of his cock has barely breached me and already I feel stretched beyond belief.

"Zalenyk—"

"Shh, you can take it. I own this pretty pussy and it will welcome me." He leans down and plants a kiss on my lips. "I just need to give it a bit of a push."

I can tell he tries to be gentle, but between his size and my small frame, there's no way to avoid the uncomfortable pressure. Realizing with some mild horror that he isn't even halfway inside of me and I already feel like I'm about ready to burst. He stills, letting some of his own natural lubricant help the situation. It does the trick and he slides a few more inches in. My breath catches. We do this same motion over and over again until he's fully seated inside me.

There was a slight tear and a small pinch that brought a rush of tears to my eyes. Zalenyk wipes them away with a tentacle. He remains still while my body adjusts, giving me a few shallow thrusts.

"You're doing so well, sweet one. You take me so well in this little cunt of yours."

Sliding himself back so that only the head of his cock remains in me, he thrusts forward and I realize the pain is gone. Our combined moisture has done the trick. All I want now is more.

A tentacle snakes out and massages my clit, suctioning onto it. I feel so incredibly full, but I need him to start moving. Really moving. I start rocking my hips in order to create some more delicious friction. Those ridges and bumps I tasted earlier along his cock are pure heaven inside of me.

Helping to tickle a spot deep inside of me that has my vision blurring.

"Greedy for my cock, aren't you?"

"Yes!" I cry and he rewards me with a shallow thrust.

"You came to me a virgin but you'll become my whore in no time. Look at you, working yourself on my cock, pathetically trying to fuck yourself on me."

"I need more, Zalenyk, please."

He pulls back out of me and then thrusts forward. My breast bounce in time with his fucking and I throw my head back absorbing each blow. Zalenyk goes slow, stoking the fire inside of me. Despite his harsh words, he's being gentle with me.

Too gentle.

"I thought you were going to fuck me until I couldn't walk?" I ask in a put-out tone.

"Is that not what I'm doing?" He grits out, one tentacle coming to wrap around my throat.

"Fuck me harder, faster!" I demand, trying to move my hips to capture more of him.

He stops moving completely, his red eyes narrowing.

"You want it rough, little slut?"

"Only if you think you can do it. At this point, it seems like me, the virgin, is the one fucking you." Zalenyk laughs darkly, withdrawing from me completely. I whine at the loss of sensation. I want him back, I crave it.

His tentacles flip me over onto my front, before roughly lifting my ass high. A few limbs wrap around my arms and keep them tied behind my back. Another set slides my feet apart so I am fully exposed and unable to close them.

"You don't know what you've asked for." I watch from below as his tentacle snaps out and slaps my ass. The heat from the sting makes my pussy grow even wetter. "You're the Kraken's little come slut, aren't you? I was trying to treat you nicely for your first time, but you don't want that do you? You want me to use all of your little holes?"

"Yes!" I cry. "Use me, however, you want."

I feel him slip up behind me and line his cock up with my pussy.

"I plan to."

Zalenyk slams into me so hard that I almost tumble forward. If not for the strong grip his tentacles have on my arms and legs I would've fallen. He pounds into me so hard, over and over again. The sound of our body slapping together fills the room. The wet slide of his cock in and out of me. It is so obscenely beautiful.

I moan into the mattress, unable to do anything but accept each one of his thrusts. My clit is being sucked on by one of his tentacles, and another one prods my ass, before slipping inside. Being filled so crudely in this way turns a key in me. I love his treatment, I love everything about this.

"Such a tight cunt," he grunts, "you'll be this tight every time I fuck you? Of course, you will, you want to please me."

"Yes, yes," I pant. The sensation is too much. My hair sticks to the sweat on my brow. From my bound position, my arms are beginning to ache but I don't tell him to stop. I want it to keep going, to see what cliff this leads me to so I can be thrown off of it.

A tentacle winds around my hair and my head is snapped up. My back arches to accommodate this new position and I am vaguely aware I'm being lifted from the bed. Another pair of tentacles come up to knead and suction my breasts. My moans are louder and wilder. A warmth spreads low in my stomach. It is heightened when I watch my skin become shiny with Zalenyk's own fluid, coating me and making me tingle.

The limbs holding me aloft suddenly move and I'm being thrust back on Zalenyk as he thrust forward. These rough thrusts make my eyes start to close. That beautifully ridged cock of his tickles that hidden spot and my muscles tighten. My neck strains as it is snatched back even further. The muscles of my pussy clench down around him and I hear Zalenyk growl.

"Does my human whore want to come?" I shake my head as best I can in this position. "Beg me."

"I can't—it's—it's too much!" He freezes, and I scream at the loss of movement. Suddenly I am ripped off of his cock and I feel it press against my ass.

"Beg me, Melody or my cock goes in here and I'll make you beg me to come with it stuffed in your ass."

"No please, I'll beg, I'll beg." Still, he doesn't move away from my back entrance.

"I'm waiting."

"Please, Zalenyk, please fuck my pussy. Please come inside of me, I want you to. Reward me with your seed, I need to feel it drip out of me." My Kraken sinks back inside my pussy and begins his punishing pace again. My thighs tremble my chest heaves. I am close, so close.

"Tell me that you love that I took you. Tell me that you'll always be mine."

"I love that you took me! You saved me, Zalenyk. I'm yours, I'll always be yours."

That snaps something inside him and he doubles his efforts. Each stab of his cock inside me unlocks pure euphoria. My muscles strain and then I am thrown off of that cliff. My orgasm is ripped from me, a scream ringing in my ears as my pussy clamps down on him. This climax is painful, so overwhelming that tears leak from my eyes.

So many things clash inside me at once, but through them, the only thing I feel is how right this is. How much I completely and totally belong to my Kraken.

Just as I start to come down, Zalenyk tightens his tentacle around my throat and lets out a roar. I feel the come explode out of him and into me. Burning hot, it seeps from his cock and his tentacles until I am once again coated in his spend. He fucks it into me and that sets off another orgasm.

Not so world-shattering as the first one but definitely enough to have my toes curling.

Sticky and panting, Zalenyk releases me from his hold and slowly pulls out of me. I feel the rush of his come slide down my thighs and onto the mattress below. Smiling, I slump forward onto the mattress, unable to move.

My body is still quivering with little aftershocks as Zalenyk rolls me onto my back. Looking down at me with wonder and love in his eyes. I hope mine are reflecting the same thing because that is how I feel at this moment.

"You did so good, Melody. You are so perfect." I blush and smile softly. He comes around to lay at my side and I nuzzle into him. I know my blush is even deeper when I spy the red mark on the bed.

Just like before, another rush of warm water comes and cleans us both off.

"As soon as I can move, I want to do that again," I say,

yawning into his chest. He cocoons me in his massive, meaty limbs.

"Whatever you want, Melody, you know that."

I do, I think as I begin to nod off. Warm and satisfied with my Kraken's come leaking out of me I realize that even if I did have the choice to leave here I wouldn't. I want to stay just like this forever.

7

MELODY

It's dark in Zalenyk's room when I finally open my eyes.

My Kraken is still asleep beside me, massive body rising and following with each great breath. I could've only been asleep for a few hours. His tentacles are still curled around me, one is even stuck to my cheek.

There was a reason I woke up? I swallow and then I am reminded. Gently disentangling myself from his hold, I grab a discarded blanket, damp and cold, and cover myself. Going in search of a glass of water, I pad down the sodden hallway.

This area of the palace will definitely need some touch-ups.

Making this palace my home warms something inside of me. I was never allowed to decorate at my father's home and while I'm sure gold-crusted light fixtures aren't readily available in this part of the country I can still make it my own.

Even if I wanted gold fixtures I know Zalenyk would find a way to get them for me.

As I make my way down the hall, I realize more of his come leaks out of me and I am a bit tender between my legs. He was so deliciously rough. Once I quench my thirst perhaps I will wake him with my mouth on his cock.

Then we can fuck again. That sounds good to me.

There is a light up ahead and that is what I am following. I'll need a proper tour of this place because this area is completely unfamiliar to me.

As I get closer to the light I can hear raised voices. Moving on quiet feet I duck into what I assume is the kitchen. Finding my discarded glass of wine from dinner, I take a sip. There are a few shouts and loud bangs from the other side of the door.

I should go and wake Zalenyk, perhaps someone is in trouble.

The doors swing open and I can't even comprehend what I am seeing. It is the human captain, unbound and staring right at me as if he also can't believe his eyes. My wine glass slips from my hand and shatters at my feet.

We stare at each other for a beat. I should scream, do something, anything, but fear has frozen me to the spot. He is holding something in his hands that I can't make out in the dim light.

His mouth curves into a smile, exposing his yellowed teeth. "This is perfect."

That's the last thing I hear before he strikes out, hitting me in the side of the head with whatever he was holding. The world around me goes dark as I crumple to the floor

Zalenyk

The lack of Melody's warmth is what wakes me.

Her small breasts are no longer being pressed into my side and that will not do. The area where she was nestled next to me is still warm, so wherever she went she could not have left that long ago. If she needed something she should've woken me up, I would've gladly gotten it for her.

She is mine. All mine, she admitted as much and I will treasure that fact for the rest of eternity. I should be showing her right now how much I love her, to prove to her that she is not wrong for loving me back.

Slipping from the bed I go in search of my sweet little human. What should I do first? Feast on her pink cunt? Lick her little asshole until she shakes? Maybe I'll fuck her with my tentacles until she begs for my cock?

The possibilities with Melody seem endless.

I follow her scent, one that has now mingled with mine, to the kitchen. The honeyed smell of it is so rich, I could come just from inhaling it deeply. Bursting through the kitchen doors I expect to find her there, waiting for me with a smile, naked.

However, she is not.

With some growing alarm, I can also smell another scent in here. Male. Human. I notice the shattered glass in the corner and a small pool of blood. My heart begins to race.

"Melody?" I call. "Melody!"

I barrel into the front room and my servants are scrambling. They all stop in their tracks and turn to look at me.

"Where is she? What has happened?" None of them speak and my anger and confusion only grow.

"Speak," I command, snatching one of the servants and dragging him in front of me.

"The hu—humans escaped, Your Majesty. Your human bride went with them. We saw her climb onto their ship and sail away."

Melody...is gone? She left me?

"Why was I not informed of this?" I growl, gripping him tighter.

"The patrol last night was all killed. A few of us ran after them down the beach to try and stop them and that's when we saw her board and begin to sail off. We were too late to stop them."

My heart sinks. Perhaps I was wrong, perhaps she only said those things to placate me. Has she been plotting with them all along? Knowing they would be her best option to hatch an escape plan. Did she only agree to fuck me so I would be tired enough for her to escape?

Even as I think about it, I know that isn't right.

Melody is brave and strong and she would never have given herself to me if she did not wish to. My gut tells me they took her and if that is the case then they are already dead. She is mine, she belongs to me and I will do whatever it takes to get her back.

"Which direction did they sail?" I ask, my voice deeper. The magic I've contained for so long is released, unfurling from inside me. My servant gulps as I drop him, rising up and expanding to fill the entire front room.

"E—east, Your Majesty."

I haven't been forced into this legendary size in decades, but these humans who dared steal my treasure will face the full force of my wrath. I slither out of the palace into the waiting cold water. Smelling Melody in the air I hold onto that sent, tracking it as any predator would.

I will get back my treasure and those who dared to take her will be led to their watery deaths.

8

—

MELODY

My head is throbbing and I am freezing cold.

How did everything go from perfect to horrible in the span of a few minutes? I shiver and try and wrap the blanket tighter around myself. The captain is close by, directing the members of his crew and casting me lecherous looks. I shiver again and this time, not from the cold.

"You're lucky I found you when I did," he sneers, coming to loom over me. He smells of sweat and sour ale. "You should be grateful I'm saving you from that creature. And with you on board, he'll think twice about attacking our ship."

He reaches out and takes a lock of my hair between his fingers and I jerk away.

"This hair will fetch a high price when we get to port. You all together will. That'll serve that bastard Kraken right for stealing our cargo. We'll sell his treasure to the highest bidder."

"The only bastard here is you!" I seeth. "He will come for me and when he does you will all be dead."

The captain laughs, grabbing a fist full of my hair so I have to look up at him. The pressure on my scalp makes my eyes water.

"I doubt he's even realized your gone, by the time he does we will be far away from here." He releases me and stomps away. "Now be quiet or I'll have to find some way to keep you silent. You really wouldn't enjoy that."

The sky is still dark as we cut through the open sea. I try and make myself small, tucking into the corner of the deck. The skies open up and rain descends down upon us. I'm soaking and so cold, and my breath curls in a white cloud in front of me. Zalenyk, where is he?

Surely he has noticed my absence by now.

The only reason I boarded this ship is by the time I came too I was already being hauled onto the deck. A few of the crew members tried grabbing at my covering and I yanked it free of their grips. If I had the chance to run I would've at least tried.

I can only send a prayer up that Zalenyk notices and he gets to me in time before we make it to port.

"Brace yourselves!" yells the captain.

The water has gotten choppy. Large waves are illuminated by flashes of lightning. The air is salty. Cold, dark water splashes over the sides of the deck and soaks me. Between the rain and the water, I may freeze to death before I make it to our destination.

Perhaps if I drown, my soul will be sent back to Zalenyk.

I shake myself from that dark thought. He has to be coming for me, I know he is. Our ship continues in the rough water. Dipping and bobbing, a few of the crew are sick over the side of the boat. There is an ominous creak and crack. A flash of lightning illuminates something in the distance.

"What is that!" someone cries, but I see it all the same. I see him.

Zalenyk is here, just like I knew he would be. His massive frame rises out of the water. His tentacles were far-reaching, his head as large and as wide as four ship lengths. The power radiating off of him makes me grow wet.

I love him and he's here to rescue me.

This form is the one legends were born from. He is formidable and scary, a god of the sea. A god that I am raising on shaking legs and walking towards the front of the boat to go and see. Salty water doses me again and those massive red eyes track my every movement.

The crew scatters behind me, cowering in fear.

"Zalenyk," I cry, waving my arm. "You saved me again. You always save me."

"I'd do anything for you, Melody." I laugh and tears stream down my cheeks.

I need to be back in his embrace, to feel his warm body against mine. To burrow so far inside of him that there is no separating us. Dropping the blanket, I step over the railing at the front of the ship and plunge into the dark water below.

It's so quiet underneath the surface I almost forget what is waging above. Then I feel it, a meaty tentacle slipping between my legs and along my front. It is so wide I can barely get my arms and legs around it but I hold on for dear life as it lifts me out of the water.

Zalenyk brings me in front of his face, so large and so worried. I must look like a doll to him at this size. He pulls me in closer until I am flush against his cheek. I run my hand along it and nuzzle into the tentacle holding me.

"Are you alright, my love?" he asks, his voice so deep it sends ripples into the ocean below us.

"I am now. I knew you'd save me."

"So you did not wish to leave with them?" he asks carefully, and my hand freezes. I squeeze his tentacle and he circles me around to the front of his face.

"Zalenyk, I told you I never want to leave you. I'm yours forever, just as you are mine."

"My Melody, my treasure," he murmurs reverently. "They tried to take you from me and they failed. Watch what happens to anyone who dares to try and steal you."

With a powerful rush of water, I can see Zalenyk lift one meaty tentacle from the water and smash it down onto their boat. I hear the wood splinter and the crew scream for mercy. I watch as Zalenyk holds them all below the surface, locked in a tight grip of his tentacles until they drown.

The wicked shiver that passes through me at the sight does not escape his notice.

"Did that make your little pussy wet, Melody? To see me take all their lives as payment for trying to take you from me."

"Whenever I'm around you my pussy is always wet."

"Hmmm," he groans, "let me see just how wet you are."

Then I am being dangled in front of him. His massive pale blue tongue slips from his mouth and runs up along my body. My arms are held tightly in his tentacles and his tongue keeps me seated. It's easy four times my size and licks me from between my ass to my nipples.

"At this size, you really are my little fucktoy."

His tongue is so warm and wet and before long my toes are curling. Zalenyk is everywhere, as soaked with him as I am with the rain. He owns me but I own him too and that's why he is the only one who will ever get me this way.

"I love you," I babble, my orgasm quickly approaching.

"I love you, Melody."

My body seizes and my Kraken is there, licking up my come and tucking me against him. Curling into his warmth I do not stir again until the morning sun has risen.

EPILOGUE

ZALENYK

One Year Later

Life in the Drowned Palace is absolutely perfect.

Especially because Melody is there. Every day with her is more perfect than the last. In the past year, I can honestly say that my life has never had more meaning, being filled with so much joy and love that I can hardly believe my luck. Melody is my treasure and each day with her is a gift.

But a gift is what I have left the warmth of her thighs to go and find.

While I call her my bride I have yet to make her my wife. It is a small thing, a human thing, but I want Melody tied to me in as many ways as I can get her. That is why I have ventured so far from the sea and into *The Woods*. Why I stand before the door of the demon who lives in them and knock once.

Behind it, I can hear the faint sound of a woman's cries. I think she could be in pain but then it is followed by a moan and I realize what keeps this beast from answering my summons. Even if I understand the feeling. If it was a choice between Melody and talking to this beast, I wouldn't answer my door either.

Still, I knock again.

There is a small giggle, followed by thunderous footsteps. The old door is nearly torn from the hinges and the demon of *The Woods* stands before me naked. Eyes of pure fire glower at me.

"What do you want, Kraken?" He grits out, I've clearly caught him at a bad time so better to make this quick.

"The pearls that a fisherman traded with you to steal my fish, do you still have them?" The demon smirks and reaches to the side of the door. Chuckling, the demon squeezes the small bag of pearls in his clawed hand and shakes his head.

"An unwise bargain for that fisherman I take it."

I am poised to agree but then I remember what I got out of it. Melody. Without his theft, I would've never met her.

"On the contrary, this turned out quite fruitful for me."

"My love?" calls a delicate female voice from deep inside the demon's cottage. He practically shoves the pearls in my hands, bracing his hand on the door frame.

"Be gone, Kraken, I have more important matters to attend to."

"You do not want the rubies I brought? Stole them from a king's merchant ship." I tap the pouch at my side. "My Melody doesn't much care for them, but I thought you might have some use for them."

"A human?" asks the demon, pausing in shutting the door, his nostrils flaring as he registers the other scent on me. From the scent inside the house, I can tell he has one himself.

"I see you've found yourself besotted by one as well." The demon smiles slightly and nods.

"My Irys doesn't have much care for them either. The Dragon's Lair isn't too far from here, if you really want to part with them he'll surely take them off your hands."

"He's stirring again? It's been decades since I last heard he was awake."

"He was always the most miserable amongst us," the demon replied. Another call from deep within the house stops me from asking any more questions. "Be gone."

The door slams with a final thud.

I'm still standing on the stoop when I hear the moaning pick back up again. It reminds me of Melody and how I need to get back to her as soon as possible. This trip to the Dragon's Lair will be fast and then I will be back inside her again.

Cutting through *The Woods* it is not long before I find myself at the mouth of a giant cave. Even with the bright sun beating down on me, only about five feet into the mouth of the cave are visible. I've never been inside of it, no humans have and have lived to tell the tale.

My natural aversion to fire has never made me want to stay in this place for very long, nor in the presence of the dragon himself. Asgorath is right, he was always the most miserable among us.

Though a curse will do that to you, I suppose.

Setting the bag down I leave it just inside the cave's mouth. Within a second two fiery eyes emerge from the darkness. The sun illuminates shiny scales and razor-sharp black claws that snatch the bag away from the opening and deep into the darkness.

"Silly creature," I say, not knowing or caring if he can even keep me. "I hope one day you find that there is something more precious than jewels and gold out there."

Mine is currently waiting for me in our bed.

I move quickly back out of *The Woods*. The river is rushing nearby and I transform as I close in on it. Changing from my humanoid form to my real one and using the power of my tentacles to swim me home as quickly as possible. I keep the bag of pearls tucked in my tentacles. The water moves past me in a flurry of bubbles. I barely spare a passing glance at the creatures I swim by.

My mind is focused on my treasure.

It takes me too long to make it back to the palace. Too long until I am inside my bedroom and come face to face with Melody. She's still asleep, her red hair fanned out all around her. Our lovemaking last night and into this morning was particularly vigorous so I know she's wiped out.

One long, pale leg lays above the sheets and I cannot resist running a tentacle along it. Her blue eyes blink open and she smiles, stretching her arms out and sitting up. The white sheet slips down her body until her breasts are free, covered only by the tresses of her hair.

I slide onto the bed and wrap her in my tentacles. Kissing my lips, she burrows into my side.

"You smell like the ocean. Where have you been?" My tongue suddenly feels too big for my mouth and I swallow loudly. She furrows her red brows. "What?"

"I went to retrieve something." A tentacle I had tucked tightly to my chest, unwinds from me holding out the small bag of pearls. Melody gasps and grabs it from me. Her delicate hands are shaking as she holds it, as she opens it, and sifts through the contents.

"Zalenyk," she gasps, "how on earth did you find these?"

"The demon and I have known each other for ages. I persuade him to let me have them."

Her hands dig through the bag and pull out a small stand necklace of pearls.

"She always wore this." Her voice is hoarse with unshed tears. Next, she pulls out a small ring with a pearl at the center. The rest of the bag is just filled with loose pearls. Black, white, and silver.

Melody cradles the ring to her chest. "This was her favorite ring, the one she wanted my husband to give to me when he proposed." Her laugh is watery. "Thank you, Zalenyk, there are no words to describe what this means to me. What you mean to me, my love."

She smiles up at me and I gently take the ring from her, holding it out to her.

"Melody, I love you. I'll love you forever. I want to make you my wife, my partner, and when the time comes, the mother of my children." She nods and with the help of my tentacles, I slide the ring onto her finger, a perfect fit. "There is no service that needs to be performed. I am king here and I declare us wed."

"There you go again, making your own rules." She flings herself at me, peppering my face with kisses. "Husband." We both moan over the title.

Then our mouths are connected and everything inside of me is right once more. I can feel her pussy dripping onto me. My tentacle comes up to circle her entrance before slipping inside. Nice and deep until she moans into my mouth. I swallow the sound.

"Which hole do you want me in first, wife?" Her smile is deviant and daring and so full of love.

"All of them."

The End

The firm, wet glide of my Kraken's tentacle along my inner thigh rouses me.

Smiling into my pillow, I let out a soft sigh and open my legs wider to accommodate his movements. In the five years we've spent together, our morning routine rarely changes. Thanks in part to our never-changing evening routine.

Each night my husband—the Kraken of the Dark Sea—takes me to bed, where he wrings every ounce of pleasure from me with his tentacles, cock, and tongue until my body is limp. My sleep is dreamless and restorative. Each morning, I am awoken by the familiar touch of my Kraken's tentacles and my body is more than ready to welcome him inside once more.

My life in the Drowned Palace is perfect. Every day is filled with love and exploration. Zalenyk has shown me wonders beyond my wildest dreams. We've traveled the world, swam in the bluest water I've ever seen and made love on white sand beaches. I've seen the finest markets and been to cities covered in sparkling lights with buildings reaching the sky.

It's been perfect and I am content.

However, there has been a piece missing between us. A piece that I'm finally ready to embrace with my love. Today, I'll delight in our familiar routine because if I have my way, it will change sooner rather than later.

"Sweet one," Zalenyk whispers in my ear. "I know you are awake."

A tentacle skims over the bare skin of my shoulder, gently sucking my skin as it goes. Another tickles my ear as it tucks a strand of my hair behind it. With a final stretch of my deliciously sore muscles, I blink open my eyes and stare into the dear face of my love.

Zalenyk stares back at me. His fathomless eyes feel like a caress. There are so many emotions swimming in his gaze, and I know they mirror my own. Reaching a hand towards him, I cup his slick cheek as his tentacles press wet kisses to the back of my hand.

The tentacle between my legs pauses its exploration to suck gently on my flesh. Soft waves of pleasure crest over my body as I snuggle deeper into Zalenyk's embrace. His tentacles wrap around me, holding me close and stroking me reverently.

My smile widens at the familiar comfort.

"What brings a smile to my beautiful wife's face this morning?" my Kraken asks.

"Pleasant thoughts," I say, pressing a soft kiss to one of the short tentacles dangling from his face. "Shall I share them with you, husband?"

"Yes," Zalenyk growls, his tentacles pulling me deeper into the cool, slickness of his body. Even though we are pressed together it seems my Kraken cannot get me close enough. I let him tug me into him, disappearing into the mass of moving muscles that is his body.

"You know I want to hear every thought in your head, Melody," he continues.

I nuzzle into his tentacles, my lips seeking his amongst the appendages. Placing soft kisses along his jaw, I press a chaste kiss to his waiting mouth. He growls as I pull back, but I can't stop my giggling.

"Brat," he chastises without heat.

"Are you going to punish me?" I tease.

"After you tell me what thoughts were occupying your beautiful head."

His tentacles drift over my chest, sucking on my naked skin and leaving behind red marks.

"I was thinking," I begin.

Zalenyk's tentacles move lower. Two work in tandem to squeeze my breasts before suctioning my hard nipples. I let out a soft moan at their attention. Liquid arousal slicks out from between my thighs. That errant tentacle still lingering between my legs moves to continue its exploration.

"I was thinking," I start again, pleasure making the words leave me. "That we...we should—"

His tentacle grazes my slit and my whole body freezes. Gently, the appendage parts me and glides over my clit. Applying gentle pressure, the firm muscle coats my pussy in Zalenyk's slick wetness that mingles with my own. The tentacle rubs circles on my clit and my hips cantor in time with the movement.

"Are you having trouble thinking, sweet one? Am I distracting you?"

"Yes," I moan.

"Shall I stop?" He asks, pausing the tentacle on my clit.

"No," I snarl.

"Then continue telling me what you were thinking and I'll reward you."

Despite the onslaught of pleasure his tentacles are bringing my body, I'm able to clear some of the lust-filled fog to give him an answer. Once I make this declaration, everything will change. I'm ready—I know it in my heart, but is Zalenyk? He always gives me what I want, but I want him to desire this as much as I do.

I hesitate for only another moment, before remembering myself. I've never shied away from my desire—especially with Zalenyk—and this is my ultimate dream.

"I want a baby," I say.

Zalenyk freezes, his eyes meet mine in a searing gaze. I lick over my suddenly dry lips before continuing.

"You've shown me everything you promised to. We've had adventures and I know I said I wanted to wait, but I'm ready. I love you so much and I want us to have a family together."

Zalenyk remains silent. His tentacles grip on me tightens slightly, the only indication that he's heard what I said. I begin to shiver in his cool embrace as seconds—perhaps minutes— pass in heavy silence.

My familiar ire begins to spark and I lower my brows at him.

"Well, what do you have to say?" I ask. Still, he remains quiet.

Taking a tentacle that's curled around my wrist I give it a harsh tug.

"Zalenyk!" I snap. "Answer me."

"I—" My Kraken breaks off with a shudder.

Unease turns my stomach. Does he not want a child? He told me of his father's history and how he came to be. Has he decided he no longer wants a family? I'll be devastated if so.

"Melody." Zalenyk says my name like a prayer. "Sweet, sweet Melody."

His tentacles begin moving once more. They are frantic as they skim over every part of my body. The one between my legs works my clit while the ones holding my breasts begin their ministrations once more. Is he attempting to distract me with pleasure?

"Zalenyk, do not—"

"Of course, I want a family with you. That's all I've ever wanted. To see you grow round with our child—to know that we've created life from our love has been a dream of mine since I claimed you. I'm sorry I caused you worry." His tentacle skims over the furrow of my brow. "I just couldn't believe you were ready. I've loved our adventures. I wouldn't mind spending the next hundred years exploring the world with you."

Ah, yes, my new eternal life. Our souls and lives had been bound together in a simple ceremony that ended with my Kraken fucking all three of my holes and filling me with enough of his seed to fill a lagoon. Honestly, it's surprising the contraceptive herbs have been able to combat how often he's filled me with his come over the years.

"We will still go on adventures, only now there will be three of us," I murmur.

My heart overflows with love as his gaze turns tender.

"Yes," he whispers, a tentacle skimming over my flat stomach. "Are you ready right now, sweet one?"

"I've thrown out the last of the contraceptive herbs." His tentacle slips from my clit and spears into my entrance.

"I want to begin trying immediately," I moan as a fresh wave of pleasure washes over me.

"Greedy brat," Zalenyk snickers. "Let me make you come before I give you more of my seed."

Who am I to argue with that?

His mouth finds mine as the tentacle inside me pushes deep. The sleek muscle presses against my womb before curling inside me. It tickles that hidden spot that causes my hands to grip the tentacles surrounding me harder.

Zalenyk's lips are cool against mine. The firm press of them makes my head spin. I delight in his salty flavor and eagerly open my mouth to accept his tongue. It tangles with my own as his tentacles cover me in his slick goo. My skin is cool and sticky and I absolutely love it.

My Kraken's tongue thrusts into my mouth in time with his tentacle in my pussy. The tentacle encircling my left breast slides down my stomach, lovingly rubbing around my navel before dipping lower. The first brush of it against my clit has me moaning in Zalenyk's mouth.

He swallows it down as his tentacle gently suckles me. My arousal coats his tentacle and the sounds it makes as it pumps into me are deliciously erotic. Pleasure permeates my body and my climax looms. My hands dive deeper into his mass of tentacles and hold firm.

Zalenyk moans into my mouth as I grip him.

Two tentacles wrap around my ankles and hold them open. He quickens the pace of his thrusting tentacles and breaks our kiss. His mouth glides down my neck, kissing and sucking as he goes.

"Are you close, sweet one?"

My mouth won't work and I can only nod. My Kraken nips my neck and my eyes fly open. While I love his tentacles, I'm desperate to have his cock inside of me. I want to be filled with his come again—there's a new desperation to my need.

"I want your cock," I groan. "Give it to me."

Quick as a whip, one of his tentacles smacks the cheek of my ass. I hiss at the sting, but the pain only causes my pussy to grip down harder on the tentacle fucking me.

"Not yet, brat." Zalenyk's mouth ghosts over my ear before licking the shell.

"Yes, now!" I demand.

My Kraken only chuckles before delivering another smarting spank to my backside.

"In time, Melody, I'll fill your greedy cunt with enough seed to drown a fleet of ships in. You'll never know a moment where my come isn't dripping out of you."

"Mmmm," I moan, my thighs beginning to tremble. "Zalenyk—"

"I've heard enough of your whining, naughty brat. I can think of a better use for your mouth."

I open my lips to voice my protest, only for a tentacle to slip inside my mouth. I moan at the musky taste. The sleek texture coasts along my tongue and tickles the back of my throat. The suckers play with my tongue and it fucks my mouth in the same devastating rhythm as the one inside me.

Heat spreads throughout my body. My stomach clenches at the feeling of being filled by my Kraken. His tentacles immobilize me and I can do nothing to fight the rising tide of pleasure. I can only suck on his tentacle and ride out the storm of my climax.

With one last suck on my clit, my body erupts. My pussy clamps down on his thrusting tentacle and my scream is garbled around the appendage in my throat. Zalenyk fucks me through my climax over and over. My vision blurs as my back comes off the bed.

It's perfect—the pleasure is almost painful, and yet it is not enough. It will never be enough, especially when I am delirious with my need for his come.

Slowly, he slips from me and I watch through heavy eyelids as he licks my come from his tentacle. The slick muscle in my mouth retreats, and I suck down oxygen. My smile is lazy as my body falls to the bed.

Zalenyk keeps me close as his body rolls on top of mine. Inside his nest of tentacles, I can feel the hard ridge of his cock as it meets my wet pussy. My climaxes always leave me depleted, but not this time. I'm ready to go and I show him that by grinding against his hard length.

"This needy cunt is desperate to be filled." Zalenyk presses a kiss on my forehead. "My wife demands I get her pregnant, and who am I to deny her?"

"Smart husband," I commend, lifting my mouth towards him.

His cock brushes me once more and I groan.

"I'm going to fuck you, Melody," Zalenyk whispers into my ear. "All day, all night—forever."

"Please."

His tongue licks up my cheek as his cock pushes against my entrance. So close—so fucking close.

"Just not here."

My Kraken's words don't register until he's pulling me from the bed.

"What?" I ask.

Wrapped in his tentacles, he carries me from our bedroom and deeper into the palace. As we pass the dining room, I thrash in his hold and turn to face him. His face is set in harsh determination as he moves confidently towards the watery exit.

"Zalenyk, where are you taking me?"

He remains quiet as we make our way out of the palace into the waiting warm water. Still locked in his grasp, he swims us far away from our home. The water glides past us in a rush as we swim past the dense foliage of *The Woods* our house is situated against.

Zalenyk guides us deeper into his territory. Soon, the familiar terrain becomes foreign, and a large cave looms ahead. My Kraken swims faster until we reach it. Nestled inside the stone walls and the high rocky ceiling is a magical-looking lagoon. The water glows bright blue and green. A few aquatic flowers decorate the surface as Zalenyk drags me into its waiting depths.

The water is indecently warm.

"I want to bring you somewhere special," my Kraken says. "I stumbled upon this place by accident a few years ago and knew it was the perfect place to ravish you. Now, it will be the perfect place to put my baby inside of you."

"Zalenyk…" My voice trails off as tears fall down my cheeks.

His tongue licks up my tears and I laugh at the sensation.

"I love you, Melody. Let me show you how much." His kiss is claiming. "Let me give you what we both want."

Zalenyk hoists my dripping body onto the edge of the lagoon. A fine layer of moss has grown over the stone floor and it cushions my back. Steam rises from the surface of the water and curls over the rocky lip of the pool.

My wet hair plasters to my naked skin as I extend a hand towards the pool—towards my love.

"A moment, sweet one," Zalenyk groans. "The sight of you laid out and dripping—eagerly awaiting my cock—I *need* to savor it."

My cheeks warm as a smile curls my lips.

"Anything for you, husband," I say, dropping my hand to the moss and spreading out under his gaze.

There's a soft splash as tentacles emerge from the water. Their touch is gentle as they explore my smooth calves all the way up to my hip bones. Another tangles in my hair and smooths over my face as if memorizing every detail.

"Beautiful," Zalenyk breathes. "There's no one in this world as remarkable as you, Melody. You are my heart—my love."

"Zalenyk," I say, tears blurring my vision. "I love you—make love to me."

His tentacles trace up and down my leg one more time before there is a loud rush of water, and my husband is dripping warm, salty water all over my naked flesh. Each droplet sends a rush of pleasure through me as I stare up at his face. His eyes glow with intensity. Raising my hand to his face, I sigh as his shorter tentacles latch on my skin and plant gentle, sucking kisses.

"What will it be, wife? How would you like me to fuck you this first time?"

It's a question he's asked me hundreds of times, and yet my face still warms at the erotic words.

"You know how I like it," I reply primly.

Zalenyk's lips twist into a feral grin as his suckers latch onto my hand harder.

"Greedy girl." The words are whispered as his tentacles slide against me.

My skin is slick as he coats me in his wetness. The glide of those sleek, seeking appendages makes my breathing turn ragged. He gently suctions to my skin as his tentacles coast over every part of me.

"Tell me to stop if it's too much, do you understand?" Zalenyk's voice is firm.

"It's never too much—you'd never hurt me."

"Melody," Zalenyk rumbles, "tell me to stop if it's too much. The idea of getting you pregnant has... incensed me. I don't know how gentle I can be."

My hand tangles in his tentacles until I find his cheek. Bringing his face closer to mine, I press a brief kiss against his cold lips. Meeting his burning gaze I give him a short nod.

"I'll tell you to stop if it's too much." My lips drag against his. "Now fuck me until I can't walk—fuck me until I carry our child within me."

With a roar, Zalenyk unleashes himself upon me.

The cave echoes with his claiming snarl, and my pussy turns wet and hot. Tentacles race over my damp skin. Instantly, my arms are bound up to my elbows and held above my head. Next, two tentacles wrap around each of my thighs, pulling them open, and dragging me closer to Zalenyk's hungry gaze.

The first lick of his tongue against me has my scream echoing around us. The glide of his wet tongue against my heated flesh is obscenely decadent. Sucking gently on my clit, my thighs threaten to close around the sensation but his tentacles hold me wide open.

As he tongues me another tentacle slithers over my folds before gently pushing at my entrance. It's a tentative invasion but one that has my vision blurring. As Zalenyk works my clit, his tentacle begins pulsing inside me. It's tortuously slow but I wouldn't have it any other way.

"You taste like honey," Zalenyk says, placing a kiss on my clit. "You live up to your name, sweet one."

"Hmm," I moan, the tentacle inside me slipping out before being replaced by Zalenyk's tongue.

Two more tentacles trail up my chest in a slippery glide before latching onto my nipples. The light suction on my sensitive peaks causes my back to rise from the ground. His tentacles roughly shape each breast as they continue sucking on me.

I long to touch him, but with my bound hands, I am helpless—entirely left at my husband's mercy. His tongue fucks my pussy with renewed vigor. Zalenyk tunnels that incredible muscle deep enough into me that my blood starts to heat.

My belly pools with desire, and my muscles tighten.

A new tentacle slips between the cheeks of my ass to gently push against my back entrance. Tracing the tight ring of muscles, it uses my dripping arousal and Zalenyk's moisture to ease itself inside of me.

"Prettiest little cunt and tightest little ass in all the realms. You truly are a treat, my Melody."

The burn is sweet—obscenely so—and that's all it takes to shove me off the edge.

My pussy clamps around Zalenyk's tongue as my body turns into a roaring fire. I thrash in his hold as pleasure crashes over me. A torrent of moans leaves my lips and fills the cave around us. My Kraken continues to lick me, sucking up every drop of my arousal as he rubs his face against my sensitive flesh.

Our hearts and souls thread together with the force of my orgasm.

In the aftermath of my climax, my muscles feel languid but I know we are far from done. Placing one last kiss on my pussy, Zalenyk licks a path up my chest until his lips are mine again. I taste my musky flavor on his tongue and moan into his mouth.

His lips leave mine as his eyes glow anew.

"I think you need my cock in your mouth."

I let out a whimper. I've come hard but somehow more liquid arousal slips out from me at his words. Nodding vigorously, Zalenyk smiles down at me.

In a flurry of slithering blue-green appendages, Zalenyk twists me until my back leaves the cave floor. The breeze is cool on my heated skin as his tentacles wrap around my middle to keep me aloft. He lowers me until my favorite sight greets me.

Zalenyk's cock is a thing to behold. Dark blue and an imposing length that makes my mouth water. I need his taste on my tongue. I need to feel him brushing up against the back of my throat.

Letting out a content sigh, I open my mouth as I try to reach for his length. Only to remember in an instant that my hands are still bound. I look up at Zalenyk's face, a pout already pulling at my lips.

"Release me," I command. His tentacles on me only tighten.

"I don't think I will," Zalenyk says. "I think I'm going to fuck that pretty little mouth of yours while keeping you entwined with me."

"Zalenyk," I moan as his tentacles twist me once more.

I'm still far enough above the ground—suspended by his tentacles—only for my back to be facing towards the ground. My head falls back as my arms are pulled tighter behind me. His cock looms before me, already leaking with seed. Licking my lips, I open my mouth in invitation.

"Perfect little slut," Zalenyk compliments. "Shall I feed you my cock?"

"Please"

His cock traces along my lips, smearing me in his sticky come. I eagerly lick my lips and his velvety tip. I try to trap the head of his cock between my lips but he pulls back before I can.

Letting out a frustrated growl, I pull against his restraining tentacles.

"Greedy brat," Zalenyk laughs. A tentacle delivers a sharp smack to my ass. My answering moan indicates how much I enjoy the lingering sting.

"Give me your cock, Zalenyk. I need it, I w—"

My tirade is cut off by his cock surging into my mouth. He is hard and slick and salty against my tongue. Unable to control the pace, all I can do is relax my throat and let my husband take his pleasure from my mouth. I love his length with my tongue, delighting in the smooth texture of his cock.

He pushes deeper into my throat and I cough, tears burning in my eyes.

"Do you have any idea how lovely you look while I fuck your face, sweet one? How perfect you look with my seed smeared on your lips as you choke on my cock?"

My response is garbled around his length. My pussy is a mess of slick arousal and his saliva. A tentacle slips down my body and discovers just how wet I am between my legs. My moan is once more growled against his cock as the appendage rubs tight circles on my clit.

"It seems I'm not the only one enjoying this," Zalenyk purrs. "Your cunt is so wet, sweet one. Listen to it."

Indeed, the wet, sloppy sounds of his tentacle entering me echo around us in the cave. His tentacle sucks on my clit in time with his cock in my mouth. Over and over, he thrusts into me. Saliva pours from my mouth and mixes with my Kraken's wetness to aid his length in pushing farther into my mouth.

Zalenyk groans above me, his movements becoming halting and jerky. I relax my throat further and let him in deeper. Tears sting my eyes, and a few fall down my cheeks

His tentacle continues to work me until my hips begin grinding against the sensation. I'm close, my peak barely a whisper away.

"Melody," Zalenyk grounds out. "Keep your eyes open as I feed you my seed. Swallow it down—every drop."

I nod my head, renewing my efforts, and give his cock a brief skim with my teeth. Zalenyk's tentacle sucks harder on my clit and I'm lost. My climax hits me at the exact moment Zalenyk's takes him under. His whole body jerks as his cock hardens further in my mouth. With one last mighty groan, he releases a torrent of seed.

Warmth slides down my throat as his salty seed fills my mouth. He comes and comes, thrusting against my tongue and feeding me every bit of his pleasure. My own body is buzzing from the effects of my own climax.

With one last thrust against my tongue, Zalenyk pulls out. A rope of sticky seed clings to his tip and my lips. He smears it around my mouth and I eagerly lick it clean. I make a show of swallowing down his come, and Zalenyk growls.

Without a moment to react, my Kraken flips me again until my back is settled against the comforting moss. His tentacles release my arms and legs. The slick muscles rub against my sore ones as I try and slow down my racing heart.

Zalenyk huddles me close to him, raining soft kisses all over my forehead and cheeks.

"Melody, Melody." He says my name like a prayer. "Tell me you're okay."

I smile at him.

"I am well. Desperately in need of more."

Zalenyk pulls back and stares down at me. Biting my lip, I lift a hand and drag it down his body until I feel his hard cock against my palm. He's deliciously slick with his come and my saliva. I give him a rough pump and he groans.

"Fuck me, Zalenyk. Fill me with your seed. Let's create life together."

My Kraken captures my mouth with his, and his tongue spears between my lips. My thighs open eagerly as he settles between them. His cock glides up my slit before rubbing harsh circles onto my clit. Mewling sounds leave me as I raise my hips to try and sheath him inside me.

With a loud groan, he sinks the tip inside me.

"Tightest fucking cunt," he snarls. "Look at your glistening pink flesh—look at how greedy your pussy is. It's already trying to suck me in deeper."

"Give it to me," I whine. "I want it."

Always one to fulfill all my desires, Zalenyk fills me with one harsh thrust. He stills as we both acknowledge our connection. Looking down, I can see his hard cock disappearing into me, and my head spins. The sight is as familiar as it is decadent.

Retreating his hips, he thrusts into me once more. My breasts jostle in time with his force. My hands reach out and sink into his mass of tentacles. They eagerly greet me and coat my body in their wetness. I'm sticky and slippery everywhere.

A tentacle wraps around my waist and tilts me upwards. Its grasp holds firm as Zalenyk pulls back his hips and begins a punishing rhythm. Our skin slaps together as he pounds into me. My body slides against the moss on the ground until his tentacles come between my head and the wall, keeping me pinned and unable to escape the pleasure he's giving me.

"Zalenyk, Zalenyk," I chant his name.

His cock butts up against my womb. I'm so full I can hardly stand it. A tentacle slithers over my hip and begins working my clit in time with his thrusts. My muscles are tightening and my peak is looming. Another tentacle slides between my ass and gently—using its wetness—slides into me.

If I thought I felt full before, I feel like I will burst now.

The tentacle in my ass fucks me gently, just enough to feel

the burn and stretch of my husband fucking both of my holes at once. My legs cinch around him. I begin to tremble, yet his thrusts never falter.

"Tell me you want my come—beg for it, sweet one," Zalenyk commands.

"Please, please," I whimper, trying to remember any words beyond his name. "Give me your come. Fill me—breed me. Please. Fuck me, Zalenyk. Come inside me!"

Zalenyk growls and somehow manages to fuck me even harder. His cock brushes my inner walls. The head of cock presses up against that spot inside me that has my vision going dark. My thighs tremble and my hands grasp onto a couple of his tentacles and hold on.

"Come, sweet one."

I am powerless and obey his command instantly. My scream hurts my ears as I erupt with the force of my orgasm. My pussy clamps down on his hammering cock. Zalenyk fucks me through my pleasure, heightening it and extending my orgasm before I feel him give me one last hard thrust.

He comes inside me, releasing an obscene amount of seed that I've never felt before. It's as if his body knows what we want and is giving him even more come to complete it. My pussy greedily sucks it all down. Giving me a few more gentle thrusts, my body hums with little aftershocks of pleasure.

His cock slips from me and I feel a rush of seed seep out from my pussy and coat my thighs. Gently he removes the thrusting tentacle from my ass. High on pleasure, my eyes begin to droop as my arm wraps around Zalenyk's neck.

My lips manage to find his and we communicate all the love and passion we need to without speaking. Lovemaking always brings us closer, but this time, it felt special. I know it's improbable that I am pregnant after this one time, but I can't help but feel like it's true.

If it's not, Zalenyk and I will keep trying until my belly grows round.

"Sweet one, how are you feeling?" he asks, pressing a kiss to my cheek.

"Perfect," I say. "Once I can feel my legs, I want to go again."

"Insatiable."

There's so much tenderness in his gaze it brings tears to my eyes.

"I love you so much, Zalenyk. Thank you for saving me—even if it very much felt like you were kidnapping me at the time."

"That's because I was kidnapping you, sweet one." Zalenyk smiles. "I am just lucky that you chose to love me, rather than flee me."

"What can I say? I love being unpredictable."

His tentacle skims over my stomach, gently tracing around my naval.

"The future is unpredictable—save for my love for you—for this baby we will create. Taking you as my bride was the best thing I ever did."

I snuggle deeper into Zalenyk—my husband, my love, the father of my children. Our love story was unorthodox, something out of a dark fairytale. Yet, I wouldn't change a thing about it. Whatever is in store for us—for our family—I know we will face it together.

"I love you, Zalenyk," I repeat, kissing him with all the love in my heart.

"I love you, Melody."

The kiss turns heated and I'm once more turning wet between my thighs. It causes more of his seed to leak out of me and soak the ground beneath us. Zalenyk helps roll me on top of him. His hard cock tickles my entrance as I let out a sigh.

"Now, let me show you how much."

His tentacles aid me in lowering down on his cock.

"You're not leaving this cave until I'm certain you're pregnant."

"That sounds perfect, my love."

No more words are necessary as he gives me a gentle pump of his hips. Everything is about to change for us and I welcome it. A new life will be created in this cave and I cannot wait to start that new adventure with Zalenyk in the same way we've taken on everything for the past five years.

Together.

A KISS FROM A DRAGON LORD

KISS FROM A MONSTER SERIES BOOK 3

1

———

ANWYN

I should've left this small town weeks ago.

It's always a risk staying too long in settlements like this one. It's easier to go unnoticed in larger towns; people hustling from their homes to work don't give someone like me a passing glance. In places like this, everyone knows each other. And a stranger taking up with the elderly woman in town, claiming to be her long-lost sister's granddaughter, arouses suspicion.

Mrs. Hitherbend is pushing her eightieth name day, and her memory has faded with time. Our paths crossed when I arrived by rowboat two months back. The town I was in previously had noticed me skimming some money from the mayor I was working for. He was a callous old man with wandering eyes and hands. He's lucky I just took his gold, not something he had a more permanent attachment to.

I had just enough coin to bribe a tradesman to take me as far as he could. That's how I ended up here. Mrs. Hitherbend saw me as soon as I docked and said I looked like her sister she hadn't seen in years. The lie I told her just spiraled from there until she gave me lodging in her house.

To be fair, I haven't completely exploited the woman. I've kept up with her washing, cooking her meals, and helping her with the tasks she's too frail to do. She's even given me a few gold coins for my work. Honestly, this is the best job I've had in a while.

I learned at a young age that we only have ourselves in this world. My parents died when I was young, leaving me penniless and with few options. I could either work myself to death as a servant to a noble family or sell my body to one of the brothels.

Instead, I decided to travel. Taking odd jobs in each town and creating aliases wherever I went in case the ones I took from tried to come after me. My crimes are minuscule compared to the ones I watched the wealthy commit on a daily basis. Each one of them using their wealth to circumvent justice or exploit those beneath them for sport.

After living so many years on the run, I began to see people as opportunities.

Life with Mrs. Hitherbend is monotonous, but an opportunity to acclimate smoothly to this new town nonetheless. It only took a short while for the townsfolk to accept me. The original plan was to stay through the winter, but as I was absorbed by the routine tasks, I let my guard slip. I had gotten too comfortable, and someone had finally taken note of me.

Mr. Wicksome.

A foul man, who I am now pouring tea for as he sits in Mrs. Hitherbend's kitchen. She absentmindedly prattles on about her chickens while his eyes rake over me. I was aware of his suspicions since I first arrived in this town. Two weeks ago, I overheard him talking to the blacksmith, saying there was something off about me and he was going to get to the bottom of it.

I should've left then, but the tradesman who brought me here before is returning tomorrow. I just have to make it through today, and tomorrow I will be on to my next destination. It's exhausting going from one place to the next but better to leave than be stuck with no way out.

"Ethel?" I cringe at the use of my fake name. "Could you fetch Mr. Wicksome and I some of those biscuits the Lees brought over last week? We rarely get visitors, and a man of your importance, Mr. Wicksome, deserves the best."

Forcing myself to smile, I nod and head into the kitchen.

Reaching up onto the top shelf, I pull down the jar of biscuits. The ceramic container sits heavy on the counter as I unscrew the top. My stomach sinks when I hear the wooden legs of a chair squeak against the stone floor.

There's heat at my back. I don't need to turn around to know who's standing there.

"I know your secret," Mr. Wicksome whispers near my ear, his hot breath making bile rise in my throat. "Anwyn."

Fuck.

I straighten my spine and turn towards him, meeting his beady eyes. His dark brown hair is graying at the temples; his skin is wrinkled and pot-marked. His clothes are made of quality wool but overly done, making him look less like a nobleman and more like a gaudy bird.

"I don't know what you're talking about."

He chuckles and shakes his head.

"You may be shocked to learn that I know a few people from that town you claim to be from. I gave them your name, and no one had heard of you." He steps closer, and I back up a step until the counter's edge presses into my back. "You haven't been very good at hiding your trail."

Mr. Wicksome curls a loose piece of my blonde hair around his finger.

"The butcher in that town recognized you from a coastal town down south. Only you went by Lila there. There is a shopkeeper down there who you worked for, but he knew you as

Sophya in an eastern farming town. I was able to track down that farmer who remembers you staying with his family as a young girl named Anwyn."

My mouth goes dry; my palms begin to sweat.

"And in each of those towns, under each of those names, you are wanted for something, isn't that true?" My blood ices over.

"What do you want?" I spit out. The way his eyes linger on my chest tells me all I need to know. There are men like him everywhere. I've always been able to outsmart them before they got too far. My stomach curdles as I realize I may be out of moves. One word from him about where I'm located and all of my pasts may find me here.

"I am a powerful man, Anwyn. With the sway over this town to protect you if the people here found out what you truly are. They would not take too kindly to a thief and a liar deceiving them."

He drops the lock of my hair and steps back.

"What I want, Anwyn is for you to repay me for my silence."

"What would that entail?" Mr. Wicksome smirks as he walks back over to the table.

"My wife died a few years ago—"

"Yes," Mrs. Hitherbend interrupts, "what an unfortunate accident that was."

The room begins to spin and my knees begin to shake.

"Quite tragic, you are right. She was barren and left me without an heir. You appear `healthy enough to bare me a few. Therefore, I will take you as my wife and you will come and live with me as a part of my household."

"I—"

"How wonderful!" Mrs. Hitherbend cries, clapping her hands together. "I just got done telling Ethel she needs to find a good husband. One who will love and care for her when she's old and wrinkly like me."

I swallow as Mr. Wicksome grins, turning back towards the table. He digs around in his coat pocket until he produces a small bag of coins. Setting them down in front of Mrs. Hitherbend, he nods to her and then back to me.

"It is settled then. I will arrive at dawn with the priest, where I will take you as my wife." I just manage not to bare my teeth at him as he leers down my body again. "Make sure to get plenty of rest. You'll be needing it. I'm looking forward to you showing me just how grateful you are that I'm keeping your secret."

Reaching behind me, my fingers curl around the butter knife left out on the counter. The old metal grows hot in my hand. I should drive this dull blade into his neck, that would be another way to assure his silence.

However much I want to, I can't. Not as Mrs. Hitherbend leads him to the door and bids him farewell. I haven't moved from my spot in the small kitchen. My knees shake in time with my pounding heart.

"You are lucky, my dear," Mrs. Hitherbend says, sitting back down at the table. "Mr. Wicksome is a wealthy man who will take care of you."

"He's evil," I say.

"Nonsense child. Though I will miss your help around here, your place is at your husband's side. Giving him children. If only my sister were still alive, she'd be thrilled to hear about your good fortune."

Mrs. Hitherbend takes a sip of her tea that has long since gone cold. I let the knife clatter back onto the counter behind me. *Good fortune?* Any luck I may have had over these last years has finally decided to run out. Time is not on my side and one thing is certain: I can't stay in this village a moment longer.

Looking out the window, the cracks in the glass appearing like a cluster of cobwebs, I sigh deeply. I wish I had time to wait for the tradesman, but I can't risk it. The walls are closing in on me, and if I want to put enough distance between me and this town by morning, I'll need to set off now.

This village is the most remote place I've ever sought lodging. It's the last settlement for miles and is completely surrounded on each side by dense foliage. The townspeople all claim that *The Woods* are inhabited by nightmarish creatures who kill anyone who ventures inside. Tales to keep children from misbehaving if you ask me.

Besides, in my experience, humans are scarier than any creature this forest could conjure up.

Leaving Mrs. Hitherbend at the table, I quickly go to my room and pack the few items that I have in a worn leather bag. The only things to my name are a small bag of gold coins, an old book, and my mother's gold necklace. I need to travel light so I can make it through *The Woods* quickly. There has to be a town on the other side where I can seek shelter.

The leather on my boots is worn down, but it will hold for this journey. I cover my thin, gray wool dress with a dark cloak before slinging my bag across my shoulder. Quickly braiding back my hair, I walk into the kitchen and head for the door.

"Where are you going?" Mrs. Hitherbend asks.

My hand tightens on the doorknob as I dare a glance back over my shoulder. The deep wrinkles around her brown eyes stretch as she squints at me. Mr. Wicksome's dowry for me sits heavy on the table. I should take it, but I won't leave Mrs. Hitherbend with nothing.

Turning from the door, I march over to her as she leans back slightly in her chair. Scooping up the small bag of coins, I thrust it into her hands, closing her bony fingers around the purse.

"You don't have a sister," I say. Mrs. Hitherbend lets out a gasp. My hand tightens on hers, holding the coins. "A tradesman is coming in the morning. Buy passage on his ship and have him take you to the next town over. There is a doctor there who can help with your memory. Use this to pay for the treatment. Leave while Mr. Wicksome is busy searching for me."

"What do you mean—"

I don't hear the rest of her question. Moving quickly on my feet, I push through the door and onto the barren town street. No one is milling around; the dark rolling clouds overhead signal an impending storm. It's not ideal traveling weather, but that means no one is around to see me slip behind the house and walk fifty feet to the edge of the forest.

It's silent beyond the tree line. The sounds of twigs snapping and wildlife running through the leaves are absent. I chance one last look back at the village. A small pang of regret at the lies I told Mrs. Hitherbend threaten to weaken my resolve. Even after all these years of lying to survive, I'm not immune to the toll dishonesty can take on a person.

I shake myself from those thoughts. My guilty conscious isn't enough to make me marry a lecherous man like Mr. Wicksome. With a deep breath, I march forward, allowing myself to be swallowed up by the tall trees around me.

2

LASSAR

Is there anything more beautiful than sparkling gold?

Rubies and sapphires have their appeal, emeralds too, but nothing compares to the brilliant sparkle of gold. I can taste it in the air, its sharp metallic flavor coating my tongue and invading my lungs. The sound it makes as it clanks over my scales and shifts through my claws. Even now, as I dig my tail into the pile of gold coins I'm lying atop, their hard texture soothes me and makes me question what I could ever desire more than this.

When I was a human man, there were things I enjoyed. As the soon of a rich lord and a future lord myself, I partook in many luxuries. I enjoyed hunting with my father, large dinners filled with exotic dishes, and dancing until the early morning hours. All of those hobbies paled in comparison to the feeling of gold in my fingers.

From the first coin I received from my father on my tenth name's day to the large fortune he showed me would be mine upon his death, I began to crave it like no other. I found myself spending hours in the family vault, counting and cleaning each coin until they sparkled in the candlelight. Betting with the stable boys all night and feeling such deep hopelessness when I would lose my precious gold to them.

I had mourned my parent's passing, but that melancholy was quickly overshadowed by my need to be reacquainted with my new wealth. I had become so preoccupied with it that my town and its tenants suffered. It wasn't long before they came for my gold. The townspeople demanded it for food and repairs. They said it was once theirs and that I owed it to them if I was not going to make sure they were provided for. With little choice, I was forced to give it up, or they would've gleefully removed my head from my shoulders.

Desperation sent me stumbling into *The Woods*, clutching a handful of gold coins I had managed to save. I threw myself at the mercy of the demon who lived there and begged him to fulfill my desires. I said I would pay any price to be able to find and keep as much gold as I possibly could forever.

I'll never forget his smile, his long tongue sweeping over his sharp teeth, and the pain that followed as we shook hands on our deal. I watched in horror as my skin began to peel back and green scales began to surface. One after another, overlapping until I was covered in them. Razor-sharp claws grew from my fingers. I remember stumbling back a step as I felt a new weight on my back and at the base of my spine. Wings and a tail sprouted from me, and as the demon cackled, I shot into the sky, illuminating it with a burst of fire from deep within my stomach.

It burned my throat and clogged my nostrils. I wasn't the most graceful flyer but I somehow found this cave. One that I've been filling with my treasures ever since. I take from the rich, the people I once was just like. I rob them of their spoils before someone else can take them. I keep them here with me, where I can protect them, guard them...*watch* them.

I've lost track of how long I've been like this. Centuries if I had to guess. Everyone who once knew the man I was is long gone, and I'm beginning to realize all these years spent alone with my treasure have turned me into more of a beast than a man.

Old memories are hazy at best. The only thing I am certain of is that I need more gold. I always need more gold; it's the only constant in my life. Without it, what would I do? I couldn't lead a normal life, not like this. I could never find a wife or make a family, the humans I come in contact with flee upon seeing me.

No one dares venture this far into *The Woods*. A few of the other creatures used to try and trade with me, but they've all gone quiet these last few years. The Kraken came by and gave me a bag of jewels. It feels like it was only yesterday, but I know that was at least a decade ago. He said something as he left them, but I can't remember it.

I've never desired anything more than gold, but it's not fulfilling me like it used to for the first time in a hundred years. A part of me, perhaps the last part of my humanity, wants to feel more. That small part demands we try and make something out of this eternal life. But what? What else can we do but get more gold and ensure it's never taken from us?

"What do you think?" I ask the coins in my hand, their smooth surface glimmering in the cave's dim light. There's a storm raging outside, and the thunder rattles their piles. I can only imagine they don't have a fondness for this type of weather.

I wait for a response like the metal will grow lips after all these years and converse with me like a companion. Alas, they remain silent.

"Is there more out there for me than this? Then my daily hunts to find more gold and jewels and keep them safe with us?" I pause. "You have always been my most trusted confidants and treasured possessions; talking to you does make me feel better."

Looking around my cave, I see all of my riches laid out. Fine silks, crowns made of the heaviest gold and brightest gems, bags of diamonds, and many, *many* gold coins. They are mine, all of them, but perhaps it wouldn't be so bad to share them?

"That wouldn't be too terrible, would it?" I ask the ten gold plates stacked on my left. "Perhaps someone out there would appreciate you all as I do. Though, where I would find such a person, I don't know. It's not as if one would just walk—"

Another clap of thunder echoes through the cave, but that isn't what has me pausing. Rising from my perch on my coins, they clink as they hit the stone floor. My claws click along the cave wall, my tail dragging gently behind me. Listening carefully, I can just make out a sound over the downpour happening outside.

Footsteps. Human footsteps.

Someone is in my cave. My scales rise as smoke puffs out of my nostrils. Who dares enter my cave uninvited? Of course, I was just considering finding a companion but one with some manners, not one who just enters my dwelling unannounced.

They could be a thief coming to take my gold from me.

That thought has me charging toward the mouth of my cave. I will make whoever stumbled into my home regret doing so. My mouth opens, fire already building in my lungs. I will roast their corpse, char their flesh until—

My flame goes out when I see it. My heart beats faster; my wings sag in pleasure as I behold it. Even in the dark cave, it glows and sparkles. It is the most beautiful gold I have ever seen. Soft as silk, the pale gold flows along the dark stone floor. It's as if thousands of stars are woven between the strands. My mouth salivates; the rain must've washed in this treasure.

This is one I will delight in keeping more than the others. This rare, golden beauty is for my eyes only.

I creep closer to my prize, extending a clawed hand toward it when I stop. This isn't gold; this is hair. How had I forgotten all about the footsteps that sent me charging up here to investigate? This is my intruder?

My eyes adjust to the dim light, and I can see her fully.

She's small, shivering in a damp cloak. A human woman with beautiful golden hair and matching eyebrows. Her skin is smooth, glowing like a polished pearl. My tail sneaks out from behind me and trails up the side of her body. Her brows furrow at the touch.

Eyes like opals blink open at me. It's like she's made from jewels, a human constructed from the finest gems. The ultimate treasure for a creature like me. I open my mouth to tell her as much, but then a small flame bursts from my mouth. The embers float in the air, and my precious human shoots upright and scrambles back, shrieking.

She can't get too far, the boulder she was sitting behind stopping her movements.

This small human shakes in front of me, her soaked cloak draped around her. Her gorgeous hair is plastered to the sides of her face. I watch her chest rise and fall and feel something happening inside my own. The more I gaze at her I realize how wrong I have been.

Was there anything more beautiful than gold? Yes, her.

She who is gold come to life. A possessiveness that I've never felt before shoots through me. My desire for her eclipses the one I've felt for any other treasure. She's the ultimate find.

The only one I will ever need.

When I was a man, I wanted a family. I wanted lovers to warm my bed. Those wants faded when I found my need for gold. Now, looking at this precious human, the desires I had wanted as a man are colliding with the ones I have as a dragon.

My golden human rises on shaking legs, glancing behind her like she has a chance of escaping me. Before she can think to move, I act. Wrapping my arm around her waist and tossing her over my shoulder. She screams again and claws at my back while she tries to wiggle away from me. Her soft breasts press into my shoulder as even more desire rushes through me.

I'll never let her go, I'll explain that to her once she calms down. She'll never want for anything, I'll protect her and care for her better than any human man can. They wouldn't know how to protect something as precious as her. She is my prize now; she belongs to me.

Forever.

3

ANWYN

A dragon...a *fucking* dragon.

I've gotten myself into some interesting situations before, but this one may be the most absurd. I will myself to remain calm as he carries me deeper into the cave. He's massive, easily over seven feet tall, made up of hard muscles and tough scales. My hands brush along their cool, rugged texture as his shoulder digs into my stomach. I watch with disdain as his tail flicks back and forth in front of my face. He snatched me with precision as if kidnapping women is common for him.

For a dragon, I suppose it is.

I had been trying to find shelter from the storm. As soon as my feet had crossed into *The Woods,* the dark clouds above had cracked open on a clap of thunder, and the rain began to fall. I was soaked in an instant, slipping and sliding in the mud of the forest floor. Searching for any start of overhang to wait out the downpour, this dry cave looked like the safest place to find shelter.

Now, I wish I would've decided to rest under a tree instead.

I let out a sigh in frustration and smack my hands against his back in a feeble effort to get him to drop me. He's no more than an animal, right? That's what I remember from the stories of dragons. He's a beast. Like any wild animal, perhaps I can startle him enough to let me go and escape. My hits to his back seem to do nothing, his measured steps never faltering. From my upside-down vantage point, I can see we are getting closer to a glowing light.

His den where he's about to char and eat me if the stories are to be believed.

Not if I have any say about it.

"Let me go!" I cry. With one last ditch effort, I wrap my hand around his massive tail and give it a tug. That makes him halt, a snarl coming from his throat. Whoops. Now, I've seemed to anger him. His hands tighten on my waist as he yanks me off his shoulder and cradles me in his arms.

"I—" Searching for something to say, I stare into his yellow gaze. His eyes are so bright they make me squint as if I was staring into the sun. His lips pull back to reveal two rows of sharp teeth. A forked tongue licks over them, making me shiver. His scales cover him completely, their green color glimmering in the low light. He exhales deeply, a puff of smoke containing a few embers dancing in front of my face.

The burnt smell makes my eyes water.

"Watch it, or you're going to burn my hair off."

I try to keep the tremble out of my voice. It's not like he can understand me, but I have to show him I'm no easy prey.

Those big yellow eyes blink at me again before he continues walking us deeper into the cave.

"Sorry," he says, the words swallowed up in a growl. My mouth drops open. Not only have I been captured by a dragon...I've been captured by a *talking* dragon. That's an interesting development, one I can use to my advantage.

After all, I have no plans on being anything's dinner.

"You can speak?" I ask for confirmation.

"Yes." He continues walking, the light in front of us getting brighter.

"I didn't know dragons could talk. All the ones in the stories are just fire-breathing village destroyers. Too busy kidnapping princesses and holding them for ransom to make small talk." The dragon merely inclines his head as if thinking over my words. The sound of the storm outside fades with each step we take.

"I've kidnapped you."

I huff a laugh and shake my head.

"I'm far from a princess, dragon. You're not getting any money for me."

If he desires a ransom payment, I can try and barter my freedom from him with the few gold coins I traveled with. I'd hate to part with them, but it's better than being eaten.

The longer he holds me I wait for fear to take over. He could easily crush me with his strong arms or slice my neck open with one of his sharp claws. How easily he could incinerate me with one deep breath.

Yet, the more he looks at me, the more I get the sense that he wants something else. There's an emotion in his gaze that I can't name, and it unsettles me. I've relied on my ability to read people for years, but this dragon confuses me. No matter what happens, I can't let my guard drop around him. The first moment I have to escape, I must take it.

"You're far more precious than gold," he says finally.

My brows furrow at his statement. Men have flirted with me before, way before an age where it was appropriate to...but a *dragon*? Now that's a new one. None of the stories about dragons I've ever encountered mentioned them wanting a human beyond ransoming or eating. He shifts me closer to his chest, and I gasp when I feel something hard pressing against me.

His cock is pushing softly against my side. I look up at him wide-eyed and realize what that unnamed emotion in his gaze is. Desire. He wants me. It's easy enough to surmise for what as my breathing speeds up. I could use this to my advantage as I have before. Play into his lust for me and then give him the slip.

It may prove harder to do with a dragon, but he's a male. All males think with their cocks. It won't be the first time I've flirted with one, only to take what I've needed and fled.

The glowing light ahead gets more intense, breaking me from my thoughts. The dragon carries me into his lair, where another shocked gasp leaves my lips.

Surveying my surroundings, this predicament may turn out to be quite a lucrative situation.

Gold, so much gold it hurts my eyes to look at it. Piles of sparkling coins cover the entire stone floor. There are massive chests with their lids peeled back, revealing heaps of glimmering jewels and polished gold bars. Crystals, necklaces, and even a few crowns litter the stacks. There is a pallet in front of an unlit firepit made up of a dozen overstuffed pillows and the softest-looking silks. Scones and torches hang from the stalactite on the cave ceiling.

One bag full of treasure in here would keep me set for life. My mouth waters at the thought of the security these riches could bring me. No more odd jobs, no more running. I could buy a place of my own and live there comfortably for the rest of my days.

My plans have changed. The goal now is to escape from the dragon with as much of this gold as I can carry before he's the wiser.

The dragon walks me over to the silk pallet and sets me down. Without this body heat, I'm aware of how soaked my clothes are and begin to shiver. The dragon's eyes narrow on my shaking form, and he turns towards the fire pit. His shoulders move as he inhales deeply, producing a burst of hot, orange flames that ignite the dry logs in the center of the pit.

It is not long before the space becomes deliciously warm, and I extend my hand toward the fire. The flames warm my fingers as the chill from the storm is melted away.

The both of us stand there for a moment, facing the flames and absorbing their warmth. My eyes close as the heat dries the hair around my face. Untying my sodden cloak, I let it pool at my feet. I hear the dragon's tail slide through a few coins littering the ground around us. His large chest rattles with each deep breath as I feel him move closer to me. Before I can open my eyes, I feel his claw slice through the leather band holding back my braided hair.

Shock at his actions renders me immobile.

My blonde tresses spill down my back as his claws shift through the strands. His touch is gentle. He works his way from the bottom of my hair toward the top of my head. His claws lightly scratch my scalp, and I have to swallow my moan. I shouldn't be enjoying this, but my hair seems to be distracting him enough to keep from eating me.

Over and over, his claws glide through my hair and brush along my scalp. My eyes feel heavy at the sensation. I can feel his large body at my back, his warm breath tickling the tops of my ears. I'm distracted by how good this sensation is I don't register just how low his claws have traveled until I feel them at the back of my gown.

With one quick cut of his claw, the lacings of my gown are severed, and the wet garment hits the floor with a soft smack. My eyes fly open as I wrap my arms around myself, naked except for my thin shift. I spin towards him as he rears back at my sudden movement.

Now I'm shocked for a new reason.

"You can't just undress me!" I don't care who this dragon is; if he can talk, then he might as well have some manners. My eyes stray lower to the simple leather breeches he wears. The outline of his hard cock is easy enough to spot. My heart pounds at the sheer size of it. If that is what he desires from me, he won't get it. Especially not after he disrobed me without permission.

Dragon males are no different from human men, it would seem, taking without asking.

"Your clothes were wet," he says simply as if that justifies it.

"That doesn't matter. You can't just undress a person without asking." I bend at the waist, pick up a silk blanket, and cover myself. His yellow eyes follow my every movement until we are staring at each other once again. He looks like he wants to say something, but then my stomach growls. The sound echoes in this deep cavern.

"You're hungry?"

I shake my head at his question; eating is the last thing I want to do despite what my body has indicated.

"I'm just tired." My traitorous stomach growls again.

The dragon gives a sharp nod and then takes a step back from me.

"I will get you food." He turns and takes another step, his tail overturning a golden goblet sending it clattering to the floor. I gasp at the blatant disregard for it. A dented cup seems to mean very little when you have this much wealth.

The dragon pauses, casting a glance at me over his shoulder.

"You are not to leave the cave."

I raise my brows. I'm not agreeing to that; as soon as he leaves to hunt, I'm gathering as much as I can carry and bolting out of here. I could fill the goblet he had just knocked over with enough diamonds to buy a hundred dresses to replace the one he just destroyed.

The dragon turns back to me and stomps closer. His body is mere inches from mine, and I have to crane my neck up to make eye contact with him. His nostrils flare as he breathes in my scent. His fork tongue slips out to lick over his scaled lips.

"What is your name, precious one?" he asks.

"Anwyn," I say. There's no need to waste a good alias on a dragon. His tongue licks over his lips again, savoring what I just said. He inhales deeply once more, his scales flexing with the movement, before shaking himself slightly.

"I'm sorry, my precious Anwyn, but I can't risk it. I must keep my treasure safe."

Before I can ask what he's doing, he moves, grabbing me by the waist and dragging me over to a stalagmite on the cave floor. I thrash in his grip, but he holds firm. My eyes widen in horror as I see the golden shackle already mounted into the stone. Grabbing my wrists, he chains them each in a golden shackle.

They are not tight enough to hurt, but there is no way to break free unless I plan to shatter my hand. I pull against the restraints, the cold metal pressing into my skin. The dragon takes a few steps back from me, his eyes remorseful.

"What are you doing? Let me go!" I screech, trying in vain to break free. The shackles clank against the rock. With one last mighty pull, I sink to my knees as my bound wrists hang in front of me.

The dragon opens his mouth but quickly shuts it. He's gone from my kidnapper to my jailer. He may desire me, but I am no more than a trinket like the ones that litter this cave. I will break free of these chains and make him regret ever capturing me.

With that resolve in mind, I watch silently as massive wings peel and snap from the skin of his back. They expand behind him, the green scales glittering in the firelight. Comprised completely of thick muscles with sharp claws decorating the bottoms, they are as deadly as they are magnificent.

The dragon says nothing more as he launches into the air. His wings thunder with each powerful flap, causing the air to swirl around me and tangle my hair. His clawed feet leave the stone floor as he turns and flies swiftly toward the mouth of the cave. Leaving a trail of rattling gold coins in his wake.

4

LASSAR

nwyn.

It's fitting that a woman as lovely as my precious Anwyn would have the most perfect name ever crafted. *Gods*, she is beautiful. Each moment I spent in her company, she only became more beautiful.

And when she spoke? I could barely hold back from claiming her right then and there. She wouldn't have liked that, my precious one. Undressing her had been a mistake. I had only desired to help relieve her of her wet clothes, but she was right. I shouldn't have done it without her permission. I've been in this beastly form for so long that I hardly have any memories of how you are supposed to court a woman as perfect as Anwyn.

She told me she is no princess, and that is true. Anwyn is more than just a title. More than any station or jewel or fine cloth. There is a fire roaring in her opal eyes, one that matches my own. I feel it simmering under the surface.

When I brought her down to my lair, I felt many emotions from her. Apprehension, which is reasonable. Then anger when I cut her dress, followed by rage when I chained her to the floor. I meant what I said to her; I can't risk my treasure. She is the best treasure I have ever found and I will not allow her to sneak off while I gather food.

The thought of providing a meal to her makes my mouth water and my cock harden. To be able to provide for my precious one is a treat I've never experienced. My cock has been hard for her since I first saw her behind that boulder. It only got more persistent the longer I carried her in my arms. Her skin is as smooth and pale. It begs for my touch, my tongue.

I shiver at the thought of tasting her bare skin. Of tracing those delicate curves hidden by her shift. I'd sever the wings from my back for just one lick of her little pussy. To spread her out before me and feast on her warm, wet flesh. It would fill me with more satisfaction than a hundred trunks filled with gold.

Damp leaves snag in my scales, and I realize I've dropped into the tree line. Thoughts of Anwyn have made me lose focus on my task at hand. Bringing her food so that she is comfortable and will see me as someone who can take care of her as she needs. She'll never want for anything in my care.

I'll make sure of it.

I hit the edge of *The Woods* with a silent thud. The storm is still raging. Freezing rain covers me. I puff a small flame in between my hands to warm them. It was a miracle my treasure found her way to my cave. I can't even think of what would've become of her had she tried to push through this storm.

In front of me is a small village. A long time ago, when I was still more human, I would barter with a few of the townsfolk. Over the years, I've slipped a few trinkets from the more wealthy inhabitants. One of whose home sits just in front of me. It is about five times larger than any of the ones around it. A warm orange glow can be seen through the windows while its chimney sends smoke into the storming sky.

The wealthiest member of the town has always lived in this house. It's been a while since I pilfered through a human's home, but my Anwyn deserves the finest things. This house will surely have what I need, and then I can return to my precious one.

Overhead, the storm rages on. The sheets of rain conceal me in the dark as I fly to the top of the house. Landing silently on the sod roof, I peel back enough of the grass and soil to peer inside. My wings keep my peephole free of any rain so I don't risk exposure by the home's inhabitants.

The inside of the house is warm. Everything is cast in a golden glow by the roaring fireplace. Fine china and silver goblets decorate an ornately carved wooden table with matching wooden chairs. There are fine paintings and tapestries that line the walls that would normally snag my attention first. However, I can't help but compare their brilliance to Anwyn's.

Now that I have glimpsed the rarest jewel, all other treasures are as unremarkable as tin by comparison.

What does capture my attention is the wide assortment of bottled wines decorating the far wall. Reds, whites, sparkling...I wonder what kind is Anwyn's favorite? I shall have to get her a variety and see.

The smell of roasting meats wafts toward me, making my mouth water. The closest I've come to cooking in years was charing the animals I killed with some of my flames. However, this roasted chicken looks beautifully prepared. Garnished with whipped potatoes and green beans, the hardy meal should provide my Anwyn with enough sustenance for all the things I want to do with her.

My cock hardens even further as I break from those thoughts. I must stay focused on getting her food and less on getting her naked even if it is the most difficult thing I have ever done.

The home below me is quiet. I watch as a servant in simple wool clothes makes a plate from the roast and sides dishes cooking over the fire. With shaking hands, he walks the plate back over to the table and sets it down at a place setting. The goblet of wine sitting there is filled with dark red wine.

It isn't long until the hinges of the old wooden door creak open. A new scent enters the home, and I peer through the sod roof to inspect who's just arrived. The man is wealthy, which is evident from his fine clothing, but they are almost too gaudy. Unlike the fine attire I was used to as a Lord, his garments are not comprised of good quality materials but rather of those that sparkle the most.

His thinning dark hair is damp from the rain. The wooden table rattles as he sits down and gulps down the wine, wiping his mouth with the back of his wrinkled hand. Even as a dragon, I balk at his overwhelming lack of manners.

"That will be all tonight, Jonathan. See to it that you get some rest, for I will need you back here before first light." A cruel smile tugs at the lips around his goblet. "I am to wed at dawn."

A pang of reget hits me. My humanity may have lessened over the years, but for Anwyn, I feel some of it slowly creeping back. I want to be better for her, someone worthy of her. Would she be okay with me stealing from a man before his wedding night? My precious one has a kind heart, I can tell.

I will just take what's necessary for her and find more legitimate ways to secure the supplies she needs in the future.

The old servant snaps up straight.

"Married?" Jonathan chokes. "I mean—who is the lucky bride, Mr. Wicksome?"

"The girl who's been living with Mrs. Hitherbend." Mr. Wicksome stabs the roast chicken and takes a meaty bite, the grease coating his lips. "Anwyn, she calls herself."

My chest tightens, and the fire in my throat gathers, demanding I release it on this foul creature who covets my precious one.

"Anwyn? But she is but a girl—"

"She is young and healthy. And I think I will very much enjoy bedding her until she is with child." Mr. Wicksome's tongue licks over his teeth. "Unlike my former wretch of a wife, I have no doubt Anwyn will give me the heirs I need."

"Very good, sir," the servant mutters, slipping on his coat. "I shall be off then."

I watch Mr. Wicksome gulp down more wine as a rage I have never known spreads through my body. It tickles every scale and makes the sod roof shred in my claws. My wings draw back tight as my vision is consumed in red.

The last time I was this angry was just after I had been cursed. The rage then didn't burn as acutely as this.

Mr. Wicksome pours more wine into his goblet, laughing to himself.

This is why my Anwyn ventured into the storm. I should be grateful; his clearly unwanted proposal of marriage sent her right to me. However, I find myself anything but. This man, this *vermin*, covets my treasure. He seeks to steal her from me and keep her for his own. He'll never touch her; no one ever will. She is mine.

Mine to keep, mine to possess, mine to protect.

He thinks to bed her? To breed her? He is the reason she was almost lost to the storm tonight. And for that, as the protector of my precious one, he must pay with his life, of course. Endangering my Anwyn deserves the most severe punishment.

No longer caring about keeping my presence a secret, I rip the sod roof off with my claws and swoop down. Mr. Wicksome gags on his bite of chicken as I yank him from the table and pin him against a wooden beam. His beady eyes grow wide, my hand collaring his neck digs in, and my claws make his blood flow down his neck in slow rivulets.

A puff of dark smoke is expelled from my mouth, the taste

burning my tongue. With his limited air, Mr. Wicksome coughs and splutters. Water splatters at my feet. I half believe it to be more rain coming in from the ruined roof until the scent of urine invades my nose.

This weakling of a man sought out my treasure? He was never a match for her. In her name, I will eradicate this threat.

"You sought out my treasure?" I growl into his reddening face.

"I—you...I—" he chokes.

"You sought to take my Anwyn from me? You're the reason I almost lost her in the storm?"

"Your Anwyn—"

"Don't!" I roar. "Don't you ever say her name, mortal. Don't you ever think about her again."

"I won't—I swear it!" he vows. I feel my grip lessen as he sucks down more air. His promise should cool some of my anger, but it doesn't. If anything, I feel angrier. I hear his crude words about my precious Anwyn float back to me. He was going to marry her and breed her, clearly without her consent.

The more I stare at this pathetic excuse for a man, the more my beast roars at me to take action. To stop this threat against Anwyn now. And permanently. This human is a pig.

Everyone knows the best type of pig is a roasted one.

"I don't think I'm going to give you the chance to."

Without warning, I breathe in, allowing the fire in my stomach to rage and roar. With one mighty exhale, my flames shoot forward, warming the scales on my nose. Mr. Wicksome screams as his body is charred. The hands he thought to touch my Anwyn with, the mouth he thought to kiss her with are reduced to ash in a matter of moments. His smoking corpse lies at my feet.

I was wrong. My humanity is still lost when it comes to Anwyn. The only difference is I want to be that creature. The one that sends fears into the hearts of all who behold it so that she may stay safe in my company.

I have no remorse as I find a discarded satchel and stuff it full of wine, meats, and cheeses. As I load the still-warm dinner into the bag and cast one last look at the man who I killed for it.

I am happy to have eradicated this threat to my precious one. Bending at my knees, I fan my wings and take to the sky. It's time to return to her, my prize. With my supplies in hand, it's now time for me to show her I'm the only one who can keep her safe and truly provide for her.

Now, I must show her why she should stay with me forever.

5

———

ANWYN

The thunder of large wings echoing through the cave has me looking up.

With a frustrated sigh, I throw the golden coin I was using to unscrew the shackles from the floor. I've been trying to free myself for the better part of an hour but was unsuccessful. Now my jailer has returned, and my chance of escaping just became nonexistent. Sitting with my back against the stalagmite, I hear his wings getting closer.

The cool stone sinks into my skin, damp with sweat from my escape attempt.

Foolish. Instead of wasting time on my restraints, I should've tried to locate some sort of weapon. Then waited for him to unlock me and, no doubt, feast on my flesh and then take that opportunity to attack. I may not have killed him, but at least wounded him enough to flee. Now through narrowed eyes, I watch his massive form lower to the ground with apprehension.

His glowing gaze locks on me, his leather pants dripping water onto the stone floor. From around his massive chest, he loops a worn leather satchel over his head and sets it down gently in front of the pallet by the fire. The old bag looks like it's about to burst with whatever is contained inside. My stomach growls as he takes out the contents.

The bag rattles as he makes a place setting of a silver plate and matching goblet. Next, he brings forth a still steaming roasted chicken, followed by a bowl of potatoes and green beans. There is an assortment of bread rolls, cheese, and ten different bottles of wine. My mouth is surely watering by the time he steps back.

His yellow eyes return to me as if seeking my approval. My stomach clenches, and for the moment, I don't care what his motives are for this food. I would be a fool to refuse a hearty meal like this one. At the very least, it will give me enough strength should the opportunity to escape arise.

The dragon is still looking at me expectantly, and I raise my shackled wrist, letting the metal click together. He moves quickly, using a dark claw to unlock the clasp. I rub my wrists and watch remorse swim in his eyes. He's the one who chained me up so I wouldn't rob him. Of course, that's exactly what I intend to do.

Silently, I follow him to the pallet on the floor. He watches me again, his massive chest rising and falling as I sink to the floor, careful to avoid his tail that lies at my feet. I pick up the fork left out for me and take a bite of the potatoes. Their rich, creamy texture melts on my tongue. I have to swallow down a moan as I go for another bite.

"How is the food?" the dragon asks, his massive wings folding into his back.

I toss my hair over my shoulder and shrug.

"The potatoes are cold."

His head snaps back, and I think I've angered him. I don't know what possessed me to say it. Perhaps it is my frustration with the situation. If he wanted a nice dinner companion, the first step would be not kidnapping and chaining them to his floor.

His massive shoulders sag, and he snatches my plate from me.

Oh great, now I've done it. I watch as he walks over to the roaring fire, his clawed feet clicking along the stone. The fire has burned down, but he quickly adds more logs until it is roaring once more. My eyes begin to water, knowing I'm about to watch him burn the food he brought me. Mouthing off to a dragon was going to have consequences, and now I'm going to spend what could be my last night in this world starving.

I should've just eaten the cold potatoes.

The dragon spends a few minutes over by the fire. With each one that passes, I grow more and more curious when I don't hear the sizzle of the food being dumped out on them. After another moment, he returns the plate of food steaming in his hands. He sets it down in front of me.

"Be careful, my Anwyn, the plate will be hot. I do not wish for you to burn your precious skin." *So he can do it himself later*, I think, but I only nod my head. Perhaps, I am being too harsh on this dragon. After all, none of the stories mentioned them braving a storm to ensure their victims were fed. Of course, he could have his own motives for this, but the look of absolute pleasure on his face as I eat my meal tells me there's something else going on here.

Still, I'm just grateful to have a meal.

Once I have polished off most of the food, he uncorks a bottle of red wine with a claw and fills my goblet. I take a small sip. It is just as delicious as well. The meal and now the wine has caused my body to become more relaxed. The dragon next to me takes another deep inhale through his nose, his tail grazing the bottom of my feet and the sides of my legs ever so often.

"Do you like the wine?" he asks. Reaching over, I pluck the

bottle up, wondering if I smashed it, would a jagged piece of the glass be enough to penetrate his scales? Surely not, but I file that information away for later.

The bottle almost slips from my hand as I see the seal stamped onto the front of the bottle. The Wicksome seal. My head jerks up as I look the dragon in the eyes, my mouth parting.

"Where...where did you get this wine?" I gesture down to my lap, where my plate sits. "This food?"

My heart pounds and blood roars in my ears. The dragon sits up straighter, a fierce look on his face.

"From the human man called Wicksome. The one who wished to marry you," he growls out. His yellow eyes blaze hot, turning into molten gold. A puff of smoke exits his nostrils, warning of the fire inside him.

"Did you tell him you had me?" I ask. If Mr. Wicksome comes here, I'll be trading one jailer for another. At least with this dragon, my suffering will be short. Mr. Wicksome intends to make me suffer for the rest of my life. I can't afford to be found by him, I won't be. The broken glass may not be enough to puncture this dragon's scales, but it will be sharp enough to slice a human throat.

The dragon shakes his head, his tail whipping behind him.

"I've taken care of him. I'd never endanger my most precious possession."

"He'd want your gold to be sure," I say, gesturing around me. "But I'm worried he'd follow you here and take me back to the village. I have no desire to marry a man like that."

Any man, really.

The dragon shakes his head again.

"He will never come after you, my Anwyn. I left his burning corpse in his dining room before I returned to you."

My mouth drops open as my heart thunders in my chest.

"You killed him?" I ask incredulously. "Why? To steal all of this?"

His golden eyes are tender on my face. He reaches out a clawed hand, and I will myself to remain still as he tucks a stay piece of hair behind my ear. Goosebumps break out along my skin as his claw tickles the shell of my ear.

"To make you safe. That man scared you so much with his threats of marriage you set off into a storm that could've killed you. I would not allow such a man as that to live." The dragon takes my plate and rises. "I will get you more food, my Anwyn."

I'm at a loss for words as I watch him at the fire. The flames illuminate his muscular back in greens and yellows. As he prepares more food for me, I let my mind fully absorb what he's just told me.

Mr. Wicksome is...*dead*. Burnt to a crisp. I'm free from that danger, because of the dragon in front of me.

Something unnamed worms its way into my chest. *To make you safe. That man scared you so much...I would not allow such a man as that to live.* The words the dragon said float back to me. For the first time in a long time, I feel...protected.

Not since before my parents both perished have I felt this way. That someone was looking out for me, taking care of me, solving my problems for me. It's always just been me, fending for myself. However, this dragon solved a major problem for me. Albeit with a more permanent solution but he did it for me.

Because Mr. Wicksome scared me.

When another plate of steaming food is set down in front of me, I look up at him. Have I been too swift to judge him? Are his true motives as nefarious as I believe? If he just wanted to eat me, surely he wouldn't have gone to all the trouble of getting me food.

I allow myself to relax for the first time in a long time. There is no danger present here, and it's clear he's not going to try and eat me. Yet, that is.

"Thank you," I say softly, not knowing if I'm giving him thanks for the food or for slaying Mr. Wicksome. He nods, his scaled lips twisting, making me believe he's trying to smile. That hardening bulge in his leather trousers is ever-present. While it scared me before, I now see it as something else entirely. An assurance that this dragon's lust for me, as ludicrous as that sounds, may just outweigh his desire to eat me.

At the very least, I can play into it and try and convince him to release me. My tactics have been all wrong. Brute force and surprise attacks won't aid me. As nonsensical as it sounds, it's the option I've been presented with: I'm going to flirt with a dragon.

Relaxing my shoulders, I tuck some more hair behind my ear and reach for the plate. Taking another bite, I moan softly, noting his changing posture. I chuckle quietly and look up at him, where he looms above me through my lashes.

"What is your name? I assume you have one. After all you've done for me, I find it rude to keep referring to you as *dragon*."

"Lassar," he says, coming down to sit beside me. I lean back, letting the silk blanket I'm still wearing drop off my shoulder. His gaze licks over the slope of my shoulder as my stomach flutters. This feels different than when I've flirted with men in the past. It was about stroking their ego, making them feel powerful. But the longer I say under Lassar's golden stare, I find myself becoming the powerful one.

It seems this dragon would be content to just stare at me until the end of time.

"Interesting name, for a dragon, I mean." I furrow my brows. "Though, I don't recall the dragons in the stories ever having any names. Beyond *destruction-bringer*, of course."

Lassar nods his head, his lips pulling into what I can now confidently say is his version of a smile.

"I was not always a dragon."

"Oh?" I ask.

"I was a man once. A lord. From a kingdom on the other side of *The Woods,* a long time ago." There's a sadness in his honey eyes, and my hand moves to touch him, to comfort him. I stop myself before I do, shocked by my body's response. This is a part I'm playing, I don't care about this man-turned-dragon at all.

Right?

"How did you become like this?" I ask. Lassar is silent for a moment, and I think he isn't going to answer. His claws scrape along the floor, picking up a gold coin. The metal shimmers in the dim light, and Lassar shakes his head.

"I made a bargain with the demon who lives here. I came to him a greedy mortal; my only care in the world was gold. Having it, keeping it, hoarding it, and then finding more. It consumed me day and night. I came to him asking if there was a way for me to have endless amounts of gold." He closes his fist around the coin, scales flexing over his knuckles. "The demon told me there was a way to have more gold than any man in this land. In my desirous state, I took the deal, and it wasn't until a few moments later when my bones began to snap, and scales grew through my skin, I realized that I had made a terrible mistake."

"Lassar, I—" But what can I even say? His anguish is clear. A greedy man who has amassed such wealth all for it to mean nothing ultimately. No one to share it with, no companions. A lonely, sparkling life. The demon of *The Woods* is just as foul as the rumors about him suggest.

More than anything, though, I understand Lassar a bit more. More gold would certainly fix my problems. After all these years of running, I could buy my own home and be safe and alone. As I look around this beautiful cave, filled with treasures only kings would dream of, I wonder if my own life isn't heading in the same path as Lassar's.

"I do not wish to burden you, my Anwyn, with such a sad tale." He reaches out slowly and skims a claw down the side of my cheek. "The curse is not all bad; it's the reason I have you now."

I laugh and shake my head.

"That's true, it's odd that my path would cross with a dragon before a rich lord, but here we are."

"And I am grateful for it. A rich lord wouldn't have appreciated you as he should," he says, and I duck my head. The raw emotion in his eyes makes me look away. My hand rubs along my wrist, no marks are left, but they still feel sore. Lassar makes a sound in his throat. "I'm sorry for shackling you. I just couldn't risk it, Anwyn, especially not now."

I look up and meet his eyes.

"I understand, Lassar. You gave up your humanity for this gold. It's reasonable that you would want to protect it at all costs."

His mouth opens slightly, and he leans forward. My spine straightens as his face comes closer to mine. For a moment, I think he may kiss me. Instead of being scared or disgusted, I find myself intrigued by the possibility of what those scaled lips would feel like against my own.

An absurd thought.

I don't find out what his lips are like, but the breath is stolen from me all the same when he speaks these next words against my lips. All of them are far more precious than jewels could ever be.

"My gold isn't the treasure I was worried about keeping safe." My heart pounds in my chest as his eyes glow brighter in the dark cave. My thighs squeeze together as his warm breath bathes my lips.

"It was you."

6

———

LASSAR

Anwyn is not asleep, though she pretends to be.

I've stuffed enough pillows and silk blankets under her to make sure the hard floor doesn't come in contact with her delicate skin. The fire burns next to her, the flames licking over her small body assure me that she is warm enough. However, I can tell she's awake. Her form is too stiff under the silk blanket, her breathing too uneven.

Still, I stay vigilant as I watch over her from my perch in the corner.

Now that I have my precious Anwyn, I must always stay on guard so she can rest peacefully, knowing I'm watching over her. My Anwyn is so lovely. Albeit a bit quiet. After I had confessed to her being my treasure and not this frivolous gold around me, she had polished off her wine and gone silent. Only spoke to tell me she was ready for bed, and I got to work making her pallet on the floor.

From the moment she settled into the mess of blankets and pillows, I have watched over her.

Anwyn gives a sigh and rolls onto her back before rolling onto her side to face me. The firelight makes her glow like a goddess, and I lean forward. Is she too cold? Too hot? Is she hungry again? Her cheeks are too hollow for my liking.

It's late, but if I set off now, I could—

"I can't sleep with you watching me like that," she says, her soft voice echoing around us. I gesture toward the mouth of the cave with my claws.

"You are my most precious possession, Anwyn. If I lower my guard, someone may come and try and take you from me." I cross my arms over my chest and give her a sharp nod. "I will not fail you. I will keep watch over you while you sleep."

Anwyn wrinkles her small nose.

"No one is coming after me now that you've roasted Wicksome."

"Is there no one else looking for you? A family?"

Anwyn shakes her head, her golden hair moving about her shoulders. A loneliness swims in her eyes, one that I am all too familiar with. We are both lonely creatures. There may be more similarities between me and my precious one than I thought.

Anwyn lets out another sigh and sits up, the blanket wrapped around her revealing her shoulders. My mouth waters at the sight of her. Tucking some loose hair behind her ears, she squares her shoulders at me.

"Look, you need to stop staring at me." She takes another breath as if summoning her strength. Her eyes are wary as they bore into mine, and I brace myself for what she is about to say next. "I'll need to be well rested so I can set off in the morning."

My flames roar in my stomach and climb up my throat, begging me to expel them. She wants to leave. My precious Anwyn wants to leave me. The way she's holding herself, I can tell she's waiting for me to explode, to forbid her from going. I suppose I could do that, but I want her willing. I would never imprison my lovely Anwyn; only for her own safety did I keep her.

I am a monster, to be sure, but I will be a monster *for* her, never towards her.

The flames inside me fizzle, and my shoulders drop. I did not provide my Anwyn with enough. Even though I tried my best to show her I was the only one who could keep her safe, it's clear it was not enough, and she has decided to set out on her own. I've failed, I've lost my chance to keep her forever.

Now that I know she is alive, I'll watch over her from the shadows for eternity. Protecting her in the best way that I can until she thinks to give me another chance. And if she does not, watching over her will give me more pleasure than a million gold coins.

I give a sharp nod, the only response I can muster towards her statement that will not show the pain her choice has caused me. The acute disappointment I feel towards myself.

Anwyn's opal eyes glow with surprise, but she says nothing, just lies back down on her mountain of pillows. The moments tick on as I watch her beautiful face look up at the ceiling of the cave. Her head turns toward me again.

"You're still staring."

"I can't risk it. I must keep watch over you." This I will hold firm on. I will never let harm come to her. Anwyn gives another sigh and then pats the space beside her. My brows lower at the action.

"If you're so worried about someone coming and stealing me, then you can lay right next to me. I can't sleep feeling your eyes on me like that."

My heart pounds in my chest. Lay beside her? Feel the warmth of her body? My mouth begins to water in earnest. My precious Anwyn has given me the ultimate gift. To spend this last night in my lair pressed close together.

I try not to trip over my own tail in my haste to make my way over to her pallet.

Anwyn shuffles over and turns onto her side, facing away

from me. Her sweet scent invades my senses; the warmth of her body soaks into my scales. My body screams at me to touch her, trace her curves with my claws, and taste her skin with my tongue. I burn with the need to grab her and hold her to me, to show her the pleasure I and I alone can give her.

That's when it hits me.

I haven't shown her the extent of my devotion, the pleasure I wish to bring her. Sure, I've gotten her food and made her warm, but I haven't shown her the euphoria I can bring her with my mouth and my cock. Would she like me to? It may be the only way to keep her with me. If I give her a taste of the pleasure that could be hers for eternity if she chose to remain at my side.

It's worth the risk.

Her body shifts next to mine. I turn to face her, leaving only a few inches of space between us. With another sigh, she tries to relax her body. The movement causes her to slide the reaming distance towards me. The supple mounds of her ass press into my cock. Anwyn lets out a small gasp as her body goes still.

With a few small manipulations from my tail, I slowly drag the silk blanket covering her down her body. The fire and my body will keep her warm enough. It's not long until the smooth skin of her arm is revealed. My tongue tries to slide out of my mouth to lick it, but I hold back. Instead, I carefully run my claw from her shoulder to her wrist. Her precious flesh breaks out in goosebumps, and she lets out a moan. My cock is so hard that I fear it may shatter before I've gotten the chance to pleasure her with it.

I trace up the side of her exposed arm one more time before she twists to look at me. Her opal eyes are heavy-lidded.

"What are you doing?" she asks.

"Making sure my precious Anwyn is relaxed."

"I—" Anwyn lets out another moan. This is my opportunity

to show her what I can provide her, I will not waste it. She is not pushing me away, and that strengthens my resolve.

"Will you let me help you sleep, my Anwyn?" I whisper near her ear. She shivers and turns so that our eyes meet. There is so much swirling in her opal irises, different emotion warring there. I wait for her answer, my heart continuing to pound. With another deep breath, she closes her eyes and gives me one small nod.

I let out a growl and waste no time servicing my precious one.

Wrapping my arm around her waist, I pull her back tight against my front. She releases another moan as my hard cock presses more firmly against her. Leaning my head down, I run my nose along her neck, reveling in the feel of her soft skin against my hard scales. Her scent consumes me, sweet like the ripest fruits, I want to swallow and drink it down. To bathe in her essence for the rest of my days. My forked tongue slips from my mouth and follows the path my nose just made up her throat.

Her scent deepens as I take my time on the delicate skin of her neck. Licking and biting and sucking until a pink mark is left behind. The sight of me marking her has my blood pumping even faster, the fire inside of me growing even hotter. Anwyn's plump lips puff open, and my mouth seeks to claim them, but not yet. I need to savor her; if I taste her now, I won't be able to control myself.

My clawed hand skims over her stomach and up her chest. I feel her pounding heart as my fingers slip just inside the top of her shift. I wait for a moment to see if she protests, but when she continues breathing heavily, her eyes glassy with lust, I continue. Slowly, I slip beneath the neckline of her shift and trail along the soft swells of her breasts.

I grasp one in my hand. Her breasts are perfect, small, and round. I gently knead one while she writhes and moans, stopping only to thumb her hard nipple. I had lovers as a human, but none of them made me feel like how Anwyn does. To allow me to do this to her in this monstrous form? She truly is a gift I don't deserve, and I will do everything to make sure she doesn't regret this.

My tail follows my hand's lead. Gently it creeps up the hem of her shift; it traces up the side of her calf, over the soft skin of her knee and thigh. Her skin is deliciously warm. Back and forth, it skims over her inner thighs, inching closer to that sweet spot between her legs. Already her thighs have grown damp for me.

Anwyn looks back at me, her opal eyes wide and wild.

"N—no one has ever touched me there," she says breathlessly. My snarl is ripped from my lips. My Anwyn has saved herself for me. Even if she didn't know she was, I'm the one who will win the honor of being able to claim her.

My tail trails up higher and traces her wet slit with its blunt end. Her little cunt is soaking wet and hot. Anwyn thrashes next to me, her moan singing in my ears. I rub her over and over again, my tail becoming slick with her arousal. Her chest rises and falls, my claws lightly digging into the skin of her breast.

"Are you going to let me make you come, my precious Anwyn?"

Again, my tail presses more firmly against her clit. Her back arches, and her small hands grasp my forearm around her waist. Her eyes are wild as they look at me, and she nods furiously. With a growl, I double the efforts of my tail. Rubbing her, gliding through her wet flesh, pressing gently into her entrance. Over and over again until her whole body is trembling.

"Please, Lassar. Please kiss me," she moans, leaning her head back and bringing her lips close to mine.

Who am I to deny my precious one?

My mouth comes down on hers, and my head spins. Her

lips are full and soft as they gently press against mine. She holds on to my arm tighter as she sighs, my tail never ceasing its movements between her legs. My other comes up to cradle her head, my scales snagging in the long tresses of her hair. Anwyn gives a surprised gasp as my tail nudges her entrance again.

I take that small opportunity to taste her fully.

My tongue licks over the seam of her lips as they open slightly. Rolling her gently onto her back, I devour my sweet Anwyn. Her body is small beneath my own frame, reminding me to be gentle with my precious one. Her mouth opens for me, and I sweep my tongue inside. Hers is tentative as it tangles with my own, her sweet taste amplified.

Her legs fall on either side of me as I settle between them. The delicious heat from her pussy warms my cock through my pants. I grind against her, swallowing down each moan she gives me. Anwyn's small hands glide up my back, sinking into the muscles and scales there.

"Lassar," she slurs, "please, I need more."

"Then I'll give you more, Anwyn." My tongue licks up the side of her neck, its forked end tickling her ear. "I'm the only one who will satisfy this pussy. This is what you need from me, isn't it? To take care of the ache between your thighs."

"Yes!" she cries, her pupils blown wide with pleasure.

My hips drop down as I grind against her mercilessly. Her arousal soaks through my pants as I dry-fuck her over and over again. Soon she'll be wrapped around my cock, where I can spill my seed inside her. Marking her as mine from the inside out.

I return to her pink lips for a moment before my hands tangle in the neckline of her shift. With one tug, her breasts are freed, and I go to claim nipple with my mouth. I pull my hips back slightly and let my tail press firmly down on her clit. Her legs tremble as they lock around my hips. I continue biting and sucking her breasts. A lock of golden hair sticks to her sweaty forehead.

"Lassar, I'm going to—" Anwyn lets out a scream that echoes in the cave around us. Moisture rushes from her pussy, and my tail is there to gather as much of it as it can. Her pussy clamps gently around the tip of it while she rides out her orgasms. I look down at her breasts, covered in my marks, and my chest glows with pride.

She is mine. She was always mine.

Her legs drop from around my waist, her eyes are wild, and a delicate sheen of sweat coats her body. I stare into her brown eyes as I bring my tail to my lips and lick her come off of it. Sweeter than any wine. More color rises to her cheeks, and she tries to duck her head. Leaning down, I kiss her again, sharing her taste with her.

"Beautiful, my Anwyn. You taste like the sweetest fruit." I brush some blonde hair off of her brow. "Never hide from me, not after your little pussy just came all over my tail."

Her face warms even more.

"Lassar, that was...there are no words for it."

Anwyn lays back down on the pallet, and I watch a yawn sneak up on her. Falling down beside her, I gather her to my chest, her ass once again resting against my hard cock. It begs me to show her the pleasure I can give her with it, but not tonight. My Anwyn is tired.

"Sleep, my precious Anwyn. The sun will rise before long."

She nods, her hair tickling the underside of my chin. With her warm body in my arms and the taste of her arousal on my tongue, life seems perfect for the first time since I've been cursed to live in this infernal form. That's all thanks to the treasure who is snoring softly in my arms.

7

———

ANWYN

Without opening my eyes, I can tell I'm alone.

The cave is eerily quiet, with only the sporadic pops and cracks coming from the fire to break up the silence. Stretching my arms above my head, I let out a deep sigh, happy to be on my own this morning so that I'm able to reflect on the absurdity of last night.

I still feel his claws on me. Pulling down the top of my shift, I can see the faint impressions of his claws on my breasts. I've never let any man touch me like that; a few have stolen kisses in the past, but nothing like what Lassar did. He devastated my mouth with his own. His kiss was filled with so much reverence. Thinking about them, I feel my pussy growing wet again.

Watching him lick my come from his tail had almost made me climax again.

Which is ridiculous, given that he is a dragon. A dragon who kidnapped me, if nothing else. It makes little difference if he was once a man. Doesn't it? I honestly don't know. All I do know is that when I told him my plan was to leave this morning, he didn't say I had to stay.

He didn't say anything on the subject if I recall correctly;

my mind still racing with the memory of what we did on the silk sheets. Perhaps it is the oddity of the whole situation, but I don't regret what happened. He had made me warm, fed me, and provided me with a mind-altering orgasm. There is a part of me, a small ridiculous part, that wants to stay here longer. Which, again, is absurd. What type of future would I have here?

A good one, a voice whispers in my head, but I ignore it.

I do plan on leaving. Now that he's gone and I have been left unshackled, I need to get a move on. Enjoying that last bit of warmth from the fire, I rise, covering myself in another silk sheet. I should ask Lassar if I can borrow this for my journey. And a few coins; it's not like he can't spare them.

My plan to slip away quietly is quickly thwarted when I hear a commotion at the front of the cave. It's only a few moments until Lassar's massive wings swoop down in the middle of the lair. His muscled back flexes as he collapses his wings. The torches have been lit, and they illuminate his emerald scales. They sparkle in the light. My cheeks heat as I remember how those scales felt on the delicate skin of my thighs.

His eyes meet mine, their gold color glowing with a hundred emotions that I have to duck my head. Again, this whole situation is ridiculous. Why am I being shy around a dragon? A dragon who protected me and killed Mr. Wicksome for scaring me. Who went out into a storm to make sure I had something to eat.

His claws click along the stone floor, his tail rattling through scattered gold coins and goblets. I keep my head down until I see him set two large leather bags at my feet. They are covered in raindrops; if I listen closely, I can still hear the storm raging overhead.

I suppress a groan. Travel will be miserable. That is if I am still permitted to go...

As if he heard my thoughts, Lassar takes a step back and clears his throat.

"These looked like your size."

I look up at him with a brow raised, and he gestures toward the bags. Curious, I drop to my knees and begin unloading their contents. My hands tremble as I realize what he's brought me. Gowns, wool ones, and simple cotton ones in a myriad of colors. A few pairs of shoes ranging from dancing slippers to thick leather boots that will aid me today as I travel through the mud.

A loud clap of thunder echoes through the cave. My hands grip one of the wool gowns. It's so warm in this cave. The thought of traipsing through icy rain has me reconsidering leaving. Would it be so bad to stay? A least for a little while longer?

Again, as if he can read my thoughts, Lassar takes a step towards me.

"Would you like breakfast before you head out? I want to make sure you're fed, my Anwyn. You will need your strength navigating *The Woods*."

"That would be wonderful, Lassar. Thank you." Rising, I slip the new wool gown over my shift. It fits me perfectly. Smoothing my hands down the gray fabric, I look up to see Lassar back at the fire. A pan is heating over the open flame as he cracks a few eggs into it.

"Where did you get all of these things?" I ask. While I am happy to be in possession of these fine items, whoever their original owner is will need them come winter. It's not as if I haven't stolen before, but for some reason, the thought makes me regretful. Ashamed even, and I don't know why.

"I scared a human trader enough cutting through *The Woods* to take my coin in exchange for giving me what he was meant to be delivering to a nobleman's daughter." Lassar looks over at me, his scaled lips tipping into a smile. "Of course, after I assured him I was not going to eat him."

"I'm sure that was his first thought."

"Is that what your first thought of me was? That I was going to eat you," Lassar asks.

"Well—" I start, cringing at his question.

"You know I have no desire to devour any part of you." His tongue licks over his lips. "Except your pretty little cunt."

My face flames as I look away. I don't know what to say to that. I thought I'd be able to sneak away this morning before talk of last night came up but clearly, that is not the case. Lassar continues to cook in silence; the sizzling of bacon soon fills the lair with a wonderful smell. My stomach growls.

Over on my left, I notice a small wooden side table with two ornate chairs. Walking over to them, I sit down in one of the seats, my knees feeling weak after our conversation. This whole encounter has thrown me off kilter.

Lassar walks over to me and sets a steaming plate of eggs, bacon, and bread in front of me. Butter and jams are soon pulled from another bag. Picking up a jeweled fork he placed beside the plate, I dig in.

To his credit, Lassar does try and sit in the other chair. It's comical the size difference. His large body causes the delicately crafted chair to whine with each shift. With a sigh, he forgoes the chair and sits on the ground. From that height, he's more level with the table anyways.

I can't help but smile.

"Thank you," I say softly. Lassar's eyes find mine. "Not just for the food. For the clothes...and for everything else."

The dragon's smile is equally as soft.

"You had nothing, Anwyn. I couldn't let you set off unprepared. The journey is dangerous enough."

"Still," I say, "thank you. You didn't have to do all of this."

"I did, Anwyn." His voice is so earnest it makes something warm bloom in my chest. My heart, cold and iced over from years of solitude, feels like it's beginning to thaw in this warm cave.

"You're welcome, all the same." His smile is wide, showing me his sharp teeth. "For the clothes and the food...and everything else."

I giggle into my breakfast plate.

He really is a kind dragon, and I am beginning to feel bad for my earlier thoughts of killing him. If I'm being honest with myself, this is the best I've been treated by anyone in a long time. Not saying much for humankind. This dragon may care for me because he wants my body, but he's been respectful toward me.

Though, I wouldn't mind a few more orgasms before I left. I've lived a lonely life. What can I say? The pleasure he gave me is a thousand times better than what I've been able to do with my own hand.

My chest feels funny again as I look toward the mouth of the cave. The pounding of rain and the claps of thunder sound ominous in this quiet cave.

"That storm sounds terrible," I venture. Lassar nods, eating the last bit of his bacon between two claws before licking them clean. I wouldn't mind knowing what that forked tongue feels like on my pussy, either.

Maybe I've truly lost my mind in this cave, but I can't bring myself to care.

"It's a strong one," Lassar agrees.

With a sigh, I turn towards him. His eyes are so bright they warm my face. I don't break his stare as I ask the next part before I lose my resolve.

"I was wondering if you wouldn't mind, of course, if I could stay here. Just a little longer until the storm passes." I let out a laugh and shrug. "I'd hate to get all the nice dresses and shoes you bought me ruined with mud."

"You can stay as long as you want, my Anwyn." His smile is as bright as his eyes. "When the storm clears, I can fly you to where you want to go. If that sounds alright to you?"

My heart pounds in my chest as I nod. The warmth in my chest spreading down my arms, into my stomach, and dancing along my fingertips.

"That sounds perfect."

THE STORM DOESN'T LET up for three days.

Each one of those days became more precious to me than the jewels littered around this lair. They were each nothing but pure, peaceful bliss. Passing so quickly that when I woke this morning with Lassar's strong body next to mine and did not hear the usual pounding of the rain, a deep sadness clogged my throat.

We had settled into a comfortable routine. Lassar cooks me a delicious breakfast each morning, and then we will explore the cave. He found me a drawing pad, and I will sketch for a few hours. I'm not very good, but Lassar says I show great talent. My sweet, lying dragon.

In the evenings, he will leave to get more supplies, and he no longer chains me up. We spend our nights talking. Sharing stories, mostly from his past. The life he lived as a mortal man. When we first met, he was so animalistic, but now he's almost human again. Well, as human as someone who breathes fire can be.

I don't do much sharing, and Lassar doesn't press me. Mostly, I'm just content with being in his presence. That is more than evident each night when we go to sleep on the floor together. Lassar wraps himself around me, my spine molded to his chest. The first night was strange, but it didn't take long for me to settle.

He hasn't touched me like he did the first night, and I haven't asked him to. I desire his touches, but the longer I've spent in his company, I realize I desire him as well. He's protective of me, caring, and kind. Not since I was a child have I felt this relaxed and looked after. Lassar always makes sure I have exactly what I need. Some would find his attentiveness stifling, but I crave it.

Like now, as he sets down another hot plate of eggs and bacon, sadness takes hold of me as I realize I may never find this attentiveness again if I leave. A human man could never do this, provide for me in this way. Lassar covets me like a treasure in a way only a dragon could.

We eat in silence for a moment as my new feelings war inside me. Lassar seems to be aware of the shift in weather as he picks around the food on his plate.

"The storm seems to have passed," I say softly, my stomach curdling. I am hungry, but I can't bring myself to eat.

Lassar's eyes find mine, and he nods. The loneliness that has been gone from them for the past three days swims in his gaze once more. From the tales he's told me, he is truly alone in this world. Just like me. No one from his past life is alive anymore.

"I should probably get going," I say into the silence. It feels like a mistake to leave. Where will I get comfort like this again? Is my independence worth forsaking this? Having the means to live alone and my own freedom has been the one thing I've craved for so long.

Lassar has me questioning if it would really be so bad to belong to someone else.

My dragon nods his head and collects my plate. I go to the leather bags and begin stuffing them with the items Lassar got me. My eyes burn as I secure the tops. This feels wrong, so incredibly wrong.

When I stand and turn, Lassar is right behind me. Making

me gasp. His large hand comes up to my face, gently rubbing his claws over my cheeks. The look in his eyes is devastatingly soft.

"I wanted to thank you," he says, his voice deep with emotion.

"For what?" I ask; surely I should be the one thanking him. Look at all he's done for me.

"For showing me what it's like to be a man again, for making me remember how wonderful life can be. Over the years, this curse has taken much from me. There was a time when I could barely remember anything beyond my desire for more gold. But no longer." He leans in, pressing his lips against my forehead. Tears leak down my cheeks.

"Getting to know you, my precious Anwyn, was the greatest treasure I have ever found. No gold or jewel or silk could ever compare to you," he says into my hair. With one last kiss to my forehead, he steps back and turns, walking towards the mouth of the cave.

"Lassar, wait!" I shout, his whole body freezing.

Perhaps it's reckless, foolish, or any number of unsavory words, but I don't care. I can't let this end here, not yet.

I do some quick math and speak to Lassar's scaled-back.

"I arrived here four days ago," I say. Lassar slowly turns, nodding his head.

"That means it's the end of the working week." Lassar's brows lower, and inclines his head, clearly not knowing where I'm going. Truthfully, I barely know what's coming out of my mouth at this point. "Finding lodging at the next town might be difficult, as well as getting work on the weekends. Perhaps it would be best if you took me to town at the start of this upcoming week?"

Lassar blinks once, then twice before smiling. The sight makes my heart pound.

"I can take you in two days from now, my Anwyn."

I sigh at the use of *my Anwyn*. It's rare he calls me anything but his: his precious one, his treasure, his Anwyn. I find I rather like his names for me.

Letting my leather bag drop to the floor, I look at Lassar expectantly.

"Since I'm not leaving, what should we do?"

Lassar looks to his right, down a passageway of the cave we have yet to explore together. Raising his hand towards me, I walk forward and take it. His large hand engulfs mine, the scales rubbing against a few callouses I have on my palms. Lassar had lamented at those, saying someone with hands as delicate as mine shouldn't have been forced to work.

I was in total agreement with that.

"There's something I've been wanting to show you. Come."

He leads me deep into the bowels of the cave. The deeper we get, the darker it becomes until the rocks around us are illuminated in faint blue light. I've seen them before, Lassar explained they are some rock formation that glows. It helps guide us along our path until we reach an opening.

I gasp at what I see there. A large pool with still, clear water. The entire thing comprised of those glowing rocks illuminating the water.

Dropping his hand, I venture to the side of the pool. Dipping a finger in, I yelp at the freezing temperature. Lassar lets out a small laugh behind me and then comes to my side. With a deep inhale, he produces a mass of scorching flames. Their heat makes my eyes water. It's not long until the pool is bubbling and steaming, heated by his fire.

"I thought you might like to bathe."

Nodding my head, I can't think of anything better. It's been days since I've bathed, and while I don't think Lassar minds, I certainly do. I watch my dragon pull out a bar of soap and a few hair-cleaning tonics I've only seen in fancy homes.

"From the trader, he said these are the best for fine hair. Your beautiful hair, my Anwyn, deserves only the best."

I blush and nod, lifting the wool dress over my head. I'm standing in only my shift, the humid air causing it to stick to my skin. Lassar looks down at me and growls before quickly turning away.

"I'll leave you to it."

Letting him go would give me an opportunity to think. To be sure this is the decision I truly want to make. But each click of his claws along the stone floor feels like a knife in my heart. It sounds ridiculous, but I've already let this dragon give me an orgasm with his tail.

My sanity has clearly left a long time ago.

"Lassar!" I call. He turns back towards me, and with confident hands, I pull my shift off of my shoulders and let it pool at my feet. Lassar's golden eyes take in every inch of me. His tongue licks over his lips like I want it to lick over me. I see the outline of his cock pressing against his leather pants. My pussy is already turning wet and slippery.

With a small smile on my lips, I meet his stare.

"Bathe with me."

8

LASSAR

Anwyn's golden hair is plastered down her naked back as she hangs onto the pool's edge.

I'm happy my beautiful Anwyn likes this place. I knew she would. I hadn't let myself hope that she'd allow me in here with her. Not yet, at least, but she had. Now my gaze is hungry as it takes in her bare skin. My cock pushes against the front of my leather trousers I still have on as I recall what she looked like, completely naked.

Small breasts and small hips. Her nipples were the same perfect pink as her lips. Her little pussy was hiding beneath a dusting of blonde hair between her thighs. My mouth waters again at the memory. I could eat her whole, but she's not mine yet.

Even though she agreed to stay longer, she still plans to go.

Not yet. I still have time to make her mine, to prove to her that I am worthy. If she doesn't choose me, I'll spend my life following her from the shadows, ensuring she is always safe and cared for.

I should be caring for her right now.

As if my thoughts reached her, Anwyn turns towards me.

Her opal eyes peer over one delicate shoulder. The side of her breast is just visible as both hands are curled beneath her head at the pool's edge. I glide towards her in the water, droplets clinging to my scales.

My precious Anwyn smiles. She picks up the hair tonic next to her and holds it out to me.

"Would you mind washing my hair, Lassar?"

Without a word, I move quickly, snatching up the glass bottles and dumping the contents on her hair and my hands. The lavender and citrus scent fills the space around us. My claws dig into her scalp, scratching and massaging lightly as I clean her silken hair. Even wet, still sparkles in the lowlight. It is a privilege to tend to her like this.

I tell her so.

She moans as I continue to work the tonic into a lather.

"No one has washed my hair since my mother when I was a girl." My claws slide down to her neck, gently rubbing away the tension there too. Anwyn is quiet about her past, but I am as greedy as ever to know more about her. To covet each new piece of information about her like it's a rare jewel.

"Can I ask about your mother?"

Anwyn nods. "She was beautiful and kind. From what I remember, at least, she passed when I was ten. My father loved her so much that he died from a broken heart a year later. At least that's what the town told me." I shrug, emotions clogging my throat. "I barely remember anything from that time."

"And you've been on your own? Since you were ten?"

"Yes. I stayed with a farmer and his family for a few years, but they had too many mouths to feed, and I didn't want to become a burden." Her voice has so much sadness that I can't help but slide closer to her. Letting my wet scales press against her smooth skin, she takes a deep breath. My head comes down on top of hers, and she leans back against me, the round cheeks of her ass cushioning my cock.

I swallow down a hiss as Anwyn continues.

"I moved around from town to town after that. Always on guard, always looking for a new opportunity to exploit. I've seen the worst of people and done things I'm ashamed of to survive."

"You did what you had to," I say, rubbing my claws through her hair again. Anwyn is quiet as I rinse the tonic from her hair. When the suds are gone, she glances over her should at me again, a small smile on her plump lips.

"It's odd that a dragon was the one who made me have faith in humanity again. I've been so relaxed here I feel like my old self."

I suppress the urge to puff out my chest. I've pleased my precious one, I feel like a king.

"I'll always take care of you, Anwyn. Even if you choose to leave, I'll always make sure you're safe." She smiles at me again. Her smooth back is still in front of me, and I gently drape her long hair over her shoulder, exposing the expanse of it. Taking the bar of soap, I rub it along her skin until it's soapy. Using my hands, I work out the stiff muscles in her back.

Anwyn moans, tilting her head to the side.

"I'm ashamed of the man I used to be. How could I have been so selfish and arrogant? Consumed by my own greed as to enter into a bargain with a demon and to be cursed to live in this monstrous form." My hands press more firmly into a particularly tight muscle. "I thought it was a death sentence, and in some ways it was. But now..."

My hands still on her back, emotions weighing down on me.

"But now what?" Anwyn asks, her opal eyes curious.

"But now, I think it was a blessing. As I said, I never would've met you otherwise, and if by some chance we had when I was human, I wouldn't have been worthy of you. My greed would've blinded me to the treasure you truly are. Now, like this, I see what you are, who you are to me. And I must protect you with everything that I am. This curse has given me the power to do so, and for that alone, I will be grateful to the demon I once hated."

I rinse the soap off her back. Anwyn is quiet for a few moments until she turns from the edge. Treading water, her beautiful breasts are bared towards me. Her hard nipples skim the top of the water, her eyes gazing into mine. She's so gorgeous I have to look away, her body too decadent for these monstrous eyes.

"Lassar," she calls gently. Her hand finds mine in the water, wrapping around my wrist. My head turns back towards her; her eyes are darker than I've ever seen them. They could lure me to my death, and I'd go willingly. "Lassar, touch me. Please."

A need to claim pounds in my veins, but I am gentle with my precious Anwyn as I grip her around the hips and set her on the edge of the pool. She gasps as her warm skin meets the cool stone floor. She bites her lip, her hands going to my shoulders. With her like this, we are almost the same height.

My claws skim up her sides before cupping her breasts. She arches back as her own hands explore my body. I memorize every detail of my treasure, from the freckle on the side of her left breast to the faded scar on her right shoulder. Letting my tongue slip from my mouth, I lick over the raised skin, and she shivers.

She is delicious. I can't believe she's letting me touch her like this.

Anwyn's hands skim over my chest, tickling my scales there. Her fingers dip into my back muscles, pulling me closer to her.

"You're so warm, Lassar. It's like there's fire in your blood." Her thighs open, releasing the sweetest scent from her cunt. She's wet, I can smell it. I'm desperate for a taste. Her legs wrap around my waist, the heat of her pussy cradles my cock through my pants, and my control snaps. The feeling of her wet flesh unleashes the monster inside of me.

"Can I kiss you, my precious Anwyn?" My hold on my beast is breaking, but I will not fail her now. Not when she has shown me this trust. I need to hear my precious one say that she wants me.

Her smile is mischievous, her cheeks rosy from the warm water.

"Only if you promise to do a lot more than just kiss me."

I growl, the sound echoing around us.

"Be sure of what you ask me, my precious one. I've been holding myself back for days. I don't want to scare you with the depth of my desire for you."

The thought of her being frightened of me makes my stomach turn. Anwyn merely smiles wider. Her hands trace down my chest again, down the hard plane of my stomach until they reach the lacing of my trousers. With one small finger, she runs along my bulging cock.

My breathing is coming in pants as she tilts her mouth up, her lips dancing over mine.

"I wouldn't ask for it if I wasn't sure I could take it. All of it."

With a broken groan, I slam my mouth on hers. She opens for me like a flower; her moans are like honey on my tongue. My claws rake over her, kneading her breasts, skimming down her back, and grabbing her ass. She moans for me, wrapping her arms around my neck to pull me in closer. Her little cunt continues to rub against me.

I drag the scales on my chest against her nipples, and she gasps, her greedy pussy soaking me with more sweetness. Grabbing her ass harder, I pull her even tighter against me. My tongue slips into her mouth, tasting her fully. It tangles with her smaller one, gentle at first. Then I'm feasting on her. I break the kiss to focus my attention on her neck.

My tongue skims up the side of it as she grinds against me.

"Your pussy is so wet, my Anwyn. Is it wet for me? For the dragon who caught you?"

Anwyn sighs, her head lulling back. Something about me reminding her how I got her makes her work her hips faster against me. My hand slips down to her soaking wet pussy. Her flesh is warm and soft as I run a claw through her slit.

"Well? Tell me, Anwyn. Tell me why you are so wet."

"You," she pants. "You made me ache like this. Now you need to take care of it."

I smile against her neck. Take care of it, I will. I will be the only one who serves this sweet pussy. If any man or creature even dared to smell her, I'd kill them. Scorch their corpses. The monster inside me agrees.

Gliding my finger through her folds, I work her clit in tight circles. Her muscles go tight, and her mouth opens as she looks at me. Her opal eyes are hazy, lost in pleasure.

"I'll soothe you, my precious one. I know just what you need."

"Please," she begs.

My tail comes out of the water and gently pushes at her shoulders, urging her to lay back on the stone floor. The blue lights around us cast her wet body in the most beautiful glow. Like this, she is a feast I plan on devouring.

But I need my Anwyn to know what this means. If I have her this way, no one else ever will.

"Are you going to let me lick your cunt, my Anwyn?" She nods her head furiously.

"I'll be the only one who's ever tasted you, isn't that right?" Again she nods, too consumed with the need to come to answer. "No one else will ever see your pussy. Or I'd have to kill them. Wicksome wanted you, wanted my treasure, and I killed him. I'd do it to anyone who covets what's mine. Do you understand, my precious one? You are mine. Mine to keep, mine to protect, mine to fuck."

"Yes," she says. "I only want you. Taste me. I ache for you."

"I want you to soak my face. Cover it in your come." I lean down, smiling against her wet flesh. "Then I'm going to make you lick it off of me."

Anwyn screams as my tongue parts her folds. Her cunt is so pink and pretty, glistening in the glowing lights. Using my hands, I gently pull her folds apart to see all of her. I run my tongue from her asshole to her clit, and she squirms.

Holding her open like this, I spit into her entrance, watching the saliva pool there. Soon my seed will run out of this hole, but not yet. Tucking my claw just inside her, Anwyn moans. My blood is on fire, rushing in my veins as her cunt grips my finger.

"You're so tight, my precious one. Going to have to go slow at first, but you'll take my cock, won't you? I'll just have to make sure my Anwyn is soaking wet first." I laugh as more of her arousal soaks my hand. "That shouldn't be a problem. You're soaking me now."

"Lassar, please, stop playing with me."

I can't help it. When it comes to Anwyn, I need her so worked up, delirious in her need for me, that I consume all her thoughts. That she knows I'm the only one who can satisfy her like this. She likes it too. I can tell that by the arousal seeping out of her little pussy.

I breathe on her heated skin, her calves coming to rest on my shoulders.

"Do you remember when you told me all you knew of dragons was their perchance for stealing princess?"

"Y-y—yes."

"In all of the stories, did you ever read what happens when a dragon captures a princess he has no wish to return?"

"N—no. I don't think those would make very good children's tales."

I laugh against her, licking her clit with the broad side of my tongue.

"They wouldn't." My tongue licks over her pussy again. "You said you weren't a princess, my Anwyn, but I don't think that's true. Your pussy is sweeter than any wine and worth more than a million golden bars. Kings would wage war over you, and I will lay siege to anyone who dares come for you."

"Lassar," she moans, her hard nipples thrusting into the air.

"This dragon has caught you, and he's keeping you." I stare deep into her glassy eyes. "Now let's see if you come like a princess."

My tongue glides over her, sucking on her clit while simultaneously dipping into her entrance. Her hands cup her breasts, but I push them away and replace them with my own, rolling her nipple between my fingers. Her body grows tighter, more delicious nectar leaks from her, and I'm eager to lap it all up.

"Lassar, it's too much. I'm going to—I can't—"

"You're going to take it. You have no choice, I own you. When I want to lick your cunt until you pass out from pleasure, I will." I growl against her, the vibrations causing her hips to rise. "When I want to fuck you, spill my seed deep inside you until you swell with my child I will."

Children were something I mourned, along with my humanity. But the thought of Anwyn, swollen with my child, has me feasting on her cunt with more vigor.

"Lassar, I'm—"

"I think there are better uses for your mouth, my precious one."

I slip my tail up her chin, pushing it past her lips. Her mouth is warm and wet as she closes her lips around the tip of my tail. Thrusting it in and out of her mouth like I would my cock, Anwyn licks and sucks. Her mouth makes obscenely sloppy sounds. Sliding it down her throat bit by bit until I bump the back of it. My precious one coughs, her eyes watering as I retreat. Spit dribbles out of her mouth and coats my tail.

Her teeth gently graze my tail, sending a shiver down my spine. I have to will myself not to come in my pants, but my control is shattering.

"Naughty girl," I admonish. Sucking her clit into my mouth once more, I slip a finger into her entrance. My head spins at the perfect tightness of her. The way her cunt strangles one finger and then a second. Hooking them inside her gently, I fuck her with them. Careful not to go too deep. The barrier of her virginity will only be broken on my cock.

She grinds her hips against my hand, fucking herself on my fingers. All the while, her hands hold onto my tail, pumping it in and out of her small mouth. My Anwyn was perfect before, but now...there are no words.

Her body goes tight, and she's close to coming, I know just the thing that will send her over. Pulling my tail from her mouth, I slip it down her body. My fingers pump her, and my mouth works her clit. With one slight nudge, my tail slips past the tight ring of muscle of her ass, and Anwyn screams.

The sound echoes around us as she shakes through her orgasm. Her back arches clean off the floor, her legs trembling on my shoulder. There are red marks all over her from my claws, teeth, and scales, and I growl with possessiveness.

Her come flows out of her, covering my chin as I rush to catch all of it in my tongue. Anwyn grabs my face and grinds herself against it, her clit bumping up against my nose. Once I've licked every drop, I pull back, watching her small body shaking with aftershocks.

"You don't come like a princess," I say, trailing kisses up her chest and neck. "You come like my naughty human captive. A dirty little girl who spreads her legs for the dragon who caught her."

Anwyn blushes.

"I'm only naughty for you," she says in a soft voice. I laugh and kiss her lips, sharing her taste with her.

"I suppose I should forgive my naughty girl?" She nods her head.

"Please, I'll be good."

"How are you going to do that?" My hand cups her pussy, which is already growing wet again.

"By keeping my promise." Her soft pink tongue licks up my chin and lips. Licking me clean of her come, just like I told her she would. My Anwyn, a gift I don't deserve.

I cup her cheek, enjoying the high of playing these games but needing to make sure she's alright.

"Are you well? Do you need anything?"

She shakes her head but then shivers. Scooping her up, I carry her body back toward my lair. Quickly, I get the fire going as I lay her down in the pallet of silk and pillows. She spreads out on the sheet like a queen. Her eyes calling me back to her.

"Are you hungry? Thirsty?" I ask, kneeling beside her. "I'll make you some food."

Anwyn grabs my arm before I can stand.

"The only thing I need right now is you." I never thought I'd hear those words from her lips. A broken groan escapes me.

Anwyn guides me between her legs again. I am careful not to give her my full weight. Her hand trails down my stomach and unlaces the fly of my leather pants. It's not long before her curious hand is holding my cock, stroking it. I growl into her neck, pumping my hips into her fist.

I don't need to see her to know she's smiling as she whispers, "My turn."

9

———

ANWYN

Lassar is everywhere as I hold him in my hand.

His claws skim over every inch of my naked skin. Just like in the pool, the sensation causes goosebumps to break out along my body. What he did to me then lit a fire inside of me. I've never experienced the type of pleasure I felt at the hands of my dragon. No human man could do what he did to me. I know that in my heart.

The silk beneath me is cool against my hot skin.

His mouth consumes mine. Over and over, his lips press into mine. They're scaled texture is rough, while his forked tongue is soft as it tangles with mine. He tastes like fire, smoky and heady and I want to drown in it. I give his cock a tentative stroke. I've never done anything like this, but I know human men are not this well-endowed. Or covered in soft ridges that mimic the scales on his body.

I shiver as Lassar lets out a groan.

"Does my cock please you, my Anwyn?" he asks. I nod my head. "Say it."

"Your cock pleases me, Lassar," I pant, his mouth sucking on my neck, biting the skin gently.

"Pleases you enough that you're going to open your pretty thighs for me? Going to let me fill you with every inch of it? Even if it's a tight fit?" His claws knead my breasts as my hand continues to explore his shaft. Our mingling growls and moans echo around us in the lair.

"Even if it hurts, Lassar," I say, meeting his eyes.

"You're so perfect, my Anwyn. My most precious treasure. Now that I've found you, I'll never let you go. I'll have claimed you forever once I fill you with my seed." His tongue licks over my ear, causing me to shiver. "I already own your pussy. Now I'm going to own your heart."

Lassar gives my earlobe a gentle bite before kissing down my neck again. He's not wrong. Something changed between us while we were at the pool. It should frighten me, but it doesn't. I can't live a solitary life anymore, now that I know Lassar exists. I thought I wanted independence, but I don't, I want to be owned. Kept and cared for by the dragon whose claw is running through the wetness pooled between my legs.

I'll let him own me, but I want to own him too.

His mouth returns to mine, and we are a flurry of teeth and tongues again. My hand slips from his pants and helps shove the garment down. We break the kiss as I get my first glimpse of his cock in the dim light of the cave. My mouth goes dry.

Feeling it was one thing, but seeing it is quite another. It's the same green shade as the rest of his body. It hangs heavy between us, a bead of white moisture already at the tip. I want to taste it, to feel those ridges against my tongue.

Lassar did say he'd always give me what I need. Right now, I need his cock in my mouth.

I nudge his shoulders, and Lassar pulls me with him as he lies on his back. His wings have spread out behind him on the silk sheet. My naked front fits along his scaled body. I marvel at our size difference, my head resting under his chin while my toes barely graze his knees. Sliding up his body, I press a soft kiss to his lips, his yellow eyes wide as I grip his cock in my hand.

"My precious one," he groans as I tug on him, running my palm along the soft scales of his shaft.

"Yes, my dragon?" I smile as I kiss him again. He makes me feel powerful. Who knew being captured could be so freeing?

Lassar's tongue licks over my lips. More of his come seeps onto my hand and the soft skin of my stomach where his cock is trapped between us. Over and over, I pump him until he is thrusting into my hand. Even his wings grow tight at my movements.

"You are too perfect, my Anwyn. I don't deserve you."

My cheeks heat, and my pussy turns even wetter. I jerk him one more time before shuffling down his body. Kissing each scaled muscle as I go until I get to his monstrous cock.

"I've never," he pants, "I've never laid with a woman in this form."

"Good," I say, licking up the wetness at the tip of his cock. His taste explodes along my tongue, and I instantly want more. "We'll be each other's first time."

"Each other's only time," Lassar growls, his tail skimming up the inside of my thighs. He wants a declaration from me. And I will give him one soon. For now, I take his cock fully into my mouth as an answer.

Slowly, I drag my tongue along his shaft, gliding over the rough texture. His skin is warm and salty and all mine. Saliva leaks from my mouth and coats his length. Pulling my mouth from him for a moment, I spit into my hand and use it to pump him as I wrap my lips around him once more. Lassar's claws fist my hair as his growls swirl around us.

"Pretty, pretty, Anwyn. How beautiful you look with your mouth around my cock." I moan around him, the vibrations causing him to groan again. "I'm going to fuck your mouth like it's your pussy. Going to come down your throat and watch you swallow it."

I moan again, and this time I feel something glide along my pussy. The blunt head of Lassar's tail nudges my fold, gently caressing my clit. I double my efforts, sucking him deeper into my mouth until he nudges the back of my throat. My eyes water, and I cough, but that only adds to the slickness. My hand and mouth work him together as his hips thrust into my mouth.

"This is what you wanted, my Anwyn. This is what brought you to my cave. You knew I'd give you the fucking that you need. First your throat and then your pussy." His hands tighten on my head, pulling it up to meet his eyes. "It won't take long for you to let me have your ass either, my precious one."

Before I register what's happening, his tail slips into my ass. It pushes gently passed the tight ring of muscle, and I squeal. The sensation is overwhelming and perfect and something I want to experience for the rest of my life. I'm close to coming, and I need Lassar with me.

Pulling my mouth from his cock, I jerk him roughly in my hand as his tail slides in and out of my ass. Our eyes lock, and I bite my lip, the tip of his cock inches from my lips.

"Come in my mouth, Lassar. Come all over me, I want to be covered in your seed. I need it." With one more harsh tug, I smile. "And then I want you to fuck me so hard I won't be able to move afterward. I want to lay in front of the fire while your seed leaks out of me from everywhere."

Lassar groans, his abs tightening, and I know he's coming. His tail pushes deeper into my ass, and my body locks up. Flames lick up my skin as my muscles tighten. All I can do is suction my mouth to his cock and swallow down his release while my body shakes through my climax.

I swallow and swallow until it leaks from the sides of my mouth down my chin. Pulling back, I make sure Lassar is watching as I lick my lips, tasting every bit of him. He groans, his eyes heating as a few more splashes of come paint my breasts.

My arousal coats my thighs as I crawl up his body, straddling his stomach as I kiss him. His claws rake over my body, squeezing my ass. Our kiss is slow and tender and full of emotion. My body is tired, but I don't want to stop. I need him, all of him.

"Are you alright, my Anwyn? Sleepy?" I simply shake my head at his question.

"I'm ready for more," I say, resting my elbows on his chest.

"More?" He curls a lock of hair around one claw. A few of the strands tangle in his scales. I place a kiss on his chest and nod before sliding off of him and laying out on the silk blanket. My skin is sweaty and sticky from his release. Lassar can wash me later. Right now I need to have him inside me.

Spreading my legs for him, he crawls towards me and settles between them.

"Anwyn—"

"I want you inside me." I bite my lip and curl my arms around his neck. "More than that, I want to give myself to you. I'm your treasure, right?"

"Yes," he growls immediately.

"Then I want you to enjoy your treasure fully. You have full control over me, do with me what you want."

Lassar's eyes darken as he stares down at me. It's a dark desire, one I'd never give to another but Lassar. He won't hurt me, I truly believe that. I've always had to be the one with a plan, making decisions. Having someone who I can give my body, my heart, my trust and know that he won't abuse that power? It's heady and what I've just given to my dragon.

"Anwyn, you trust me? I've finally earned your trust?"

"Yes," I say, pulling him down for a kiss. "Now own me."

Lassar snarls. His claws scoop me up and hold me to his

chest. My hard nipples rub against his scales. As does my pussy, covering him in my arousal. I can't get enough. My body craves the connection. Lassar's tongue licks over my ear, his hot breath tickling me.

"Do whatever I want with you, my sweet Anwyn. You have no idea what you're asking for." His claws skim up my sides and circle around my back. "But I'm going to show you."

Lassar stomps us over to the stalactite on the floor. The golden shackles are still hanging from them. It wasn't that long ago I was contemplating his death while attached to them. Now, as he locks both my wrists to them again above my head, I realize I'm going to let him fuck me in them.

A delicious shiver runs through me.

Lassar sits back on his heels, his tail flicking wildly, as he takes in the long expanse of my naked body. With my arms bound like this, I can't touch him. I'm completely at his mercy, just like I wanted. I don't feel scared giving him this control. A part of me, a part I never knew existed, settles at the thought of being owned by him fully.

"Look at you, my precious one." His claws graze down my chest, circling around one nipple. "Laid out before me like a feast. Your sopping wet pussy is begging for my cock."

"Please, Lassar," I whine.

"Shh," he says, squeezing my breast before leaning down and licking my hard nipple. "When I'm done with you, Anwyn, there won't be a single piece of you I don't own. Look around you, look at all the treasure I've hoarded, and know this. I would sell it all—burn it all—to keep you."

I moan as his other claw goes to my pussy, gently rubbing my clit. The shackles clink as I flex my hands, desperate to hold on to something.

"I scare everyone in this cursed form. But I don't scare you, Anwyn. Your pink cunt is soaking my hand, demanding I fuck it." His finger enters me in shallow thrusts. The sloppy wet sounds of my arousal cause my thighs to clench. "I'll be fucking it every day for the rest of your life. It doesn't matter if you leave to live a normal life, I'll find you. Burn your home down and fuck you in the ashes. Do you understand?"

I cry out as he slips another finger inside of me. Lassar's never spoken to me like this, and it should scare me. It has the opposite effect as I feel my arousal coating the inside of my thighs. I want what he's saying, I want to know that if I did leave, he would come for me and bring me back here. That I truly do belong to him.

"Y—yes!" I shout as his fingers continue to pump me over and over again. Lassar slides between my thighs as he pulls his fingers from me. I watch through heavy lids as he grips his massive cock in his hands and rubs it through my wetness. I sigh as he drags those ridges along my clit.

"You're mine, precious one. Mine, say it." The head of his cock pushes into me, and my body tenses. I already feel full, and he's barely inside me. My hands tangle in the gold chains.

"Say it, Anwyn," Lassar demands again, giving me another few inches before retreating. My legs curl around his hips, holding me tightly to him. Lassar rears back to give me another few inches.

"Say i—"

"I'm yours!" I cry, raising my hips to meet his thrust and sealing him fully inside me. There's a pinch of pain from being stretched so wide. Lassar doesn't move, only breathes hard as he stares down at me. My own chest is rising and falling in time with my wild heartbeat. His hand cups my cheek, his claw pushing into my mouth where I suck the tip of it.

Lassar groans, slipping his hand down my throat and collaring me there. His touch is light but controlling all the same. I love it.

"You don't know how beautiful you look like this. My claw around your throat; your tight little pussy wrapped around my cock." Lassar gives my throat a gentle squeeze. "Are you alright, my precious one? Is my cock too much for you?"

I shake my head, the pain stopping and a deep desire for my dragon to fuck me like he promised.

"I need more, Lassar. I need you to fuck my pussy, to own me, I'll die without it."

It's euphoric, not just the feeling of being stretched by him but to be able to admit my desires to him. This dragon owns me, and I want him to enjoy every bit of it as much as I know I will.

"My beautiful Anwyn wants me to fuck her?" Lassar's hips pull back before he slams back into me. My breasts bounce in time with his thrust. "The little human who stumbled into my cave now opens her legs for me. Begs me to ravage her pretty cunt and fill it with my seed."

Lassar fucks me even harder. His hands hold up my hips to get an even deeper angle. The soft scales of his cock graze my inside walls, the sensation making my toes curl. My mouth hangs open as I moan with each delicious thrust.

"There's no mention of dragons fucking the human princess they capture in your stories, Anwyn. We can make our own story." His tongue slips out of his mouth and licks over each of my nipples. "They'll tell our story in every town. The human girl on the run and the dragon who captured her. Every day he provides for her, kills all those who would come for her, and at night she thanks him with her beautiful pussy. Letting him use it and fill it over and over until she grows round with his child."

I groan, my hands yanking hard against the shackles. I'm surprised they don't rip from the stone.

"That's your legacy Anwyn. To live as the dragon's pampered fucktoy. His ultimate treasure. That's what you want, isn't it?"

"Yes! I want it!"

"I'll always give you what you want." His lips come down on mine, and our tongues tangle as he powers into me over and over. My body tightens, and my thighs begin to quiver. His thrusts turn more frantic. I feel his tail glide through the cheeks of my ass before pressing into me there.

That's all it takes, the sensation of him filling both my holes at once as my climax barreling into me. My body erupts into flames as my heart pounds in my chest. I scream his name into the cave, the sound echoing throughout. My pussy clamps down on his cock as if it knows what's coming next.

Lassar is quick to follow, his body freezing before he gives me one more thrust. His hot seed fills me, leaking out from my pussy and sliding down towards my ass. My dragon fucks it into me, making sure I have every drop.

"My precious Anwyn, my beautiful Anwyn. Tell me you're mine for as long as I can have you. Tell me your mine for eternity," he murmurs, pressing kisses to my open mouth.

Reaching up, he unshackles my wrists, my arms falling limp to my sides. My whole body is trembling. Lassar holds me to his chest, carrying me over to the pallet on the floor. He doesn't set me on it. He keeps me in his arms, his chin resting on top of my head.

His request still lingers between us. There's so much that I want to tell him, but my body is exhausted. In the morning, I'll share everything that's in my heart, but right now, I just need him to hold me. My whole world has changed in this cave, and I don't fear it.

As my eyelids close, I'm able to slur one last word before the darkness consumes me.

"Forever."

10

ANWYN

These past two days have gone by in a blur.

Since the first time Lassar took me, it has been a nonstop cycle of fucking. The comfortable routine we had before has changed slightly. Now, every morning he wakes me with his head between my legs, his tail gently pushing into my entrance or my ass, depending on his mood. He makes me come with his tongue and then with his cock, pushing into me and fucking me while my screams echo through the cave.

Then he feeds me breakfast before we return to bed. Sometimes he will shackle me or tie my hands with silk fabric and make me ride him. We don't stop until we're both exhausted, and my stomach growls. Lassar then cooks me a filling meal before we start touching each other again. It's not long before I'm on my back, and he's inside of me, filling me with more of his seed.

As I lay in the silk sheets now, his come from last night is still drying on me. This morning is different as I pat the sheet next to me and don't find my dragon. Perhaps he has gone to get more food? Our supplies were dwindling last night, and he couldn't pull himself away from me long enough to get any more.

The thought makes me smile. As absurd as all of this is, I can't deny the truth. I'm falling in love with a dragon. He makes sure I'm safe and cared for. He fucks me without mercy. Lassar is everything I need, but more importantly, he's everything I want. I've been meaning for us to have a conversation, but there hasn't been much time for talking.

When he gets back, I'll make time for it, I want him to know how I feel.

Stretching my arms above my head, I realize just how sore I am. Every muscle aches, and there is a dull throb between my legs. I need another bath, but I don't want to wash Lassar from my skin. Each time he fucks me, he makes sure I'm soaked with him. I remember his words from our first time together about making me round with his child. My hand rests on my stomach.

We haven't taken any precautions. Could I really get pregnant by a dragon? What would that even look like? I can't say that the thought doesn't appeal to me. I missed out on my family, I would love to be able to have my own with Lassar.

I'm due to get my courses in the next week. If they come, then I'll start on the contraceptive herb, and if they don't, I guess Lassar will have to share me sooner than he anticipated. A giggle bursts from my lips as I flop back down on the silk sheets.

It's quiet outside the cave, sunlight filtering in between a few of the rocks. Maybe Lassar and I can explore *The Woods* together today. Fuck outside for a change.

Movement sounds at the mouth of the cave, and the sound of Lassar's claws along the stone floor has my pussy heating. I'm addicted to him. I push up onto my elbows and watch him enter into the lair. His eyes find mine, and I smile, but his face remains serious.

Looking at the bags in his hands, my brows furrow. One is filled with supplies, while the other is empty. Lassar looks at the floor, his shoulder hunching.

"This bag will be able to hold a substantial amount of gold coins. Enough to buy a house should you need it. I got you some new dresses as well, in case if you end up somewhere warmer, the wool of the others will be too thick."

My heart pounds in my chest.

"Am I going somewhere?" Lassar's shoulders grow tighter at my question.

"The weather is mild today, perfect for flying. My offer to take you where you want to go next still stands."

My mouth falls open. Oh, my sweet dragon, how can he think I'd want to leave him? We hadn't discussed my staying outside of the declarations given during our lovemaking. What I said then stands now. I'm staying with him forever.

I'll just have to show him that I mean it.

Rising from the floor, I let the silk sheet fall from my naked body. Lassar's eyes lift from the ground and take in my body. My hard nipples, my thighs still coated in his come, and my wet pussy that is begging for his attention. I pad over to him. His chest rises and falls. His wings spread out behind him.

When I'm right in front of him, I push onto my toes and kiss his mouth.

"I'm not going anywhere, Lassar. I'm staying here with you forever."

Lassar growls, his hands gripping my head. Our kiss deepens, his rich flavor exploding in my mouth. Our tongues tangle together. He walks me backward but I stop him. I want him to fuck me, but not yet. I want to show him that I meant every word I just said.

Sinking to my knees before him, I undo the lacings of his leather pants.

"You've given me everything I could ever need. Let me show

you how much I want to be owned by you." I groan as his cock springs free. Reaching behind me, I grip an overstuffed pillow and kneel on top of it. To cushion my knees but also to give me some height and position his cock right at my lips. There's a bead of come at the tip that I lick off.

"My precious girl. You. Are. Mine." Lassar growls each word.

"Yours," I agree before taking him fully into my mouth. My tongue glides along his soft scales. My hand pumps him into my mouth. His length bumps the back of my throat as his claws cradle my head. I bob up and down on his cock, saliva coating him. His hands tighten in my hair.

"My Anwyn sucks my cock like she was born to do it. Were you, precious one?"

"Yes." The word is muffled with his cock still half down my throat.

I work him over and over again. His hips moved in time with my mouth. He grabs fistfuls of my hair to hold me steady as he fucks my mouth. Mercilessly until I'm gagging, my eyes water in response.

"This throat is mine, I'll fuck it how I want, and you'll take it. Until I slip down your tight little throat."

I nod my head as he continues to pump into me.

"I'm going to come, Anwyn. Keep your eyes open. I want you to see what you do to me." I keep my eyes wide as I watch Lassar lose control above me. His movements become sloppy until his body locks up, and he spills down my throat. I swallow his seed, loving the taste of it before he pulls himself from my lips and coats my breasts with his come. It's warm as it lands on my skin.

Running my finger through it on my chest, I lick it clean as we lock eyes.

"I love that you were willing to let me go, Lassar if that was still what I wanted to do. That's why I'm yours. You're the only one who's ever cared this much about me. Ever wanted ~~to~~ me this much. I love that, I crave it. Almost as much as I love you."

Lassar's eyes go wide, his whole body ridged. He doesn't say anything for a moment. I wait for his reply as he stomps off. My brows lower as I watch him dig through a pile of gold. The coins hit the stone floor with soft clinks before he returns back over to me.

He crouches down before me to show me what he's collected. It's a simple gold band. My eyes water as he holds it out to me.

"My precious Anwyn, I was a cursed creature before I found you. I thought I would spend forever miserable and greedy. Now that's all changed. I have you, my Anwyn, and you require this form in order for me to keep you safe. You are my human captive, my most precious treasure." Lassar snags my hand and slips the ring on my left hand. "You are my wife, I declare it to be so. You are my everything Anwyn, just like I am yours."

My laugh is water as I loop my arms around his neck. It's unorthodox, it's strange, but I've never lived a normal life. This is perfect. Lassar is everything to me. I don't see the future as uncertain or something I'll have to navigate my way through. My future is with Lassar, and it's filled with love and happiness.

Our mouths meet, and Lassar lifts me. He carries me and sets me back down on the silk sheets. He settles me on my back, but I smile, gently pushing at his shoulders. Lassar obliges me, and I crawl in front of him. He growls as I walk on all fours and thrust my ass out towards him.

He loves having me on my hands and knees. My dragon moves behind me, his claws holding me firmly by the waist. I look over my shoulder and watch his fork tongue slip from his mouth. Lassar buries his face into me from behind. He licks my clit and my entrance with broad strokes of his tongue.

Over and over, he licks me until I'm moaning, my hands fist the sheets below me. His tongue slips out from my entrance and licks my asshole, dipping just inside. It's decadent and obscene. It's wrong, but the pleasure is too good.

"I'll fuck this little hole soon enough." Lassar's claws spread my cheeks open, his tongue licking me over and over again. My pussy is so wet my arousal is running down my thighs. Lassar's claws return to my hips and hoist me up.

He gives no warning before he plunges inside of me. My back arches as I moan. He's so deep this way, the scales of his cock sliding along my inner walls until I'm panting. Like this, he's able to hit a spot deep inside me, making my toes curl. His clawed hand smacks down on my ass, and I feel heat bloom there. His tail slips between us to rub my clit. It's too much. It always is from this angle.

Now slick with my arousal, his tail slithers down to my ass. I cry out as it begins to enter me there. The stretch from his tail and his cock feel like I'm being split in half. I don't dare tell him to stop.

"Look at you. Both of your holes being filled—"

There's a noise from the mouth of the cave that has both of us freezing. Lassar stops pumping into me as the sounds get closer. It's voices. At least a dozen different ones. Lassar's hands snag my waist as he snarls. One voice is clearer than the others. My mouth opens when I recognize who it belongs to.

Mrs. Hitherbend.

"Dragon!" she yells. "We know you killed Mr. Wicksome and have the girl. Let her go, and there will be no trouble."

Lassar growls again.

"Stay here, my precious one. I'll deal with whoever has dared to enter our cave."

Lassar moves to pull out of me, but I reach back, holding him still. I don't want violence to come to these people. I'm sure my dragon won't think twice about burning their bodies. Mrs. Hitherbend was kind to me in her own way. I don't want her to meet the same fate as that evil Wicksome.

"Don't stop fucking me just because they're here," I say, encouraging him to move within me once more.

"But Anwyn, I need to make you safe. I—"

"Oh, dear gods!" Mrs. Hitherbend cries as she enters the lair. The ten people from the village she brought with her also pause in shock. One could think it was because of all the immense wealth right in front of their eyes. However, something tells me their shock is coming from seeing me being mounted by a massive green dragon.

"Let her go, you foul creature!" A few of the townspeople point pitchforks and torches at Lassar. He snarls at them, but I grip his hand on my waist. My eyes meet Mrs. Hitherbend as I shake my head.

Lassar begins to move inside of me, and the townsfolk gasp in horror.

"Sweet child, we've come to save you from this beast. Look at how he defiles her!" she shrieks towards the townspeople. "I went to that doctor you told me about, and he's helped me remember things. I know you aren't my sister's, but I can't let you be this creature's plaything."

"I chose this," I moan as Lassar hits that deep spot inside of me again. His claw wraps around the back of my neck, holding me down as he pounds in and out of me. My body is fully covered by the sheet and the pillows, but the scene before them is clear.

"You should be happy for me, Mrs. Hitherbend. I did what you said," I pant as Lassar doubles his efforts. His tail moves at the same punishing rhythm in my ass. Our skin slapping together echoes around the townspeople. "I found a man I love to take care of me."

"Child, this beast—"

"Has taken her from all of you. She is mine," Lassar growls, his tail plunging in even deeper into my ass, making me moan. "Look at how she screams for me. Hear how wet her pussy is.

She loves this, loves being owned by this beast. Tell them, my Anwyn."

"Yes! I love it, I need it." His hand smacks my ass again.

"She's so hungry for my cock, I wake in the middle of the night to find her slipping me inside of her. Insatiable, my little human." I moan. It's true I need him all the time. "I wear myself out in this little cunt every day. Just like I will for the rest of our lives. You can't take her from me. She's mine."

I should be appalled at the words he's saying, but I find myself craving more of them. I want them to know he owns me. This is what they need to hear, so they'll never come looking for me again. I never want to see another person beyond Lassar for the rest of my life. He's all I need, and I'm ready to seal my fate.

"My dragon, I'm close. Come inside me, I need more of your seed."

Mrs. Hitherbend looks pale, as do the townsfolk around her. Lassar's hand on my neck pushes me down onto the floor. I'm completely helpless as he ruts into me at a punishing pace. I feel him breathe in deeply before the smell of fire permeates the air.

I look up in time to see the flames he's roared at the townspeople. Not enough to hurt them but enough to have them scurrying away.

"Leave and never come back, Anwyn is mine!"

My body tightens, both my holes clamping around his cock and tail. His clawed hand slips to my throat and pulls me up, his tongue running along my spine.

"No one but me gets to watch you come," he growls.

"Forever?" I ask.

"Forever." I'm helpless to do anything but obey. My body is awash in pleasure as he fills me to the brim with more seed.

EPILOGUE

LASSAR

5 Years Later

My beautiful wife is being naughty.

Does she think I can't smell her sweet scent on the wind as I soar above the trees? I returned to our cottage only moments ago, expecting to find her just as I left her. Relaxing in our bed where I could feed her before fucking her again like I had this morning. She prefers to stay indoors when I have to venture into town.

I typically travel into town under the cover of night with a dark hood in order to prevent giving the sellers there such a fright. However, my Anwyn has been craving oranges, and the trader who sells them was only passing through town today. I slipped him a little extra coin, and my scaly skin and claws were soon forgotten.

Those oranges now sit abandoned in our cottage while I search for my wife. We left the cave a few months after our mating. Anwyn had gotten her courses and decided to start taking the contraceptive herbs. While getting her pregnant would've been a joy, it just wasn't the right time for us.

Instead, we decided to move deeper into *The Woods*. Somewhere remote but close enough to a town for me to get the things my Anwyn needs. Those early months were heady. I barely left her thighs long enough to feed her. Our love is less frenzied now but nonetheless all-consuming. Recently it's been ramping up again at Anwyn's insistence, and I will never deny her pleasure. Each moment we spend together, we somehow sink deeper into our feelings for each other.

Every day that I've spent with Anwyn, she has become more and more beautiful. My gold helped us buy the supplies for the cottage and will keep us and whatever children we may have in the future comfortable for the rest of our lives.

This curse has given me the perfect life, and I never thought I'd ever be grateful for it. But I am.

I growl as I see a flash of blue from below. Swooping down, I swallow a snarl as I see the blue dress Anwyn was wearing earlier hanging from a tree. We are deep in the woods as I begin my descent toward my wife. There is a meadow bursting with all types of beautifully colored flowers off to the side. They all pale in comparison to the beauty of my precious one.

She is oblivious to my approach, completely naked and spread out atop a silk blanket. Even though I've tasted every inch of her skin, and been inside her countless times, when I see her like this, it's just like seeing her for the first time.

Silently, I creep up beside her. Moving quickly, I cover her mouth and pin her to the ground. The setting sun illuminates her golden hair, making it blend into the silk sheet. Her opal eyes are wide with surprise as she screams into my hand. It's not long before they lower, joy replacing the surprise.

"I've caught you, my precious one. The dragon has you now. No ransom will be enough for me to give you back." Anwyn moans into my hand. I slip between her thighs, her pussy soaking through my leather pants to tease my cock. She's so perfect. It's a mystery she's real.

Anwyn raises her hips to drag her pink cunt along my cock, needing the friction. She loves this game we play. Her the helpless captive, and me the dragon who's come to claim her. It's because she knows that she holds all the power between us. I live for her, I breathe for her, and that's how I gained her trust, and with it, her surrender. A loud ripping sound cuts through the air as I shred the fabric she's resting on with my claws. I quickly use it to bind Anwyn's wrists and hoist them above her head.

Her naked body is laid out for me to use however I want. I press a soft kiss to her lips.

"Lassar," she moans as I break it.

"What was your plan, precious one? Did you think you could really escape me?"

She shakes her head, her breasts jiggling with the movement.

"The evening was lovely, I just came out here to enjoy it."

"You mean you wanted to show your body off to anyone who saw you. Wanted to let them catch a glimpse of your pussy." My claws close over her wet flesh. "My pussy. Did you think I would allow that?"

Anwyn smiles softly, my claws parting her folds and rubbing her clit.

"I don't care who sees. But you're the only one who gets to touch."

My blood heats as I look into her beautiful face. She always knows exactly what to say to have my cock painfully hard. Leaning down, I run my tongue from her pussy, up her stomach, over each hard nipple, and then along her neck.

"That's right. I'm the only one who gets to have you forever. Let me make sure you remember that," I whisper against her ear.

Without warning, I plunge two fingers into her wet cunt. Her arousal coats my hand and allows me to get nice and deep, scissoring them within her until her back is arching. Her beautiful breasts are thrust into the air as I claim a nipple.

"Even after all these years as my captive, your cunt still begs for my touch." I pump her a few more times before pulling them from her entrance and dragging them lower. I slip one finger into her ass as she squeals and thrashes in her restraints. "This hole welcomes me just as much, doesn't it?"

"Yes! You own them," Anwyn pants.

I've only taken her here with my cock a few times. She's so tight in her little ass I can barely last a few thrusts. Tonight, I'll use my tail. When we're back in our bed, I'll make her grip the footboard as I also push into this hole.

"Beg me to fuck you. Show me the treasure I got when I captured you."

Anwyn's cheeks are pink, but she's a good girl. Her thighs spread wide on either side of me. Pressing up on her heels, she presents her wet cunt to me. It glistens in the setting sun, her scent strong and sweet on the wind.

"Fuck me, Lassar. Fill me with your come. Use me however you want. You own every inch of me."

With a roar, I rear back and push my cock inside her tight pussy. She's slick and hot and grips me tight enough to make my teeth clench. That storm that sent her into my cave was a gift. A chance to prove that I had learned from my past life. That there was more to life than gold and greed. There's Anwyn. Every thrust inside of her body is more precious than a million gold coins.

The greatest treasures in this world are priceless, just like my Anwyn.

My tail slips beneath her to press into her ass. She loves being filled like this. Her thighs tremble where they're locked around my hips. Bracing both clawed hands under her thighs, I push them up and back to expose her to my eyes fully. Her wet pink skin looks perfect, being stretched by my cock and tail.

Anwyn's eyes are clouded with lust, and I know she isn't going to last much longer.

"Say it, Anwyn." I spit down on her pussy, watching the saliva catch around my cock. "Say it, and I'll make you come."

"I love my dragon! Make me come, please."

My claws pinch her clit, and she's done for. Her little cunt locks around me, milking every ounce of my seed that I'm more than happy to spill inside of her. My spine locks as I pump her full of my come. It splashes between us, covering both of our thighs. I love making a mess of her. She loves it too.

Reaching up, I gently slice through the tie on her wrist and cuddle her against me.

"How are you, my precious one?" I ask, tucking some hair behind her ear.

"Perfect, I love when we play our game," she sighs, cupping my cheek. She nods towards the meadow beside us. "We should take some of those flowers back to the cottage. They'd really brighten up the sitting room."

Glancing behind me, I shake my head.

"Those belong to the Faerie King. Anyone who takes from his meadow must serve him in his court below *The Woods* for eternity." My arms tighten around her.

"Too bad I'm already serving someone else." She winks at me as I press a kiss on her forehead. Gently, she takes my hand and holds it to her stomach. "Though, you might have to get used to the idea of sharing me."

My heart stops. Anwyn's cheeks are rosy as she smiles up at me. The setting sun paints her in gold. This may be the most beautiful she has ever looked. I register what she is saying, and now it all makes sense. The cravings, how insatiable she's been to fuck lately. My grip on her flat stomach tightens.

"I've missed my last two courses," she says softly.

"You're pregnant?" I place a kiss on her stomach as she nods.

"Are you happy?" she asks.

"Yes. This means we're going to be a family."

"I know," she says, her eyes rimmed with tears. "It's something we've both wanted for so long. I can't believe it's finally happened."

"I love you, my Anwyn. My precious, precious wife. My life was nothing before you. You've given me everything."

"I love you, Lassar. You take such good care of me, I know that you'll love our child just as much." Anwyn's mouth presses against mine. A cursed dragon lord and an orphaned human. Brought together by chance. With the evidence of our love now growing inside my Anwyn. This life is perfect, something gold could never buy.

Anwyn kisses me hard, rolling me onto my back as she climbs on top of me. My cock is instantly hard again as she braces her hands on my chest. My hands hold her hips as she rubs her clit along the scales of my stomach.

"What do you say we give that old Faerie King a good show?"

My hands on her hips tighten as she grips my cock and rubs it along her wet slit. Both of our come leak out of her and allows the head of my cock to slip inside her easily.

"I'll always give you what you need, my wife."

Anwyn sinks fully down onto my length, her moan loud enough to send the birds scattering from the trees around us. I raise my hips, meeting her thrust for thrust. Over and over again.

The life we built together lays out before us, worth more than any amount of gold.

BONUS SCENE
ANWYN

As much as I love Lassar, I don't always like him.

Especially in this moment, where I'm laid out on our bed completely naked, and instead of ravishing me until the evening, he's slowly backing away with a familiar —*unwanted*— conflicting emotion swimming in his yellow eyes.

"Anwyn, precious one—I'm not sure—"

I sigh and my head falls back against the overstuffed pillows beneath me.

"If you keep denying me, Lassar, I shall be forced to believe it's because you no longer desire me." My hand trails over my round stomach.

In an instant, Lassar is at my side, kneeling next to the bed. His clawed hands tangle with mine, cradling my belly. I turn to look at him, tears burning my eyes. I'm only a few months into my pregnancy and my emotions have been all over the place from the start.

My husband refusing to fuck me when I'm burning with lust at all hours of the day would make anyone feel like bursting into tears.

"My love, never think that. You are more beautiful now—carrying our child—than you have ever been before. My hesitation is not from a lack of desire. In truth, I want you too much. That's what frightens me. I would rather die than hurt you or the babe."

I shake my head. "You won't hurt either of us."

Lassar still looks unsure. His hand trails over my stomach and cups me between my legs. I hiss as he gently rubs circles on my clit. He's trying to distract me, and it feels so good that I might just let him.

"Are you aching, my love? Let me lick your sweet pussy. It'll make both of us feel better."

His fingers part me and I moan, already on edge. All of my senses are heightened and it doesn't take long for me to come—a side effect of the pregnancy, we should both be enjoying.

"Your cock would make me feel better. I miss having my husband inside of me—you don't even allow me to take you into my mouth," I whine, much like a petulant child.

"Let me pleasure you, precious one. You'll feel better once I do."

"I'll better when you—oh."

My protests are cut off as Lassar falls between my legs and licks up my pussy. His claws grip my thighs and hold them open. He is gentle with me—gentler than ever and while I love it, I also despise it at the same time. His gentleness is why he won't give me the fucking I thoroughly desire.

It's been weeks since he's been inside me, and the last time had been before I started showing. In the previous two weeks, I've almost doubled in size, and while I know he loves me—my body is different and his refusal to be inside of me hurts.

I'll just have to make him see the error of his ways, which I will do, as soon as I reach my climax.

Lassar gently sinks a finger into my pussy and I clamp down on it. While it's nowhere near as pleasurable as his cock, it's still enough to take the edge off. He sucks my clit firmly and my hips rise from the bed.

"You have the most delicious cunt, precious one. Soak my face with more of your sweet come."

"Lassar," I moan his name.

He adds a second finger inside me and curls them expertly. They brush up against that spot deep inside of me. With one last lick to my clit, my orgasm consumes me. Fire erupts along my skin, and I throw my head back into the soft pillows and scream.

Sweat beads on my brow as Lassar licks up every last drop of my pleasure. His fingers pump me until I am spent. My eyelids feel heavy. Another side effect of this pregnancy is how tired I constantly am. Before, I was able to go round after round with my dragon. Now? As soon as I come, my body is begging for sleep.

My muscles feel relaxed as Lassar crawls up the bed towards me. He licks his fingers clean before pressing a gentle kiss to my stomach. The sight brings more tears to my eyes. Laying down beside me, he curls me into his side and holds me close. His clawed hand splays across my belly.

"Rest now, my love. I will give you more pleasure after you've napped."

"This isn't over," I say, breaking off in a yawn. Damn him for being so deliciously warm.

His hand threads through my hair before gently scratching my scalp. Goosebumps break out over my skin, and sleep threats. My husband knows all my weaknesses it seems.

"Sleep, Anwyn," he commands.

Powerless to do anything else, I succumb to my exhaustion and let slumber take me.

Lassar

My naughty wife is up to something.

When I left her resting in bed an hour ago to tend to things around the house, I expected her to be in the same place when I returned. Instead, all I found were cold sheets and my Anwyn's scent on the wind.

My heart broke when she asked if I no longer desired her. As if her being pregnant with our child could make her look like anything less than a goddess. I want to be buried deep inside her more than she knows.

But I can't. Not while she's in this fragile state.

Though, I must admit my refusal to fuck my precious Anwyn is seemingly causing her more distress than I'd like. Still, I won't take any chances with her. She grows more uncomfortable by the day and my job as her husband is to take care of her and everything in our home. The only time I'm away from her is to tend to the house and ensure we have enough food and supplies.

My Anwyn has had some particularly intense cravings, and I indulge her with every single one. I'll give her whatever she wants. Just not my cock—not yet. I'd rather die than hurt her. Despite her and my cock's protest, I will hold fast and delight in the pleasure my fingers and mouth can give her until our baby is born.

Once she is ready, I'll fuck her until she can't move. Until I get her pregnant once more. My cock hardens at the idea, but I cast it a disapproving scowl. Standing in the doorway of our empty bedroom, I take one last lingering look at our vacant bed and exit the room.

I follow Anwyn's honeyed scent out the front of the house. Our modest cottage has been our primary residence for the last five years. Together, we've made it into a home. A home that my very pregnant wife should be resting in, instead of sending me hunting after her.

The thought of her being in trouble spurs me to quicken my steps. Maybe she went for a brief walk and tripped—fell—now she's somewhere in pain, bleeding.

The *baby*, is it—

My steps slow as I take the stone path deeper into *The Woods* surrounding our home. The late summer breeze perfumes the air with the scent of wildflowers and fresh grass. However, all those scents pale in comparison to the intoxicating aroma of my pregnant mate.

My very naked, pregnant mate.

Anwyn's brown eyes sparkle under her blonde lashes. Resting on top of a silk sheet, she's devoid of any clothing save for the metal cuffs binding her to the base of a tall oak tree. She looks gorgeous—a goddess that I'll worship for eternity, thanks to our binding ritual. Anwyn will be by my side and in my bed forever.

Time is no longer an obstacle for us and I am grateful for that. I never want to be apart from her. She should always be in my arms where I can protect her.

Now, I find her out here, at the mercy of the elements and the creatures in the surrounding woods. They know better than to venture close to our dwelling but still. Anywyn is in a fragile condition and now she's made herself even more vulnerable.

Despite the lust roaring in my veins and hardening my cock to stone, I cannot allow her to take such risks. Even as I glimpse the pink, wet flesh of her pussy and catch the musky scent of her arousal, I cannot let her gorgeous body weaken my resolve.

"Anwyn," I say, my voice sharper than I intend. "What are you doing out here? Do you have any idea the danger you've put yourself in?"

The easy smile on her beautiful face falters and I want to howl. Walking swiftly towards her, I kneel at her side and force my eyes to stay on the golden cuffs around her wrists and not on the teasing swells of her breasts. They've gotten fuller, and I long to fill my hands with them again.

Using my claws, I gently unlock the metal bindings and let them fall from her. They hit the silk sheet with a light clink. I reach for Anwyn but she smacks my hands away before folding in on herself. Her golden skin sparkles in the evening sun and I want to taste every inch of her.

"Anwyn—"

"Go away, Lassar," she snaps.

Her eyes meet mine in a blaze of fury, but I don't miss the sheen of tears collecting along the bottoms. My heart shatters in my chest as I take in the sight of her despair. She should always be happy—I haven't seen her cry anything but tears of joy in years, and to know I'm the reason—

I let out a pitiful growl as I watch her slight body shake. Salt water replaces her honeyed scent and I want the ground to swallow me whole. With her facing away from me, I slowly reach out my hand and comb it through the ends of her silky, golden hair.

"Precious one," I whisper. "Don't cry. I'm sorry, I didn't mean—"

"Why don't you want me anymore? You say it's because of the baby, but how can I be sure?" Her voice is a broken whisper. "I need our connection, Lassar. The one I feel when you're inside me. Without it, I—I don't feel whole."

Anwyn turns to face me and her brown eyes are rimmed with red. A tear streaks down her cheek, and I catch it on my thumb before cupping her face. Slowly, I pull her into my chest and hold her soft, supple body in my arms. I turn her so as not to crush her round stomach and tuck her head under my chin.

Her body is limp in my hands and I can't bear it. My brave, bold, and beautiful Anywyn seems lost—she doubts my devotion to her. How could she ever think I no longer desire her?

Because you've made her believe you don't, an angry voice whispers in my ear.

I've been so preoccupied with protecting our unborn child that I've neglected my sweet mate. How could I be so ignorant of her needs? It's clear making her come isn't enough. It's as she says. She needs the physical intimacy between us and so do I.

I must make things right. I'm worried over the safety of the baby but I can be gentle. My precious one needs me and I will not fail her.

"My precious Anwyn," I say, gently cupping her chin and lifting her face to mine. "I desire you more than anything. You and our child are the most important things in the world to me. The fact that I've made you doubt that makes me want to burn myself alive."

Anwyn lets out a gasp and curls her hand around my cheek. "Lassar—"

"Let me finish, Anwyn. I've been scared of hurting you or the baby. That's the only reason I haven't made love to you. I've been dreaming about the day until I can be deep inside you again—fucking you for hours until your stomach grows with our next child."

She shivers, her gaze turning hazy with lust.

"But I've been foolish. I thought if I could just pleasure you, then that would be enough. I could hold off on my need to be inside you if it meant that I wouldn't cause you harm. But I've done exactly what I hoped to prevent, haven't I? I've hurt you, Anwyn, and I am so sorry. Let me make it up to you—let me give you what we both need."

"You mean..." Her sweet voice trails off as she looks at me, her tears drying instantly.

"I'm going to fuck you, my precious one. I won't stop until you're coming on my cock."

Her mouth parts and I meet her pink lips with my own. She moans into my mouth as I taste her fully. My tongue glides against hers as they tangle together. This feels perfect—our souls reacquainting with each other.

Her lips are eager as they press against mine. I break our kiss to trace my lips along her jaw and down her neck. I bite and suck as I go. Her skin is sweeter than the ripest fruit. Anwyn's hands fall to my cheeks as she holds my head to her. The delicious scent of her arousal grows stronger and I'm reminded that she's gloriously naked in my arms.

"Hard," Anwyn sighs as I nip under her ear.

"Hmm?" I give her a question look.

Dark, lust-filled eyes sear into me.

"You're going to fuck me hard, Lassar," Anwyn states.

My whole body freezes. My idea was to lay her as carefully as possible on her side and settle behind her. Then, using the utmost care and consideration I would gently pump into her and rock her until she came. Once she found her peak, I would carefully inspect that she was no worse for wear before carrying her back to our home and demanding she remain in bed for the next two days.

"My love," I say in protest but her lips find mine and silence me.

"Hard, Lassar. It's been weeks since I've had your cock, and I'm going to enjoy it on my terms."

"But the baby—"

Again, she silences me with a press of her full lips.

"Will be fine. However, its mother will not be if her husband doesn't fuck her in the next five minutes."

Her beautiful eyes implore me and I'm powerless under her stare. I kiss her once more. Licking into her mouth, I swallow down more of her moans as my hands drift to cup her beautiful breasts. They fill my palms as I tug each nipple.

Anwyn thrusts them farther into my hands as I kiss along her cheek. Licking the shell of her ear, I delight in her soft sigh.

"I'll fuck you, my Anwyn, exactly how you want. Just promise me two things."

"Anything," she moans, her hands digging into my back.

"If something is uncomfortable, tell me to stop immediately. Do you understand?"

"Yes."

I smile against the side of her head as my left-hand drops lower. It traces down her chest, over her round stomach, until my claws graze the sopping-wet flesh of her pretty cunt. Cupping her firmly, her head jerks back.

"Promise me that when I make you come, you'll scream loud enough so that every creature in *The Woods* knows who's pleasuring this perfect pussy."

"Lassar," she gasps. "Please."

Licking up her neck once more, I gently lower her back down to the silk sheet. Crawling around to her front, I press a kiss to her belly before cupping her soft knees. Gently, I spread her open and reveal the most glorious sight I've ever seen.

Her pussy is dripping with arousal, and my mouth waters. Hoisting her legs over my shoulder, my mouth falls to her waiting flesh where I get to work. My tongue flicks over her clit over and over until her hips begin to grind against my face. My claws find her entrance and gently part her. Using a finger, I pump into her tight channel.

"Lassar, I'm close," she moans.

"Already, my precious one? I've barely touched this greedy cunt."

Adding a second finger, I scissor them inside her until I feel her body going taut. Her inner muscles clamp around my fingers as she comes on a silent scream. Her body shakes as I continue to lick her. Removing my fingers, my tongue spears into her entrance and licks up every drop of her sweet come.

Once she is clean and her body falls limply to the sheet, I gently roll her to her side and slink up behind her. Shucking my pants, I grip my hard cock in my grasp. Lifting her top leg gently, I push against her heated flesh and listen to her moan.

I'm dangerously close to coming already.

The head of my cock presses against her entrance. Her wet heat is making my head spin. Surging my hips forward, I'm just about to enter her when Anwyn's small hand wraps around my length.

"Wait," she whispers, giving me a gentle squeeze. "I want to taste you."

"Precious one," I snarl, as a rope of my come bathes her pussy. "You will not get on your knees when you are so heavy with child."

She looks at me over her shoulder, mischief dancing in her eyes as she gives me another stroke of her hand.

"I don't need to be on my knees. Just lay on your back, Lassar—let me pleasure you."

"Fucking your tight pussy will please me."

Anwyn merely bats her lashes at me; again, I am nothing more than her servant. With a groan, I roll to my back and pull her on top of me. My precious one lets out a giggle as my cock grazes her wet flesh. Pressing a chaste kiss to my lips, she crawls down my body, tasting me as she goes.

Her wet tongue licks over the scales of my stomach muscles. It seems impossible but my cock hardens further as if it knows what's coming. As much as we've both missed me being seated deep in her cunt, her mouth is a particular delight I've been depriving myself of.

"You taste so good," she murmurs.

"My precious girl needs to suck my cock, doesn't she?"

"Yes," Anwyn moans.

Settling between my splayed thighs, she grips my shaft in her tiny hand. Giving it a tentative stroke, I nearly come off the sheet. Molten pleasure erupts in my veins. A fresh bead of come lingers on the tip of my cock and Anwyn's curious tongue licks it up immediately.

"I love taking you into my mouth." Anwyn's eyes find mine. "Promise me you won't deprive me of this anymore—of us."

"Precious one—"

"Promise me, Lassar. I can't live without this. The baby and I will be just fine."

Her face is lovely and dear. Reluctantly, I find myself nodding.

"I promise, Anwyn."

"Good."

Her pink lips pull into a smile before she sucks the head of cock into her waiting warm mouth. I let out a snarl as she works me deeper into her throat. Her tongue licks me in time with her fist pumping my shaft. She sucks me deep, gently grazing me with her teeth.

Against my better judgment, I raise my hips to meet her mouth. Anwyn makes a slight gagging sound as her eyes begin to water. I lower my hips to the sheet, ashamed that I couldn't control myself.

"Anwyn, I'm sorry. I—"

My precious wife growls against my length and takes me deeper into her incredible mouth. Butting up against the back of her throat, my wife gags in earnest on my cock as saliva coats my length. She uses that wetness to pump me harder. Pleasure spears through me.

I'm lost to her in this moment. My hands thread through her long hair as she tastes me completely. The scent of her arousal grows deeper the longer she works me into the wet cavern of her mouth.

She's perfect in every way. I knew it from the first moment she stumbled into my cave that she was it for me. I did everything I could to keep her safe and no matter what the future holds for us, that is one thing that will never change.

Suddenly, I'm overcome with love for her. This deep well of desire that I have for my precious Anwyn somehow grows deeper and I can't wait any longer to claim her. I lurch up and pluck her from my cock.

Her lips are swollen and red. Saliva is drying along her chin as she makes a noise of protest.

"I wasn't done!"

"Apologies, precious one. You can suck my cock later. If I don't fuck you in this moment, I'll set fire to this whole forest."

Her eyes turn heated as a small smile curls her lips.

"Well, we can't have that."

The idea of fucking her on her side is long forgotten as I settle her on her hands in knees before me. My Anwyn needs it hard and I need to be as deep inside her as possible. Leaning over her, I trail a path of kisses down her spine. My claws sink into the globes of her ass and gently spread them wide.

Without warning, I plunge my tongue into her back entrance and she lets out a scream of pleasure. The tight ring of muscles is resistant to my invasion at first but it doesn't take long before I'm swirling my tongue inside her and stretching her in the most delicious of ways.

I hear her arousal hit the silk sheet below us, and I know she's ready.

Rising behind her on my knees, I pull my tongue from her and use my hand to line up my cock with her dripping cunt. Pressing into her tight entrance she lets out a soft keening sound.

"Remember, I love you, Anwyn. Remember that you wanted it hard."

Before she can answer, I push into her. She falls to her forearms and grips the silk sheet in her hands. I don't stop thrusting until I'm fully seated within her. My cock butts up against her womb and we both groan at the reconnecting of our bodies. How could I think to be without this for the next few months?

I won't make that mistake again.

"Lassar, you feel so good."

My claws reach around her and find her breasts. Cupping them in my hands, I pull my hips back only to slam into her again. The moan she gives is filled with pleasure, with no hint of discomfort. I give her another harsh thrust and revel in the tightening of her little pussy.

"Did your pretty cunt miss me, precious one?" I ask.

I slam into her once more and tweak her nipples with my fingers.

"Does this sweet pussy need to be pounded every day?"

"Yes, Lassar. Fuck me—every day, forever."

Leaning down, I sink my teeth into her shoulder as she cries out. More liquid arousal soaks me as I withdraw nearly all the way out of her tight heat. Removing my teeth from her soft skin, I lick over the bite and feel our souls lock as I mark my wife. Anwyn is mine. *Mine.*

Now, I must claim her.

"As you wish, precious one."

Thrusting forward, I'm sheathed fully inside her once more. I set a punishing rhythm. Pounding against her, the supple curves of her ass cushion me as I fuck her. Relentlessly—ruthlessly. Her knees slide along the silk sheet as she tries to hold herself steady.

Her moans echo around us as I move in and out of her wet pussy. The sight of her pink flesh gripping me as I disappear inside her causes me to growl. My claws find her ass once more and hold her open so I don't miss a second of the glorious sight.

"Such a tight cunt you have, my Anwyn." My palm smacks her gently on the ass and her pussy ripples around my cock. "You came out here bare. Anyone could have seen you naked and glowing. Anyone could've gotten a glimpse of my precious pussy, couldn't they?"

"I—I," she mutters. "I wasn't thinking about that. I just came out here so you would finally claim me."

"Naughty girl," I say, delivering another sharp smack to her ass and watching the color bloom. "You didn't think someone else may come upon you and seek to claim you for themselves. Do you doubt how much of a prize you are?"

"Please, Lassar. I don't want anyone but you. No one's ever seen me but you."

"Exactly," I snarl. Possessiveness crowds my chest. "No one ever will. Your pussy is mine—you are mine. You carry my child, and soon, I will fill you with more of my seed. Do you want that, my precious one?"

I grip her hips and tilt them. This new angle allows me to push against that secret spot inside her. Her moans turn choppy. I watch as she turns to look at me over her shoulder. Her mouth is open and slack with pleasure. Her eyes are wild with love and lust.

"Please, fill me with your come, my love. I need it dripping out of me."

I growl at her words. Reaching down, I wrap the expanse of her golden hair loosely around my fist and snatch her head back. Her back bows as I continue to power into her. I feel her body start to tremble, and I know she's close.

Reaching around her hip, my fingers find her clit and I rub tight circles on it. Her pussy tightens further, but it's still not enough. My tail curls around her and joins my cock at her entrance. Collecting some of her wetness, I coat the tip of my tail before trailing it up the cheeks of her ass.

"Lassar," she moans. "I need—I need—"

"Me," I snarl. "You only ever need me."

With a quick thrust, my tail pushes into her ass, and Anwyn lets out a scream that has *The Woods* around us shaking. I fuck her ass with shallow strokes that match the pace of my thrusts into her pussy. I let out a growl at the sight of her tight holes being filled by me.

My release is looming.

"Lassar, Lassar, Lassar."

Anwyn chants my name like a prayer. My fingers continue to work her clit as I fuck both of her holes ruthlessly. She drops to her chest on the sheet as I power into her. Her pussy tightens and her legs begin to tremble. Her pussy is so wet it's soaking my thighs with every thrust into her tightness.

"Come on my cock, Anwyn. Now," I command.

My claws graze her clit once more and her whole body freezes. Gripping my cock like a fist, I feel her climax wash over her. Her scream makes my ears ring. The base of my spine tingles, and with one last powerful thrust, I'm coming inside her. My sticky release fills her.

My vision goes blurry with the force of my climax, but I continue to thrust until her muscles go loose. Gently, I withdraw from her and watch my seed pour out of her little pink pussy.

Anwyn falls forward but I manage to snatch her into my arms. Despite my exhausted muscles, I cradle her body, that's still shaking with aftershocks of pleasure to my chest. Lifting her front the silk sheet, I rise on trembling legs. Walking with purpose, I turn back up the stone path and make my way back to our cottage.

We both remain silent until I enter our home and journey into our bedroom. Settling her gently on the rumpled sheets, I stand at the foot of the bed and survey her. Anwyn's face is flushed. Red marks from my lips and tongue decorate her neck. My bite gleams on her soft skin.

I should apologize for it, shouldn't I?

"If you tell me you're sorry, I'm going to kick you," Anwyn mutters.

"I was rough." Shame makes my cheeks grow hot.

Anwyn holds out her arms towards me and I settle down on the bed beside her. I mold her spine to my chest and rest a possessive hand on her growing stomach. Her hand comes down on mine. The baby inside her pushes against our palms, and some of my guilt lessens.

"See? We are both fine." Anwyn turns her smiling face towards me. "I need my husband, Lassar. Don't take him away from me because you're afraid."

I kiss the top of her head and pull her closer to me.

"I won't, Anwyn. I promise."

"Good," she hums deep in her throat.

Her wandering hand falls between us to find my cock. It hardens instantly in her grasp. Giving me a rough pump, her eyes dance with amusement. And love—so much love.

"Now fuck me again. In our bed this time."

She glides my cock—still wet with both of our arousal—to her waiting cunt. I should protest and tell her she needs rest, but when the head of my cock finds her entrance, I'm rolling my hips forward until we are joined again.

Each day I love Anwyn more than the last. This child will be a new adventure—a new challenge we will face together.

"I love you, Anwyn. Always."

"I love you, Lassar. Forever."

As I retreat my hips and thrust back into her, I feel that word settle in my bones. No matter what happens—what challenges or changes we face, our love is the one constant through it all. The cursed creature I once was is long gone. Now, there is only Lassar, Anwyn's mate.

A title more precious than any gold or jewel.

A KISS FROM A FAERIE KING

KISS FROM A MONSTER SERIES BOOK 4

1

LAURELLE

This dress was made to torture its wearer.

There is no other explanation for its construction. If it was not built for punishment, the designer definitely had a twisted sense of humor. Every breath pushes my ribs painfully against the unyielding fabric. My head pounds from the lack of breath. It's as if this *thing* is drowning me on dry land.

It's a slow, tortuous death, and yet it pales in comparison to what awaits me at the end of this journey.

Despite my protests, my mother had deemed my discomfort wholly necessary given who was about to receive me. It eradicates the curves my mother considers unbecoming of a respectable young woman, as if my maturing was a personal affront to her constitution.

The purple fabric of the gown is stiff and far too thick for this weather. The hot sun leaks through the carriage windows as we roll along. Sweat slips down my neck, and I know the curls framing my face that my mother had so carefully placed are damp and rapidly losing their perfect coils.

She would be most displeased if she saw the state of me.

As would my father, though nothing seems to please him these days beyond an elevation in status. Apparently, the payment for this elevation comes in the form of this satin prison and a few thousand gold coins.

I swallow. The high neck of my gown obstructs even that movement. I go to lift my hair from my neck, but the sleeves of my gown won't allow my arms to rise higher than my chest.

This journey to the palace will be unbearably long. Even my companion doesn't know where to look or what to do. I can't say I blame Caryssa. If my upbringing was hard, hers was unbearable, especially with a brother like hers.

Her brother...my intended.

Our engagement will not be finalized until I am received at court and my father ships over the dowry owed to my soon-to-be husband. What my father lacks in station, he makes up for in wealth. Our deficiency of connection has always been a thorn in his side.

It was clear to me from an early age that he would earn a title by any means necessary. His children were mere pawns in his game. My siblings had been quite a bit older than me and were already married off to various noblemen by the time I was ten.

Unluckily for me, I had the rare opportunity of marrying a prince.

My mother falling pregnant a few years after the prince's birth was no coincidence. Even if she had been older—the risks higher—none of it mattered so long as my father had a chance at infiltrating royalty. For all of her faults, my mother is a pawn in all of this as well.

I should be happy to have a title and security within my husband's household, but I cannot find it within myself to do anything but sit in quiet contemplation. To be the meek and silent girl my parents cultivated as soon as I was young enough to be paraded in front of suitors. My dreams and desires are worthless in the face of my father's ambitions.

Try as I might, my heart still holds on to them, even as every moment spent in this carriage leads me closer to a fate not of my choosing.

I glance out the window as we continue along the Lord's Road. When Princess Caryssa came to collect me, we had shopped in town. I had been informed of Prince Carysen's fondness for the color red. My mother would be proud of how well I kept my composure while my stomach flipped over the idea of dressing for his *pleasure*.

Our royal escorts advised us we needed to set off before sundown. Silently, I watched as they packed the carriage full of red fabric and gowns quickly tailored to my size. If only this carriage could've caught on fire before we climbed inside. I'd rather them be turned to ash than wear them for Prince Carysen.

Caryssa is young, barely older than sixteen, and of a nervous disposition. Even as we sit in silence, I dare a glance over to her and watch her wring her hands for the hundredth time.

Between her silence and this dress, I don't know what's making me more uncomfortable.

I can bear it no longer and decide to break the quiet myself.

"Have you been presented at court yet, princess? Your sixteenth name day was only a few months ago?" I ask. Caryssa's eyes dart up to meet mine. They are a lovely shade of blue. Her hair is just a few shades too dark to be considered blonde, as it sparkles in the dim light of the carriage.

"I—yes, my lady. I was presented when I was fourteen," she says softly.

"That's quite young." Her chin dips, and she shifts uncomfortably. Is her blue gown made of the same horrendous material as mine? I can only imagine it is. "Was it your mother's idea?"

She shakes her head.

"My father's. He feels it's best I secure a betrothal now before I get any aspirations of my own." The princess blanches at her own words, her light eyes widening as they meet mine. My stomach sinks as my suspicions are confirmed. Whatever scrupulous rules I was under in my family's home will undoubtedly follow me into my marriage.

"I understand, princess. Our fathers seem quite similar."

"My apologies, my lady. I shouldn't have spoken out of turn like that," Caryssa says, her face turning even paler. "I would never want to speak of my father that way. He is a good man—complicated in the way all powerful men are."

I nod my head, my gaze staying on her face. She looks so young. I'm nearly ten years her senior. Something in me wants to protect her from the dangers of the world. I also want to ask my own mother if I looked that young when she brought me to court for the first time as well.

Caryssa begins wringing her hands again. I dip my chin to try and capture her eye.

"Princess, you may call me Laurelle. We are to be sisters, are we not?"

"Laurelle," she says, testing my name on her tongue. "That's pretty. Call me Caryssa, though it's a name nowhere near as lovely."

"What would you want it to be?" I ask.

"Want what to be?" She arches a golden brow at me.

"Your name. If you could pick any in the world, what would it be?"

The princess scrunches her nose, deep in thought. For a moment, we seem like two ordinary girls. Sisters even despite looking nothing alike. I could befriend her, help her break free of this cycle that not even my own dreaming could save me from.

Caryssa's eyes pop open, and a smile graces her lips.

"I think I would like it to be—"

The carriage jerks to a halt, and we nearly fall off the benches. The sudden jarring movement causes my lacing to squeeze my ribs even tighter. This thing is unbearable. If I had the power to do anything in the world, I'd rip this dress off and never wear another corset again. Or another pair of stiff shoes. Every day, I would wear thin cotton and walk barefoot through the world.

I'm sure my mother's neck felt a chill by merely thinking that.

Ignoring my throbbing sides, I reach out and touch Caryssa's shoulder.

"Are you alright?"

"Fine," she says, though I notice her wincing too.

"Apologizes, Your Majesty," comes a voice through the carriage window. Glancing over, I see the silver top of a guard's helmet. "The storm last night upended a tree in our path. The road is blocked, but there's a shortcut through *The Woods*. We'll be back on our path in no time."

My heart pounds in my chest at the mention of them.

"*The Woods*?" Caryssa's wary voice echoes my own sentiments. Growing up this close to them, the stories were told throughout my village. Many said they were simple tales to scare misbehaving children, but I'm not sure. There is an eeriness to them, as if something or someone unsavory is lurking in the tree-line.

"We will be quick, princess," the guard assures her. "The sun isn't setting for at least another hour. That's more than enough time to return to the Lord's Road."

"Of course," Caryssa agrees, though her face is still sallow. "Thank you."

The guard stomps off, and it's only a few more moments before we begin rolling again. Caryssa still looks unsure, especially as the terrain turns uneven. The jostling of our carriage is only exacerbating the pain from my corset.

"Tell me about your brother," I say, trying to distract the both of us from the discomfort.

"Oh," Caryssa whispers. "He's—well, he's um…"

Her eyes drift around the carriage. Again, her hesitation only serves to make my discomfort grow. I knew what I was being sent off to do. With my marriage to Prince Carysen, I'll be a princess. In exchange for my hand and a very large sum of gold, my father will become a duke. I had been less than happy when my father told me of this betrothal.

Barely managing to keep it together long enough to be excused, I locked myself in my room and sobbed quietly, hiding the evidence before word of my response reached my mother's ears. They wanted me to be grateful. Grateful that I was marrying a man who made my skin crawl. Who I had met one time and who had been obscenely drunk. Who's eyes and hands wandered. Who cornered me during the evening, and if we had not been interrupted by servants, I shudder to think what would've happened.

Grateful to be marrying a man who has a reputation for *misplacing* his brides-to-be.

If the rumors are true, I'm his tenth intended in under two years. *Worthless gossip*, my mother had called the rumors when I questioned how he was available once more for marriage. We heard he was marrying another princess from a faraway kingdom. Only for her to turn up missing a few days after her arrival.

I hope for my sake they are only rumors. Would death be better than a marriage to that beast? Is this what my life has become? When I was younger, I had so many dreams and desires. I had plans for my future. Wants and hopes, and now I'm being driven headlong into my grave.

When I was young, I fantasized about my marriage. It was usually to a faceless hero, a knight who had saved me from a dragon, or a handsome king who saved me from my arithmetic lessons. When I was older, my desires matured with my body. A few of our cooks passed around short novels filled with the most salacious passages. My mother confiscated it and fired them all, but not before I could steal a few sections of the book.

I read the pages over and over until they disintegrated in my hands. Those wanton activities intrigued me because they were in such sharp contrast to my cold, demure life. I dreamed that my marriage bed was the time I could lie in a man's embrace and bring my pleasure-soaked fantasies to life.

To have my hero tame the ache between my legs formed by those smut-filled stories.

The thought of sharing a bed with Prince Carysen has my stomach cramping. I can't go through with this, but what choice do I have? I can't return home. I have no money of my own. Where would I go?

A part of me says it doesn't matter; anywhere is better than arriving at the palace. As my eyes glance out the carriage window, my hopes of escape are dashed even further. The foliage around us is thick. Even if I managed to escape the carriage, how would I navigate this harsh terrain? Especially in a dress this restrictive.

I huff a humorless laugh. Caryssa's eyes land on my face before quickly glancing away. Is this my life now? Uncomfortable silences and unfulfilling marriage. Is a title worth giving up on everything I ever wanted for myself?

Is it worth giving up the chance of finding true love?

"Be honest with me," I say, finding Caryssa's eye again. "I will find out the truth soon enough. What is your brother really like? Please, Caryssa, tell me."

The princess bites her lip and glances through the window. Her voice is low when she speaks as if someone is just outside the carriage listening.

"He's cruel, Laurelle. Very, *very* cruel. My father was thrilled when he made that deal with yours. Our money...is gone. The royal banks are empty. The people have already begun to starve, and we are surely next. Your father offered a much-needed solution. Beyond that, my brother needs to be married off...his reputation...I mean, you must've heard the stories."

My palms begin to sweat.

"Are the stories true, Caryssa?" I ask. Her paling face is all the answer I need.

"They didn't run away. My brother can be rough, and the things I've seen him do..."

She trails off, and my ears begin to ring. I fall back against the bench seat. The carriage tilts around me, and I can't suck down enough air. My bones feel like metal, weighing me down.

How could my parents give me to a man like that? The answer is painfully simple. I've never been more than an opportunity. I'll die for my father's ambition. Will that make it worth it to him?

"What do I do, Caryssa?" I ask, my voice barely above a whisper. Moisture stings my eyes, but I refuse to cry. I will not be scared. Carysen doesn't deserve my fear or my tears.

"I—" Caryssa begins before a loud crash rips through the carriage's interior.

The carriage jerks and twists, dumping Caryssa and me to the floor. The impact rattles my ribcage and steals my breath. Caryssa lands on top of me, our heads knocking together. We both grunt in pain. The carriage lurches again, and we are jolted once more.

"Fuck!" someone shouts from outside.

"Grab hold of it!"

"Princess, are you hurt?"

The carriage comes to a harsh stop before the door is yanked open, and two guards reach in to pull us out. I wobble on my feet, touching the tender spot where our heads smacked together. My fingers come away clean. Caryssa comes stumbling out and is a bit worse for wear.

Her palm is cut, and crimson blood seeps into the sleeve of her gown.

I blink my eyes and take in the sight of the carriage. It's completely flipped onto its side. The cause of the accident lies still spinning a few feet away. The front right wheel has completely snapped off. The spindles are in splinters, and the axle is ripped off.

"What happened?" I ask the nearest guard. He shakes his head, his helmet obscuring his features.

"We're not sure. It was rolling just fine until...it wasn't. As if some unseen force just broke the wheel off."

"It's this place. It's cursed," Caryssa whispers, coming to my side. I look down at her and gently take her uninjured hand.

"Are you hurt beyond your palm?" I ask. She shakes her head.

"What about you?"

"I'm fine. Let's get you cleaned up."

"Stay close," the guard next to me says. "We'll work fast to fix this while we still have the light. However, we don't know what prowls these woods, and the king will have our heads if you both aren't returned."

I gulp but nod as I lead Caryssa towards the back of the carriage.

The guards crowd around the broken wheel, leaving us unwatched—the hairs on the back of my neck rise. *The Woods* are unsettling. It feels like a million eyes watch me as I tear a strip of fabric from my dress and bind Caryssa's hand. She hisses slightly before biting her lip in discomfort. Her light eyes dart towards the guards.

Even at a distance, I can hear them grunt and curse. There's no way this wheel will get fixed anytime soon, and I don't feel like spending a night in these woods.

"Well, it seems like fate is granting us a bit more time together before we return to the palace," I say, giving her a soft smile. Her eyes are still on the guards as she chews her bottom lip. "Are you sure you aren't hurt worse?"

I place my hand on her forehead and try not to recoil. She's as cold as ice.

"Caryssa, you're freezing. Here—"

"Laurelle," she whispers, capturing my hand. "You need to run."

Her words cause my own blood to ice over.

"What?" I ask, glancing at the guards, who are still gathering around the wheel.

"You can't go to the castle. He'll kill you."

"Caryssa, where would I go? I have a duty to—"

"A duty to nothing," Caryssa spits. Her eyes were like blue fire, a fury I'd never seen before kindling them. "You are kind and caring. I was too young or afraid to save the others, but I can't let their fate befall you. Run, run now."

My hands shake as her words wash over me.

"Here." Caryssa is already moving and leaving me no time to consider her words.

She shoves a small coin purse into my hand. My fingers curl around it.

"There's a town a few miles down the Lord's Road before we pulled off. A merchant is there who can give you passage somewhere else—somewhere safe. I've been in contact with him myself. For when the time comes where...I need to make my escape."

"Caryssa." My hand curls around hers. A girl as young as her shouldn't have these worries. "Come with me. I can't leave you behind."

She shakes her head.

"I'd only slow you down. Don't worry about me, but go now. Before the sun fully sets and you lose the path back towards the road."

I grip her hand again, giving it a gentle squeeze.

"Thank you, Caryssa. Truly."

I lift up my skirt and slip off my uncomfortable slippers. My toes dig into the soft grass of the forest. With a harsh jerk, I rip my gown off before loosening the laces of my corset. I suck down my first mouthful of air, savoring the crispness of it. Caryssa's eyes are round as she watches me.

"I can't run in that thing."

Caryssa nods and nudges my shoulder.

"Go, I'll distract them."

"How?" I ask. She bends down, picks up one of my slippers, and holds it towards me.

"Hit me with this."

"What?" I whisper, my mouth falling open.

"Just hit me with it and run. I'll do the rest." I grip the silken slipper in my hand. I cringe as I raise my arm above my head.

"Sorry," I whisper before bringing the slipper down on the side of her head.

Before the slipper hits the ground, I'm already running. I hear Caryssa's scream and rush towards the guards. My braided hair whips in the wind as I pump my legs. I haven't run in a long time, and it's showing as I'm quickly winded.

"Hey! Grab her. Get back here!"

"Lady Laurelle, come back!"

The guards shout after me, but my steps don't slow. *The Woods* swallow me up the deeper into them I get. I don't know how far away the road is or if I'm even traveling in the right direction, but I don't stop. My corset still constricts me, so I rip the laces off and let the damn thing fall behind me, never slowing my steps.

Metal clanks behind me as I careen sharply to the right.

"Stop running!" a voice calls from a few feet back.

My legs burn, and my feet are cut on sharp sticks. The cold air licks over my heated skin, and sweat pools along my spine. I take another sharp right and fling myself behind a large boulder.

Panting, I slap a hand over my mouth to silence my breaths. Metal footsteps continue past me as I sit still in the fading light. My thick shift is a mess. Shredded along the hem and the sleeves. I gently peel it away as I survey the damage to my feet and legs.

The cuts aren't deep, but I must clean them before they fester. I sit in the dark until I hear an owl hooting overhead. The sun has fully set. The large, pale moon illuminates the forest. The stillness of it all is unsettling. No animals beyond the owl rattle the branches or bushes around me. I would think I was if it wasn't for the feeling of being watched.

I don't know how long I sit in the dark, but I know it's not wise to linger. I need to make it to that village. The guards have missed me for now, but they could return at any moment.

Limping forward, I continue on the dimly lit path. The night air is cold, and I begin to shiver, remembering that I am half-naked. It takes only a few minutes of aimlessly walking before I realize I'm truly lost. The trees I'm passing seem like ones I've already walked by.

My shoulders slump. This is my first taste of freedom, and I will perish in *The Woods* before getting to fully enjoy it. The grass turns damp beneath my feet as I continue forward.

A breeze blows my curls into my eyes. First, it's gentle, then more forceful. I let it guide me. It's as if *The Woods* are taking me somewhere, and I can only hope it's a way out—my heart lodges in my throat as my eyes adjust to the scene before me.

The tree line is thinning, and there is a clearing up ahead. My steps speed up. Have I reached the forest edge? Crossing through the tree line, I let out a groan. It's just a meadow with dark trees surrounding it on all sides. The moon shines overhead and illuminates the open space. This isn't an ideal place to be.

If the guards come upon me, there's nowhere to hide. I go to turn and head back the way I came when something stops me. Slowly, I twist back around and blink my eyes to focus them. My feet move of their own accord as I take in the sight.

What I'm seeing doesn't seem real. It looks as if it's from another world.

A single flower sits in the center of the clearing. The thick blue petals glow softly, already covered in a glistening dew. It's as if it's made from crystals and sapphires the way it sparkles in the moonlight. It's a siren's song, luring me in. The bright petals are in three full layers, surrounding a bright-white center.

It seems to pulse, and as I kneel before it. The bloom casts my skin in a blue glow.

I'm transfixed, and even as the brightness burns my eyes. I wipe the tears sliding from my eyes as my hand extends towards it. Tracing one large petal with my fingertip, I shudder at the softness of it. What's happening to me? Have I lost my mind in these woods? Did I hit my head in the carriage crash, and now I'm hallucinating?

Whatever is happening to me, I feel like a bug caught in a spider's web. The pain in my legs and the fear of being captured by royal guards fade from my mind. All there is is this flower. My fingers trace along the velvet stem.

I want it—more than I've ever wanted anything. Something must've happened to me during the crash. Nothing makes sense, but the only thing I care about is having this flower. I shouldn't pluck it. My intuition tells me it would be wrong, but I can't help it.

I need it, I need it, I need it.

"I'm sorry," I whisper toward the flower. It's too pretty to be plucked, but I'm selfish. I want to keep its beauty all to myself. My hand grips the stem as I yank it from the ground. Its roots seem impossibly long, as if growing here for centuries. I pull it towards me, enjoying its sweet scent...before my eyes widen as the petals atrophy. They turn dull and brown before curling in on themselves. It's only another moment before they turn into a cloud of dust that blows away in the night air.

"No!" I shout, my heart crumbling along with the bloom.

What have I just done? Why would I do that?

I don't get to answer those questions as the ground below me shakes. The solid soil beneath my knees breaks away and disintegrates just as the flower's petals did. My scream is swallowed up by the dark abyss I'm sent tumbling down into.

2

____

EMRYS

My subjects could try the patience of the most even-tempered king.

The Great Oak knew in all its infinite wisdom that only a creature as strong-willed as myself could keep them in line. My power contains them in our realm far beneath the human world. Far away from *The Woods* our beloved oak tree sprouted from below. Its gnarled branches reached through the soil to separate our two worlds. It wasn't long before it became teaming with creatures from all manner of ilk. Flocking towards its ancient magic, they find their home amongst the dense foliage.

Deep beneath the ground, *The Great Oak's* roots grow strong and feed off the magic from our realm. Whether the magic existed because of the oak tree or the oak tree exists because of magic is one of our greatest mysteries. Regardless, I've always been its keeper. My reign has been from the beginning and will continue until the end.

As of late, it's been boringly tedious, as no one makes a fuss anymore.

There were centuries where I could hardly keep the

humans and other creatures from falling into my kingdom at an exorbitant rate. I had to put safeguards in place to keep them at bay, and they have worked, unfortunately, for my restless spirit. Now, I only have a few lost humans or a misbehaving sprite to entertain me. The creatures of the above world have decided to rule over their sections of *The Woods* and don't care to venture too close to mine.

Leaving me to toil away in my underground realm, the guard of the unchanging great tree, of the everlasting oak spirit...that is, until a few decades ago.

When *The Great Oak* lost its first leaf.

The sprites came to me, horror on their little glowing faces. Even the faeries—a naturally mischievous bunch—had looked solemn. Their dark eyes and two-foot-tall bodies were tense with unease.

Indeed, dread is what I felt watching that first golden leaf fall—floating on a gentle breeze until it landed softly on the damp grass. Shrieks rang out as it browned and curled before turning to ash in the wind.

The pain came next. A deep ache rattled my soul and caused me to double over. My pain was linked to it as its guardian. If I wanted to save myself, then I had to save it.

I knew the solution before the sprites flew to my ears to whisper it to me. I've always known what obligation I must fulfill, but even so, these meddlesome creatures don't give anyone, least of all me, their king, a moment's reprieve.

Even now, as I sit, the twilight setting in and coating our meadow in rich blue hues, their voices plague my ears. The three sisters, Puddle, Pond, and Port, are the most staunch weavers of this tale.

"This kingdom is sick," says Puddle.

"Sicker than sick," agrees Pond.

"Without a queen," Port rasps in my ear, "the plants won't grow."

I wave my clawed hand, scattering their plump, pink forms. Their clear wings sparkle as they dodge my movement. Their skin glows brighter, a glimpse at their dismay.

"That one didn't rhyme," I remark, scratching the base of my crown. It's a permanent fixture I was born with. Two mighty branches sprout from my forehead, their limbs reaching toward each other like interlocking fingers. Some days, especially recently, make it feel heavier than ever.

The sisters are right. Poor rhyming skills aside, the sentiment rings true. *The Great Oak* is dying. Countless leaves have been lost since the first one broke free. Each one wracks my body with excruciating pain. When it finally goes rotten, will I decay along with it? Each morning, I check for a decline in my outward health: a rotting tooth, a missing finger, or an eye turning milky and unseeing. Nothing has happened, but I have the distinct impression something will soon if I don't act.

"Plant the seed," the three sisters whisper. "Pull the weeds."

Their squeaky voices chant the saying in unison over and over. I bare my teeth at them, but they merely float to my shoulders. Weaving themselves in between the strands of my white hair, I can never stay mad at the sisters for too long. With a deep sigh, I rub the base of my crown once more.

"What would you have me do?" Their pink bodies zip in front of my nose. "To complete the ritual, I must mate in the heart of *The Great Oak*."

That is what legend says will save us all. If ever the power of the tree should wane, an offering of body and spirit made inside its heart will reignite it. Magic is created when two souls become one during the intimate act. It's primal magic—the type of magic that may have created *The Great Oak* in the first place.

It seems like a simple enough ritual to complete- except for one key component that's been missing these past centuries.

"I don't see you volunteering to complete it with me."

I raise a brow as the sisters burn into a hot magenta. Their wings flap quickly as the three of them fly in a circle.

"Oh no," sighs Pond.

"Not us," sings Puddle.

"Never, ever," cries Port.

"Don't act modest. I've seen what you three lustful creatures get up to. Together...and apart."

The sprites are as wanton as anything. I can hardly judge them. When you are nearly a millennia old, the list of things you haven't done is much shorter than the inverse. Still, the sisters are right. It can't be either of them, as I have no doubt they are about to remind me.

"Must be a human," chimes Pond.

"That's the only way," chuckles Puddle.

"Find one now," chirps Port.

I lift my hand towards the meadow around us.

A few unlucky humans mill about down here. The punishment for breaking into my realm is an eternity of servitude. Not that any of them seem to mind it. They're drunk on pleasure and an odious amount of faerie wine. I watch one human woman pass. Her eyes glazed over and heavy-lidded. She's been here for almost a century. Her bare feet snag in the damp grass as she's led by the sleeves of her sheer dress towards one of the many alcoves.

A debauched scene of her and some of my faeries will ensue shortly. The meadow does that to everyone. Wildflowers weave together in a mass of colors and fragrances while each is laced with magic to lower your inhibitions and heat your blood. A novelty I enjoyed for many centuries that I now find no longer holds much appeal.

My heart longs for more—a meeting and binding of my soul with another's. Part of that desire stems from my guardianship of *The Great Oak* and a need to complete the prophecy. However, I felt this restlessness within me before the first leaf fell. An unease that no amount of faerie wine and naked flesh could solve.

Despite the confusion within myself, one thing is clear: the human I need to complete the ritual is not currently in my service. It's been a few months since the last one slipped through. My faeries and sprites quickly sank their claws into them before I even got the chance to consider them as a partner in this ritual.

A part of me knows that even if my faeries hadn't gotten to our last human first, they wouldn't have been the right choice. I will not take just anyone into *The Great Oak*. Whoever I choose to complete the ritual will be it for me. My mate, my queen...I would not sully *The Great Oak* with anyone less than that.

Sitting on my oak throne, a gnarled branch digs into my back as my crown tightens at the base. The wood of my throne feels weaker—hollow—indicating that I'm failing at the one role I was created for. Closing my eyes, I inhale deeply. The sweet and smoky scent of the meadow fills my lungs as my hair blows in a gentle breeze.

Great Oak, I pray silently, *hear me. Guide me and help me so that I can serve you. Bring me the one I need for the ritual before it is too late for us all.*

The wind shifts as the leaves above me rustle softly. I would take it as a sign that *The Great Oak* heard my plea, but this isn't the first time I've called and been ignored. If the human I need doesn't arrive soon, we may be doomed.

"Tick-Tock," says Pond.

"Tick-Tock," repeats Puddle.

"Time's almost up," declares Port.

Breathing deeply through my nose, I raise my hand to swat at the pestering sprites when my whole body goes rigid. It's faint—barely rising above the earthly scent of the meadow— but it's there. Sweet and warm and unlike anything I've smelt before. My mouth waters from just the barest hint of it as I rise from my throne on wobbly legs.

The three sisters notice the change in my demeanor, but before they can give another infernal rhyme, a shrill scream cuts through the tittering of the faerie gathering. I huff a breath as the faeries around me shiver and shake, their excitement palpable as they shriek in unison.

"Human!" they wail, buzzing on translucent wings towards our latest arrival.

My subjects swarm towards the clearing—where the veil between my realm and the human world is thinnest—and I am powerless but to follow them. Rubbing the base of my crown, my head feels twice as heavy as I remember I am king.

My curiosity is peaked but I will wait for them to return with our *guest*.

There are various entrances all over the human world above that allow them access to my realm. Most find themselves here by accident—a few hedonistic souls do, however, seek us out. Less so now, as I'm sure the tales of my realm have turned into foreboding myths and legends.

This particular entrance has entranced even the most cautious human.

Though, if they have ventured this far into *The Woods*, aren't they looking for ruination somehow? Only a truly desperate soul would come this far, and the fate befalling them by plucking my flower is better than one at the hands of the other beasts who roam the world above.

My lips pull back at the thought of this being another fur trader. There's been an influx of them lately—greedy souls who don't make for fun playthings. Dreadfully dull—even for humans. Their profession of killing and skinning for coin does not mix well with our faerie wine. The dozen of them wandering the fields with their open mouths and milky eyes is a testament to that.

If nothing else, I hope this thief who tried to steal my blossom is at least pleasant to look at. Their scent alone is more intriguing than a dozen fur traders.

Shrieks and screams of delight echo around me. Even the damp grass of the meadow seems to lean towards our newest arrival. The trees that encase my meadow sway on a gentle breeze. A few glowing bugs weave between their strong trunks. This meadow—my realm—seems foreign, yet I know it to be as familiar as my hand.

Something cold skates down my spine. I glance behind me to see if it's one of my subjects, but only a gentle wind greets me. I'm not given long to ponder my unease as the wails of pleasure from my faeries get closer. The hum of their tiny wings echo through the tree line.

I hold my breath as they approach. My lips twitch, urging me to pull them back from my teeth. *No need to snarl at our guest*, I think. *Yet, at least.*

Branches snap as they pour through and into the meadow. My faeries' bodies glow as they fly around. They float through the grass, dance along the branches of the trees, and with all their force, yank whoever was unlucky enough to try and steal from me.

A decidedly feminine whimper has my ears perking up. My shoulders droop slightly as my subjects drag her into the clearing. She swats at them, but it's useless. My faeries cover her completely, and I can only make out her hand. Then, only a glimpse of her foot and a curling tendril of her dark hair.

This angers me more than her intrusion.

"Enough!" I command.

In an instant, my faeries stop their frenzy and retreat from the human. Settling their sparkling forms into the grass at her feet, casting her a dim glow. The moon overhead illuminates her enough. My heart pounds as I take her in. This is no intruder—no thief in need of punishment. She is a goddess who walks the world above. The sun cast in mortal flesh. The moon sculpted into a female form.

She's perfect. She's *mine*.

Her simple cotton shift does nothing for her. Even if it seems it was once good quality, it's been tattered and torn, leaving swaths of her golden brown skin exposed to the glowing light. Her legs and arms are slim, but I won't be satisfied until I can see, touch, and taste every inch of her skin. The graceful slope of her neck leads up to a delicately pointed chin. Full lips and cheeks are surrounded by thick, shining black curls. My claws itch to thread through them, to watch the coils slip between my fingers and reform into their magnificent shape.

Delicate dark brows arch over the most beautiful eyes I've ever seen—a warm brown with honey swirled into her irises framed by thick lashes. They stare at me in shock—in fear—and my stomach lurches. She shouldn't be anything less than happy and pleased in my presence. Even as she looks unsure, warmth pours from her and heats my blood clear across the meadow.

Her full lips parted with a gasp as she trembled slightly. The wind blows her tattered shift, carrying her delicious scent. My cock stirs in my thin pants, and my mouth waters. It's sweet, sweeter than honey, than the ripest fruit. Like sun-drenched wildflowers, her scent has me taking a dazed step towards her.

"Who are you?" Desire has turned my voice to gravel.

Her wonderful eyes shift away from me before returning, kindled by fire.

"Laurelle," she says, her voice making my knees buckle. "I was—I was just passing through."

My beauty—she dulls the meadow around her—blinks her eyes rapidly as if waking up from a dream. The wildflowers are muted and lifeless in comparison to her. She is a true blossom, an indulgent temptation.

"Where am I?" Her voice is a mere whisper. "How did I—"

She swallows hard and takes a shaky step back. I go after her, itching to touch her, but I hold back. She's skittish now, and I won't scare her further. My eyes are the only thing that will give away my hunger for her.

"Laurelle." I savor her name on my tongue. "Did you try and steal from my meadow? Plucked a flower that did not belong to you?"

"I," she gasps, "I didn't mean to. I'm sorry. Please, just let me go. I swear—"

I lick over my sharp teeth, pulling my lips into a smile.

"Humans come into my realm," I state. "None of them get to leave. It's the price for trying to take from me."

Laurelle takes another shaky step back and looks down. Quickly, as if finally noticing her state of undress, she wraps her arms around herself. I can't manage to swallow down my snarl. She should never cover herself. I'll show her that she is a treasure to behold.

There is no shame in my realm.

A grazing of soft wings tickles my ear as the three sisters weave between my hair and longue along my crown. I'm too transfixed by Laurelle to swat at them.

"The human we need," says Pond.

"The human to feed," agrees Puddle.

"The human to seed," states Port.

My heart pounds as I take in their words. Never has another affected me like this. Sure, I've spent years, decades, centuries engaging in illicit trysts fueled by lust, maybe even strong affection. However, this is...something bigger—deeper. Laurelle is different, and I can only hope that, for once, *The Great Oak* has finally answered my prayers.

The three sisters fly away as I move closer to Laurelle. Her sweet scent invades my lungs and settles in my stomach. Her eyes remain fixed on the ground as she takes deep breaths. Her shoulders rise and fall rapidly as I approach.

I stop just before my body grazes hers. My claws move slowly before gripping her chin. Her skin is warm and soft as I gently lift her beautiful face towards me. Being this close to her makes breathing hard, but somehow, I manage.

"Forgive me, I haven't properly introduced myself." My grin is as wide as her eyes. "I am the faerie king Emrys, and you, my blossom, belong to me now."

My thumb brushes her bottom lip, and she whimpers. Leaning in closer, my lips are a breath away from her ear. My tongue longs to taste, but instead, I settle for using it to deliver a promise.

"*Forever.*"

3

———

LAURELLE

I tremble in the faerie king's solid grip.

Standing this close to him, I'm acutely aware of the fact that his hands are tipped in black claws that could easily shred my throat. I'm out of my depth here. Part of me feels like I'm trapped in a dream. A horrible, unnatural dream. How had I gotten to this place? Had I truly tumbled through the ground into a portal and...ended up here?

Wherever here is.

A chill runs through me as I consider the very real possibility that one of the royal guards caught and killed me. Now, my soul is trapped with these creatures for the rest of eternity as punishment for defying my father's wishes.

The king's grip tightens ever so slightly, and I'm jolted back into reality and into the strange world I now find myself in. This is all real, too real. The meadow's grass is damp against my bare soles. The night air is perfumed with the wildflowers that cover the ground. The creature in front of me smells like soil and crisp air.

Nestled in his white hair sits a crown of gnarled branches

that sprout into deep green leaves. A seemingly uncomfortable accessory to highlight his importance. His skin is pale, milky green save for the dark ends of his fingers. His eyes are completely black and glossy. He doesn't so much as blink as he surveys me from head to toe. His gaze is hot and curious as it runs along my body.

I may not have died, but I most definitely hit my head because my body isn't reaching as it should. I should be clawing at his grip, fighting to escape his heated stare. Instead, my body feels...strange. Aware and warm and not entirely unpleasant.

This creature seems to know this as his lips twist into a smile, revealing two rows of sharp teeth.

We stare at each other momentarily. My breath hitches as he drops his hand from my face. His gaze lingers down my body, and I'm reminded that I'm practically naked in my thin shift. It's tattered and torn, exposing more of my body than I ever have, save for my lady's-in-waiting, who helped me bathe.

Instinctively, I wrap my arms around my chest. My captor only smiles wider.

"Pond, Puddle, Port!" he growls, his voice practically feral. I watch with wide eyes as three plump sprites break from the others and shimmer before me. They glow a deep red before tangling in the king's long hair.

"Yes?" they giggle in unison.

"Prepare our guest." His tongue licks over his teeth on the last word. "We will have a feast tonight to celebrate her arrival."

Before I can unstick my tongue, the three shimmering beings lounging on the king's shoulders fly towards me. The three sprites glimmer and shake until they transform with a gentle glow. They land at my feet, larger than before but barely over a foot tall. However, they pull me with the strength of full-grown men.

The whole meadow around me erupts in cheers as they drag me over the slippery meadow. Two of them pull me by each arm while the other yanks me by the tattered hem of my shift. My head whips back as I stare at the king. His dark eyes narrow as he licks over his sharp teeth, causing me to shiver.

What is going on? Where am I? What's happening?

Why couldn't I voice my protests? I suppose they don't matter. I'm stuck here despite...everything. How have I managed to escape one unfortunate fate only to end up trapped in another?

The evening breeze on my heated skin feels real. Once again assuaging the idea that this is some delirious dream I'm having. The grass squishing between my toes feels sticky and familiar. The hands of the faeries dragging me are small, but they pulse with life and warmth.

Again, my voice is trapped inside my throat as my three chaperones lead me toward an opening in one of the larger trees. Its branches are lined with rich green and gold leaves. It's larger than any tree I've ever seen, with the hollowed-out trunk being wide enough for three of me to fit through. Once we pass through the wooden arch, the breath is stolen from me, and my feet pause.

"Keep walking," one sprite chirps.

"No stopping," complains another.

"Time is ticking," states the last.

They murmur to each other in more riddles, but I am transfixed on the sight before me. We're inside the tree, yet we are in a palace. A grand one with an entryway and tile-lined floor. A sparkling chandelier hangs from above, illuminated with golden candlelight. It is in the shape of overlapping branches, matching the crown around the king's head. This place appears to stretch far back—seemingly endless despite us being nestled inside a tree.

It makes no sense, yet nothing here seems to.

"Hurry, you're too important to delay."

Small hands yank me again and I follow. The air inside is crisp and fresh. The three of them pull me past different rooms. A few are bedrooms with their beds decorated with fluffy pillows and silks. We pass another set of doors that seems to lead to a kitchen. The scent of fresh bread and roasting meats makes my stomach growl.

"What is this place?"

My voice is rusty from disuse. It sounds foreign to my own ears.

"The king's palace, of course," the one holding my right arm says.

"Quickly, Puddle, in here. Time is ticking," the one holding my left arm whispers.

"Don't rush. She must be perfect, Pond," responds Puddle.

"She will be. Right, Port?" asks Puddle.

"She already is."

The three of them continue their chatting before yanking me into another room. My eyes adjust to the bright light. Candles cover every surface. The walls are painted gold, and it matches the metallic veining decorating the pale tiles on the floor. Along one side of the room are three massive wardrobes. I watch in shock as they fill with an array of items. Silks and fine linen dresses hang from the inside. There are fresh shifts to replace my tarnished one. I'm unfamiliar with an array of short, silk garments I see being hung next to the rest of the items. It takes me a moment to recognize them, and only because of those salacious novels I once read. Nightgowns, they were called. Short and in every color of silk imaginable.

My face warms as the three faeries pull me in front of a large mirror. I gasp at my reflection. The evening has taken a toll on me. There are a few faint scratches along my cheek. Dirt is smeared across my forehead and nose, and I know there's plenty stuck under my nails. My curls are limp as they cling to my neck. My hair is one big tangle, having come loose from its braid.

"Come sisters, let's get to work," says Port. "Puddle, fetch material for her dress. The green will make her eyes glow. Pond, tend to her cuts, and clean her. I'll handle her hair."

The three turn their full, unblinking attention on me before they break into a flurry of activity. Their glowing bodies sparkle in the candlelight. Pond appears in front of me with a pair of golden scissors. I jerk back as she glides the cool metal up my shift.

Port pushes my shoulders and forces me into a plush, white velvet chair.

"What are you—"

The question dies on my lips as Pond uses her wings to fly up and slice my shift clean up the middle. With a wave of her hand, my shift slips off my shoulders and pools on the chair around my hips. I yelp and try and cover my breasts, but that only makes the three faeries around me giggle.

"Stop this!" I shout. "You can't just cut my clothing off."

The three sprites stop their laughing, and their glow dims a little. They don't seem remorseful. No, they seem more *confused*.

"But," whispers Puddle, "it was filthy."

"You can't just strip me. Not without asking me first. Bring me a robe to cover myself," I order, trying to remember my old life. Nudity is immodest and not something to be so cavalier about. I'm sure these three sprites, dressed in a mere smattering of leaves, have no concept of shame.

"A robe?" Pond asks.

"Humans," Puddle huffs. "So fickle. Just like all the others."

"No," Port chimes, "she's different. Even if she can't see it yet."

A damp cloth appears in Pond's hand, and she buzzes on her wings towards my face. I wave my hand to stop her movements as she leans towards the marks on my cheek. A new feeling settles into my bones. Anger. How dare these creatures drag me into their debasement? I am not like them. I do not want to be special to them.

"Don't touch me. I demand you let me go at once."

I pray they can't hear my shaking voice. It's hard to be authoritative while sitting naked in a chair. My cheeks heat as I catch a glimpse of myself in the mirror.

"You're never leaving," states Pond.

"I'm not staying." I cross my arms over my chest, my face flaming even further. "Wherever it is that I am. I need to get back to my world."

"You are in the faerie kingdom. *The Great Oak* has sent you to us," chimes Puddle, who's half buried in fabric from the wardrobe. "You will bring back life to our realm."

My brows lower. *What does that mean?*

I must've voiced my confusion because Pond swiftly responds, "The king will choose you."

"You will serve him," adds Puddle, floating towards me with gossamer green fabric.

"He will serve us," finishes Port, producing a wide-tooth comb and slowly brushing through the ends of my hair.

Her skin glows a deep magenta at my tangles before she produces a bowl of water and a thick jasmine-scented cream. Her small hands rake through my curls, saturating them until she easily glides the comb from bottom to top. It's not an unpleasant sensation. It reminds me of the handful of times my mother was ever gentle with me as a young girl.

Still, I can't let this pleasure distract me from what they've just said.

"Serve him? What does that mean?"

That sets the three sprites into a fit of giggles once more. Their laughter echoes around the room. Pond dabs a wet cloth on my cut cheek, and I gasp as the scratch heals instantly. She gently wipes behind my ears and along my neck. I jerk as she grazes under my breasts and down my legs. My face warms as the the three share a look with their wholly black eyes.

"An innocent, I can smell," sings Pond.

"The king will be pleased, I can tell," chuckles Port.

"We must hurry. No time to dwell," chastizes Puddle, who's finished with my hair. My curls are perfectly formed and glossy in the light. Carefully, she drapes a few dark tendrils along my temple before braiding a top section of hair back from my face.

"Can you three stop speaking in riddles and give me a full answer?" I ground out.

"No," they say in unison.

I roll my eyes as they continue working on me. They're stronger than they look, and I'm certain I couldn't fight them off. Besides, where would I even escape to? I fell through the ground. I'm sure there's no way back to the surface unless one of them helps me, and if they already believe I belong to their king...

My options for escape are slim, so I shall do what I have always done and bide my time. When the opportunity to flee arises, I will take it. I have to. I can't stay here even if I have nowhere to return to.

Pond rubs her warm hand across my cheeks to add a bit of pink dust to them. Next, she uses the same hand across both my eyelids and lashes to darken them. Lastly, a dark-colored berry appears that she rubs across my lips, turning them into a deep red. This is no modest amount of make-up. My mother would be horrified at my wanton appearance.

When they slip the sheer gown over me, I know for certain that my mother would've keeled over at the sight.

The thin green fabric hugs my body, molding to each curve that was deemed unladylike even when I was still a girl. The fabric is thin enough to show everything from my hard nipples to the shadowy place between my thighs. The color warms the golden brown of my skin and makes my dark eyes shine.

My chest rises and falls as I take in my appearance. I look strange—like I belong in a place like this. I should feel ashamed or uncomfortable, but as my bare feet curl onto the cool tiles, I feel...free. The strict rules of society don't apply here, and for a fleeting moment, I let myself consider the life I'd have down here. Of course, there's always a possibility that their idea that my *service-to-the-king* will result in my beheading.

Though, judging by the hot stare the king looked me over with, I think he has another plan for my body rather than turning it into a corpse. What would that be like? To be owned by a creature like him? Would it be as freeing as I feel now?

The three sisters sigh and break me from that thought. I'm trapped here and need to figure out a way to escape. Whatever the king's ownership of me entails, I am certain I do not wish to find out.

"She looks just right," Port states. "The king will be pleased with our work."

"I can't go out there like this." My protests sound half-hearted even to my own ears. "It's immodest—immoral. To show this much skin is unbecoming."

"Those words don't exist here," snaps Puddle. "Forget them, or you will be punished."

I swallow hard as they take my arms and skirt once more and pull me from the room. The palace around us passes in a golden blur. My feet feel the cool grass as we reemerge outside. The sun has set, and there is a chill to the floral-scented air. Glowing bugs and faeries weave between the thicket of trees. There is a hum of life as the large, pale moon hovers above, casting us all in its blue light.

How is the sky visible if we are underground?

The three of them lead me back towards the king's throne.

Faeries and sprites of all shapes, sizes, and colors sip from golden goblets. They dance, their bodies shimmering and naked. Music floats through the air as a few engage in some sort of dance. It looks more like a mating ritual with their grinding bodies and wandering hands.

Do they expect me to allow the king to touch me in such a way?

My breath catches as I register more figures in the meadow's clearing. They're too big to be faeries or sprites. Their skin is too dull. Tucked amongst the creatures celebrating are humans. Or at least the husks of some of them. Their hair is long and unkempt, as is their clothing. Their eyes are milky—clouded as they drink from their own goblets. Their mouths are red, like mine, but twisted into pleasured smiles.

Any thought that they could help me escape is quickly forgotten.

"That could've been you," whispers Puddle, who returns to her original small size and perches on my shoulder. "Still could be if you're not careful."

I suck in a breath as the other two sisters continue pulling me into the clearing. I try to delay as best I can, but it is of no use. My toes curl into the grass as we stop before the king. He sits shirtless. His pale chest is muscular, as are his arms. He's a large man—male? Whatever he is, his figure is most imposing.

His throne is carved into the base of a large oak tree. Hallowed out to accommodate his strong thighs that are barely contained in his dark linen pants. His black eyes miss nothing as they survey me from head to toe. My nipples harden further, and I wretch my arms free from the sisters to try and cover myself. A reflex I can't help.

The king growls, baring his sharp teeth, and I dip my head. My face heats, and shame curdles my stomach. Am I embarrassed of my body? Am I uncomfortable because that's how I feel or because I was taught to be?

The music around me stops, and my heart speeds up as I hear the creaking of wood followed by strong footsteps stomping towards me. The king's scent reaches my nose—dark and woodsy. It invades my mouth and chokes me, turning my skin warm and my lips dry.

His feet come into view. Before I can say anything, his strong hand wraps around my neck and jerks my face upwards. The touch doesn't hurt but leaves me in no doubt of his power. His thumb drags along the pulse at the side of my throat. My heart beats wildly as I meet his unrelenting stare.

At this angle, he's easily a foot taller than me. My neck cranes all the way back to look up at him. His crown cast in moonlight makes him look even more dangerous. I should be immobile with fear. I most certainly shouldn't be overcome with this foreign yet not entirely unpleasant sensation. A warmth spreads from my stomach and into my lower extremities, causing them to prickle with awareness.

"Do not hide yourself from me," the king, Emrys, growls. His sharp teeth gnashing.

His power overwhelms me. My knees wobble, and shockingly, I want to obey him. Shame still holds me back, and for the first time in my life, I feel anger toward my parents for instilling it in me. I want to be wild and wanton in a way befitting of this place even if that thought is ridiculous.

I couldn't possibly stay here.

I swallow against his hold and nod my head. His lips tip as his hand lets go of my throat. Sharp claws skim over the exposed skin of my collarbone. I swallow down a yelp—a moan, really—before his hand encircles my arm.

"Come, you are my guest. Let me tend to you."

Gently, he leads me forward. I glance back at the three sisters, fluttering on their shimmering wings and nodding eagerly. Their color deepens before zooming away, presumably to engage in the festivities around us.

Emrys settles on his smooth, wooden throne, and before I can drop to the space next to him, he guides me towards his lap. I take a deep breath before perching on his thigh. A few thin layers of fabric separate our naked skin. A fact I'm distinctly aware of as I hold myself stiffly. The king only chuckles and curls a lock of my hair around one of his black-tipped claws.

"If you're good, I'll reward you," he states, dropping the strand of my hair. "I'll show you all you can be in my realm if you let me."

I swallow against my dry throat. I have no idea what he means, and I don't think I'll be sticking around to find out. Despite my state of undress and my confusing feelings, I reach back into myself—into the training I've had as a child when it comes to royalty. In my experience, it's best to be seen and not heard. With that in mind, I sit silently on the king's lap as the warmth of his muscular leg seeps into me.

There's a comfort from him that has my posture relaxing. As the minutes or hours tick by, my shoulders begin to droop. His claws skimming up my back don't help my steely resolve as my body weakens in its rigid posture. My eyelids grow heavy as I watch the scene before me. The music plays with a renewed fever. The band of sprites and faeries bang away on small drums and their tiny hands pluck at harps and saw at a few wooden fiddles.

More wine flows as various berries and breads are passed around.

Suddenly, I'm overcome. Too tired to fight to resist the king's pull, I let my rigid posture go. The adrenaline from the fall— from being primped, pampered, and presented to this monstrous king—leaves me as I lean more fully into this male. To his credit, he doesn't touch me more than lightly on my back. It would be easy for him to take advantage of the situation, especially as sleep threatens, but something tells me I know he won't.

If that was his goal he could've easily done it by now. Besides, as my eyelids fully shut, I have no choice but to trust him. I let his warmth thaw my icy resolve and melt away the last of my self-preservation. With a deep breath, I inhale his scent as I tumble headlong into a new darkness filled with all-seeing dark eyes and razor-sharp smiles.

4

EMRYS

She weighs nothing as she sleeps soundly against my chest.

The soft curls of her hair tickle my cheek as she shifts her position. The thin fabric of her dress renders her practically naked in my arms. Her chest rises and falls—the perfect swells of her breasts teasing the low neckline. She's lovely and warm.

Laurelle glows brighter than any star above.

As content as I am to watch her slumber—no doubt she's feeling the effects of all she's experienced this evening—I want to rouse her. I want to question her and hear her voice once more. I want to watch fire rage in her warm, brown eyes, and more than anything, I want to know what or who she was fleeing that sent her right into my trap.

Not that I'm complaining. I would've found her eventually somehow, but if she has enemies above, I need to know about them.

So I can eradicate them for her, of course.

Then there is the matter of her shyness. The three sisters had whispered in my ears after she fell asleep. They worried about her...*skittishness*. The shame she feels over being exposed. My teeth grind together as I remember her trying to cover her body from me. I will rid her of that shame—the word does not exist in my realm.

A few of my faeries and sprites fly up next to us. They come carrying overflowing goblets of sweet faerie wine and a variety of bread and cheeses atop golden serving platters. Settling the trays on a small table next to my throne, they quickly flutter away on their sparkling wings to rejoin the revelry happening around us. The air is thick with excitement and lust. The music filters through the trees, and the moonlight illuminates the night-blooming flowers all around us.

However, it all pales in comparison to the blossom in my arms.

Dear *Great Oak*, she is so gorgeous. In sleep, she is the picture of relaxation. Her golden brown cheeks are full and dusted with a smattering of freckles. I long to count and taste each one. Her dark lashes fan over them like delicate lace. Her nose is small and slightly upturned, dotted with more delicious freckles. Her mouth is slightly parted as she sleeps, inviting me in to taste her red lips. The make-up the three sisters put on her only enhances her beauty. When she was fresh-faced before me earlier, she was just as tempting.

I should let her rest, to not overwhelm her, but I am a weak king. I know it to be true when my finger lifts towards her cheek, and I gently trace her soft skin with the tip of my claw. She lets out a soft moan that has my cock jerking in my pants. I've been painfully hard all evening. Only she can take away this ache, but not yet. I must be patient, even if my finger continues its journey along the smooth contour of her jaw and down the delicate skin of her throat.

Her mouth opens wider on another moan, and I watch in delight as her nipples harden against the front of her gown. Her sweet floral scent deepens, and I swallow down my own responding growl. Tracing my claw back up her face, I gently rub her lips with the pad of my thumb. Would she welcome my kiss?

Her eyes blink open, and I hold my breath. As if waking up from a pleasant dream, her eyelashes flutter as she yawns. In a flash, she goes from languid to rigid. Her small hand flattens against my shoulder and shoves me back. She's surprisingly strong for such a little thing.

Golden eyes blaze with newfound fury as she scurries from her place on my lap. She doesn't get far, but I do let her retreat further down my thigh.

"What are you doing?" she seethes, giving me another shove and fighting my grasp. I love her fire and will carefully stoke it for the rest of our life together.

She gives me another shove before freezing. Her face leeches of color as her mouthparts. My brows lower as her hands fold into her lap.

"I'm sorry," she whispers, staring at her clasped hands. I almost growl at her lack of eye contact. Her eyes should always be on me. "I shouldn't have—I mean, I didn't mean to—"

"Shh," I say, gently clasping her chin and forcing her stare back on me. Does she think I am upset by her resistance? If anything, I am hungrier for her after that show of strength.

Besides, it is me who should be apologizing, and I don't hesitate to do so.

"Relax, my little blossom. I am the one who's sorry. I moved too fast for you. I'll wait for you to be ready and welcoming to my touch."

Laurelle dips her chin, but her body remains stiff. As if remembering herself, her arms wrap around her chest, and she crosses her legs. A growl escapes me, and my claws sink into the arms of my throne.

"Why do you do that?" I ask through gritted teeth.

"Do what?" Her eyes shift away from me.

"Hide your beautiful body. Nudity is more than welcome here. It is encouraged."

I wave a clawed hand towards the clearing in front of us. Her cheeks color as she surveys the scene before us. Most of my faeries are naked in their small forms. Our human captives are as well. The sound of skin slapping together and high-pitched squeals of pleasure mix with the music. Pleasure is freely given and taken in my meadow. I want Laurelle to under-stand that. This will be her life now—with me—and the sooner she embraces it, the sooner we can begin partaking in it together.

"It's not," she pauses, her eyes returning back towards mine, "proper. A lady should be modest at all times. This type of behavior is unbecoming."

I bark a laugh. The words don't seem to be her own. They lack the conviction she's trying to convince herself they have.

My hand cups her petal-soft cheek, gently tracing her blush.

"You are no lady," I state.

Her head rears back as if she's been struck. Water pools at the bottom edge of her eye. She looks away, fighting to remove herself from my hold once more. The look of hurt splashing across her face has me reaching for her. Grasping her beautiful face once more, I let her see the earnestness of my words. I lay my desire for her bare in my gaze.

"You are no lady, Laurelle. You are much, *much* more than that. A gift—my gift. A goddess of old. My prisoner, one who's punishment is to be pleasured for eternity." She licks over her lips as I groan. "Not that that sounds like much of a punish-ment now, does it?"

Her lips curl into a smile before she shakes herself, her gaze guarded once more. We're making progress. I can see her fighting against her need for modesty. Her eyes drift back to the meadow before us.

"Will they be doing the...*pleasuring*?" She whispers the last word as if afraid someone may overhear.

I look over to the groups of faeries, sprites, and humans locked in *faerie-wine-fueled* couplings. I've had no qualms and have even been a willing participant in these wanton orgies in the past. However, Laurelle will not be partaking in them. I'd slaughter anyone else who dared touch her.

"No, my blossom, your sweetness is just for me."

Her body seems to relax, and I revel in her closeness once more. Who put these notions in her head? Who taught her to be afraid of her desires?

"You should feel no shame here. Lust and desire are natural feelings. There's nothing wrong about wanting to give yourself over to them," I tell her.

"I don't know," she says softly. "At first, I thought this place was a dream—that I'd wake up asleep in *The Woods*—but it all feels too real, and I don't...I don't know what to think now."

"It's best you forget whatever rules you lived by in the mortal realm. The sooner you understand that, the better." I renew my hold on her cheek. "I will not hurt you. No one here will."

"Because I'm special? The three sisters said I was meant to serve you," she whispers, her eyes straying towards my mouth. Her body is warm and pilant, and I'd do anything to peel her out of her gown and ravish her in front of all those gathered here. I won't—I will wait.

She's too important. Too *mine*.

"Busy bodies, let's not think of that this evening." I lean towards the opposite side of my throne and grip one of the golden goblets. The faerie wine is dark in color, and golden flecks decorate the top. Its honey scent tempts my nose. "I want to know more about you."

"You do?" she asks.

"I want to know if you're willing to take the first step of

letting go of who you were before. If you want to stay sheltered and shamed or if you wish to begin anew here, wild and wanton."

Taking a sip of the faerie wine, I let its hedonistic magic wash over me and overwhelm my senses. My desire for Laurelle was already strong, but the wine intensifies it further. I hold the goblet out towards her. The choice is hers. Whatever she chooses, I will accept.

I hold my breath as Laurelle licks over her lips. Her pupils dilate as she stares down at the wine. Slowly, she brings her delicate hand up to wrap around the base of the cup. Lifting it towards herself, I watch her take a deep breath.

Her eyes meet mine, and my blood grows molten.

"Wild," she answers softly.

Taking a small sip, she moans at the sweet taste. Her cheeks color, and her whole body warms further. It becomes pliant in my lap, her eyes bright and glowing. I gently pluck the goblet from her hand. She fusses, but I merely shake my head.

"One sip, my blossom, is more than enough for you. Lest the sugarplum wine turn you into one of them." I nod towards the glazed expressions of the humans littered around the clearing. "It will help you relax. Help you let go. Enjoy yourself, I'll keep you safe."

Her smile is brilliant, showing her perfect white teeth. Her expression is all innocence and sweetness. I thought there was no way she could be lovelier, but I was wrong. Laurelle, open and smiling on my lap, is a newfound pleasure. One that rakes its nails down my spine and makes the blood rush in my ears.

I want to devour her whole, but her growling stomach stops me. Plucking a piece of bread off the tray next to me, I bring it to her plump lips. She opens her mouth, her pink tongue inviting as she leans into my side. The softness of her breasts meets the muscles of my chest, and I growl.

Her cheeks color further as she chews and swallows. I feed

her more, delighting in the pleasure of caring for her. I bring a few pieces of sugar-coated fruit to her mouth. She moans at the taste, a few sugar crystals collecting at the corner of her mouth. I catch them on my thumb and lick them off.

Laurelle's eyes track the movement. One deep inhale tells me the delicious state her pussy is in. I want to drown in her sweet scent. Fighting the urge to sample the sugar straight from her mouth, I produce a small piece of hard cheese and feed it to her. Over and over again, I give her bits and pieces until she shakes her head.

"I can't possibly eat another bite. I'll burst," she giggles.

Without her walls erected between us, she seems younger —more carefree. I can't help but curl her even deeper against me. She doesn't protest. In fact, one of her arms folds around my shoulders, absentmindedly playing with the strands of my hair.

"Are you feeling better? Was the wine too much?" I ask, needing to know how much that small sip is affecting her.

"I feel...wonderful." Her smile is small and secretive. "This place is—I've never seen anything like it."

"Really? Your human lands don't engage in orgies under the full moon?" I deadpan.

Laurelle chokes on her gasp before giggling. Her side vibrates against mine.

"No, definitely not." She shakes her head, her curls brushing my shoulder. "If my family could see me now, I'm sure they'd drop dead from shock just from how I'm dressed."

Laurelle shakes her head again, breaking out in another fit of giggles. The wine is definitely working. Her tongue is loosening, and I want to use it to my advantage. I'm greedy for any knowledge of her she's willing to share.

"What were they like?" I swallow, unsure if I should ask the next question. "Do you miss them?"

"Miss them?" she laughs. "I—no, I can't say that I do."

"Why?" I ask.

Her eyes grow distant before she speaks again.

"My father was a wealthy man—very wealthy. The fact that he wasn't born into nobility was always a point of contention with him—until recently—I guess that doesn't matter now either." Her fingers curl into one of my locks of hair. "I was merely a pawn to be used for his ambition, a servant to my father's unfettered ego."

"I don't like the idea of you serving anyone but me," I growl, my grip on her tightening.

Sadness dances in her beautiful eyes, shredding my stomach. I hold her tighter and run my hand through her hair. The silky locks slip through my fingers as they reform into perfect spirals.

"They mistreated you," I say softly. Laurelle shrugs, and her eyes move to the debauched scene in front of us once more. Her breath hitches at the sight of those twisting and mashing glowing bodies.

"I had to keep myself hidden and demure in order to fit into their plans. Any inkling of desire was snuffed out and replaced with duty and modesty. My mother said it was the only befitting way for a lady to live. It was the only way I could be worthy of the smarmy prince they wished me to marry."

My claws tighten in her hair. Hot and burning rage laces through me at the thought of another claiming her. Of having her and filling her with this shame she suffers from. Laurelle is a well of desire; I can see it in her eyes, and it begs me to set her free.

I will do it, and I will slay anyone who comes to take her from me.

"You were only meant for a king. Someone with the means to protect you and help guide you in your cravings. That weak mortal prince was never worthy of you. He wouldn't have treated you like the jewel you are—not as I will."

"Hmm," she moans deep in her throat. "Presumptious are you? We barely know each other, yet you've declared I'm yours?"

My claws skim down her back and tangle in her waist.

"Make no mistake, my blossom. You were always mine. I would've found you. Our fates were always meant to intertwine."

Biting her lip, Laurelle's hands explore me. Her speech is clear, and her eyes are bright, telling me the wine has eradicated her apprehension. She's in control of herself and her thoughts. While she may not be drunk by typical human standards, the effects of the wine should not be understated.

However, I see the real her as she sits in my lap—the one I will endeavor to ensure never hides herself in shame. It will be my pleasure to awaken this side of her when the wine is not calling it forth.

My hand skims up her exposed leg, and she shivers. Her fingers trail over my collarbone as I match her breathy moan with one of my own. Her cheeks flush as she explores my jawbone. Warm fingers drag down my throat, then double back to smooth over my cheeks. I want to haul her against me, to meet my mouth with hers and devour her whole. Yet, I hold back and allow her to explore me on her own terms.

When her curious fingers brush against the base of my crown, my groan is ripped from me. Laurelle bites her red lip but doesn't stop. I revel in the comfort she's feeling in touching me. My leaves shift through her hands, the sensation sending a pleasant tingle down my spine. They are a part of me, and as such, they delight in her attention.

"Does it hurt?" my blossom asks, eyes wide as she combs through the foliage on my head once more.

A breath puffs from her full lips in surprise as my crown transforms in her grasp. I don't need to see it to know what it looks like now. Instead of two strong branches, it has become smaller, merely a dusting of fragile twigs and a few leaves woven together. It's lighter in this form, but its significance is still great.

"I was born with it. It will always be a part of me until all of this is nothing but dust and dirt."

She wrinkles her nose slightly before saying, "That sounds like a big responsibility. Did you not have a choice?"

My claws snag around her waist, pulling her in closer and inhaling more of her floral scent. Her bare leg brushes my raging cock, but she says nothing, even as her cheeks fill with more color. My chest feels tight, but when she doesn't move away from my hardness, I let go of a deep sigh.

"*The Great Oak* chose me as its protector. It made me out of its magic. The same magic that made everything around us. It was what I was born to do—what I will always do until the end of time."

Her eyes go round, and her teeth sink into her lower lip. My free hand cups her cheek, and I pull her chin down with my thumb until her mouth opens slightly. How easy it would be to kiss her—how sweet would she taste?

I shake myself.

"What were you born to do, my blossom?"

She tries to shrug, the movement only causing more of her soft hair to brush my chest.

"I don't know," she admits. "To secure a higher social standing for my father? That's all my parents intended for any of their children, but as far as what I wanted for myself...I don't know. I had to let go of my desires—my goals and ambition—a long time ago."

My hand tightens on her cheek at her obvious mistreatment. I will enact revenge on those who put these doubts inside her beautiful head. Those monsters taught her to be timid when she is a wildfire. She is the sun—meant to burn brightly and to be adored by the masses.

And none will be more adoring than me.

"You were born to be here, Laurelle," I say softly, even as doubt begins to creep into her irises. Before she can shift away from me, I continue, "Let me prove it to you. If only for tonight, give yourself over to this place. Dance, eat, run—let yourself revel in what we have to offer."

Her brown eyes blaze with longing before cooling in an instant. My lips twist as her shoulders curl in on herself.

"I'm not sure. I mean—"

My hand frames her jaw.

"You are mine now. Remember that. No one will touch you but me. Ever."

I snarl the last word as she lets out a whimper. A part of me panics, thinking I've scared her, but then I smell it. Her floral scent is deep and inviting—begging me to sink to my knees and throw her legs over my shoulder. To feast between her thighs, right here on my throne, so everyone gathered knows she is mine, and she is their queen.

In time, I shall do just that. For now, I gently help her to her feet and groan at the feeling of her pert nipples brushing against my chest. Standing, she barely reaches the center of my chest. Taking her arms gently, I turn her towards the party around us.

Bodies of all shapes and sizes work together in a symphony of erotic sounds. Sprites and humans twirl and dance while spilling sweet wine into their mouths. The night has only just begun, and it's time for my sweet blossom to enjoy it.

"Go," I say.

She hesitates for a second before nodding. Her feet seem stuck next to me, so I shift my hand lower and swat her gently on the supple mound of her ass. She squeals before her bright eyes find mine. The look of scandal on her face is adorable. Her lips twist into a smile as she shakes her head.

"Enjoy yourself, Laurelle. I'll be watching, so be a good girl, but have fun."

With a deep breath, Laurelle throws one more smile my way before walking into the fray. I watch her dark curls disappear into the crowd. My claws scratch at my chest as she gets further away. This space between us is necessary. I want her to be comfortable here, and she needs to see what all is on offer in my realm.

Secure in the knowledge that she'll be back in my arms before the night is done, I sit back on my throne and watch my little blossom bloom into the wildflower she was born to be.

5

EMRYS

The longer I watch Laurelle dance in my meadow, the more I turn into the primal beast my magic demands I become.

How long have I sat on my throne just taking her in? Hours? Days? I do not know, and I do not care. I could spend the rest of my eternal life enjoying the rush of color flooding her cheeks as she spins on the green grass.

Her hands are high above her head, showing off the perfect, curvy expanse of her body. The sheer gown barely conceals her and a growl worms its way up my throat. Her curly head is thrown back in a rich laugh as she spins faster. Sprites and faeries gather around her, none of them daring to get too close and risking my wrath.

Clever little creatures.

Sweat glistens on her face, and a few pieces of dark hair stick to her temple. She is such a treat. Her body moves like water as she flows with the beat. Laurelle has ingested no more faerie wine, and as I suspected, one mouthful was more than enough for my little blossom.

She's unafraid and unleashed. Sensual in a way I doubt she is even aware of.

My Laurelle was born to be a wanton creature just like me. It's evident in the way she moves. Her laughter tickles my ears as she whirls again before falling to the ground. Her whole chest heaves as she giggles before rising again and continuing her dance.

The sight makes me smile even as my thoughts turn dark.

I'll murder her family for keeping her caged. My claws curl into my palm as I think about how they kept my blossom rigid when she was meant to grow free and wild. There is nothing shameful about desire or about expressing it. There is nothing wrong with enjoying life's pleasures and reveling in them. Needs are meant to be met.

And I will satisfy each one of hers, especially when I take her into the heart of *The Great Oak*.

She is mine. I feel it in my bones—my blood. She is the one I've been waiting for. Together, we will restore this land, but more than that, she will belong to me. As I already belong to her. Waiting is torture, but I must. My queen will only find comfort in my company, and if that means swallowing down this lust until it chokes me, I will do so. I will wait for her to be ready and for her to call to me.

And call to me she will. Over and over again, and I will prove to her why I am the only one who will ever rule her—her heart and soul.

Laurelle's body twists once more in tempo with the music. Her arms come down from above her head, and with them falls one of the straps of her dress. Golden skin sparkles under the moonlight, and my mouth waters to taste her. Her chest heaves as a result of her exertion. The fallen strap leaves the swell of her breast dangerously close to spilling out of the top.

The growl I've been holding in echoes from my lips and reaches her.

She turns fully towards me, her face flushed and her eyes bright. As if she's not seen me in years, her lips pull into a surprised smile as she waves. Gathering her skirts, she rushes along the damp grass back over to me.

Out of breath, she grabs my hand and declares, "You must come dance with me!"

I hesitate for only a moment—not because I do not wish to join her but because I want to revel in her smile, in the warmth and affection on her face as she looks at me. Guarded Laurelle was hard enough to resist, but this Laurelle, who looks at me with curiosity and heat, may break my resolve to be patient.

She gives my hand another squeeze.

"Please," she whines.

Licking over my teeth, I rise from my throne.

"Of course, my blossom."

Laurelle lets out a delighted squeal and yanks me towards the clearing. Damp grass and trampled flowers squish between my toes as we fold ourselves in and amongst the bodies. My subjects dance and couple with a frenzy, but with me now in the mix, their attention turns towards us.

Watching and waiting to see if this is the night I claim her.

The crowd pulses with a new energy. Laurelle looks up at me, her small hand still in mine, and with a small grin, turns her back towards me. I want to demand her eyes remain on mine until the supple curves of her ass press against my hard cock.

I let out a hiss and she giggles.

"This is how I saw the others dancing together. Something tells me a formal two-step dance wouldn't be appreciated here," she says, her voice rising above the music.

Wrapping my arms around her waist, I haul her back against me. She gasps at my hardness but doesn't move away. If anything, she grinds herself closer to me. Her hands circle mine, and I lean down and inhale her floral scent. Our bodies move and mash in time with the upbeat song. The sprite on the fiddle works overtime to get the crowd into a fevered frenzy.

Laurelle arches her back ever so slightly and moves side to side in a deliciously maddening way. Dipping my head lower, I skim my nose up her neck and delight in her small gasp.

"Be careful, my blossom, or I'll take you right here in the middle of my subjects."

I wait for her to shove me away, to say I've gone too far, but she doesn't. Instead, she shivers before twisting around to face me. Her eyes are wide with lust, and her cheeks are rosy and gorgeous. Her hands intertwine behind my neck, and she pushes up on her toes. My hands remain on her waist, stroking her warm skin through the fabric.

"Really?" she asks softly. Her lips are so close for the taking.

"Would you like that? To have the others watch as I lay claim to your little pussy?"

The old Laurelle has been eradicated. That question would've had her fleeing and calling me a disgusting beast. This Laurelle, my queen, only lets out a soft moan. Her hands thread through my hair, and she rubs her hard nipples against my chest.

"I've," she pauses and licks her lips, "always been curious about these types of things. I never let myself explore with anyone—I never felt safe to. But now...I want to."

"With me?" I must hear her confirm it.

She nods before wrinkling her small nose.

"I sound absurd, don't I? Hours ago, I was about to be given to a cruel prince, and now I'm telling the king of the faeries that he makes me feel safe enough to be pleasured. Is this some trick? A game?"

My hand cups her cheek, and I shake my head.

"No trick, my blossom. You desire me as I desire you. There is nothing to fear or be ashamed of. I will keep you safe, always."

"That's the thing," she says. "I don't even know what to desire. I used to have some idea before, but now I—"

"I'll show you," I growl. "Everything. Things even your human mind couldn't dream up. Pleasure will be pulled from your body. You'll beg me to stop because you don't think you can take anymore, but you will."

She lets out a sweet moan and yanks my head down towards her. Tilting her face up to meet mine, I should kiss her. Should make good on my promise to take her right here and now.

Yet, I won't.

Not after she just revealed to me the depths of her innocence. I won't allow her first time to be witnessed by others. In the future, if it's what she desires, then I'll fulfill her in that way, but not yet.

For now, I opt for the second-best option.

Without warning, I scoop her into my arms and turn us away from the crowd. She makes a noise of protest but clings to me nonetheless as we leave the meadow. With my arms under her knees and along her back, I gaze down into her lovely face. Exhaustion dances in her gold-flecked irises.

"I think you've had enough fun with the faeries for one night," I say, rounding down a corner until my palace comes into view.

"Wait! I want to dance more. And you! I thought we were going to—"

My grip on her tightens as I growl through my teeth. She's too tempting for her own good. Passing through the wooden archway of my palace, I race us down the tile floor until we reach the furthest back bedroom.

This palace felt so empty before. Now, with Laurelle in my arms, it glows with new life.

"Are you going to fuck me tonight?" she asks bluntly.

I can't conceal my surprise at her direct question, and my steps stumble.

"That's not a very ladylike question," I chastise.

Her smile heats my blood as she gives a gentle shrug.

"You're the one who said I was no lady." Biting her lip, she glances down. "And you said you're the only one who gets to touch me."

We make our way into my bedroom. Even though I want to keep her locked to me, I gently set her on her feet at the foot of my bed. It can easily sleep ten full-grown humans. The sheets are made of the softest silks, and the pillows are stuffed with goose feathers. If she hates the gold and green color scheme, I'll get rid of it.

Whatever she wants, I will always make sure she has, except tonight.

"Be sure, my blossom, that I would claim you tonight—all night." She moans at my words, taking a step closer to me. "But that sip of faerie wine has lowered your inhibitions. I want you to have a clear head the first time we lie together."

Laurelle looks scandalized as she shakes her head.

"I'm not drunk!" she declares, crossing her arms over her chest. The picture of a petulant child. An idea sparks in her brown eyes as she drops her hands to the neckline of her dress.

"I'm not drunk," she repeats.

With a forceful tug, she shreds the dress clear down the center. All thoughts empty out of my head as I take in her naked body. The smattering of freckles on her chest and stomach. Her full breasts and her hard nipples are at the center of them. My gaze drops lower to the patch of dark curls hiding the one place I want to be inside of forever.

Her voice is shaky, but her touch is firm as she reaches out and places my claws on her hip.

"I want you, Emrys." My name on her lips, while she's

naked, has a trickle of seed seeping from my painfully hard cock. "I've never been so sure of anything in my life."

This is going to be a long, *long* night.

My claws tighten on her hip, my other hand feeling the fleshy swell of her ass and dragging her towards me. Her skin is hot and smooth. I will spend an eternity tasting and memorizing every inch of her.

"In the morning, my blossom," I growl near her mouth, her warm breath bathing my lips. "If you still want me like this when the wine is out of your system, I'll fuck you within an inch of your life."

She thrusts herself more against me as I give her backside another squeeze. Her floral scent grows richer, and I can only imagine the amount of sweetness coating the inside of her thighs.

I drop my hand from her ass and take a step back. Laurelle's eyes lock with mine as she lets out a particularly adorable growl. Without warning, she shoves hard against my chest and knocks me onto the bed. The cool silk meets my skin as she crawls on top of me.

Her wet cunt cradles me through my thin pants. Rubbing herself back and forth against my hardness, I let out a growl, and my claws find her hips to stop her. More seed leaks from me, and I can't allow that.

I need to save it all for her perfect pussy.

Small hands fall to my chest as her breasts dangle before my eyes. I long to have her hard nipples in my palms—and most definitely in my mouth. Her curls tickle my skin as she leans down into my face. Her lips are pouty as her eyes plead with me.

"Emrys, please, I need you. You were the one who told me to be free," she whines. "You unlocked this part of me I had buried away. I burn for you."

With a growl, I lift her off my lap and toss her to the bed

beside me. Not giving her a moment's reprieve, I climb on top of her and skim my nose up her neck. Her hands go to my back and dig into my muscles. My tongue licks up the shell of her ear, and I delight in her sigh.

Pressing my lips against her, I say each word carefully.

"Hold on to that lust, Laurelle. I'll reward you for it." My smile is wicked against the side of her face. "Tomorrow."

Laurelle lets out a scream of frustration and rolls on her side, facing away from me. I laugh but slip off from atop her. Pulling back the sheets, I curl her back to my front and lay my arm along her waist.

Turning her head, she appraises me with unhappy brown eyes.

"You really are a cruel captor," she huffs. "Is this how you decided to punish me for my crimes after all?"

My laugh rubbles from my chest as I pull her tighter against me. Her warmth soaks into my skin and dances with the inferno running through my veins.

"Trust me, my blossom, you're going to thoroughly enjoy being punished by me."

6

LAURELLE

Golden light streams into my face, rousing me from a deep, dreamless sleep.

Never in my life have my muscles been this sore. Last night, I used parts of my body I haven't in a very long time. The dancing, the music, the wine—all of it feels like a dream. As my eyes adjust to the room around me, a small part of my brain still believes this is a dream.

How could it not be?

The utter decadence of last night. The way I had barely been dressed, and yet I moved without a care in the world. My body had twisted and swayed in time with the salacious drums and fiddles. I had sat in the king's lap and touched him with reckless abandon before leading him to the dance floor. It had been me who guided him behind me. Me who had allowed him to touch me in a way I've never allowed another male—human or not—to.

Then he carried me back to this room and—

A strong male arm rests heavily against my bare hip, and I'm shocked back into reality. This is very much real. From my sore muscles to the heat of another body pressing into my spine. My eyes focus on the room around me. It's comprised of gold and green fixtures. A gentle breeze blows through the open window and disrupts the emerald curtains. The bedding is made of fine gold silk, and my head rests on the softest pillow.

There are a few pictures on the walls—sketches of the oak trees and the meadow and even a crude portrait of Emrys himself. I'm sure the sprites had a hand in crafting it. There are a couple of wardrobes and a short table surrounded by velvet-covered chairs.

Emrys breathes deep, his breath tickling my ear, and my face heats as I remember our exchange last night. While the faerie wine heightened my senses, I was not drunk in the typical sense. The night isn't blurry in the slightest. I remember how I had danced with him under the moonlight, how pleasure had slid down my spine at his closeness, especially when his hardness pressed against me.

The same hardness I can feel against my backside now.

I had practically thrown myself at him when we had arrived in this room. Disrobing and grinding against his hard cock, it would've been easy for him to take advantage of my desirous state. Yet he hadn't. How many human men would've been so noble?

A woman's willingness is never of great concern to them.

Yet it had been to Emrys. And if I'm being honest—with fresh morning light pouring into the room—while a part of me is a bit embarrassed at the level of my eagerness, my desires have not changed.

I want him as much as I did last night. He teases these desires out of me. Pleasures and feelings I thought I'd never experience now seem within reach.

It's in the way he touches me—how his black eyes seem so

cold but only fill me with simmering heat. The ache he created inside me has only intensified. The wine may have helped loosen me up to the idea of staying here, but now, as I sit sober in the warm morning light, I only wish to continue my exploration of the king.

To see how deep this well of desire goes and allow him to wade through it with me.

I sigh deeply and twist onto my other side to face him. In sleep, his face is relaxed. I take in his magnificent features. Did I think him a monster before? Surely not. He's handsome in a way no human man could ever be. Ethereal and otherworldly, and the sight of him has my inner thighs tingling with awareness.

When he tells me he desires me, I believe him.

The taste of freedom I had last night is heady, and I want so badly for it not to be a trick. For the first time in my life, I want to lower my guard and keep it down. I desire him—want him to pleasure me in the way he threatened to, but do I trust him? It's too soon for me to decide, but I won't hesitate to explore.

Brushing my curls out of my eyes, I tuck the strands behind my ear and slowly extend my finger toward his face. Gently and slowly so as not to rouse him, I explore the strong planes of his face. I smooth over his brow and each angular cheek. He's strong and solid. Being naked in his arms should have me blushing and fighting to cover myself, but I don't want to. I love how his smooth skin feels against mine.

I skim my fingertip down the strong column of his nose. Emrys lets out a breath and tips his head towards my touch. My heart pounds as I trace over the pointed shell of his ear before reaching his crown. While it's made of twigs and leaves, it pulses with life.

The pure power of it hums under my fingers.

How can someone so strong be so gentle with me? In my

experience, the more power a man has, the crueler he is. Could this faerie king be different than all the others? Could I be happy here with him? He's already claimed ownership of me. My mind wills me to fight against it—to remind myself that I don't want to be owned by anyone. Yet my heart begs me to give in and enjoy all the entrapments he has planned for me.

Skimming my fingers back over his brow, I'm inclined to listen to my heart. My lips itch to follow the path of my hand. I lick my dry lips and shift closer to him.

Slowly, his dark eyes blink open. We stare at each other for a moment, and I allow his woodsy scent to invade my lungs and cause my body to hum with pleasure. His arm tightens around me before his hand skims up my bare back.

I shiver before whispering, "Good morning."

"Good morning, my blossom. I feared I would wake this morning, and you would only be a delicious dream." Emry's lips twist into a self-satisfied smile. "I'm pleased to have awoken and found that you are very much real and that your sweet pussy is soaking me through my pants."

I gasp as he shifts his hips, and I realize just how entwined we are. My leg is slung over his hip while his thigh presses against my heated center. He rubs me there once and gauges my reaction. I only moan and grind myself down against him.

This unbridled yearning is headier than any faerie wine.

Emrys slides his hand up my back to tangle in my hair. Gripping my head, he tips it back and stares down into my eyes. His desire burns through me, igniting my own further.

"Do you feel the same as you did last night?" he asks softly.

My cheeks heat despite myself, and I dip my chin. He growls against me, the vibrations rattling my own chest. He forces my head back up to stare at him.

"You will not hide from me anymore, Laurelle." My breath hitches at his command. "Last night, you were a woman who demanded what she wanted. That is who you shall be here. Let me ask you again, and you will answer me with your words. Do you feel the same as you did when I brought you to this room?"

Meeting his gaze, I shake my head. His eyes fill with disappointment, but his grip on me loosens. Before he can misunderstand me, I wrap my arms around his neck and bring my body flush with his.

"The ache is even worse than before, Emrys. I want you—I need you," I whisper against his mouth. "I don't know why, and I don't care. This desire...it feels too right to deny."

His groan tickles my lips as his hands dig into my ass and bring me even closer. Pressed like this, I can feel every rise and fall of his chest. Every cut of his muscles presses into my curves.

Emrys's smile is all sharp teeth as he says, "Your body knows who it belongs to. It's mine to praise, to punish, and to pound. That's what you wanted, after all. That's what you begged me for as you rubbed your little wet cunt on me last night."

My face burns at his crude words but I only nod my head.

"Yes," I sigh, "please take the ache away."

His lips skim over my forehead as we strain against each other.

"As king," he says, "I expect to be awoken each morning with breakfast."

That breaks through my lust, cooling it for a moment. Shame threatens to overwhelm me as I remember once more that I am his prisoner—at the very least, his subject. I guess some things about royalty don't change. We are all meant to serve them in the end.

Shifting slightly back from him, I try to hide my disappointment at his abrupt change in personality.

"What would you like to eat? We had cooks while I lived at home. I can make a few dishes, but nothing—"

I let out a squeak as his claws sink into my hips, and he pulls me up his body. Planting my knees on either side of his head, his soft hair tickles the skin of my inner thighs. In this position, my naked body is exposed to the morning light. The urge to cover myself never comes as my hands come down on the wooden headboard to balance. Looking down, Emrys's black eyes sparkle while the bottom half of his face is dangerously close to my molten center.

My breath catches as he presses his face against me. His nose inhales deeply, and I feel his groan permeate his chest.

"This is the only thing I'll need to eat for the rest of eternity."

I don't get a chance to respond as he gives me one thorough lick. My hands grip the headboard even tighter, and I hear the wood creak beneath my hands. The taste is gentle and exploratory. My thighs clench on either side of his head.

Pleasure sings down my spine at the realization that he wasn't commanding me to be his servant but that he wished to give me pleasure. I've heard about this act from the pages of my novels. I had a lady-in-waiting who whispered about it once and said it was nice but not all that pleasurable.

Her partner must've not known what he was doing because this is the most pleasure I've ever felt. Even the fleeting times I touched myself over the years don't compare. Emrys licks me once more, and I moan, thrusting my breasts forward. His hands skim up my sides and cups one in his hand. He rolls my hardened nipple between his thumb and forefinger.

My curls stick to my back as I through my head back.

His mouth works me over and over again, lick after lick and bite after bite. With broad strokes of his tongue, he focuses in on my clit before licking back down to prod at my entrance gently. It's not long before my hips are working in time with his movements.

"Delicious, my blossom," he growls against my feminine

flesh. "Too delicious for mere mortals. Has any man ever had a taste?"

My thoughts are scattered as he continues licking me, but somehow, I manage to find my voice.

"Never. Only you."

"Good girl," he states, his claws sinking into my ass once more. The hint of pain only heights my pleasure. Working my hips, I grind against his face. His nose bumps my clit as he tastes my entrance against and again, swirling his tongue around the whole.

"Look at you, riding my face for all that you're worth. Tell me what you're feeling, Laurelle."

"I—I," I murmur, swallowing against the pleasure racing down my spine and pooling in my stomach. "I feel free."

"What else?" Emrys demands.

I whip my hips against him as he sucks my clit into his mouth. My arousal makes it easier to glide over his face. The wet, sucking sounds of him working me only enhance my pleasure. Despite the soreness in my legs, I could stay in this position forever and let him feast on me.

"Pleasure. I feel so much pleasure I could burst with it," I admit.

"Good girl," he praises again. I preen at his words. "My perfect blossom, do you want to know what you taste like?"

"Yes," I moan, my stomach tightening.

"You taste like sunshine and sugarplums. This pussy is too sweet and perfect. I'll guard it from anyone who seeks a taste of their own. From anyone who seeks to even smell you."

His hands slip from my ass to underneath me. One claw dances around my entrance while his mouth returns to my clit. He swirls it inside of me once, twice, and on the third time, he eases it inside of me.

"Emrys, please, I—"

"Come, my blossom. Flood my face with your sweetness, and watch me swallow it down."

Pleasure races through me, and I erupt. With a scream, my body clenches, and I grind and buck against his face and finger. His finger pumps inside me as I squeeze it. The intrusion is foreign but not unpleasant in the slightest.

I whip my body back and forth and wring every ounce of pleasure from his attention. I feel my come flood from me and cover his face. He doesn't stop working me until my stomach heaves, and I float back into my body.

Emrys growls and nips my clit one last time. With one final pump of his finger, he eases it out of me and cups my hips once more. Breathing deep, my chest rises rapidly as Emrys slides me down his body. Sweat drips down my neck, and a curl is stuck to my temple.

My cheeks warm as I stare at Emrys. His handsome face is shiny with my arousal, and I watch rapt as he licks it off of his lips.

"Best meal I've ever had," he declares with a wink.

Leaning up, I don't know what overcomes me, but I run my tongue through my arousal on his cheek. I taste myself mixed with his salty sweat and moan. My mouth hovers over his and I'm dying for a taste of him.

Emrys groans but merely shakes his head.

"Not yet, my blossom."

"You don't...want to kiss me?" Old insecurities sour my stomach.

"Laurelle, of course I do." His eyes are earnest. "I want to do more than just kiss you, but I can't. Not yet."

"Why?" I ask, my voice sounding wounded.

"I—" My rumbling stomach cuts him off, and his white brows lower. "It doesn't matter now. Let me feed you, my blossom. I must tend to your needs."

I want to protest, but after what we've just done together, I feel relaxed, and I want to be close to him. I want to let him take care of me and keep me safe.

His arms lift me from the bed, and he sets me down gently in front of one of the wardrobes. Opening the heavy doors, he shifts through the barrage of hanging fabrics until he selects a simple blue silk gown. Lifting it over my head, he lets it slide down my body. I watch as his hands go to his pants, and I turn, not sure if I'm ready—or trust myself not to jump on him—to see the cock he's kept concealed from me.

Instead, I wander over to the vanity and find a wide tooth-comb, a pot of hair cream, and a ribbon the same color as my dress waiting for me. I smile as I begin detangling my hair. It takes a few tries, but I manage to secure my curls into a loose braid and secure it with the soft ribbon. Flinging it over one shoulder, I look at my reflection.

Something is different about me, but I can't put my finger on it.

Emrys approaches from behind me, his hands resting on my bare shoulders. The dress is only held up by thin straps, and the heart-shaped neckline shows off the tops of my breasts.

"You are the most beautiful thing I've ever seen." His eyes darken. "And now I know from first-hand experience, the sweetest."

My cheeks fill with color even as I rise from the chair and turn to shove him.

"You have a filthy mouth." I try and fail to sound chastising. My voice is far too breathy.

"A filthy mouth?" His mouth presses against my ear, sending a chill down my spine. "You didn't seem to mind when you were grinding your needy clit against it."

I giggle and shake my head.

"You are incorrigible."

"And you are delicious." His lips press against the side of my head. "Come let me feed you."

Taking my hand, he leads me from the room before I pause.

"Wait, do I not need shoes?" I ask, looking down at my bare feet. The grass stains from last night have mysteriously disappeared. I glance towards Emrys's naked feet before meeting his amused eyes.

"There's no need for shoes in my realm."

That's the most wonderful thing I've heard in my entire life.

7

LAURELLE

With my hand locked in the faerie king's, he guides me from his room and into the hall.

Our bare feet smack lightly against the tile. The whole palace is filled with golden light filtering in from the carved windows. The fact that we are inside a tree really demonstrates the grandeur of Emrys's magic and how free-flowing it is in this realm. I try to take in as much as possible, but many ornate doors are shut.

A few sprites fly in from the window as we continue down the hall. Their thin wings buzz as they soar towards us. Glowing bodies barely bigger than my finger dance in front of my face before weaving themselves into my curls. A few perch on my shoulders and whisper riddles into my ears.

"The time has come," one whispers. "It must be done."

"Lest our realm turns to muck," another adds, "you and the king must fu—"

"Be gone," Emrys commands, waving a clawed hand through my curls and disrupting the sprites. His dark eyes blaze with authority. Even the few sprites collecting on his shoulders follow his command—their colorful bodies cooling to paler shades.

"The sister said something similar. What am I meant to do for you?"

Unease tickles my stomach. Am I no more than a pawn to Emrys as well? Is he using me for his own means, just as my father did?

Emrys is quiet as he leads me through a set of wooden doors. They are ornately carved with pictures of oak trees and a pair of antlers circling above them in a simple replication of Emrys's crown. Gently, the king takes my arm and helps me to the table. It's a long, glistening creation comprised of pale-colored wood. Around it sit ten velvet chairs, but only two place settings are arranged across from each other at the middle of the table.

The king pulls out my chair, and I slip onto it. I wait for him to move to his own seat until I feel his claws on my shoulders. Giving them a gentle squeeze, I look up at him. His face is earnest, his dark eyes swimming with a depth of emotion.

"All I want from you right now, Laurelle, is to feed you and make you happy. What my subjects keep pestering you about isn't something I want you worrying about."

"But I will worry if you aren't honest with me." My voice is small but clear.

"Soon, my blossom. All will be revealed, but for now, I need you to eat."

With a wave of his hand, platefuls of delicious-smelling food cover the table. There are several jars of fresh jam in all different colors. Dark and light-colored bread lay steaming inside towel-covered baskets. There's an array of fried meats and soft cheeses.

My apprehension is quickly forgotten as my stomach growls loudly.

Emrys rounds the table and stands across from me.

Reaching out, his claws clink on the ceramic plate as he begins piling food high on my plate. My tongue licks over my lips as I watch him expertly butter a piece of brown bread before laying a glossy helping of scrambled eyes on top. This is a feast even my wealthy father would be envious of.

The glass goblet in front of me fills with a pale gold liquid. I raise my brow at Emrys as he sets my overflowing plate in front of me.

"Apple juice," he explains.

I giggle despite myself. It's such a mundane drink for somewhere so...otherworldly. Or is it laced with something like the wine had been? I grip my fork and meet his stare again.

"Is it...like the wine? And the food, will it make me drunk like last night?"

"No," he says, piling a helping of bacon onto his own plate.

"Do a lot of humans live here?"

I remember the ones I had seen last night. Their eyes milky and unseeing. Their mouths open in erotic sighs—drunk on wine and pleasure.

"Only naughty ones." Emrys's grin is wicked, and it sends a thrill down my spine.

One glance at his mouth, and I remember how it felt against me. How his tongue had tasted and feasted on my most private flesh. How I had ridden—

I cough before taking a small sip of my juice. The crisp tartness explodes on my tongue. There's no need to get carried away with those thoughts already. Besides, I am starving.

I devour my pile of eggs and take a few bites of the cured ham. The salty taste leaves me in need of something sweet. Reaching for a pot of red jam, I slather it on a buttered roll and take a bite. The jam is thick and sugary as it coats my tongue. It takes of strawberries and some other fruit I can't place.

Moaning again, I say to Emrys, "This is delicious."

He chuckles darkly. "I'm sure it's only second in sweetness to your pussy."

My face warms, and I shake my head. "You don't talk like a king."

His grin is all teeth. "Then all the kings you've met must have been quite boring."

I nod. They were nothing like Emrys. Not as caring or considerate. They didn't look at me as if I hung the moon in the sky or was the sun in which his world orbited. No, they looked at me—at everyone—only to assess how they may be of value.

My father may not have been a king, but he was cut from a similar cloth.

Unease rakes its icy nails down my spine as I think back to how Emrys avoided my question earlier. As much as I want to trust him, a small bit of apprehension holds me back. My heart screams at me to submit to him fully, but my mind can't stop questioning everything.

Setting my fork down, I take another sip from my crystal goblet before squaring my shoulders.

"Emrys, what is meant to happen to me here?" I ask.

"You belong to me." His answer is quick. "Your place is here with me, forever, as is your punishment for plucking my flower."

Again, I raise a brow and gesture towards the table.

"This doesn't seem like much of a punishment."

Emrys's grin deepens. "Punishments can always be pleasurable."

I smile slightly before biting my lip and looking away.

"Why not turn me into one of the other humans? What's all this talk from the sprites? The sisters said I was different. What are they talking about?"

The king shakes his head, his white hair floating around his shoulders.

"I don't want you thinking about that. It's not—"

"Please," I interrupt. "Please, be honest with me, Emrys. I want to trust you, but I can't if you are keeping secrets from me."

I know it's quite a demand to make of a king who has ruled for centuries. To demand he lay all of his truths at my feet is laughable. However, I have to know. I can't enter into any sort of relationship with him without understanding my true purpose for being here.

After a moment, Emrys sighs and rubs a clawed hand down his face.

"This is going to be a problem," he sighs.

My heart pounds. "What is?"

"You, my blossom," he says, "when you use that word. When you beg me so prettily, I find I can deny you nothing."

"Oh," I say. "Well, good?"

"Good," he chuckles. "You're going to bring me to my knees, Laurelle. Never has anyone had this much power over me."

My lips twitch even as my cheeks warm. "I'm sorry?"

Emrys laughs and reaches towards me. His thumb wipes at the corner of my mouth and comes away sticky with remnants of my strawberry jam. Licking it off his finger, he groans.

"Too sweet for your own good," he states. "Alright, my blossom, I will tell you all you need to know. In due time."

"But—"

"I know that's not what you want to hear, but I promise you will not make any decision without being fully informed. Do you trust me? At least in that regard?"

My throat feels dry. To take this leap of faith with a faerie king, no less, is asking a lot. Yet Emrys has shown me more kindness and understanding than anyone in a long time. I owe it to him to extend the same courtesy, at least for the time being.

"I do," I respond. "But I want to know the full truth before long."

Emrys nods. Looking around the room, his dark eyes connect with mine. They've cooled a bit, and I watch him inhale a great breath.

"Do you want to return to the world above?"

The question is asked so softly that I almost don't hear it. At the abrupt turn in the conversation, my heart kicks up as I consider his question.

"If I said yes, would you let me go?"

Emrys's eyes flash and his pale lips flatten into a hard line.

"I wouldn't," he pauses, "I wouldn't like it. A part of me says no. It says that I would chain you to my bed before I ever let you leave."

I suck in a breath, but the king continues.

"Yet, I know I couldn't do that. To cage you—even to keep you—isn't something I could stomach." His eyes pour into my mind as if he can see my very soul. "Know this, Laurelle, if the time comes when you want to return above, I will let you go. It will always be your choice to stay with me or not."

"To stay with you and be punished with orgasms and bountiful breakfasts?" I ask.

Emrys barks a laugh, the tension leaving his shoulders. "Exactly."

I think about his question. When I first arrived, I would've seized this opportunity to leave. Was my arrival only a night ago? Regardless, I was content on biding my time and escaping as soon as the moment presented itself.

Yet, now that it's been dangled in front of me, I no longer want it. It's not because I feel under the influence of any magic or wine. No, it feels as if I know Emrys. Like we've spent weeks together rather than just a night.

It's strange, but I don't want to leave for now. Besides, I have nowhere to go back to.

"My family will wonder what happened to me." My body

shudders. "I don't even want to think of how the prince will react when I don't show up for our engagement."

The king raises and brow and asks nonchalantly, "Would his head ease your concerns?"

My mouth drops open. Surely, he is kidding. He has to be. To imply that he would—

"I'll kill him for you, my blossom. You need only say the word," he continues.

Shock ices over my veins. I knew Emrys was powerful, but to show it in this way...I should be appalled at the depths of cruelty and be standing to flee—demand he take me to the above world. I shouldn't feel warmth spread throughout my stomach and pool between my thighs.

"You would do that?" I ask, my voice barely above a whisper.

"There's nothing I wouldn't do to give you peace of mind."

I consider his offer before shaking my head. "That's not necessary. Whatever anger the royal family feels towards my disappearance can couple with my family's. For the first time, I didn't do exactly what they wanted. I wasn't the perfect, dutiful daughter forsaking her own desires in order to help my father reach his."

Emrys's dark eyes bore into mine.

"What did you desire, Laurelle? Back when you were able to dream?"

I bite my lower lip and think back. When I was a young girl, I had been afforded a bit more freedom. Before I became of age, I still had to hold myself to a high standard, but I was still young enough not to face the entire scrutiny of my mother and father. I remember summers spent in the garden, reading all manner of tales under the warm sun. I remember wanting so badly to have adventures like theirs.

To find true love that only seemed to exist inside those pages.

That is my deepest desire. The only desire I've held on to even when all hope seemed lost. Can I really share that with the king? Will he think me foolish? Does true love even exist for faeries? Lust and ownership are clearly present, but what about something beyond that?

I huff a laugh and shake my head, falling back on my old training to keep some secrets to myself.

"It's ridiculous—frivolous nonsense. A childish desire."

Emrys's eyes harden, and his mouth thins.

"If it's something you want, then it isn't nonsense."

"It's nothing, really," I say, trying to end this line of questioning.

"Tell me," he commands.

"No," I snap. His eyes flash and I have to look away. I'm not angry with him. Truth be told, I'm not even upset. The reminder of what I've always wanted—even in a place like this—seems still out of my reach. If my lust for Emrys turned into love, would his infatuation do the same? Or will I always be his pleasured prisoner? Something to be kept and not to be treated as the other part of his soul like I desire.

Why am I already considering loving a faerie king I barely know?

"Laurelle." His voice is soft like spring rain. "Please tell me. Whatever it is, I will not find it foolish, I swear to you."

Licking over my dry lips, I hesitate once more. Can I really do this? Trust him with this deep desire? My parents both drilled into me that it was a foolish want. That I should be ashamed for even wishing for such things when my purpose was to make connections—to gain power for my family. Is that why I am so afraid to tell him? To have my parent's sentiments be echoed by his own?

Giving myself no chance to reconsider, I jump off the cliff and wait for the sea of my truth to swallow me whole.

"Love," I whisper. "True love, the kind from legends and tales. That's all I've ever wanted in life."

I hold my breath and do my best not to avert his intense gaze. Something shifts in his dark eyes. They fill with a new light. His mouth parts, revealing some of his sharp teeth. He's handsome—so handsome that it makes me ache anew. There's danger written in every line of his face, yet his eyes show his true, gentle nature.

Seconds pass and then minutes. I wait for him to laugh at me—mock me as my parents have. I don't expect him to slide his black-tipped hand across the table and cover mine. The silky warmth of his skin causes more fire to roar in my blood. Gently, he squeezes my hand as a small smile plays on his lips.

"Then I will earn you love, my blossom," he declares. "It will be the sweetest thing I've ever claimed."

Shock has me stumbling over my words.

"I—Emrys, that's not entirely what I—"

"If I prove myself worthy of your love, will you stay with me? Claim this as your home for all eternity? Will you give me the chance to earn your trust and safeguard your heart?"

My mind races. I had expected Emrys to say...anything else. For him to plead with me to earn my love...isn't this exactly what I've always wanted? Sure, he may not be a shining knight coming to rescue me from a locked tower, but he is in a sense my savior.

By plucking his flower, I was saved from my cruel husband-to-be.

In return, I now have my own king, giving me pleasure and treating me with kindness. Do I not owe it to myself and to him to see if this can blossom into more?

Before I can answer, Emrys pushes back from the table. Rounding it in the blink of an eye, he falls to his knees beside me. Turning my chair, he clasps my hands in my lap. In this position, our faces are nearly the same height.

"I'll give you everything, my blossom. Every want and whim of your heart, I will lay them all at your feet. Pleasures unknown to mortal kind, I will bestow on your beautiful body. All the freedom you can dream of will be granted to you, so long as you share my bed every night."

I shiver at his words. My thighs clench together.

"Why would you do all that? If I am meant to serve you already as my punishment, surely there is no need to...earn my affection." Why am I trying to fight this? Have I been so conditioned that my body's response is to fight even when presented with what it desires most?

Glancing away, my face warms as I say, "After last night and this morning, you see how willing I am to share your bed already."

Emrys growls, his hands tightening over mine.

"Lust and pleasure are one thing, Laurelle. Both of them are important things, but they are fleeting. Love—like the kind you dream of having—is for eternity. I have searched for it myself over the years and never thought I would find it. And then you fell into my realm, and I realized that I had been waiting for you all this time."

Tears prick my eyes.

"Emrys—"

"I've had centuries to prepare for you. Experiences that make me certain of who and what you are to me. You have not had that luxury. Let me earn it—let me show you that I am worthy. Let me show you what could be yours if you choose to stay with me." One clawed hand cups my cheek and forces my eyes on him. "As for your...service to me—the whispering from my meddling subjects—I will explain all of that to you in time."

I nod my head, accepting his words, as I stare at the truth in his dark eyes.

"A noble king puts his realm's needs before his own, but I will not put their needs above yours." His words send a hot trick down my spine. "When I claim you in the way I have wished since the moment you dropped from the sky, it will be because you beg me to. You will commit yourself to me—bind yourself to me—and fulfill the prophecy of your own free will. And you will do it because I have earned it."

"Prophecy?" I ask. The sister never mentioned anything like that.

"All will be revealed later, my blossom. For now, let me commence with making all your wishes come true."

I can't help but chuckle. Rising from the floor, he gently pulls me with him. I crane my neck back to stare up at his face. Twisting one of my brown curls around his finger, he raises a white brow.

"Tell me something you wish to do. Anything, and I will make it yours."

I consider his words. Going back into my mind, I try to remember the young girl I once was. If she was given unbridled freedom, what would she have wished for? The realization shocks me like a bucket of cold water. I can smell her choice. Salt on the air and hot sand pooling between my bare toes.

Only this time, my mother won't be here to condemn me for getting the bottom of my gown wet.

Biting my lip, I smile up at my faerie king.

"I really want to go swimming."

8

EMRYS

Laurelle was made for the sun.

Her soft skin welcomes the heat of its rays. Standing along the sandy shore, crystal blue water laps at our feet. It's shockingly cool against the humid temperature.

A gentle, salty breeze blows a few of her curls that cling to her temples. A cluster of white birds caw overhead, and I can see a pair of sparkling fish swimming close to shore a couple of feet away. I rarely come here. This part of my realm is tucked away—far from the prying eyes of my subjects. What *The Great Oak* needed with a beach, I do not know, but I've never been more grateful for it.

Whisking Laurelle here and watching her brown eyes glow with excitement had been worth it. Her plump lips remain slightly parted as she takes in the rising tide. My blood screams to kiss her—to lay her out on the sand and claim her in a soul-connecting way that would leave no questions about my devotion to her.

My new goal quells my rampant lust. Earning her love.

The meadow has been dying for years at this point. What

will waiting a little longer to complete the ritual with Laurelle hurt? Especially when the prize at the end is as sweet as my blossom.

Does she think her desire for love is foolish? It is not. If only she knew that I am way passed loving her. I'm obsessed—hungry and all-consumed by her mere presence.

Not just for her body, even though I can't wait to be inside of her and feel her smooth thighs against my hips. I'm obsessed with her. I want to hold her down and demand she tell me everything she's ever felt. Every thought she's ever had. I want to know her fears, her dreams, and above all else, her desires.

My chest feels tight at the thought of her. Her beauty is beyond compare. Especially now, as she sparkles in the sun. Her body is soft and supple, her curves highlighted in her thin dress. The hem of which is already covered in sand.

"This is so lovely," she sighs, her sweet voice catching me off guard. I want to swallow the sound of it. "How is it possible? For us to be this far underground, how is there a full ocean?"

My mouth twists into a grin as I look down at her.

"Anything is possible in the faerie realm. Magic makes it so."

Laurelle giggles, and her hands go to the tie on her braid. Gently, she pulls the silk ribbon free and shakes out her curls. Raking her fingers through her hair, she gathers it at the top of her head before twisting it into a loose knot. Her hands work to secure the ribbon around the bun once, then twice, to no avail.

I chuckle before capturing her hands with my own. Using my claws to scratch her scalp she sighs. Twisting my wrist, I reform the bun before tying it securely with the ribbon. A few loose curls cling to her graceful neck and along the sides of her face.

I can't help myself, and I lean down to inhale more of her floral scent. I meant what I said before: she's too sweet for her own good.

Blushing, Laurelle smiles up at me.

"Thank you," she says.

I nod and gesture towards the water. "Ready to go in?"

Laurelle wrinkles her nose and says, "Actually, I thought we could just sit here for a bit."

I watch as Laurelle sits down on the white sand. Her toes dig into the ground as she sighs. I follow suit, sinking down next to her and allowing our bare shoulders to brush. The water comes racing towards us and spills over the tops of our feet.

We breathe in comfortable silence. Have I ever felt this content in the centuries I've been alive?

Laurelle's eyes close as she lifts her face to the sun. A single bead of sweat glides down her forehead, and my tongue is eager to taste it. I have to dig my hands into the sand to keep from grabbing her. My blossom tortures me in the best way.

"My mother never let me sit in the sun this long," Laurelle says, breaking me from my salacious thoughts. "Thought it would age me prematurely."

I chuckle. "Never fear. The faerie world will keep you just as you are now."

Lifting my hand from the grand, I gently trace a claw down her graceful neck. Snagging on her collarbone, I savor her sharp inhale.

"Besides, wrinkles or not, you'd still be the most beautiful woman in existence."

My claw slides over her soft shoulder and underneath the delicate strap of her dress. With a gentle push, it slips off her shoulder. I quickly give the other one the same treatment. The two green straps rest against her upper arms, and while I'd love nothing more than to continue until her breasts are bare, I don't.

"Tan lines," I explain at Laurelle's raised brow.

She smirks and shakes her head.

We remain quiet on the sand for a long time. The rushing of water and the gentle calling of birds lull us both into relaxation. The sun overhead soaks into my bones, making my muscles loose. I inhale the saltwater and Laurelle's scent and feel nothing but peace. The worries and stress of my kingdom are gone—there is only her.

I watch Laurelle through heavy lids. Her face is flushed, and sweat beads along her temple. It glides down her neck and soaks the top of her gown. She fans the back of her neck, even as she continues to bask in the sun's warmth.

"You can take your dress off," I offer.

Even with her eyes closed, she smiles at my words. "You'd like that, wouldn't you."

"No need to play demure, my blossom." I lean closer to her side and whisper the words near her ear. "I've already tasted your sweet pussy, and you all but begged me to fuck in you in front of everyone gathered in the meadow."

Her golden-flecked eyes slide to mine.

"You were very kingly in the way you put a stop to my wanton advancements."

My smile is all teeth.

"My resolve is stronger than most. Even if your temptation was more than I could bear."

Her face turns from me but I softly grip her chin and force her eyes back on me.

"You don't have to hide. Any part of you from me. My desire for you is evident and unending. You can revel in it without worrying that it will dissuade me or that it may tempt me to go farther than you'll allow." I squeeze her chin. "You are the only thing that matters to me, Laurelle. You decide the pace between us. Whatever you wish to give me, I am more than eager to have."

She considers my word, her head tilting to the side. I watch her chest rise and fall rapidly before lifting her small hands to the top of her dress. With one smooth motion, the silk slips down her body, baring her breasts. She tugs it the rest of the way and pulls it off at her feet.

I suck in a breath. I've seen her naked—and tasted her sweet flesh just this morning. However, it's like seeing her for the first time. Her skin glows as she meets my gaze. I nearly come in my pants at the defiant look she's giving me. Free and confident.

Her breasts are perfect, round, and more than a handful. Her hips flare before tapering into her shapely thighs. Her nipples harden under my gaze. My eyes only dip lower to her pretty little cunt hiding between her legs.

Taking the dress from her, I lay it on the ground beside us. I shed my own pants, wanting to be as naked as her. Waving my hand, I motion for her to lie atop her dress while I fall to the warm sand beside her.

Stretching beneath the sun, my mouth waters as I take in every line of her body. I count the freckles on her cheeks and chest. A small smile curves her mouth as she rolls onto her front.

"This feels very wicked," she sighs, her ass thrust into the air.

My cock hardens, rising up to brush against my stomach. Her eyes drift there, her flushing face the only indication that she's pleased by what she sees. That and her deepening scent. If I reached between her legs, I knew she'd be soaked for me.

Skimming my claws down her soft skin, I trace the indentation of her spine. Goosebumps break out along her flesh as she sighs.

"Is this okay?" I whisper. At her nod, I continue.

I trail my hand lower, over one cheek of her ass. I give it a gentle squeeze as her thighs clench together. Not trusting myself to get any closer to her wet flesh, I double back and run my claws up her side.

Laurelle lets out a breathy giggle and squirms away from my touch. A soft laugh escapes my lips, and I brush up her side once more. She groans and flails her legs.

"Are you ticklish, my blossom?" I chuckle.

"Yes!" she cries, trying in vain to escape my fingers. "Will you torment me with this knowledge?"

My grin deepens as I lift off the ground.

"Perhaps," I say and double my efforts.

Using both my hands to touch her. I skim up her sides and her hips and even reach beneath her to the soft curve of her stomach. She thrashes in my grip, rolling onto her back to shove me off as she laughs. Tears form in her eyes as she babbles and tries to push my tormenting hands away. Her legs tangle with mine.

With her thighs open, I settle between them as my hands fall to either side of her head. Our chests meet as we breathe in deep. Both of us are acutely aware of how close we are. How easy it would be for my cock to slip inside her. How her hot cunt is warming it even now as if inviting me to take her.

Our lips are barely a breath apart. Her hands come up to my sides and curl into my shoulder blades. Her brown eyes are alluring—encouraging me with no words to kiss her. I wait for her to command me, yet it doesn't come.

That's the only reminder I need before I get too carried away.

Pressing a kiss to her forehead, I pull back.

"I'm being a poor host."

Laurelle lowers her dark brows as I nod towards the water.

"You said you wanted to swim, and we haven't even taken a step into the water."

Sinking her teeth into her lower lip, Laurelle averts my eyes.

"Oh, I don't mind. Laying in the sun suits me better anyway."

When her eyes meet mine again, I see the wariness

clouding them. Her mouth mumbles something about there being sharks or other creatures who could eat her. I shake my head, gently pulling back from her body.

"The Kraken knows better than to send his vermin to my realm. The water is safe. I promise."

Still, the wariness remains in her eyes.

After a moment, it clicks. My hand is gentle on her arm as I pull her up and brush the sand from her soft skin. I keep my voice even and meet her gaze.

"Can you swim?"

Laurelle grimaces and looks away. Capturing her face in my hand, I don't let her hide from me. After a moment, she sighs and shakes her head.

"One of our servants taught me when I was little. We'd sneak off to do it at this small pond right outside my family's manor." She wrinkles her adorable nose. "That was until my mother found us and forbade me from ever doing it again. The next morning, that servant girl was sent to who knows where."

After another beat of silence, Laurelle continues.

"I thought being here—doing this—would be the first step in reclaiming some of the freedom that was stolen from me. But now...looking at the water...it's so much bigger than the pond where I learned. What if I've forgotten or—"

Rising to my feet, I offer her my hand.

"I'll teach you. You're safe with me."

Laurelle hesitates before I feel her skin slide against mine. Pulling her to her feet, I walk her towards the open water. We both let out a yelp as the cool water reaches our knees, then our hips. Being a good foot taller than her, I can still stand long after she can't. Once the water hits her shoulders, I grip her waist in my hands.

"Kick your feet and your arms at the same time, that will help you stay afloat."

She does so. Her legs brush mine as she treads water. The

foamy spray tickles my nose as I hold fast. My feet drag along the sandy bottom as she continues to move in my grip.

"Move with the water, not against it."

Slowly, her moves are less silted and more fluid. She glides against the incoming waves. I watch her long limbs slash through the calm surface as she keeps herself upright. She barely notices when my hands leave her skin. Laurelle's face is a picture of concentration as she keeps herself above water.

Her face turns back towards me and she gasps, her efforts failing when she sees how far I've let her drift from me. I'm at her side in an instant, helping her regain her leverage and floating once more.

"You're doing so good, Laurelle." Her cheeks warm at my praise.

She kicks her legs before lying on her back. The water keeps her body buoyant as I float beside her. The sun has brought more freckles to her nose, and I count them. Saltwater collects on her dark lashes.

"I used to do this before my mother caught us. I'd float in the sun wearing only my shift," she admits. "I'd dream of a life where I could do this forever—where there were no rules."

Her eyes blink open towards me. "I never could've dreamed you or this place up. Not in a million years."

My hands find her waist once more and pull her into my arms. Her legs wrap around my hips as we stare at each other. Tendrils of her hair cling to her face, and I brush them back with a claw. Her breasts press against my chest, and suddenly I'm overwhelmed with greediness again.

I want to fulfill her in every way I can. I have to.

"What else did you dream of doing?"

She shifts against me, her pussy brushing my hard cock and eliciting a groan from me. Her dark eyes sparkle as we stare at each other. Wrapping her arms tighter around my neck, her head fits perfectly in the groove of my shoulder. Her mouth moves dangerously close to my own.

"I dreamt hundred of dreams in that pond," she confesses. "I dreamt of baking enough pies to fill a whole room. Of having a library with a million books. Of being able to paint with an unlimited supply of colors. To count the stars until the sun came up."

She pulls back, a small smile on her lips.

"Silly nonsense, you see."

My grip on her tightens. I squeeze her sides until her eyes meet mine again.

"Easily met demands for a faerie king," I correct.

Her smile is beautiful enough that my chest begins to hurt. Once more, I am renewed with purpose. My queen has given me a list of demands, and I will see each one fulfilled.

Her pussy grazes me once more. The pleasure of being inside of her will destroy and remake me. I will be a new king after filling her with my seed and claiming her as my own. For now, in this moment, it is more than enough for her to look at me like she is. With openness in her eyes and a soft smile on her lips.

To share in her joy and know that I am the lucky male who procured it for her.

I'll win her smile every day. I'll be worthy of it. Giving her waist another squeeze, I slide my hands along her sides until she's breathless and thrashing once more.

"We'd better get started," I whisper in her ear. "We have a long day of making all of your dreams come true."

9

LAURELLE

"There," I say, wiping my flour-covered hands on my smock.

The white powder mixes in with the paint stains already smeared across the front. After we finished our swim in the sea, Emrys took me back to his tree palace and let me wash the salt and sand from my skin and hair. Despite asking him to join me in the tub, Emrys merely growled before kissing me on the forehead and saying he had things to attend to.

I scrubbed away my disappointment—and lust-filled frustration—with a bar of jasmine soap. Once I was dry, I slipped on a new, fresh dress. This one was light pink and silky with thin, short sleeves. It clung to my chest before flaring out to a fuller skirt around my waist.

When the king reappeared, I had just finished twisting my curls away from my face.

Without so much as a word, he merely took my hand in his and led me down the golden hallway. We walked in comfortable silence until we paused outside of a set of double doors. With a wave of his claws, they both swung open and revealed the most incredible sight I had ever seen.

A small room illuminated by a stained glass window opened to let in the fresh smell of the meadow below. There was an easel and an endless supply of blank canvases. They ranged in size and lined the stone walls. Stacks of sketchbooks with pencils and pens were collected in cups beside them.

However, the shelves along the far wall were the most marvelous. They were easily seven feet tall, and I noted a small wooden stool had been provided for me to reach the top. Easily two feet deep, they were filled to the brim with every color imaginable.

Dark purples bled into vibrant teals that turned into hazy blues. Golden yellow, sunshine yellow, and daisy yellow covered another shelf. There were so many colors—some of which I'd never seen before—that my eyes could barely take them all in.

I turned towards Emrys, his dark eyes glowing.

"Is this what you dreamed it would be like? To paint with never-ending colors?" he asked softly, waving a claw toward the room. He seemed to hold himself still in anticipation of my answer.

There were no words to describe this wonder. No words seemed appropriate to thank him, so I merely pressed my lips to his cheek and gave his hand a squeeze.

It was all a blur as I sat down in front of the easel. Emrys asked me what I wanted to paint first, and after a moment, I thought of my answer.

In my mind, I saw a river—great and roaring—while above it, the sun began to set, casting the world in dark purples and warm pinks. I told Emrys of my vision and gasped when he wiggled his fingers. Just beyond my easel, I watched the stone wall adorned with the stained glass transform into my sunset scene. It was real enough that I swore I could feel the mist from the water.

I didn't dare ask how it was possible because I already knew. Magic. Such wonderful, splendid magic.

Emrys used his powers to help me paint vision after vision. From my family's estate—cast in dark colors and rainclouds—to Emrys's palace—warm and golden. I don't know how much time had passed before I stopped. My fingers ached from holding the brush, and my back was feeling tight.

My faerie king had watched me contently from his place on the stool beside me. He didn't offer critiques of my novice art skills. In fact, he praised my color choices, causing my face to tingle throughout the afternoon. A few sprites had breezed in, tangling in my hair and smearing the paints on my palette before Emrys ran them off when they started whispering riddles about the prophecy.

I welcomed their company, but my king seemed to be in no mood to share my attention.

That had sent a pleasant thrill through me. I loved his unbridled attention—the heat in his gaze. I even enjoyed the chaos and frenzy of his world. It was intoxicating being surrounded by so much life and magic. Emrys himself was intoxicating.

After my paintings were left to dry on the wooden tables, Emrys fed me meat and cheese until my strength was renewed. My eyelids felt heavy for a moment before he helped me from the painting studio, down the hallway, and through another set of doors.

Behind which sat the kitchen of my dreams.

Spacious and open, the stove and oven are made of white stone, and the counters are carved from golden quartz. The fires were already roaring by the time we entered, and my eyes snagged on the workbench in the center of the room. It was stacked full of ingredients for every type of pie.

Candied fruits and melted chocolate were set next to roasted chicken and vegetables, depending on whether I wanted to make a sweet or savory pie. There were fresh crust rolled out and hundreds of pie dishes to bake my creations in.

That is where I have spent this whole evening.

With Emrys by my side, we roll out the dough before more is magically made for the next pie. We place it gently in the dish before filling it with whatever concoction I'm feeling. Emrys uses his claws to pinch the sides, while I use excess dough to create a design on top.

I've just fasted the wildflower-shaped dough over the top of my glossy blackberry pie when a buzzing sound goes off. With a wave of his claw, the oven doors open for Emrys, and the latest batch of pies fly out on a sweet-smelling cloud. They land with a soft thud on the counter to cool while our new batch replaces them.

They smell delicious, but the king and I have eaten so many slices over the past few hours that I can't possibly ingest anymore. I told Emrys it felt wasteful, but he assured me these pies would be offered to his hungry subjects in the meadow.

I glance down at the pies fresh from the oven. The chicken pie bubbles up through the lattice top. Its rich gravy containing carrots and celery makes my mouth water despite my fullness.

Emrys's soft steps echo behind me while his claws dig softly into my waist. I sigh and snuggle back into his body. Have I ever felt this content? This safe? Everything I've ever dreamed of, he's brought to me. All day, he's catered to my every whim, listened to my every word, and given me something I haven't had in a long time.

Happiness.

More odd still is I feel like I know the faerie king. Something in my heart tells me that I do. Throughout our time together, we've talked and shared stories. I revealed more of my time living under my father's thumb, and Emrys made several offers to bring me his head as well. Again, I told him it wasn't necessary.

Just being able to confess to my mistreatment had me feeling lighter.

A closeness has formed between us. One that makes me feel as though we've spent lifetimes together, and I should embrace these feelings. My soul belongs to him—or at least it wants to.

How can I feel this way after only a day?

Albeit one full day. My body is bone tired. It's lived a dozen lives between swimming this morning to putting these final pies in the oven. A yawn sneaks up on me as I watch the sun through the glass window finally begin to dip and darken.

Gently, Emrys's claws go to the tie at my back. Once the smock is loose, he slips it over my head and turns me in his arms. Using his thumb, he gently wipes some flour from my cheek. I smile up at him, the small gesture feeling extremely intimate.

"Did you enjoy today?" His voice is rough with desire.

"Yes," I say, wrapping my hands around his neck and molding my body to his. "Doesn't it feel like we've spent weeks together?"

Emrys chuckles, and his hands skim up my sides. My thighs clench together as more heat licks up my spine. The longer I stare into his eyes, the more truth spills passed my lips and pools on the floor between us.

"I want you," I sigh. "I want to give myself to you."

I want to love you. The thought steals my breath as I manage to conceal that final confession.

Emrys lowers his face to the top of my head and inhales deeply.

"I'd be a poor king if I did not inform you that time moves differently here, my blossom."

Leaning back, I look up into his handsome face with a raised brow.

"Moves differently, how?"

His claws skim down the side of my face.

"Faster or slower, depending on my mood."

My heart pounds, and I lick my dry lips.

"How...how long have I been here?"

His smile is small, but I notice the way his body stiffens.

"By human standards, maybe..." he hesitates. "Three weeks? A month at most."

The world around me freezes. The warmth of the ovens only adds to the heat of my body. His words bounce around in my head. Three weeks? No more than a month? He can't be serious. He can't mean—

"I've known you a month?" I choke out.

"Only in human time," he reminds me.

I wait for the shock to render me motionless. I wait for anger to course through me and propel my arms to shove away from him. Yet, nothing like that happens because...I don't care. This has been the most wonderful day—month, I guess—I've ever had. Beyond how kind he's been to me, I feel the rightness of us in my bones.

Knowing him for a month doesn't feel like a shock. It feels...*right*.

This also clears up one of my last hesitations. We've known each other a month in my world, that's more than enough time to give my body the last push it needs into this waiting pool of desire. I've known my faerie king longer than it takes some people to be married. There's no need to hold back when it comes to each other.

Not that I've been doing that since last night.

My hands tangle into his hair. I scratch at his scalp until his rigid posture melts into my curves. His hands on me tighten, causing more moisture to pool between my thighs.

"Why did you do all of this, Emrys?"

He presses his forehead to mine.

"To prove to you that I meant what I said. You are important to me—you are the only thing that truly matters. If you choose me, this can be our life together. Whatever you want, I'll make it yours without hesitation."

"And if the time came when I wanted to leave, would you still permit me to go?"

I don't know why I ask. Perhaps it is the last tendril of self-preservation moving my lips.

Emrys pulls back slightly and averts my gaze.

"I won't lie to you, my blossom. After spending this time with you, it would be...difficult to let you go. Unbearable even. I would do anything in my power to persuade you to stay. Use tactics I wouldn't be proud of to keep you with me."

I hold my breath as his dark eyes return to mine.

"But," he says softly, "even as much as I want to, I could never keep you caged. Not even if it was in a gilded one by my side. That's why I would only ask you to make me one promise in exchange for your release."

"What kind of promise?" I ask. His lips are close enough to feel his soft breath.

"Promise me you'll never return to your family."

I raise a brow as he continues.

"I've glimpsed your spirit, Laurelle—your soul. It is too beautiful to be stifled by societal rules. If you grow to desire a human life, I want you to be free. No matter what you choose, I demand that you never hide yourself again."

Water pools in my eyes and slides down my cheeks. I don't give myself a chance to think. His words threaded through my heart; like a puppet, they yank me towards him. Gripping his head, I pull his face towards mine and slam my lips onto his.

They are motionless for a moment, my brain trying to warn me that we're making a mistake, but I don't listen. I just feel. Emrys realizes I'm kissing him in an instant and lets out a strangled growl. It echoes down my throat and into my racing heart.

His lips are feverish against mine. I've only kissed one other person, and that was years ago. If my technique is bad, the king surely does not notice. I whimper against his soft lips as we turn into a frenzy of touches and clashing teeth. His taste is crisp and sweet. Perfect. He tastes like forever.

Who needs faerie wine when his lips make me feel like this?

I don't want to stop, but I have to breathe and tell my faerie king my truth. All of it.

"I want to stay," I whisper against his mouth. "My heart knows we belong together. My soul demands yours, and I want to be with you."

I barely get the words out before his mouth is back on mine. Our mouths feast on each other as if we can devour the other. My hands leave his neck and slide down his naked back, sliding along the strong planes of muscles. I dig into his shoulder blades and moan.

With my mouth open, Emrys seizes the chance to plunge his tongue into my mouth. It dances with my own—tasting and taking all that it can. We kiss as if we are fighting for dominance. It is delicious chaos, and I want more of it. I'll never get enough of this feeling—of him.

I need more. Now.

My hands drop from his back and go to the top of my dress. I manage to slip one sleeve off before Emrys stills my hands. Growling my own protest against his mouth, my eyes pop open.

"Not yet." His kiss is searing, even as he slips my sleeve back on me. "One more surprise, my blossom."

"Your cock can be the surprise," I whine, trying to pull his mouth back to mine.

He laughs before giving me another hot kiss.

"I won't let my need to fuck you stop me from spoiling you utterly rotten." Another hot kiss makes my lips tingle. "Or giving you the truth."

His lips press against my cheek. Softly, he kisses under my ear before gently nipping at my lobe. I gasp, my pussy turning even wetter. My thighs are surely soaked. His lips trail down my neck, biting and sucking as he goes. Claws skim down my sides until they tangle at my hips.

"But I am not a cruel king," he whispers before nipping under my chin. "I'll take the edge off for you."

With a gentle push, I fall backward onto one of the tables we had used to make the pies. I land with a gentle thud. Together, we push bowls and pans out of the way and listen to them clatter to the tile floor. I don't care if we're ruining all these beautiful pies. I need Emrys to touch me again. I need to feel him, or I'm going to die.

A bowl of jelly splatters to the floor, and I pay it no mind. Just like I pay no mind to the flour coating my hair and dress as I reach down and yank up my skirts. Emrys's claws tangle with mine until my pussy is completely exposed to his greedy eyes and the evening air.

"So pretty." Emrys trails a claw up my wet slit, eliciting a moan from me.

"Emrys," I whine. Opening my legs wider, I watch as he tosses them over his shoulder and grips my hips. Yanking me towards his face, he inhales against my wet flesh as my hands tangle in his white hair.

"This perfect pussy needs to be worshipped." He inhales deeply once more. "It needs to be kept safe at all times. It's the ultimate treasure—one humans were never fit to behold."

His tongue licks up my center, and I scream. I'm already dangerously close to climax. I always am whenever he touches me. My back arches, and a cloud of flour coats the air around us.

"Look at how wet you are, Laurelle. You're soaking the table."

With his tongue returning to my clit, I feel his claw circle my entrance before gently pushing inside. The stretch is decadent, and my moans become louder. My chest rises and falls as he pumps me with his finger. Closing his lips around my clit, he sucks gently, and I scream out his name.

My body is teetering on the edge when I feel him pull his finger from me. New heat pools in my belly as I feel him skim that same claw down between the cheeks of my ass. My face flames as he gently prods my back entrance, as his tongue spears into my pussy.

"Emrys!" My hands tighten in his hair.

"Before the night is over," he growls against me, "you'll beg me to be in both of your little holes. In your mouth. You'll demand my cock fill you with seed everywhere it can."

"Yes," I agree, lost to my pleasure.

"I can see it now, my blossom. You spread out before me like this. So sweet and tempting. Your body is covered in my bites. My back is red from your nails gripping me."

He sucks my clit again as he pushes his finger all the way into my ass. My scream echoes around the room. The heat from the ovens causes my body to break out into a fine sheen of sweat. My hair clings to my temples.

"You know what else I'm going to see, my love?"

My heart catches at the term of endearment, but I manage to ask, "What else?"

"I'm going to see my seed seeping out from your sweet pussy. I'll see some of it dried along your breasts. And the corner of your mouth. But it's your pussy that will be overflowing with it. Filled to the point that it will seep out and soak the sheets of our bed. Isn't that what you want?"

I nod my head, the muscles in my body tightening.

"And you know what you'll say to me?"

"What?"

His breath hovers over my clit, and I feel him smile against me.

"You'll beg me to use my seed to fuck your ass. To stretch you open and flood you with my come there. It'll hurt, but you'll love it."

Clamping his lips over my clit once more, he shoves a second finger into my back entrance, and my body erupts. Molten glass seeps through my veins as my thighs tighten around his head. The hard twigs of his crown dig into my thighs as I thrash through my orgasm.

My pussy clamps around nothing as I rock my hips against his face.

Emrys never falters as he sees me through every second of it. He pulls his fingers from me and licks me clean. His tongue tastes every inch of me until my hips lower back down to the workbench. He doesn't stop, even as I shake through the final waves of my orgasm.

My eyes are heavy as I watch him spread me wide and feast on me again. I shiver—my body is too sensitive from the intense climax.

His dark eyes find mine as he lowers my legs from his shoulders and pulls my skirts from my waist. Gently, he pulls me up before kissing me softly. My taste mingles with his. His hands brush through my curls as he holds my body tight to his.

Lifting me in his strong arms, he cradles me to his chest as we exit the kitchen. Walking us down the hall, my breath is still shallow, and my body feels utterly relaxed.

We must've gotten truly carried away in the kitchen because when we emerged outside, the sky is already an inky black. The stars above twinkle down at us, and a cool breeze tugs at my dress. It feels nice on my warm skin.

Emrys takes us through the meadow until we are once again at the clearing from last night. A silk sheet is laid out, and the sprites and faeries hug the tree-line. Gently, Emrys sets me down on the covered ground before sitting behind me. My back rests against his chest, and his hands hold me to him.

The sprites float towards us and illuminate the space with their glowing bodies. My head falls back against Emrys's shoulder as I absorb his closeness. Raising a hand, Emrys directs my attention to the night sky.

"Watch," he whispers in my ear.

As if they are alive, the stars begin to move. They swirl around in a dazzling circle. My breath hitches as they cut through the sky like water. Such beautiful magic.

The stars slow their movements until they form a massive tree. Its trunk is tall, and its branches are far-reaching. The stars file in on each other to create the great mass of leaves.

"Long ago, there was *The Great Oak,* and from it sprouted all faerie life," Emrys explains, his voice clear and strong.

I watch as a new scene is illustrated by the sparkling embers. They form the bodies of sprites—buzzing around and wreaking havoc. The scene transforms into the meadow, but one that is trampled and unorganized. A far cry from what it is now.

"But *The Great Oak* knew that they could not be left to their own devices. They needed a ruler to keep this realm in order," Emrys continues.

I watch the scene in the sky change again, and the massive tree is once more illuminated. From its strong truck, a cluster of stars breaks off and swirl into a familiar figure.

"From it's magical bark, I was born. The faerie king. Given my power from *The Great Oak* to control the meadow and maintain order."

Emrys's handsome face is cast in glowing stars and my heart speeds up.

"But *The Great Oak* had a secret." The scene changes once more into the tree. I watch in silent shock as golden stars fall from the branches and fade to nothing before reaching the bottom of the thick trunk. "It was dying, and with it, so would the meadow and all who inhabited it."

I open my mouth to say something—the sprites around me pale and hang their heads. Even Emrys's clear voice has become tinged with sadness. The truth of what he's explaining to me spears into my heart. My hand grips his as I turn to face him.

"Unless the prophecy could be fulfilled," he says softly, his hand cupping my cheek.

Gently, he tips my face back up to the sky and I gasp. It's Emrys and I, made out of glowing stars. Hand in hand, we walk towards *The Great Oak* and slip inside. The stars twist and shift, and the scene becomes more erotic. We are both naked—our bodies moving with each other while the tree around us glows brighter.

"As the prophecy goes, the king must take a human into the heart of *The Great Oak* and claim her. To restore its power by infusing his back into it. Only then could *The Great Oak* be revived by the offering of two souls and the primal magic that is made when they fuse together."

The stars glow bright once more before spreading out. The story ends, and they resume their typical place in the sky. Turning back towards Emrys, my eyes search his. Raising his hand, I notice a laurel of wildflowers. They are a riot of colors —blues, oranges, pinks, and whites—and smell delicious. Emrys smiles as he sets it on my head.

"The prophecy," I whisper.

I feel the flower crown settle there. With a gentle tug, the crown does not budge from its place on my head. Power flows through me and feels like Emrys—exciting and heady. It's not painful. It feels right. Permanent. As if I've always belonged here and always will.

"I've waited a long time for you, my blossom. All of my realm has, but they will continue to wait until you are ready. I won't complete this prophecy without you. It is you who hold the power," he whispers.

I lick my lips. "You've never taken anyone inside *The Great Oak*?"

He shakes his head. "Never."

"And you want to take me?"

"More than anything," he confesses. "You're the most beautiful woman I've ever seen. I want to own and keep you. I want to possess you. Laying claim to your soul during the ritual will be the greatest honor and the most wonderful pleasure. I want nothing more than to bind your soul to mine because you've owned me since the moment I saw you."

I stare into his earnest eyes. I can feel the sprites and faeries humming around us—willing us together. Who am I to deny them? I want to keep this realm safe, but more than that, I want Emrys. I want his kindness—his devotion and desire. He's given me my freedom and stoked my pleasure, and now I'm ready. To be a permanent fixture of this land and to do it by his side.

If I've owned his soul since the moment we met, then he most assuredly has owned mine.

My mind whispers that this has to be some sort of trick, but that voice sounds an awful lot like my mother and father's. I shake myself gently. No more will I think of them. No more will I let myself be ruled by their expectations and rules. I will be just as free as my king demands me to be.

The king who I love.

The realization makes the silence between us stretch. I love him. I do. It's too fast, but it's true. I should tell him, but not yet. First, I want to show him what he means to me—what he'll always mean to me.

Winding my hands through his soft hair, I twist until I'm straddling his lap. My legs lock around his back as I bring our mouths together. The kiss is soft and claiming. It's the first one of the rest of our lives together. Pulling back slightly, I touch our foreheads together.

"Take me to *The Great Oak*."

10

LAURELLE

Emrys carries me like I'm made of delicate glass.

His steps are quick and sure as we pass through rows of sweet-smelling flowers. Sprites fly up around us—cheering and offering congratulations. A few faeries throw white petals that cling to our knees. I'd say they seem more excited than me, but that would be a lie. My body hums with anticipation.

We cut through a row of thick trees beyond Emrys's palace. A few leaves tickle my cheeks, but Emrys's hold stays locked on me. I snuggle into his warm chest. Any nerves I have fade, and only eagerness swirls in my stomach.

Soon, I will have him, and soon we will be one.

While the prophecy is important, it isn't the only factor driving me and Emrys together. I want and care for him, and because of that, I want to help him save this beautiful, magical realm. The fact that he's never taken anyone else in here tells me all I need to know. If his depth of feeling for me wasn't clear before, it surely is now.

Pushing through the dense foliage, we emerge in a moonlit clearing. It's easily triple the size of the one the faeries and I danced through a few nights ago. This one is sequestered away, hidden to conceal an ancient secret. The sprites fly towards it and lounge on the branches of the surrounding trees.

A new sensation tickles my body. It pulses with energy—a different sort of magic zips through the air. A dense fog obscures the center. The damp wind tugs at my thin dress. Still, Emrys presses on until the cloudy air recedes, and my breath stills in my lungs.

It's magnificent. Even compared to all the things I've seen, *The Great Oak* is beyond compare.

Glowing with a pure golden light, the massive tree reaches into the sky at a shocking height. It's made up of hundreds of strong branches—all of them decorated in golden leaves. It feels warm despite the cool evening air. Its trunk is wider than a castle wall. Sprites and faeries swarm it, allowing their glowing bodies to add even more light to its impressive structure.

My eyes snag on a few bare branches, and my heart dips.

Emrys raises a hand at the tree, and the trunk gently peels open. Its golden bark folds in on its side. A gentle, crunching sound fills the clearing until there is a hole big enough for the two of us to step through.

Emrys takes us through the opening as I stare at my surroundings. The walls and floor are bare oak wood. Inside glows from an unknown light source. Magic, I assume. A few windows are carved along the oak walls of the room. They peer out into the dark night sky.

I'd expected the inside to be more similar to Emrys's palace— a tree that opens into a swath of rooms—however, we seem to be in a sort of wooden pocket. It is just one simple room carved into this wide trunk. Simple, its purpose clear, and my face warms.

Emrys gently sets me on my feet, and I sag back against his chest.

He says nothing as he takes my hand and raises it up before

us. A slight sting tickles my palm, and I watch in shock as the empty space before us is covered in fine silks and over-stuffed pillows. There's a thick mattress that looks akin to a cloud. The fabrics sparkle in the light, and I know in my heart that I've summoned these things.

I have magic—somehow. Part of me wishes to explore this newfound power, but as I watch the final pillows land softly on the bed, I only care about being with my king.

As if sensing my thoughts, Emrys collects me at my waist and deposits me on the bed. Despite the open windows, the inside of the tree is pleasantly warm. The floors and walls seem to pulse with life as if we are inside something living.

Emrys stands before me, his eyes dark and hot. We gaze at each other—our desire stealing our words. His hands skim up my sides, and I let out a soft sigh. My own hands curl behind his neck and yank his face down to mine.

Our lips connect, and the tree around us blazes in a new wave of golden light. My eyes pop open to see what just our simple touch has done. His lips on mine never waver, and I let myself be overwhelmed by his delicious taste.

There is power in here—heady and all-consuming—and I'm happily giving myself over to it.

Pulling him fully on top of me, I shimmy up the bed until he falls between my splayed thighs. Our mouths collide in a frenzy of kisses and bites as our hands tangle together. This kiss is a glimpse, a taste, of our future together. I moan as I swallow it down.

His tongue dances with mine as his claws shred my gown, leaving my hot skin exposed to the room.

Breaking for air, Emrys stares down at my naked body. His claws close over one of my breasts and give it a gentle squeeze. My eyes are heavy as I feel the soft skin of his sides slide against my inner thighs.

"I don't know what to do," I whisper. "How am I supposed to perform this ritual?"

Emry's smile is all teeth.

"By letting me pleasure you, my blossom. That's all *The Great Oak* demands of us. Look at what we've already done."

Indeed, the room glows with more golden light. The tree pulses with fresh power and Emrys has barely even touched me.

His lips return to mine, and I tangle my hands in his silk hair. His tongue tastes my lips before gently biting down on my lower lip. The little nip of pain has more wetness slicking out of me. I have to be soaking the silk below us.

Emrys's mouth traces down my neck. Biting and sucking as he goes, and my toes curl into the sheets. We've done this before, and yet it feels like the first time. It's familiar yet foreign.

Laying open-mouth kisses along my chest, he gently squeezes my right breast before his tongue swirls around my other nipple. I moan as he sucks it fully into his mouth, rolling the hard bud between his teeth. I'm panting as I watch him give my other breast the same treatment.

My body is on fire, and he's only adding more fuel to it.

His claws skim up the sensitive skin of my thighs before reaching my pussy. I gasp as his claw parts my soaked flesh and gently enters me. My eyes flutter close at the sensation. He's gentle as he fills me, pumping his finger slowly until my teeth clench. Carefully, he works another finger inside of me, the stretch decadent.

He's preparing me for his cock, and that realization makes more arousal surge from me. It seeps down my thighs, and I can hear the sloppy, wet sounds his fingers are making as they pump me. Emrys nips the fleshy swell of my breast, and my eyes pop open.

Black eyes sear into my soul.

"Are you going to be a good girl, Laurelle?" he asks. My

reply is a moan as he works a third finger into me. "Are you going to let me put my cock in this tight little pussy?"

His fingers still deep inside me. I try to move my hips to get some friction, but his claws pin my hips to the bed.

"Yes!" I cry out. A smile curves his lips as his fingers curl inside me. They brush up against a spot deep inside me, and my stomach clenches. Pleasure sings down my spine, and my groans become more unabashed.

"Even if it hurts?" he asks. "If only for a moment?"

Words escape me as I nod my head. My eyes threaten to close at this new onslaught of pleasure. I'm close, and I feel my thighs tremble along the sides of his hips.

Using his grip on my hips to leverage me, Emrys pushes me further onto my back until my hips tip up. This exposed, I can fully see his fingers—pale green and tipped in black—disappearing into my soaked pussy. Wetness shines on the inside of my thighs. My legs threaten to close, but he hooks his hand under my left knee and keeps them open.

Being this exposed, I wait for shyness or shame to steal my pleasure, but it doesn't. I want him to see me like this—to know that all of this is because of him.

"Use your words, my blossom," my faerie king growls.

"I want—I want—"

Words are hard when his fingers are fucking me this good. They work that secretive spot inside of me over and over again until my peak is just within reach.

Then his hand stills once more, and I let out a frustrated growl. My eyes blaze fury into his. Emrys merely smirks.

"Tell me what you want, and I'll continue."

"I..." With my pleasure so close, I let the truth of my heart spill free. There's no reason to hide anymore. There never was any reason. "I want you fuck me. Make me come—first with your fingers so I can lick them clean. Then I want your cock inside of me. Stretching me and filling me with your seed until it seeps out of me for hours, like you promised. I want to feel you every time I move tomorrow."

His fingers hook inside of me as he growls.

"Be my first," I cry, pleasure barreling towards me. "Be my only."

A warm, wet tongue licks my clit, and my whole body erupts. I arch clear off the bed, my muscles clamping so tight around his fingers that I fear I may break them.

I feel my come seep from me and soak his hand as he continues to pump me through my climax. It soaks my thighs—the smattering of curls covering my pussy. Still, my king doesn't stop as he wrings more pleasure from my body.

My muscles were tight, and now they are decadently languid. I feel like I am floating. Aftershocks of pleasure make me shiver and gasp. Faintly, I am aware of Emrys pulling his fingers from me. I open my heavy eyes to meet his gaze.

It's filled with affection and lust. He extends his hand towards my mouth and smears my release on my lips and chin. Clasping his large hand in mine, I suck his finger into my mouth. I taste myself and his skin. Moaning around his finger, I gently nip at the tip of his claw.

His eyes grow wide as he growls.

"Such a good girl," he praises. "Suck me. Taste yourself and understand the delicious treat you are."

I feel him shift between my thighs as I move on to the next finger. Emrys tosses something behind him, and I realize a moment too late it's his pants.

His finger leaves my mouth with a pop as I feel his cock push into my entrance. The tip is round and smooth. Glancing down, I get my first real look at his cock, and *Great Oak spare me...*

It's massive. Slightly darker green than the rest of his skin. Thick and already dripping with milky white seed at the tip. That wetness, mixed with my own, helps him glide just past my entrance. He's barely inside of me, and I already feel full. His hand traces down my chest, giving my breast a gentle squeeze before cupping my hip.

"Are you ready for me?" His voice is barely audible.

I nod my head as he shifts his hips slightly forward. The stretch and burn are great. I force my eyes to stay open as I watch his thick shaft part of my wet flesh. He's not even halfway in. His cock is a blessing—and also my greatest adversary.

"Words, Laurelle. I need the words."

Pressing up on my heels, I slip more of him inside of me with a strangled moan. My hands find the muscular curves of his backside and give a gentle pull.

"Take me. I was born to serve only you. A vessel for your pleasure."

With a strangled groan, Emrys goes to slide inside me more, but I'm impatient. Using what little strength I have left, I haul him the rest of the way inside of me. There is a pinch of pain— the feel of him stretching me is not without discomfort. Yet, I don't shift away. If anything, I drag him closer until our chests are pressed together. Opening my legs wider, I let his hips become flush with mine.

His breathing is ragged as he stays still inside of me, allowing me to adjust to his great length. My hands skim up his back and tangle in his hair. Emrys lays kisses on my forehead. His lips press against the tip of my nose before working their way down my neck. His deep voice murmurs praise with each kiss.

"Beautiful," he whispers. "Perfect. Your cunt was made for me. Tell me you're okay, my blossom."

His eyes find mine—concerned etched on his face. I cup his cheek and give him a gentle smile. Our lips press together, and my heart overflows with emotion. This is perfect. It's beyond anything that I could've ever imagined. Those old novels I used to read are nothing compared to this. The feeling of him inside me is beyond words.

And I want more.

Looking him in the eye, I break our kiss and say against his mouth, "Fuck me."

The command is simple, but it unleashes my faerie king.

His hips pull back before thrusting inside of me. The force is strong enough to have my breasts jolting. His hard cock fills me completely and presses up against my womb. He's so deep and wide, and if there was any question that I was meant for him, they're quickly done away with. I shouldn't be able to take him like this, but I can't get enough.

As if we were truly crafted to become one.

"Yes!" I scream as he thrusts into me again. "I have to have this forever. I can't live without it—without you."

"I'll never deny you a thing."

He pulls out of me until only the head of his massive cock remains inside me. My moan catches in my throat as he tosses my legs over his shoulder and shifts our angle. When he pushes inside me again, it will be even deeper, and anticipation tightens my muscles.

"You're too tight, too perfect."

"Impossible," I whine, trying to sheath more of him inside of me. "Please, *please*, give me your cock. Don't deny me the one thing I want the most."

With a strangled groan, he plunges deep inside of me. My hands cover his as he holds onto my hips. The sharp pricks of his claws only heighten my pleasure. I hope they leave behind a mark.

Mercilessly, he fucks me. His thrusts are hard yet gentle. Our bodies slap together in a symphony of sweaty, sticky skin. It's indecent, and it's exactly as it should be. I feel our hearts beating in time—our souls being threaded together. His earthy scent overwhelms me, and I taste it in the air.

"Look at how greedy you are for my cock," he says. "This little cunt is soaking me. It knows who's laid claim to her. Who owns her for the rest of eternity."

"It's yours. Just as I am," I pant.

"Greedy girl. A human man could never have given you this. Isn't that right?"

"Never!"

"Only me. Only this cock can truly satisfy such a sweet pussy."

His hips smack into my ass, causing my body to slide up the bed. My hands sink into the silk sheets and curl into fists. My moans are sloppy and loud. Lifting my legs from his shoulders, he folds them together before twisting my bottom half onto its side. Sliding into me once more is deep and tight. My king easily steals my breath.

"Emrys," I moan, my muscles tightening once more.

My eyes find the open window and gasp as I take in the glowing bodies there. The faeries and sprites watch through unblinking eyes. They lounge on the open window and float on their gossamer wings.

Emrys thrusts into me, and a moan slips past my lips. The sprites cheer in a flurry of glowing bodies. Should I be embarrassed that they're watching? I'm not. In fact, I enjoy their eyes. After having to hide myself for so long, claiming my desire and freedom so openly heightens my pleasure.

My faerie king cups my knees and pulls them open. Our hips meet as he fucks me over and over again. His mouth lands on mine as he tastes and teases. His claws roll and pinch my nipples.

"Do you enjoy them watching?" he asks. My cheeks warm, and I nod.

His hand travels between my legs as he traces the tip of his claw around my clit. He smirks and shakes his head.

"Only naughty girls are so wanton in public."

Pleasure calls to me. My peak is so close I can taste it.

"I want to be naughty," I admit. "Only with you."

His smile is pure male confidence as his mouth meets mine again. His tongue licks over my lips. I open my mouth to let him in as he slams his thick length into me over and over again. With each thrust, he claims a piece of my soul for himself.

Pulling back from me, Emrys says, "They want to watch the completion of the ritual. Should we allow them?"

Biting my lip, I nod my head. Golden light pours from between our connected bodies. *The Great Oak* seems to swell with each slap of our flesh.

Quick as lightning, Emrys shifts our positions once more. I protest as he pulls out of me, and my back lands against his chest. With his legs hanging off the edge of the mattress, he lifts me onto his lap. My knees rest on either side of his thighs.

His claws grip my chin and tip my face forward. My heart races as I watch the glowing figures fill the entryway and windows. Their eyes stare at us—rapt and undivided.

"Give them a good show, my blossom," Emrys urges.

With a shaky moan, I reach below and find his hard cock. I run my hand through my come coating him, and give him a gentle tug. He hisses as he pushes my curls off my sweaty back. His tongue licks up my spine as I press up on my knees. I work him around my entrance before sheathing the tip inside of me.

"Oh, Emrys," I moan, sliding down his impressive length. This way is obscenely decadent. The stretch is otherwordly. I rise up on my knees before sinking fully onto him again.

The sprites and faeries before us cheer and dance. Their bodies hum and glow anew, just as *The Great Oak* does. Emrys's hand comes to my hip and helps raise and lower me on his hardness. Over and over again, I take his length as my moan ratchet up.

"Once my seed spills inside of you, the ritual will be

complete. *The Great Oak's* power will be restored, and you will be queen. You already wear the crown."

My hand comes up to the flowers woven through my hair. They pulse under my fingers. I feel powerful, as if each thrust is infusing me with more and more magic. It feels permanent claiming. Just as permanent as my love for Emrys.

"Come. Inside. Me." I bite out each word on a thrust. "Fill me with your seed. I need my king's come."

Emrys growls, his claws tightening on me as he pulls me off his length and throws me face down at the end of the bed.

"Then you shall have it," he growls against my ear.

He thrusts into me with one powerful stroke, and my chest knocks to the bed. He yanks my hips upward, and my fingers find the sheets. His hands are the only thing holding me up as he pounds me into the mattress. Each thrust jolts me forward and pulls my climax towards me.

Flames lick my skin, and my muscles begin to tremble.

The sprites buzz around us. A few faeries have even ventured into the room, their small footsteps barely audible. Those in the crowd mirror the sound of our skin smacking— clearly more than eager to participate in their own wanton display. My moans are choppy as he ruts into me.

His claw skims between the cheeks of my ass, and I feel him press at the tight ring of muscle back there.

"Hear me, my blossom. We won't leave this oak until I've claimed all your little holes. I already promised as much."

His thumb breaches my back entrance, and it sets off my release. When his other hand rubs my clit, I'm done for. I scream into the sheets, my whole body shaking as my come drips out of me and covers him. My muscles clamp down around his hard length, and I feel our connection between my legs and in my heart.

Emrys thrusts hard into me once, twice, and on the third, he lets out a guttural growl before his warmth soaks me. He comes and comes until I feel his seed mingling with my own and sliding down my thighs. I feel a strange tightening in my chest as it flows into me.

Looking up, the room blazes with golden light—brighter than the sun. Fresh flowers sprout up between my fingers from where my hands grip the bed. A harsh wind blows through *The Great Oak*, pushing the sprites and faeries from the room. They let out a scream as they land outside. A metallic taste coats my tongue at the abundance of fresh magic.

My body still shakes with my orgasm as Emrys embeds his teeth in my shoulder. The bite is harsh and claiming, and it sets off another climax as I feel our hearts and souls become one. Two halves finally becoming whole.

The sprites cheer and titter outside as Emrys jerks one last time inside me.

Glancing over my shoulder, my eyes can barely stay open. I watch as Emrys kisses the bite on my shoulder before gently pulling out of me. My curls cling to my sweaty temples, and I try my best to tuck some behind my ear.

Emrys's hands grip my side and gently pull me down to the bed on top of his chest. My hand lands over his heart, and I feel it racing under my palm. Even Emrys seems to glow. He hums with new power. His crown is dotted with fresh golden leaves. My own skin seems to be sparkling as if my blood flows gold instead of red.

I'm too tired to take it all in.

With a deep sigh, I snuggle into his chest and let our mingling releases dry on my thighs. I love the feeling of him seeping out of me. I love the claim.

My eyes are already closing when Emrys's claws skim down my cheek.

"Are you okay?" he whispers.

Sleep has stolen my voice, but I manage to open my eyes and smile. Giving him a small nod, he gathers me tighter against his chest. His lips brush mine, and it takes everything I have to return it.

"Sleep, my blossom," he commands. "I'll have my cock in you again soon enough."

Despite my exhaustion I manage to giggle and find my voice.

"Can't wait," I slur before drifting into a deep, boneless sleep.

11

EMRYS

Even in sleep, she is perfect.

Her gorgeous face is relaxed—her whole body is warm and trusting in my arms. I should be sleeping as well, but I can't. Not as our lovemaking still pumps through my veins and *The Great Oak* hums around us with new magic.

The prophecy has been fulfilled. Satisfaction should be coursing through me, and in truth, I am happy that my realm is no longer in danger. But satisfied? I can't say that I am anything but restless as a new hunger burrows under my skin.

This new need roars in my veins, demanding I claim my blossom over and over again. To be awake and not inside her is torture. To not hear her call my name as she comes is an unbearably cruel punishment.

At least I have my eyes on her. Even watching her, helps some of the sharpest parts of my desire dull. I'll guard her as she sleeps. I'll wait for her to be ready for me again, and I'll enjoy the warmth of her embrace and siphon as much pleasure from her as I can before she needs to rest once more.

My whole kingdom is asleep. The excitement of tonight taking its toll on everyone.

Even though my body is exhausted, my heart and mind are alert. Need, raw and hot, pulses through me. I try and quiet my mind by counting Laurelle's freckles. I've just gotten to number seventy-two when she stirs against my chest.

Her plumb lips part with a sigh as she burrows closer to me. Pride and primal urges dance in my chest. My claws skim up her back and over her delicate shoulder eliciting a small shiver from her. Tracing up her throat, I swallow my growl at my claiming bite. The imprint of my teeth is an unwavering indication of who owns her.

My cock hardens at the sight.

Continuing their exploration, my hands skim back down the soft skin of her back. How can someone be this perfect? This delicate? Her shame and shyness are gone. Eradicated by my touch and I revel in it. I laid claim to her soul—her heart—and I will keep them safe for all eternity.

My claws dig into the fleshy swell of her ass, and Laurelle shifts closer. Her warm breath bathes my throat as her brown, gold-flecked eyes blink open at me. They glow with the magic we created here. The magic that belongs to her and makes her brown skin glow.

Her lips curve into a soft smile. Affection warms her gaze.

A queen is what she is. My queen.

"Why aren't you sleeping?" Her voice is rough as she cups my cheek. Her thumb gently traces the line of my cheekbone.

"I enjoy watching you too much to rest."

She laughs, slinging her leg further over my hips and snuggling closer to me. I can feel my dried seed on her leg, and my thoughts turn wicked. I send up a prayer of thanks to *The Great Oak* for putting Laurelle in my path. She's too perfect for me and I will spend the rest of our lives proving myself worthy of having such a gift as her.

"You're not tired?" Her voice vibrates against my neck.

"Not tired enough to take my eyes off you."

She shakes her head, her curls tickling my cheeks. Rising up slightly on her arms, her naked breasts come into view, and my blood heats. Perfect. They filled my hands as if molded for them, and I long to taste them once more.

A grin curves her lips as if she knows what I'm thinking. Clearly, she felt my cock stir to life once more. My hand runs up her neck and tangle in her hair. I let her curls slip through my fingers before reaching her flower crown.

It's beautiful, made of flowers just as wild as her. Nothing is more befitting of my lovely queen. It's more than an accessory; it shows her permanent place at my side. We will rule this land together, hand in hand, and I will worship her every day of our reign.

"I don't know how you aren't sleepy," she whispers, her hand tracing the muscles of my chest. Biting her lower lip, her face is the picture of innocence. "Maybe you need some help relaxing?"

I get her meaning when her curious hand travels down my stomach. My whole body tights as she wraps her small hand around my cock. It's already hard and dripping. Even that small touch has seed spilling from the tip.

Knocking back the silk sheets, I expose our naked bodies to the room. Laurelle moans as she glances between us. Her hand barely wraps around my length as she gives me a gentle squeeze. I hiss, and she moans in answer.

Despite loving her touch more than anything, I can't help but check in on her.

"You don't have to do this, Laurelle." My claws dig into her waist. "I know you're exhausted. Sleep. My cock will still be hard when you wake. That I promise you."

Instead of releasing me, she gives another tight pump of her fist, and I groan. Wickedness gleams in her brown eyes as she rolls on top of me. Her lips press against mine, and I cup her head. I'm lost to her sweet mouth. Her small hand pumps my cock in time with her thrusting tongue. It makes my head spin.

We're both breathless as we pull apart. My shaft is trapped between my abs and her soft stomach. Pressing our foreheads together, Laurelle smirks at me. A powerful queen merely toying with her willing subject.

"You said we weren't leaving until you claimed all my holes," I growl as she places a soft kiss on my chest. "I woke up with this craving, my king. Shall I tell you about it?"

"Yes," I growl as she licks over one of my nipples. My wild and wanton Laurelle. "I command you, reveal all your desires."

She bites her lip as she stares up at me.

"Your taste," she whispers. "I dreamed of what you would taste like. Of what your hard cock sliding against my tongue would feel like. Would you deny me?"

"Never." My growl rattles the room.

"Good."

Her mouth kisses down my chest. She bites and sucks as she goes and now I bare her markings. Pride warms my chest. My Laurelle is possessive and I'm more than happy to be claimed by her.

I spread my legs wider to accommodate her between them. My cock hardens further until it stands proud—preening for her attention. Her eyes are wide as she realizes just what was inside her from earlier. And what will soon be filling her perfect mouth.

She gives me another tug before tucking her dark curls behind her ear. Bracing her hand on my thigh, her delicious breasts graze me as her pink tongue tentatively licks the bead of seed at the tip. Moaning, she swallows it down.

Hazy eyes lock with mine.

"You lie, my king," she states.

"About what?" My heart races. She licks up the length of my shaft.

"You said there was nothing sweeter than my pussy, but... have you never tasted yourself?"

"Laurelle," I growl. Her lips curve into a wide smile before she leans down again.

Wrapping her perfect lips around the head of my cock, she sucks me deeper into her mouth. It's warm and wet and Laurelle. The only thing more decadent than her mouth is her sweet pussy. Her head bobs in time with her fist as she jerks me. Her saliva coats my shaft and wet, smacking sounds fill the room.

Deeper and deeper she takes me into her mouth until I'm in her throat. She chokes once, twice, as if testing her limits. My hands tangle in her hair and lift her face towards mine. Saliva coats her lips and dribbles down her chin. Her eyes water but I can smell her deepening scent.

She loves this almost as much as I do.

More seed seeps from my tip, and she eagerly licks it away.

"Cock-hungry little girl, aren't you?"

She nods her head, working me deeper into her throat once more.

"You look so pretty with my cock in your mouth."

Releasing my length with a pop, she gazes up at me.

"Am I doing alright? I've never done this before, but I've always wanted to."

I raise a brow as jealousy tightens my chest.

"Really? Did you think of doing this with a human man?"

Her eyes widen, and she shakes her head. "Never."

My jealousy dissipates as she continues.

"I only heard about this in passing from a few of our servants. I never thought it would appeal to me, yet when I met you, I wanted to try. To know what it would be like to taste you here. I—"

She pauses and looks away, her mouth going back to my

cock. I capture her face before she can take me back inside her. I use my thumb to pull her pink lip down.

"Say the rest," I command. Her cheeks color, but she nods.

"I had this fantasy long, long ago. Something I read in a book my mother took from me. It's something I've been wanting for us to try."

"Tell me, and I'll make it yours."

My curiosity is peaked further as her cheeks fill with color and she bites her lip.

"I imagined you standing in front of me. My knees on the floor and my hands gripping your thighs." Her breath picks up, and I watch her squirm. "I thought of your claws pricking my scalp as you guide my mouth up and down your cock. I'd choke and spit, but I'd keep going as far as I could so that I could please you."

My balls draw up tight, and I'm dangerously close to spilling all over her delicate hand. Shuffling her back, I wait for her knees to hit the floor in front of the bed. Standing over her, I stare down into her face. With a wave of my hand, a couple of pillows stuff themselves under her knees so she doesn't hurt herself but also to make her the perfect height for what I plan to do.

Curling my claws into her hair, I let them press into her scalp and her mouth opens with a gasp. Seizing the opportunity, I rock my hips forward and sheath myself inside her warm mouth.

She groans, sending delicious vibrations down my cock. Her hands come up to my thighs before slipping around and gripping my ass. I thrust into her mouth over and over again. I slide against her wet tongue. I bump the back of her throat, and she gags. Tears stream down her golden brown cheeks as her eyes flame with more desire.

"Is this what you wanted? For me to fuck your face just like I did your little cunt?"

She makes a garbled sound, and I yank her off my length. Swallowing down her saliva, I revel in the beautiful mess I've made of her.

"Use your words," I command.

"Yes," she gasps. "Just like this. I love it."

"Good girl. Such a naughty little cock-slut you are."

She gasps at my words. They would've offended the old Laurelle, but this one lets them wash over her. My queen is a dirty girl who likes cock in her mouth and my fingers in her ass. She wants to be taken roughly and crudely by someone she trusts.

And I'm the lucky creature who gets to have her.

"Tell me you love being my little fuck-toy," I command.

She squeezes my ass, and I can hear her come soaking the floor beneath her. I'll lick it up later.

"I love it," she says.

"Tell me you want me to come in your pretty little throat."

"Please, come in my mouth, Emrys. I crave your taste."

"I'll feed you this cock every night. You won't even need food. This will keep you fulfilled for eternity."

She garbles her agreement before taking me back into her mouth. My grip on her head tightens as I rock against her warm tongue. She sucks and slurps me. Her mouth is tight and hot, and my spine is already beginning to tingle.

Her curious hand leaves my ass to graze under my shaft, and I'm done for. My roar scatters the birds lounging in *The Great Oak's* branches. My spine locks up, and my muscles tighten as the seed is ripped from me. Warmth spreads throughout my stomach as my teeth clench.

"Swallow it. Be a good girl."

Laurelle eagerly takes my come into her mouth. She gulps down two mouthfuls before I pull her from my length. Gripping my seeping cock, I line it up with her face.

The first spray of my seed covers her lips and chin. Her eyes widen as the next spray lands on her chest and drips down her breasts. I bathe her lips in my seed once more before shoving it back into her mouth.

Now sticky with my release, she cleans off my cock with efficiency.

Once my climax passes, I fall from her mouth once more. She licks over her lips and moans at my taste lingering there. My seed is smeared all over her perfect face and it's more decadent than I can bear.

Her thighs rub together, her floral scent drowning me. She looks up at me, a silent plea in her eyes.

"I know just what you need."

Plucking her from the ground, I toss her into the center of the bed. My face comes down between her splayed thighs, and I devour her wet flesh. It's soft and soaking wet. I rub my nose back and forth against her clit before sucking it into my mouth.

Her hands grip my head as she thrashes on the bed. The sheets around us are in tatters. Laurelle is lost to pleasure as she raises her hips against my tongue. She grinds against my face, demanding her orgasm.

My tongue spears into her entrance, and I taste our mingling releases. I groan as I lick her clean. Rubbing her clit with my thumb, her body locks. Those inner muscles clamp around my tongue as more wetness floods my mouth.

I drink her pleasure, swallowing her down just as she did for me. Her body shakes through it all. Her eyes are wide open, and her mouth is parted on a silent scream.

Slowly, her thighs loosen from my head. I expect her to pass out, but she doesn't. Her hands find my head, and she tilts my face towards her.

She's all queenly power when she demands, "Inside me."

I grin before pressing a soft kiss to her inner thigh.

Without giving her a warning, I cup her hips and flip her onto her stomach. Dragging her by the middle, I prop her up on her elbows and tip her hips up to face me. My claws dig into her ass and spread her cheeks wide. Both of her little holes are ripe for the taking.

"Emrys," she whines, not in embarrassment but in desire.

I spit down on her back entrance. Spearing my tongue into her ass as she squeals. Her muscles should be loose enough from the orgasm, but we'll still need to go slow. Incredibly slow as I ease a finger into her tight hole. I pump it inside of her slowly as she thrashes. I retreat the finger and plunge it back in, eliciting a scream from my blossom.

Perhaps I can't make good on my promise after all.

"You're too tight here," I explain. Gently, I withdraw my finger.

Her hand reaches back and captures mine. Looking over her shoulder, her eyes are firm.

"Fuck my ass."

"My blossom, I don't—"

"If it's too much, we'll stop, but I want to try." Her eyes implore me. "Please."

I growl. "You know I can't deny you when you use that word."

She giggles and props herself up on her elbows. Reaching down, I grip my cock, that's already hard, and begging to be back inside her any way it can. I press against her ass, and Laurelle moans.

Her smile is trusting as I gently push the tip inside of her.

Hot, tight muscles wrap around the head of my cock. It chokes the pleasure from me. Laurelle keens and claws at the bed. Gripping one of her cheeks, I hold her open. I have to see every moment of this.

I push in another inch, and her chest heaves. She's too perfect.

"I won't last longer than a minute," I confess. My seed is already embarrassingly close to spilling.

"Good," Laurelle groans.

I chuckle despite the onslaught of pleasure. My cock stretches her tight hole as I push as far in as I can. Laurelle's breath catches, and I hold still. Reaching underneath my cock, I push a finger into her wet pussy. It eagerly sucks me in, and Laurelle moans.

"Full, Emrys. I'm so full of you," she cries.

I retreat my hips and finger before entering both her holes again at the same time. Fucking her ass with shallow thrusts, I take some of her sweet come and begin to rub her clit. Her hips push back to meet my thrusts as her moans become incoherent.

"Emrys, I'm coming!"

Her ass tightens, and I slip my fingers back inside her pussy. Her greedy cunt clamps around my fingers as her come soaks my hand. Looking over her shoulder, her face is a picture of euphoric bliss, and it takes me over the edge. To know I'm the one who brought this pleasure to her is a privilege.

It's too fast, but I can't bring myself to care.

My seed spills into her tight ass as I gently fuck it into her. She moans softly as her muscles loosen once more. The last spray of seed leaves me, and I pull out of her tight body. I pull her cheeks apart and watch my seed leak from her ass and trail down her pretty slit. The sticky come gathers at her entrance before dripping onto the bed below.

I gently smack her ass before nipping it gently. Laurelle yelps before breaking off into a fit of giggles. She slumps forward on the bed, but not before capturing my hand and pulling me down beside her.

Curling her spine against my chest, our hands hold each other between her breasts. I turn and inhale her scent, loving the way her soft hair sticks to my sweaty skin. With a deep sigh, her ass presses against my cock, and it rises to life once more.

Laurelle's yawn quickly dispels any notion of another round.

"You have to be tired now," she murmurs. "I could sleep for a week."

I nod against her shoulder. My soul mingles with hers as I hold her. The two of us become one after the intensity of our coupling. I've never felt this way. The satisfaction I felt with previous loves is nowhere near what I feel right now.

I've had her in every way I can. I'll keep her and pleasure her and love her. Love.

It blasts through me, overwhelming all my senses. I've known that I've loved her from the moment she landed in my realm.

Why have I not told her? I should've told her every moment we've been together. She wants to stay with me. Surely I've done enough to earn hers? Maybe she's just waiting for my confession before surrendering her own.

Possessiveness—needing to lay this ultimate claim—burns my blood as I tighten my hold on her.

"I love you, my blossom," I say.

Her response never comes and as I glance down at her face I know why. She's out cold. Her breath is deep and even.

A small smile curls my lips as I wave my hand and the silk sheet covers us. I'll tell her again in the morning. After all, we have eternity together. Laurelle is mine. I've claimed her just as she's claimed me. For the first time, the future doesn't seem so much like an unending chore. It's filled with hope, excitement, and love.

My eyes grow heavy and it's not long before I'm following Laurelle into a deep restful sleep.

12

LAURELLE

Golden sunlight streams into my eyes.

Shifting slightly, my muscles protest the movement. Despite the soreness of my muscles and between my legs, I'd gladly forgo my discomfort in order to relive last night a thousand times. All of it had been wonderful. A wonderful, wild dream.

No not a dream—a real-life fantasy.

The muscular arm draping across my waist tethers me to this bed and my body. A firm reminder that everything that's happened since I stepped foot in this faerie realm is very real. My life began last night and every day will be just like these past two days. Perfect, magical, and filled with so much love it pours from me.

Emrys has done more than enough to earn my love. When he wakes I shall tell him.

Licking over my lips, I'm pleased to still have the taste of my king there. I want more of him. Forever will not be enough. He's made good on his word and has freed me from my old life. Now instead of shame, all I feel is freedom flowing through me.

Unbridled lust and desire dance in my blood and demand I give into it with Emrys.

I have to get a look at him.

Rolling onto my other side, I stare up at his handsome face. Relaxed in sleep, he looks younger. His chest moves with each deep breath. Taking my hand, I gently trace my finger over his cheeks and along his strong jaw.

He inhales sharply, and his dark eyes blink open. His hand captures mine against his chin and brings it to his lips. His mouth lays kisses along the pulse at my wrist before giving it a gentle bite. I sigh and shift closer to him.

"You made good on your word," he grumbles. "We've been sleeping in here near a week."

I gasp and pull back to look at him. His green lips curl into a smirk.

"In human time, of course. In the meadow, it's only been a few hours."

I smile and shake my head, delighting in the warmth of his naked skin against mine.

"Some beast ravaged me well into the morning. I was in dire need of my beauty sleep."

"Some beast?" He raises a white brow.

I give a prim nod. In a flash, Emrys rolls me onto my back. His body slides between my splayed thighs. His hands circle my wrists and bring them above my head. The silk sheets and pillows cushion my body and bring me even closer to his.

"If I remember correctly, it was you—naughty girl—who begged this beast to fuck your ass."

I gasp schooling my features into a picture of mock outrage.

"A lady would never do such a thing."

Emrys chuckles before joining his mouth with mine. The kiss is gentle, and tender, in a way that brings tears to my eyes. I don't let them fall, I only kiss him harder. Everything is perfect.

An old insecurity worms it's way into my heart. Is all of this too good to be true? Am I worthy of such a picturesque life?

Emrys breaks me from my thoughts as his lips tickle my ear.

"I see no lady here, only a queen. Queens demand whatever they please."

My hands cup his head as my eyes lower. I can't stop the words from passing through my lips. I hate this insecurity I still carry. Will it leave me with time? Or is this one last gift from my parents I'll never be able to rid myself of?

"Are you so certain of me? Of our connection to have bound me to you in such a way?"

Emrys pulls back, his brows lowering over his dark eyes.

"Are you having doubts?" he asks. His claws cup my cheek and force my gaze to meet his.

Biting my lip, I shake my head. Who can I share my worries with if not him? After all, he is the only one who can truly eradicate them for me.

"Just old insecurities threatening to ruin everything. I never felt good enough during my old life. I just worry that you've made a mistake. I'm sorry, I shouldn't doubt you. After all that you've done for me."

Shame, an ugly and all too familiar emotion makes my eyes lower.

"Never apologize for your feelings," he growls. "It will take time for you to unlearn the lies taught to you in the human world."

I shake my head in agreement. Emrys tightens his hold on me, and I feel his hard cock rub against my wet pussy. I let out a soft moan as he does it again, my desire replacing any other feelings. My eyes snap up to his.

"As for your insecurities..." His tongue licks over the shell of my ear. "I'll fuck them out of you. Your place is beside me. Or better yet, my place is inside of you for eternity."

I smile and lift my hips. His cock nudges my entrance as I meet his heated gaze.

"Then that's what you shall have."

Our chests speed up as we stare at each other, the desire and love we shared last night raging inside us again. Demanding we claim each other and bring the threads of souls together once more. The heat of bodies burns away all doubts.

Love. I must tell him. Now, I won't keep this to myself any longer.

"Emrys," I say. My hands tangle in his hair. "I—"

Unease curdles my stomach. Something is wrong. I can feel it. The meadow dims, and the breeze whips through the open window. It's cold and stings my nose with its metallic scent. Emrys roars, his chest vibrating against mine as he sits straight up in the bed.

"Intruders," he spits. His dark eyes glow with a fury I've never seen before. "I'll deal with them at once, my blossom."

I pull the silk sheet to my chest as I watch Emrys tear the room apart. He yanks on his thin, dark-colored pants. With a wave of his hand, an unbuttoned white shirt covers his back and flows down his arms. Anger pours from him as I watch his crown grow—the branches becoming thicker and the leaves denser.

Whoever made the mistake of interrupting us will feel the full wrath of my king.

"You will be safe here, my blossom. I'll be back to fill your needy little pussy in no time. You have my word."

My cheeks heat as Emrys heads towards *The Great Oak's* opening. Somehow, I manage to find my voice.

"Wait," I say. Emrys turns towards me, his fury melting into affection the longer he stares at me. "I am the queen now. Perhaps we should see to these trespassers together."

My hand gently touches the flower crown. The petals weave between my curls and dance under my fingers as if they are eager for my touch. This is my life now, and I want to claim it. My role here is important; while I love sharing Emrys's bed, I want to have a larger purpose than just a lover.

I want the responsibility of caring for the land and the people who set me free. Ruling over them with my king at my side is a privilege. I won't shrink from my duties.

Emrys pads over to me. His hand meets mine in my hair and gently traces over the petals of the wildflowers. It sends a shiver down my spine as I feel them revel in his attention.

"My beautiful, fierce queen. You would do me this honor of ruling by my side?"

"Always," I say. Emotion clogs my throat as he helps me from the bed.

He growls at my exposed body, the remnants of his seed still clinging to my chest and between my legs. With a wave of a hand, they are washed away, and I feel like I've just bathed in the warmest bath.

"You have *The Great Oak's* magic now, my blossom. Use it," Emrys encourages.

I stare down at my body and concentrate. Light flows from my chest as I reach inside myself, where Emrys and I are tied together. Power tingles at my fingertips as the scent of fresh flowers coats the air. Closing my eyes, I concentrate on what I want to appear.

Gasping, I feel something soft cover my body. I open my eyes to watch flowing white fabric decorated with light blue and purple flowers cover my body. The skirt is long, as are the sheer sleeves, but the neckline is low enough to enhance the swells of my breasts.

My feet remain blissfully bare.

"Perfect. You're too beautiful for any realm," Emrys states, grabbing my hand.

Leaning into his side, I press up on my toes and peck him on the lips.

"You make me feel beautiful. Powerful, too."

"As any good king should."

"How much power did you give me—or rather *The Great Oak*?"

His smile turns salacious as we pass through the trunk's opening. The cool morning air tickles my cheeks. The sharp metallic scent is still there. The wind guides us back towards the clearing where, no doubt, the intruders are being kept.

As an intruder myself, perhaps I'll show them mercy. Maybe their happiness resides down here as well.

"*The Great Oak* gave you a taste of the depth of your power. If you want more, all you have to do is ask. Or better yet—"

Emrys pulls me against his side and dives his tongue into my mouth. He kisses me thoroughly, tasting me until I forget where I am or where we are going.

"I can just fuck more of my power into you. How does that sound?"

"Delicious," I moan. He kisses me firmly once more before taking my hand again as we walk towards the meadow. "You make everything so easy for me."

"Nothing is more precious to me than you. If you wanted my crown, I'd cleave it from my head just to see you smile."

"Ugh," I wrinkle my nose at that gory image. I give his hand a squeeze. "That's sweet, but I prefer your head fully intact."

"As you wish, my blossom."

The closer we get to the meadow, the more Emrys's posture stiffens. Magic swirls around him on an invisible breeze. He glows with menace. The picture of destructive power, I almost expect the trees to tremble in his wake. Indeed, some of the sprites do as we pass. Their bodies dim as they hide under passing branches.

Emrys is every bit the terrifying king, but to me, he could only be my sweet lover.

Lover. The word doesn't sound right for what he is to me. It seems too fleeting. Yet, we've given no vows—there's been no discussion of what we are only that we belong to each other. Is that enough? Do I require such a pathetic human title from a creature with unlimited power?

My steps slow, and Emrys turns towards me. Concern is written on his face. Before he can ask me what's wrong, my worries slip from my lips. Damn my parents for poisoning me with such fickle insecurities.

"Are we married?" I blurt out. Emrys merely blinks at me. "I mean—will we be married? Is that something your kind does?"

The silent stretches for a moment I curse my errant tongue. Why did I have to make this awkward? He's made me his queen —what does it matter if I'm his wife or not? I should be grateful enough for this.

Emrys pinches my chin and holds my stare.

"I own you in every way. Just as you own me." I lick over my dry lips. "Is marriage important to you, my blossom?"

"It's so trivial, I know. It's just—"

"Nothing you want is trivial. Now, start again."

My body relaxes. I should've known he'd understand. No longer do I have to apologize for my feelings or feel burdened by them. My feelings are normal—natural. What's unnatural is disregarding them in order to appease someone else. I did so for my father and was preparing to do so for my future husband.

No more. I will never apologize for what I want again.

"Marriage is important to me. I want us to be united in that way."

Emrys nods, a small smile on his lip.

"Then, as king of this realm, I pronounce us married. Our subjects as our witnesses."

Raising his hand, I watch as he pinches the air and brings his fingers in front of my face. There, sitting between his thumb and forefinger is a delicate gold band decorated with a series of colored gemstones. It sparkles in the bright sun. My hand trembles as he takes it in his own.

"You are my everything. Wife, queen, lover. The other half of my soul," he says, sliding the ring onto my finger. It's a perfect fit. Tears rush to my eyes. "You are my heart. My mate. The one I took into *The Great Oak* to fulfill the prophecy. You are the only thing that truly matters to me."

"Quite romantic, husband." My giggle is watery. Emrys presses his lips to my forehead as the sprites around us cheer. Tucking my hand in his again, I admire my new ring as we walk the last few steps into the meadow's clearing.

The ring is perfect—just like everything else here. Nothing could ruin life here.

Until I see the humans clustered in the center of the meadow.

My stomach clenches, and my head feels strange. There's a handful of men, all dressed in the regalia of royal guards. Bile rises in my throat as I take in their discarded banner. It's the royal seal of Prince Carysen's family.

The breath is ripped from my lungs as I fully take in the scene. A pair of royal guards are swinging their sharp swords at a swarm of faeries. Their bodies are barely two feet tall, yet they have these grown men shaking with fear. I might have found the whole thing funny if I wasn't so shocked.

Especially as I watch the three sisters bang against the guards' helmets, causing them to stumble.

My heart twists as I see the pathetic figure cowering behind the four royal guards. Prince Carysen—my intended—covers his ears as a handful of sprites pull at his sandy brown hair. He waves a gloved hand at them. His clothes are gaudy, yet clearly, they are showing signs of the fall he took to get down here. Grass stains mar the silk of his overcoat, and mud is caked on the fingers of his riding gloves.

His eyes finally open and meet mine. The cruelty there

steals my breath, and I take a step back. Emrys is immediately at my side.

"My blossom, what's wrong?"

I open my mouth to answer, my eyes whipping between him and the prince. I don't get a chance to explain before a voice dripping in condemnation rips through the meadow.

"There she is," calls Prince Carysen, pushing from between his guards. "Of course, *you'd* manage to end up in a place like this."

He pays for that little show of courage when a pair of female faeries hiss at him, swiping at his pants with their claws. The guards manage to shove them back. Both the sprites and faeries retreat even as their muscles stay coiled.

I can feel their anger as if it is my own. It hums through me, as does the unease of these latest arrivals. They don't belong here—they can't stay. If Emrys feels it too, he makes no indication as he gathers me to his side, and we face the wrath of my betrothed.

"What a great fucking mess this," Prince Carysen exclaims. "A month at least, we've been searching for you. A month without the dowry I was counting on your father providing me."

Emrys's grip on me tightens, his rage hot against my side.

Prince Carysen tracks the movement. His sneer misses nothing as the king holds me, our connection clear—especially as his ring glows on my finger.

"Why am I not surprised to find you here? Whoring yourself out to these foul creatures. No doubt you've let them take turns with you. How ashamed your family will be when they learn what's become of you."

One of the sisters—Pond—buzzes in front of his face and uses her hand to smack him in the eye. He howls and doubles over. Despite his cruel words, I can't help my smile at watching him in pain.

"You fucking bitch!" he roars. Whether it's at me or Pond, I'm not sure.

Wiping at his eyes, they blaze with blue fury.

"You could've just married me. Let me put some heirs in your belly and be done with it. Now, we're trapped in this fucking forsaken land with a bunch of—"

"Enough."

Emrys's voice cuts through the clearing with authority. Even the breeze stops blowing.

His claw skims up my back until he reaches my tense shoulders. Gently, he pulls them down and uncoils me. I hadn't even realized how much Carysen's words affected me until Emrys helps me right myself. Each vile word made me turn inwards, and the wrath on Emrys's face tells me they won't go unpunished.

Tracing a claw over my cheek, I let his power flow into me. I won't hide, and I won't cower. I belong only to Emrys, and he will keep me safe from monsters like Carysen.

My king turns his dark eyes onto my former betrothed, and I watch him and his guards pale.

"How dare you insult my queen." His voice cuts through the clearing like a knife. "You hurl those disgusting words against the woman I love. Saying she is no more than breeding stock and a few bits of gold. She is worth more than any coin. Any jewel. She is worth more than life."

A shiver of pleasure sings down my spine at his declaration.

With a wave of his claws, the trees around us shake before becoming a riot of snapping twigs and cracking branches. Invisible hands rip the swords from the guards' hands. Defenseless, they can do nothing as those mighty oak trees reach with their sentient branches and wrap them around their arms and legs. They scream as they are hoisted into the sky. Bucking against their wooden shackles, their fight is futile.

Carysen's eyes are wide as his fine clothes tear against the branches. He thrashes the most, tears streaming down his ruddy cheeks. Pain and fear dance in his eyes. How many women have felt the same in his presence? All of those former betrothals ending in their disappearances—his sister confirmed to me what happened.

He deserves every moment of this pain.

"Now you will die for your insults," Emrys commands.

Like whips, branches wrap around their throats and hoist them further into the sky. They thrash and gargle. Carysen's satin gloves rip against the branch as he tries to dislodge it from around his neck.

For so long, I have been afraid of men like him—of my father and his expectations held up by my mother. Their rigid ideals stole so much from me, and I won't allow them to take anymore. Why should I hide in front of a coward like Carysen? A vermin who soaks the front of his trousers like a scared little boy.

My shoulders straighten as I feel the power of this realm—of Emrys and *The Great Oak*—flow through me.

"Wait," I command and watch as the trees listen. They stop tightening for a moment.

Emrys turns to me and awaits my command. I smile at him and let my love for him show. He loves me. He told Carysen—told his whole realm. I'll show him the same devotion in a moment. Right now, I have something important to tell this sniveling prince.

Taking a step forward, I level my gaze at Carysen and let cruelty flood my gaze.

"My father forced me to marry you in order to gain power. Power I never would've benefitted from. He did the same with my other siblings, shackling them all to their own loveless unions." I take another step as snot leaks from Craysen's red nose. Petulant child. "You would've been cruel to me. Your own sister clued me into the depths of your depravity and, with

courage—something you could never be accused of having—
helped me escape you."

"Laurelle, please, let me—"

"Silence." My voice echoes around the clearing, strong and
unwavering. "Here I am safe—important. I have power and get
to decide what I am. I have my freedom. My desires are many
and indulged in. You may call me a whore, but that word means
nothing coming from a monster like you."

"Please," Caysen chokes.

I merely incline my head, and the branch wraps tighter
around his throat. Glancing behind me, I meet Emrys's gaze. It's
just the same as it always is. Gentle and loving, clearly, he
enjoys me reclaiming my power. His cock presses firmly against
the front of his pants. I lick my lips.

Soon.

Turning back towards my prey, I grin.

"Do you know what true power is?" Carysen shakes his
head as much as he can. "It's knowing that you'll be a
forgotten human prince. It's knowing that I will live here
powerful, free, and eternal. And more than anything, It's
knowing that this creature, as you've called him, will kill you
in an instant. He only waits for my command because he
loves me."

I glance over my shoulder and meet Emrys's dark eyes as I
say clearly, "Just as I love him."

Emrys growls, taking a step towards me, but I have one final
edict as queen to deliver to our prisoner.

"Or he'll let me kill you, and I'll live in peace knowing you
can never harm another person. And as much as I would love
to be the one who ends you." I feel Emrys at my back as I smirk
at Carysen. "I need to give my husband a wedding present. My
love, would you please kill this pathetic man? I need you inside
of me again."

Carysen babbles out a plea, but I'm already turning towards

my faerie king. He smiles down at me as I wrap my hands around his neck and press our bodies together.

"With pleasure."

The branches snap together with a wave of his claws. I don't even watch as I hear the life being choked from Carysen and his guards. The cheers of our loyal subjects swallow up their last breaths. Their deaths aren't worth my note—Carysen's legacy has already been erased.

"Take their bodies away," I command my king.

The branches twist, and I hear a whipping through the air. In a moment, a distant thud can be heard just beyond the meadow. Let them be eaten by the wildlife here as their final act in this world.

My hands go to the back lacings of my gown and I undo them. Emrys's eyes heat as he watches me. Sliding the dress off my body, I hear the tittering of sprites and faeries all around us. Let them watch. I need my king.

He growls as I take his hand and place it on my breast.

"Now fuck me," I command him.

His mouth lands on mine as he gives my breast a squeeze. I'm flattened to the damp grass below us, and his tongue tangles with mine. Palming my breast, he quickly cups the other as I raise my hips, desperate to get some much-needed friction there.

The sprites and faeries cheer for us—whispering praise in our ears as they fly overhead. I can hear a few tinkling moans, and I know they're overcome just like their queen and king.

My hands rip off Emrys's white shirt before going to the tie of his pants. His teeth sink into my neck as I moan and rub my wet pussy against the bulge in his pants. His tongue skims up his bite as I thrash in his grasp. I'm soaking and desperate.

"You've bloomed, my blossom. Powerful and free. The real you is a sight to behold."

His mouth meets mine, and I moan into our kiss.

"You freed me. I'm never going back to who I was again. I can't. Not now, not ever."

He groans against me, and suddenly, his pants are off. His massive cock bobs between our bodies, the tip already leaking with delicious seed. Before I can wiggle down to taste him, he grips his length in his hand and lines it up with my entrance. Lifting my hips with his free hand, he sheaths himself inside me in one strong thrust.

My muscles are still sore, but I accommodate him nonetheless. I love the burn of him inside of me. I crave it more than anything. Pressing up on my heels, he grips my hips and jerks me forward onto his length. We work in tandem to heighten each other's pleasure. It's so deep this way, our movement frantic with lust.

His eyes heat my blood. My breasts bounce with the force of each thrust, and I know my body is hurtling towards its peak. Fire licks up me, and I can't wait to erupt.

"Watching you order their deaths made me harder than I've ever been," Emrys growls.

"Does a cruel queen make you hard?" I ask.

"You make me hard." He impales me on his length as I let out a loud moan. "I should've known you enjoyed being watched."

My eyes take in the crowd around us. The air is thick with lust and couplings. Their beady eyes watch Emrys take me in this primal way—their mouths fall open as they glow brighter. A smile curls my lips as I turn back towards my king.

"Does that make me a naughty girl?" The question is as coy as I can manage while he fucks me with renewed vigor.

"Yes," he growls. "Next, you'll ask me to share you."

"Never," I say softly. His thrusts falter, but I pump my hips in time. My climax is swiftly approaching.

"Never?"

"Unless you wish to share me?"

"No," he growls.

"That's what I thought." I smile. "I don't want to share you either. They can watch, but nothing more. You're only for me."

"Posessive for a lady."

"A lady who knows exactly what she wants."

Lifting up on my elbows, I push my chest up and wrap my arms around Emrys's neck. He leans back and pulls me with him. His length is still deep inside of me as I balance on his lap. Working my hips, I grind down on his length over and over. The force of this position has my teeth smacking together.

I need more. I need it deeper than before.

With a shove, Emrys lands flat on his back. Balancing my hands on his chest, I raise my hips and lower myself on his massive cock. At this angle, my clit brushes against the base of his cock. My knees sink into the soft ground as I slam down on him over and over again.

Breasts bouncing, Emrys grips one in his claw and snarls. Raising his hips to meet mine, his cock hits my womb, and my eyes roll back in my head. I ride him for all that I'm worth. My muscles feel like jelly, but I keep going, my climax already tightening my stomach.

Our subjects encourage us, and that only adds to my pleasure.

"A queen this wanton is perfect for our king," one whispers. "Look at that ring!"

"She takes him so well. Should we really be watching?" another asks.

"Of course we should!" replies a tinkling voice. "Now get over here, and we can do our own fucking."

A giggle bursts from me as my nails embed in Emrys's chest. My curls cling to my back as I toss my head back and let my king take over. He holds my hips and lowers me onto his length. My pleasure steals my thoughts, but my mouth manages to move.

"This is what I've always wanted. When I would dream of my future, this is what I desired."

"Participating in a faerie orgy?" Emrys quips. His brows are lowered in concentration.

Despite my impending orgasm, I can't help but laugh.

"To feel like this. To be loved and to be in love." My mouth lowers to his, and I kiss him, pouring my soul into it. "You made a dream I hadn't even remembered I dreamed come true."

His hands wrap around my back and lock me to him. Raising up, he powers into me from below. My clit drags back and forth against him, and it's all I need. I scream into his mouth as my body explodes.

Muscles tighten and strain as bliss coats my body. I shake through it all, soaking Emrys until his body jerks below me, and he floods me with his seed.

"Laurelle." He fucks his come into me as it squelches between us to soak the grass. His warmth ties our souls together as he places soft kisses against my lips.

Peeling my eyes open, I notice the wildflowers that have grown around us. My smile is small as I meet my king's stare. His hands skim up my back and tangle in my hair. Bringing our faces close together, I let him see the truth in my gaze. I let him glimpse the soul that he owns.

"I love you, my king."

"I love you, my blossom," he answers.

Sinking onto his chest, my head turns out towards the meadow. The sun is high in the sky and illuminates the nearly empty clearing. All traces of our intruders are gone. There's just calm, serene peace. Clearly, our subjects found their peaks at the same time we did.

It's absolutely perfect.

"What would you like to do on your first official day as queen?"

Emrys's voice pulls me from my daze. Turning, I rest my

chin on his chest. His smile is full of love as he curls a lock of my hair around his finger. The birds caw over my head, and I bite my lip at the idea that hits me.

"There is one thing," I say, crawling up his chest and pressing a kiss to his lips.

"Name it."

Nuzzling under his chin, I let out a content sigh.

"Is there any way you can make me fly?"

EPILOGUE

EMRYS

Many, Many Faerie Years Later

"Have we ever made it through one of these parties without you ruining my dress?"

Laurelle's question ends in a gasp as I rip open the front of her green silk gown. Instantly, her luscious breasts spill free, and my mouth comes down to claim a hard nipple. They taste sweet—just like every part of her does.

The lively music and smell of fire swirl around us as I see to my queen in this empty corner at the edge of the meadow. Usually, my queen likes a more public display, but tonight, I need some time alone with her in the dark.

"Are you asking me to stop?" I nip the fleshy swell of her left breast before sucking her right nipple into my mouth.

"Never," she moans.

Her hunger for me—just like her delicious wantonness—has only grown over the years we've spent together. She looks like same. Beautiful as ever. More so now as she glows with more golden power with each passing year.

The time we've spent together feels short in comparison to

those dark, lonely years I was without her. How much time has passed in the human world? Sixty years? Seventy? Who knows. My blossom hasn't aged a day—her life is as eternal as mine. Even more so now that we regularly venture into the heart of *The Great Oak* to renew its power.

We are two willing and diligent subjects in that regard.

"We should be entertaining them. They are our guests, after all."

Laurelle's half-hearted protests are whispered against my lips as my tongue dives back in to dance with hers. *Great Oak*, she is sweet. Sweeter with time and familiarity. I've memorized her a thousand times—could tell you the number and shape of every freckle on her gorgeous body—and yet when my lips find hers, I am just as overwhelmed as if it was our first kiss.

I won't deny my pleasure nor hers for the sake of some arrivals.

"Guests that don't need us at the present moment," I growl, my claws squeezing her breasts.

"Still." She tries to argue against my mouth even as I feel her small hands go to the tie of my pants. "It seems rude. They came all this way as a show of good faith."

Kissing my queen once more, I press my forehead to hers.

"We had one of these more than a century ago, and it was a boring and dull affair," I state. Raising a dark brow, disbelief is written all over her lovely face. "I'll concede that this time is a bit more...interesting."

Laurelle giggles. "You can say that again. They're no better than us."

Glancing over my shoulder, my blossom is, as always, correct.

I spy our guests and their mates. How interesting it is that creatures of our ilk each claimed our own human beauties. Though none of them are as gorgeous as my Laurelle, no one ever will be. Still, the delicate females are in sharp contrast to their male counterparts.

The first pair I spot is the demon Asgorath with his dark-haired human, Irys, in his lap. Golden goblets of faerie wine lay discarded at their feet. He's treated us to his demon form this evening. His skull burns with a red-hot fire that matches the blushing cheeks of his pale human lover. Together, their hands work each other through their clothing.

His hand skates under her thin black dress, and his long tongue caresses the side of her neck. Her moan echoes around the meadow as her hand curls into his dark cloak.

"I've kept you to myself for too long, little one. Shall we show them how wet your pretty pussy still gets for me after all these years?" the demon growls. His hand pumps between her legs as his other peels her long skirt higher.

"Yes, please," she whimpers.

A small smile plays on my lips as I turn to my old aquatic friend. His reign has been almost as long as mine and the demon's. He was always the most miserable amongst us, but that male is long gone. Especially as his eyes stare up at his crimson-haired human, Melody, they are just as entangled in each other as the demon and his mate are.

Albeit a bit more so due to Zalenyk's tentacles. His semi-human form is long gone, and now he is merely a slimy mass of muscles and slithering appendages. Hosting her up by her arms, his tentacles slide underneath her skirt as her eyes roll back in her head. She lets out a keening sound when a second one disappears between her thighs.

"Wet for me, sweet one. Beg for me to fuck you in front of everyone," the Kraken commands.

Melody's eyes blaze with icy fire.

"Make me," she challenges.

The Kraken shakes with dark laughter as a third tentacle hoists up her skirt. His other limbs wrap around her and bring her into his massive body, swallowing her high-pitched moans.

Lastly, there is the dragon—the youngest among us with the most unfortunate backstory. However, there is no sign of the cursed male, as he and his golden-haired, Anwyn, are a lot farther along than the other couples.

He's already drug her behind a small rose bush. His green-scaled wings thrust towards the night sky while Anywn's bare legs dangle from his powerful hips. Her blue dress is left forgotten on their shared chair, along with their food.

His tail slides towards her until she lets out a deep sigh. Wings flexing, I watch his hips jerk forward and earn a rewarding moan from his human.

"This is what you get, my treasure. Take your punishment for almost allowing them a glimpse of my precious little cunt," the dragon growls.

"Lassar, you fill me so good. You own my pussy, no one else will see it. Never," she mewls.

I watch her hands sink into his strong backside as their moans join the cacophony of the other couples. Laurelle's and I's will mingle with theirs soon.

Turning my attention back to my own treasure, she smiles up at me, and my heart stumbles in my chest. Gripping the tatters of her dress, I pull it from her as the primal part of me demands we claim her just as the others are. To show that this beautiful female is our mate and no one else will get the pleasure of her flesh.

This meeting, though momentarily paused, is an important one. It was called to establish our boundaries. While I reign over *The Woods* creator—*The Great Oak*—the realm it sprouted above has been left unruled. It hasn't been a problem in centuries yet, but our arrivals made sure to tell me of the new creatures that have begun to call it home.

Some linger on the outskirts and the undiscovered portions

of the dense forest, while each monster here today has laid claim to a different section. A portion of The Woods will be Asgortah's domains, where unlucky souls can still seek out bargains. Lassar will take the cave system and hoard treasure as he sees fit. Zalenyk will control the waterways in and around *The Woods* while I will remain here.

Securing my realm as I always have and always will with my queen by my side.

Zalenyk and Lassar have been very territorial lately due to their families continuing to grow. Both of their unions have brought forth a new species of half-human, half-creature, and their domains' safety is paramount. Whatever the future has in store for these new halfling children, we can all rest easy knowing we are in support of keeping them safe.

Looking down at my lovely queen, maybe one day, the two of us will embark on that adventure together when the time is right. For now, I am far too greedy to share her and will continue to bring her the contraceptive herbs each morning.

Her gown falls to the floor as I pin her to the nearest tree. The smooth skin of her thighs wraps around me, and her skin glows like a star in the moonlight. Entering her in one swift thrust, I weave my fingers through her curls to cup her head. Her breasts bounce with the impact of each thrust as her moans echo around us.

"Still so tight, my blossom. Your perfect cunt is too much," I groan.

"It welcomes my king whenever he wants it. You rule it just as you do my heart."

The primal surge to claim her harder rips from me as I yank her from the trunk of the tree and lay her on the soft grass. The sprites gather around us and buzz on their colorful wings. Faeries gather, too, their short bodies watching with dark eyes as I take their queen. Grunts and moans soon drown out the sound of the music as everyone in the meadow swiftly gives in to the lust permeating the air.

My realm sparkles. *The Great Oak* is pleased with the number of couplings occurring and is flooding it with primal magic.

Yet my eyes remain on my beauty. Her cheeks are flushed, and her eyes are wide as I spear into her wet flesh once more. Her legs go up on my shoulders as I hold her hips in my hands. Fucking her onto my length, I revel in the sloppy sounds her wet pussy makes as I take her hard and fast in the damp grass.

"It's perfect," she moans. "Every bit of this life with you is better than any dream."

"You're my only dream," I growl, increasing my tempo as I feel her muscles start to clench down on me. "My only desire. There is nothing beyond you. Beyond this."

"I love you, Emrys," she sighs, her hands curling into the grass beside her.

"I love you," I echo and slam into her with a force that has her body sliding along the wet ground.

Her body thrashes in my grip, but I don't stop. The wave of her pleasure is just about to crash. When it does, her pussy strangles my hard cock, and her back arches. Her mouth is open in a silent scream as I let myself go. My spine locks, and I flood her little pussy with my seed and fuck it into her so she gets every drop. It pools between us before hitting the grass below. She eagerly welcomes every drop, rocking her hips forward to capture it all.

Once my body stops trembling, I pull her from the ground and hold her in my arms. My claws skim up her back as her own wrap around my neck. Our crowns tangle together just as the threads of our souls do.

She is mine. Always.

Much has changed over these years together, and change will only keep happening. With the new creatures stirring in

The Woods and the future of these pairings and the children resulting from them still unclear, the only thing that's certain is that things will become different. I welcome it all, especially with Laurelle by my side.

The years without her were empty. Whatever these next ones bring will fulfill me in a way I never thought possible before her. Looking down at her face, I know she feels the same. As do the other monsters in my meadow. They said as much before the faerie wine really started to flow.

The power we've all wielded for so long was nothing without someone to share it with. Life without love—without our humans—isn't worth living. We will all do whatever we must to safeguard them and our futures together.

Rolling to my side, I tuck Laurelle against me. The cool evening breeze feels good against our hot skin that sticks together with our sweat. I peel one dark curl from her temple and wrap it around my finger.

Leaning down, I whisper all that I've just thought into her ear. I make promises of our future and more declarations of love than I can count. When her smile stretches so wide I'm sure her cheeks are beginning to ache, I kiss her perfect mouth and gaze into the soul I've claimed.

"You saved me. Fulfilling the prophecy saved my realm— my people—but you did more than that. I couldn't have survived another handful of centuries without you. Without this," I confess.

Her eyes sparkle with unshed tears as she kisses me back gently.

"You saved me too. From a life of cruelty, you've given me everything. You are everything to me."

The meadow around us glows as the sprites settle in, and the magic from our fucking flows through the land. I can't help my own smile as I take it all in. Things may be changing and yet my love for Laurelle will always remain.

I grin as my cock hardens against her hip. Gently, I take her shoulder and roll her onto her side with her back pressed up against my chest. My hand skims down her side, eliciting a high-pitched scream as she squirms. My ticklish little queen. I continue touching her until I reach her soft knee and lift it before settling her thigh along my hip.

Laurelle giggles and looks at me over her shoulder.

"What are you doing?" she asks.

I grin at her, showing the teeth I'll be biting her with in a moment. My claiming mark on her shoulder is starting to fade, and my blood demands I renew it.

"I haven't had your ass in a while."

Laurelle barks a laugh and shakes her head.

"You fucked me there this morning."

"See," I say, gripping my cock, still glossy from our releases, and pressing it against her back entrance. "That was a couple of days ago in the human realm."

"Instatiable beast," she murmurs. Her eyes glow with affection. "But you're mine. Eternally."

I thrust inside her tight ass, and she lets out a deep moan. Our souls sing as our connection is sealed once more. My blossom, my queen, my Laurelle. Perfection in every way. *The Great Oak* has blessed me beyond my wildest dreams.

"Eternally," I agree and thrust inside her again.

"Emrys, I couldn't possibly eat another bite."

I capture his hand, holding the jam-coated bread before my lips. Early morning sunlight is filtering in through the openings of The Great Oak. We are nestled in our bed of fine silk sheets and overstuffed pillows. I have no idea how long we've been in here.

Since the unwanted arrival of my former betrothed yesterday—and my king's swift handling of him—we've done nothing be fuck all over our realm. The first time had been in the clearing where the men who thought to take me back lay dying not too far off. Our subjects joined in with their wanton demonstration, but I only had eyes for Emrys, my husband.

It feels strange to say and yet so right.

After that, Emrys led me back into The Great Oak to discuss an urgent matter with his queen. The matter in question had been me riding his face until my legs felt like honey before he made love to me soft and sweet. We slept for a few hours but as the evening settled in all around us he had me again, and again, and *again*.

Life here is a dream—a fantasy from the deepest parts of

my heart. Yet, after that unwanted interruption by Carysen yesterday, something has been nagging me this morning. I have no regrets about leaving behind my life. My family never cared about me and never took into consideration my wants and needs.

However, there is one sore spot in all of this when I think of how I managed to end up in this realm. The one person responsible for putting me on the path to true love could be suffering in the human lands.

The thought occurs suddenly, and my veins ice over. Why had I not considered the punishment that could've befallen Caryssa for helping me? Is she suffering right now?

Shame makes my breakfast race up my throat.

"My blossom," Emrys says, his dark eyes full of worry. "What's wrong?"

My mouth opens, but I can't find the words.

"Laurelle." Emrys's voice is commanding. "You are worrying me. Are you hurt in some way?"

His clawed hands skim over my naked shoulders and down my back.

"Caryssa," I say, my eyes boring into Emrys's.

"Who?"

"Caryssa," I repeat. "She is Prince Carysen's sister. When they came to collect me, she was waiting for me in the carriage. She's the reason—"

"Has she been complicit in your mistreatment, my blossom?" Emrys's voice is lethal. "Say the word and I'll bring you her head."

"No!" My heart stumbles in my chest as I grip his claw hand. "Caryssa saved me, Emrys. She distracted the guards and gave me a chance to escape—she's the reason I found my way into your realm."

Emrys's eyes calm as he grips my hand. Gently, his claws go to my hair and tuck a dark curl behind my ear.

"Everything here has been perfect, and I'm ashamed that I haven't considered what fate could've befallen her for helping me. If she was punished, I—"

Unease clogs my throat, and tears burn my eyes.

"Shh," Emrys whispers, catching one of my straying tears on his thumb. "If she is the reason you made your way to me, then I owe her the greatest of debts. Let me help you look for her. Do you trust me?"

"Yes." My answer is instant—honest.

With a short nod, Emrys crawls behind me. Settling my naked body against his, a thrill rushes through me at the contact. *Later*, I chastise myself. My faerie king tangles our legs together and threads his arm around my waist.

Holding me flush against his chest, his long hair tickles my shoulder and I feel his lips against my ear.

"Close your eyes, my blossom. Picture what she looks like; my magic will help us locate her."

With a deep breath, I do as I'm told. My mind swirls as I remember the quiet, wide-eyed girl inside that suffocating carriage. I can see her heart-shaped face and light brown hair. Her lips are moving but I cannot make out the sound.

The room around me falls away—the only thing anchoring me to my body is Emrys's steady arm around me. The metallic scent of magic stings my nose as I feel my body dip and twirl. Cold dew decorates my skin, but I dare not open my eyes.

I can still see her—Caryssa—haunted and scared inside that carriage. Except she's not in a carriage...no, she's in a cell. One that is small, dank, and reeks of rotting flesh. Her shining hair is dull and matted to her head. She shivers in a corner, her face buried in the scratchy fabric of her dress.

Where is she? What does this mean?

"Open your eyes, Laurelle," Emrys commands.

When I do, the breath is stolen from my lungs. Before me is the scene I was envisioning. Hunched over, the princess's frail body is shaking. The dress she's wearing hangs limply from her shoulders. A loud bang echoes through the stinking dungeon and Caryssa jumps.

Clanking footsteps get closer until an armor-clad guard appears. He drops a tray and I watch in horror as gray slop sloshes over the cracked, stone floor.

"Food."

With that one word, he turns and the sad vision of Caryssa sinks to her knees. Her bony hand reaches forward, revealing wrinkled skin and broken fingernails. For the first time since we arrived at this unpleasant vision, she's finally facing towards us. Emrys's grip behind me tightens.

Her tangled hair parts, and my stomach turns. Bile races up my throat as I take in her face. It's Caryssa—in about thirty years. Her skin is sallow and marred with deep wrinkles. Her once bright eyes are dull and lifeless. Her lips part to reveal rotten teeth and a pale tongue.

"Oh dear gods," I gasp, stumbling back into Emrys.

Caryssa is looking right at me, but there is no spark of recognition. How can this be? How much time has indeed passed in the faerie realm?

"This is a vision, my blossom," Emrys explains. "She cannot see us because we are not really here. Neither is she. This is a glimpse at what may happen—of a future that can still be prevented."

I turn in his embrace and stare up into his dark eyes.

"Then we must prevent it."

Emrys licks over his lips before nodding.

The horrific picture in front of us becomes cloudy. Thick fog swirls and more metallic scents tickle my nose. My body shifts and Emrys tightens his hold on me once more. After a moment, the mist thins and peels back to reveal an ornately decorated room.

We materialize inside the stately room and a familiar dark-gold head greets us. She's standing before a large mirror. The wrinkles and rot have been cleaned from her face and she's back to the version that I remember. Dressed in a simple green gown, her eyes dart around the room.

Taking a deep breath, Caryssa walks over the creaking floor and tries the handle of the door. Giving it a harsh tug, the wooden door holds firm.

With a huff, she drops the doorknob and turns towards the large window on the left side of the room. Golden sunlight pours through the glass. Given the height at which the trees appear below, it would be unwise to use it to escape.

"How can we help her?" I ask, turning towards Emrys.

Emrys raises a white brow while his lips pull into a grin.

"Magic."

With a wave of his claws, a light breeze circulates the room —papers on Caryssa's desk rustle at the force. A few strands of her hair get tugged by the wind. Lifting her head, I follow her gaze to the old door that was firmly shut a moment ago.

I hold my breath as the door swings open on silent hinges. The dark hallway beyond it is quiet. Whatever guards were once stationed there are long gone—thanks, I'm sure, to my faerie king. Caryssa lets out a small gasp as her eyes widen.

She remains frozen for a moment, uncertain of what to do. I know Emrys's magic is strong but it will not hold forever. My eyes look around the room until they land on an old leather satchel and a cloak hanging from a peg. Instinct drives me as I wave my hand, and the bag flies towards her.

The cloak follows the same path and lands on her shoulders. Caryssa ties it around herself as if in a daze. Clearly, her desire for freedom is greater than questioning the invisible force aiding her. Items from her desk and wardrobe fly through the air until the old satchel is filled. The leather strap loops over her head and settles along her side.

"Excellent, my blossom," Emrys purrs in my ear. "You're already coming into your power."

I shiver at his praise, but I can't allow myself to be distracted. With one deep breath, I summon all my will into the final item I place in Caryssa's care. A large purse materializes. The wool is stretched to accommodate the sheer abundance of gold coins nestled inside.

Caryssa holds out her palm, and the bag settles in her hand. Clutching it to her chest, her eyes scan the room. I know she cannot see us—I know Emrys's magic makes it impossible but I swear when her eyes connect with mine she inhales sharply.

"Whoever you are—whatever you are," she says in a soft voice. "Thank you."

Caryssa tucks the coin purse inside the satchel and pulls the cloak's hood over her head. She moves swiftly on her feet and through the open door without sparing a single glance behind her. Releasing a deep breath, I sag against Emrys as the thick mist around us swirls.

My body tilts until I feel the familiar fabric of our silk sheets below me.

Emrys comes down on top of me. He's so handsome it hurts to look at him. My love for him pours from my soul and ties us together with a golden thread. My hand cups his cheek, and I trace the harsh line of his cheekbone.

"My love," I say. "You are the most wonderful husband in the world. Thank you for helping me rescue her from that deplorable fate. I couldn't bear it—to know she was suffering when she's the one who put me on the path to you—to true love."

Emrys's lips find mine in a chaste kiss. I growl in protest when he pulls back too quickly.

"Anything for you, my impatient queen."

I smile at the title and tuck a strand of white hair behind his pointed ear.

"Tell me—what happens to Caryssa? What becomes of her?"

Emrys's eyes go distance. The black orbs seem to darken further.

"She makes it onto a ship and sails far away from that blasted kingdom. She finds herself working in a tavern—free and independent. Caryssa is happy."

"Does she find love?" I ask, needing to know if her life will be as fulfilled as mine.

Emrys's light brows lower in concentration. After a moment, his lips pull into a grin, showing off razor-sharp teeth.

"Oh, yes. A certain beast catches her scent, and you should know firsthand, my blossom, how ravenous a beast can be when claiming his love."

"Good," I say. "I want her to experience the same love and joy I have."

Emrys lowers his mouth to mine.

"I need to fuck you again, my love."

"Hmm," I hum into his kiss. "In here?"

Claws skim up my naked sides to tangle in my hair.

"Unless you feel like being a bit wicked with your king?"

Wrapping my arms around his neck, I press my body into his. Emrys's hard cock pushes against the damp folds of my pussy. I writhe against his length, needing to get any friction I can. My faerie king lets out a growl before gripping my hips with his claws.

"Naughty girl," he chastises.

"You love it," I return.

"I love you," he counters. "Let me show our subjects just how much."

Without warning, Emrys scoops me into his arms and carries me from our cocoon of silk blankets. His skin is warm against me as I burrow deeper into his hold. Golden sunlight greets us as we exit The Great Oak. A sweet-smelling breeze tickles my nose as Emrys walks with purpose deeper into the meadow.

Tiny, glowing bodies rise up all around us as we travel deeper into the clearing. The sprites swirl around us and tangle in my hair and skim petal soft hands against my flushing cheeks. This is wanton—wicked—yet I can't deny the arousal slicking out of me as a large crowd begins to form.

The wildflowers seem to grow brighter in the afternoon sun. Their blooms are supple and coated in a light dew. Sprites and faeries alike pop up in the meadow, their bodies growing until they are two feet high. Their grins are all feral delight.

Emrys pays them no mind as he continues walking us towards the dais. His throne sits unoccupied and my face burns further as realization sets in.

"You are a truly wicked beast, my love," I whisper against his neck.

His grip on me tightens as a growl vibrates his chest.

"I am simply a male in love with his mate. Why would I not want to show off my blossom like the goddess she is?"

I giggle and place a soft kiss on his neck. His feet stumble and I suppress my laughter.

"Now, who's being wicked?" he asks, stomping up the step and settling us on his throne.

Seated in his lap, my ass is cushioned against his muscular thighs. I can hear the excited chattering of our subjects gathered around us.

"Look at them—it's as if we aren't here," one hisses.

"Thistle, don't just sit there and leer," another squeaky voice responds.

"You're right, we should join them. I haven't been inside you in hours, my dear."

I tune out the sounds of pleasure from the crowd behind us. Already, the riotous noise of naked flesh slapping together and high-pitched moans are echoing in the clearing. This is an indecent place, yet I've never felt more at home.

I bring my hands to Emry's handsome face and take him in. The pale green of his skin glimmers in the sunlight, while his white hair glows like freshly fallen snow. His dark eyes appraise me—heating my already scorching blood. My nipples harden and press against the muscular planes of his chest.

His hard cock lengthens beneath me and I squirm against it. My lust for him is only heightened by the knowledge that all those gathered here will watch him take me in a few moments. While I'll never allow another to share in our lovemaking, I don't mind being watched. In fact, I crave for our subjects to know just how thoroughly their king has claimed me.

My desire for him is all-consuming.

"Emrys," I moan as his length grazes my clit. "Please."

His claws grip my head and prick my scalp. That hint of pain only heightens my arousal. His lips curl into a wicked grin as he leans into my face.

"Hmm, my blossom, I finally have you exactly where I want you. My cock has not been inside you in days."

My lips tilt and I shake my head. "You were inside of me less than an hour ago, my love. Have you forgotten?"

"An *hour* in my realm, my sweet. That's easily a week in the human lands and that is far too long for me to be parted from your sweet cunt."

"You're insatiable," I say, bringing my mouth flush with his.

Emrys's lips are warm and soft as they press against mine. Our kiss starts chaste but the moment his tongue slips into my mouth, all is lost. My blood heats as my nails seek his scalp. Grabbing long strands of his white hair for leverage, I give myself over to wantonness and let my king have his wicked way with me.

There is nothing more than Emrys and I in this moment. Our connection is new yet feels as permanent and everlasting as my soul. Each day, we will revel in just how deep our connection grows.

A sudden rush of emotion hits me. Breaking our kiss I hold his perfect face in my hands.

"I love you, Emrys," I say, moisture pricking my eyes. "I loved you from the first moment I saw you—even if I didn't realize it then. You saved me and now you've helped me save Caryssa from a fate worse than death. How can I ever be worthy of a male as wonderful as you?"

Emrys presses a firm kiss to my lips as his thumb catches the errant tear escaping my eye.

"My blossom, it is *I* who is unworthy of you. I think about it every day. The Great Oak blessed me beyond reason for putting you on my path. There is no one in this world more beautiful, brave, and kind than you. I am humbled to be your mate. Every day, I will prove to you that choosing me over the mortal realm was not a mistake."

I laugh and shake my head.

"Now that I know you, I could never go back. You are my heart."

"And you are mine," he agrees. "Now let me make you come in front of our kingdom so they know I've laid claim to your pussy just as much as your soul."

His lips return to mine with a newfound frenzy. We are a mess of clashing tongues and fervent lips. Emrys's hands go to the bare skin of my waist. Skimming his claws along my sides, I am reminded of the fact that we are both very naked. The sun overhead warms my exposed flesh.

Emrys's hands find my breasts and gently cup them. I moan into our kiss as he expertly works my nipples into tight peaks. The ache between my thighs grows as I rock back and forth in his lap. His cock is hard and seeking, resting against the curves of my ass.

I canter my hips, trying desperately to give myself a small bit of relief.

"Emrys," I whine, breaking our kiss.

"Already soaking and desperate for me, my blossom?"

My head falls back as Emrys's lips bite and suck along my neck.

"Please," I sigh.

My mate sucks the soft skin of my throat between his teeth before releasing it in a gentle pop. His hands on my breasts skim lower, tracing down my ribs before settling at my waist.

"Whatever my queen wants, she shall have."

Without warning, his grip on me tightens as he flips our positions. Cool, smooth wood greets my back as I settle against the throne. I watch with heated desire as Emrys sinks to his knees before me. His pale skin glows like the moon. His full lips peel back in a wanton smile.

My eyes look beyond him. The breath freezes in my lungs as I take in the debauched scene. Faeries of all shapes and sizes are engaged in the most sensual acts. Two glittering purple female faeries lay on top of each other, devouring each other's most intimate flesh. Two male faeries have a beautiful gold-skinned female faerie strewn between them. One pumps into her waiting mouth while the other thrusts between her splayed thighs.

The scene beside them is a mass of limbs and pleasure-twisted faces. It's impossible to see where one sprite ends and the other begins. I couldn't even begin to count the number of bodies in the mix. My cheeks heat as I look up into the sparkling dark eyes of my husband.

"Eyes on me, my blossom," he commands. "Let me give you the pleasure you deserve."

"Yes." The word is barely out of my mouth before Emrys is on me.

His hands cup the backs of my knees and gently place them

on the armrests of his throne. He pushes them higher up until my thighs begin to burn. There is no hiding when you are this spread open. My wet pussy glimmers in the sunlight, and I can scent my musky arousal.

Dark claws tickle the sensitive skin of my inner thighs. Emrys's dark eyes glow as I watch him lower his mouth to my pussy. The first press of his tongue against my clit makes me toss my head back against his throne. I'm already on edge and we've barely begun.

My faerie king gives my pussy another thorough lick before parting my folds with his tongue. His lips latch onto my clit and suck with force as his fingers find my entrance and gently sink inside. He scissors and flexes his hand in a way that has white stars blurring my vision.

Keening sounds escape my lips. My mouth is open in a silent scream as Emrys feasts on me. His mouth makes deliciously sloppy sounds along my heated flesh. His fingers work me in time with his lips and tongue. Already I feel my stomach muscles tightening.

Vaguely, I am aware of the spectacle we are creating. Beyond Emrys's head, I can see a few of the faeries have stopped their coupling to watch us with fevered eyes. My cheeks heat at their frank appreciation—as they begin working themselves and each other while watching their king and queen.

"They can look, my blossom," Emrys growls against my pussy before adding a second finger inside me. "But never touch."

His declaration of ownership sends another rush of desire through me. My hands find his head and hold his mouth firmly against me. With my legs draped over the arms of the throne, it is hard to move my hips but I still manage to grind myself against him.

Emrys adds another finger inside me, and the stretch is

decadent. My eyes threaten to close but I force them open. Tunneling my fingers through his silken hair, I use it as an anchor to work myself faster against his mouth. His tongue travels from my clit to my entrance, licking around where his fingers have me parted.

"Soak my face," Emrys commands. "Let me wear my queen's come so I may be the envy of all the other faeries."

"Emrys," I pant.

My vision is blurring, and my muscles are growing taut. Sweet fire licks my sweaty skin as my peak becomes within reach.

"Come, my blossom."

With those words, Emrys slips his fingers from my pussy and presses one firmly into my ass. I erupt with the simple intrusion. The pain from the burn couples with my pleasure to make a most delicious combination. His mouth is at my entrance, and he greedily drinks down every drop of my arousal.

I suck down lungfuls of crisp, floral-scented air as I slowly regain feeling in my body. My curls cling to my naked shoulders, and the beads of sweat along my temples. Little tremors wreck my body as Emrys gives me one last thorough lick before rising from his knees.

His lips find mine and share my taste with me.

The warm, wet glide of his tongue against mine has me turning slippery between my legs once more. While I love the pleasure his mouth can bring me, I need his cock. When we are joined in that way I can feel our souls becoming one—our bond growing stronger.

"How are you, my blossom?" Emrys asks.

The sound of moans and flesh slapping together from the meadow brings a shy smile to my lips.

"Wonderful. Eager for me," I say.

"Anything for you, my love."

Emrys's hands find my waist once more and he switches our positions. Only this time, when he settles me, my back is flush to his chest as I stare out into the meadow before us. His hands trail over my chest before gently cupping my breasts. My head falls against his shoulder as his mouth presses a kiss to my temple.

"You are going to ride me, my blossom," he says, his other hand trailing between my thighs and working my clit in tight circles. "Our kingdom will watch you—will see that their king is no more than a vessel for their queen's pleasure. They will see that their queen is not only beautiful but bold—no longer that shy, timid creature that fell from the sky. She is a woman who takes what she wants. Can you do that for me, Laurelle?"

I turn my head towards him. His eyes are heavy lidded with lust but I still see the unfiltered adoration shining in them. I feel his love for me pour from him and into my soul. I let my own emotions flow just as freely. My hand falls between us and I find his hard cock.

Gripping him tightly, I revel in his sharp inhale and give him a quick tug. Jerking him in my fist, I feel his chest vibrate with a growl behind me. He works my clit just as quickly until my peak is once again approaching.

The next time I come it will be with him buried inside of me.

Summoning my strength, I settle my feet on the tops of his solid thighs and raise up. I continue to pump him, all the while guiding him to my dripping entrance. His hands settle on my waist to steady me. He presses a kiss to my shoulder before our eyes lock.

"Anything for you, my king."

The head of his cock pushes into my entrance, and I sheath him inside of me with one sharp descent of my hips. My ass rests on the harsh contours of his muscular stomach. The breath stills in my lungs at the fullness of him. His claws dig into my skin as his mouth leaves open-mouth kisses along my spine.

Using the armrests to help me, I rise up once more until only the head of his massive cock is inside me before sinking down again. Over and over, I impale myself on his length. Soon, I find my rhythm—one that is punishing and quick. My breasts bounce in time with my movements.

I ride him with all the strength I have left. My moans are feverish—all words have emptied out of my head. Emrys leverages his hips up to meet my thrusts until his cock is butting up against my womb. My teeth smack together and my head falls back. The sound of our flesh slapping together is decadent.

My pussy begins tightening on his length as my climax is fast approaching.

"Open your eyes, my blossom. Look at your kingdom."

Somehow, I manage to and the sight before me causes more arousal to leak out of me and soak his thighs.

Our kingdom is in a wanton state—each one of the countless couplings are watching us. Mouths are parted in ecstasy as I take Emrys fully inside me once more. When I let out a particularly high-pitched moan, our subjects cheer in a flurry of glimmering bodies. They clap when Emrys tweaks my nipples and they grow brighter when his hand slips between my thighs to find my clit.

"Your pleasure fuels them—fuels our kingdom," Ermys says into my ear.

His claws rub my clit as I continue to pump my hips on his length. My muscles are growing tighter and tighter with each thrust. The faeries' pleasure seems tied to mine as the closer my peak comes the more frenzied their couplings turn.

When one faerie finds their peak, they are quickly pulled into another tryst. Partners are switched and flipped. One male faerie pulls his dripping cock out of a shimmering magenta female faerie before a green male faerie sinks to his knees before him and cleans off their mingling come. Two turquoise female faeries are lying atop each other but inversely. They lick and finger each other before a male faerie settles behind the one on top and thrusts into her. Both let out a moan and glow bright blue with pleasure.

Watching all of them unlocks a deep well inside of me and I renew my efforts. Emrys works my clit and I raise and lower my hips in quick succession. My ass smacks against his stomach—the meadow swallows up the sound.

My thighs begin to tremble and goosebumps break out along my skin. His cock is impossibly deep inside of me and in this position, it brushes that spot deep inside of me that cause my vision to darken along the edges.

"Emrys, I'm close—I'm—"

"Come, my blossom. Scream it—soak me with your come."

His claws pinch my clit and my whole body erupts. My pussy locks around his thrusting cock as my eyes fall shut. White hot fire coats my body. My soul reaches out towards Emrys's and I feel them lock together. Our hearts beat as one. We are two bodies who share one heart and soul—we were always meant to find each other.

Despite the euphoric feeling of my pleasure, I am vaguely aware that Emrys didn't come with me. His hard length is still lodged deep inside of me, prolonging my release.

"My love is everything—" My question ends in a squeak as Emrys flips us.

Settling me on my knees on the throne, he guides my hands to the back of the chair and anchors me with a clawed hand on my hip. Looking over my shoulder, his eyes are wild as they stare down at my pussy. Using his leg, he gently slides my legs apart, baring me further to his eyes.

"Oh, my blossom, you should see the delicious state of your little cunt." He drags the head of cock through my folds before gently dipping into my entrance. "It's begging me to fuck her again—to own her."

"Please, Emrys," I whine. "I need your come."

His cock teases me before slapping against my wet pussy.

"And what if I wanted to come in here?" he asks.

Before I can ask him what he means, I feel the blunt head of his length pressing against my back entrance. The tight ring of muscle burns as he gently pushes inside. My nails dig into the soft wood of the throne as a deep groan leaves me.

Despite the ache, my hips push back against him.

"Naughty girl," Emrys chastises. "Is that a yes? Is that you giving your king permission to flood your ass with his seed?"

My mouth opens but only a babble of sounds escapes as he pushes deeper into my backside.

"Say it, Laurelle. Beg me to fuck your little ass."

Swallowing down another moan, I somehow find my voice.

"Please, Emrys. Fuck my ass—come inside me."

"Good girl," he praises before sinking his teeth into my shoulder.

The bite of pain distracts me from the sharp thrust of his hips. In one harsh movement, his cock is entirely inside of me. The stretch—the burn—all of it is decadent. The pain dissipates, and in its wake is a deep well of untapped pleasure. My pussy clamps around nothing, and my clit throbs in need.

"So fucking tight, my blossom. I won't last long."

"Me neither," I pant.

His hips retreat before sliding back into me. His chest molds to my spine and I feel our hearts beating in time with each other. His claws skin into my hips—only leaving to deliver a sharp smack to the fleshy mound of my ass.

A moan leaves me as I press my forehead against the back of the throne. I move my hips back to meet his thrusts as he works himself in and out of my tight hole. I feel every inch of him like this.

My breasts bounce with each thrust and my body is racing toward another world-

shaking climax. Emrys doubles his efforts as his hips slam against my ass. The sting from his spanking once again heightens my pleasure.

Emrys's hand leaves my hip and trails beneath me. He finds my needy clit and begins working it in time with his thrusts.

"Come, my beautiful queen—my wife. Let me spill my seed inside you."

"Yes, yes!"

My eyes shut, and I give myself over the pleasure he's pulling from my body. With one more press of his fingers against my clit, I'm lost. My climax takes hold and my pussy tightens before a rush of fresh arousal slides from me and soaks my inner thighs.

Emrys growls, his body freezing against me as he thrusts deep one last time. His seed is released in a torrent. Hot and sticky, it fills my back entrance until it is overflowing and slips down my legs. Emrys fucks every last drop into me as my body shakes with the force of my release.

His arms come around me and he pulls me into his chest. Vaguely, I am aware of us falling backward. It's enough of a foreign sensation for my eyes to open and to find us back in our bed at Emrys's palace. The soft silk sheets greet my skin as a yawn sneaks up on me.

Emrys chuckles and rolls my body until I'm nestled under his chin.

"I've worn you out, my blossom."

"Just give me a minute and—" A yawn cuts off my words.

Emrys's hand combs through my curls in a soothing way. It's a struggle to keep my eyes open but I manage it. My faerie king gives me a satisfied smile and presses a kiss on my nose.

"Every day with you will be a gift. I would've waited a thousand more years to have you," he says.

Tears blur my vision as I press a kiss to his jaw.

"You are my happy ending—my dream come true. Whatever life has in store for us, we shall face it together. Always."

He holds me tighter as his hand goes back to my hair.

I was born into a loveless family—sold for my father's ambition. As much disdain as I hold for them and their treatment of me, the anger I once felt slowly begins to dissipate. They will always be miserable. They will never feel a fraction of the all-consuming love I feel for Emrys.

And I pity them for it. A life without love is no life at all.

Before sleep takes me, I offer my thanks to The Great Oak. My new life has only just begun. There are many adventures I want to go on—places I want to see. I know Emrys will show me everything, and then one day—when we're both ready—we'll start a family.

"Sleep, my love. I'll be ready to ravish you once more when you wake."

I smile at his heated words and burrow deeper into his warmth.

"Ravenous beast."

My ravenous beast. My faerie king—my husband. The other half of my heart and soul. Mine.

Forever.

ACKNOWLEDGMENTS

Where do I ever begin? This novella series started off as a way for me to get more comfortable writing smut and now it is by far my most popular series! There are so many of you to thank, but first and foremost I have to start with my amazing Beta & ARC readers.

You all provide such amazing insight to me and my books wouldn't be what they are without you.

Next, I have to thank my readers. Without you I wouldn't be here doing this job that I love more than anything! A world without monster romance lovers is a world I don't want to be a part of.

I have so much planned for the next volume in this series starting with a certain runaway princess and a sexy wolfman...

See you in the next one!

xoxo Charlotte

ALSO BY CHARLOTTE SWAN

Subscribe to my newsletter for all the latest updates on upcoming projects!

Monstrous Mates Series

Available on Kindle Unlimited

Taken by the Dark Elf King

Captured by the Orc General

www.ingramcontent.com/pod-product-compliance
Lightning Source LLC
Chambersburg PA
CBHW030334010826
48973CB00004B/1001